PARIS BY NIGHT

Instead of taking her straight home, Philippe drove to the river. The Seine was especially beautiful on this warm spring night, laced with silver and gold. "It's like a fantasy," she whispered. In the distance she could see the spires of Notre Dame soaring majestically into the star-studded sky.

"You are the fantasy," Philippe responded. "Do you believe in love at first sight?"

Her smile faded. "No."

"I do. Do you know what Richard de Fournival said in the thirteenth century? He said, 'Love is a folly of the mind, an unquenchable fire.' That is how I feel about you, and I haven't even kissed you yet."

He drew her to him gently, his arms encircling her. Bending his head, his mouth found hers. She let herself taste his lips, feel the pressure of his hands splayed against her back.

"Yes, oh yes," she murmured. It was the sweetest kiss she had ever known or imagined. At that moment, she knew that for the first time in her life, she was falling in love . . .

PAMELA WALLACE

SMALL TOWN GIRLS

ZEBRA BOOKS
KENSINGTON PUBLISHING CORP.

*This book is dedicated with love
to my son, Christopher*

ZEBRA BOOKS

are published by

Kensington Publishing Corp.
475 Park Avenue South
New York, NY 10016

First Zebra Books printing: July, 1992

Printed in the United States of America

ACKNOWLEDGMENTS

I am deeply grateful to the following people for their advice, support, and encouragement: Earl W. Wallace, Carla Simpson, Elisabeth MacDonald, Elnora King, Julie Birnbaum, Dr. Alan Birnbaum, and my agents, Mel Berger and Alan Gasmer.

Most important, I would like to thank my editor, Toni Lopopolo, whose keen insight is reflected on every page of this book.

I owe a special debt of gratitude to Karen Latham, Vickie DeWitt, Judy Reynolds, and Lynda Knowles, whose enduring friendship inspired this story.

Thanks, guys.

The passage to fulfillment lies between
the perils of desire and fear.

—Joseph Campbell

PROLOGUE

I grew up in a small town.

Visalia, California, began as a Santa Fe Railroad freight stop in the marshy Kaweah River bottom in the vast San Joaquin Valley. My hometown was an oasis dotted with stately valley oaks in an otherwise flat brown landscape. The huge trees, with their gnarled trunks and dark green, leafy limbs spreading a shady, protective canopy in the blistering hot summers, lined the wide streets and ringed the small parks.

Quiet and slow-paced, with a classic broad Main Street featuring family-run businesses, Visalia was the personification of small-town America. It ran to pickup trucks, barbecues, and neighbors who didn't bother to lock their doors. The sense of community, of extended family, was inescapable, and as I grew older, I began to find it all stifling.

I didn't realize that the rest of the country was different. I was unaware that children in big cities couldn't play safely outside at night as my friends and I did, giggling as we dodged the beams of passing headlights. I assumed that everyone spent lots of time outdoors, with hula hoops and bikes and plastic swimming pools.

There was an orange grove across the county road from my front yard, and in the late spring, the scent of the orange blossoms was intoxicating as it drifted across the blacktop. I still remember the feel of the powdery dust my bare feet kicked up on hot summer days, of racing across a grassy lawn, my blond pigtails flying behind me. The heady smell of fresh-mowed grass was the essence of summer. In the autumn, I raked up huge piles of leaves only to throw myself on them, giddy with joy. The leaves, smelling musty and damp, crackled when I crushed them.

As I grew older, I was allowed to ride my bright pink bike from one end of town to the other, down Main Street to the park at the end of the business district. I passed old ladies in navy blue polka-dot dresses going to the First Southern Baptist Church, where people believed it was a sin to dance or wear makeup or smoke cigarettes. At the park, boys played Little League baseball on summer grass. On the periphery, I sat with the other girls, chattering and laughing among ourselves; we were animated, self-absorbed spectators like brightly colored petals blowing in the wind.

There is a photograph of me when I was eight years old, knobbykneed, fine blond hair hanging in thin braids, large gray eyes staring with utter confidence straight into the camera. Within the well-defined borders of that small town, I felt completely free and unafraid.

At holiday dinners, my aunts, uncles, grandparents, and cousins gathered around tables covered with hand-crocheted tablecloths. There were huge turkeys bursting with stuffing, steaming hams, a dozen different salads, vegetables, desserts. Everyone brought something to these family gatherings, and there was always more food than we could possibly eat.

The sheer abundance of food was important because my family had come through the Great Depression. A generation earlier, they had been ditchbank Okies, blown out of the Midwest dust bowl to seek a better life elsewhere. People of the land, they migrated, along with thousands of others, to the promised land of California and the agriculturally rich San Joaquin Valley. Often they set up housekeeping in wretched camps along the banks of canals. They knew what it was like to not have enough to eat. Now, when they gathered together with all this abundance, the unspoken thought was: *See how far we've come.*

The men sat around and talked while the women cooked and served and then waited until everyone else had been fed before sitting down themselves. All of those women were housewives. The men didn't have careers, they had jobs — stable, middle-class jobs that offered security for their families. When my cousin Sharon's husband quit his job driving a delivery truck to go to junior college and become a bookkeeper, the entire family was shocked and disapproving. No one could understand why he would give up a steady paycheck and risk his two small children's financial welfare just because he said he wanted something more.

I understood. I wanted something more, too.

At fourteen, I said to my Uncle Phil, a funny, gentle man who had been awarded a Purple Heart in World War II, "I'm not going to end up like my mother and my aunts." His pale blue eyes fixed angrily on me in a way I'd never seen before. "You could do a lot worse, Kate!" he snapped.

I couldn't answer him.

By the time I was a teenager, I had heard Jim Morrison singing, "Come on, baby, light my fire." I had read *Valley of the Dolls.* I knew that, contrary to local conviction, Visalia, California, was not the center of the universe. In the big cities, people had more to do than spend Saturday nights dragging Main in somebody's parents' car, windows rolled down, AM radio blasting the Beatles or the Stones or the Beach Boys, endlessly circling around Foster's Drive-In, or later, when the first shopping mall was built, congregating in the parking lot late at night after the stores had closed. In the summer, the routine varied as we made the half-hour drive up to the foothills to the Kaweah River to swim in deep,

11

cold pools and lie on hot, smooth rocks at the river's edge.

In high school, I dated a boy who was so gorgeous I could hardly breathe when he spoke to me. I pretended to be dumb because I didn't want to scare him, although I knew I was smart and had to work hard at being dumb. As it turned out, I bored him speechless. He quit calling.

In the fifties, my friends and I had giggled enviously at Mouseketeer Annette's precocious bustline. In the sixties, we discovered round, pastel-colored birth-control dispensers in our mothers' bathroom cabinets. Newspapers and television newscasts began to trumpet Kennedy and Vietnam and civil rights and womens' lib and the whole exciting agenda of that turbulent time. To this day, any member of my generation can establish an immediate kinship with another by asking, "Where were you when John Kennedy . . . Bobby Kennedy . . . Martin Luther King, Jr. . . . was shot?" "Where were you when you first heard 'I Want to Hold Your Hand'?"

Even in our remote corner of the San Joaquin Valley, that vast sea of orchards, hay fields, and vineyards bounded by towering mountain ranges, we could scent the distant, exciting aroma of change. By then, the boundaries of that small town had come to feel suffocatingly restrictive. The town was a pocket of resistance to forces of change. Instead of feeling free, I felt confined and couldn't wait to bust out, to cross over the mountains that separated the valley from the mecca of Los Angeles, to pursue my dreams.

When my application to UCLA was accepted, my mother bought me a baby's cradle. For "someday." My high school graduation photo shows a young woman with chin-length golden brown hair ferociously teased into a high bouffant. My eyes are lit by an unquenchable optimism. In my yearbook, a boy wrote, "Stay as sweet as you are," but all I could think of was getting on Highway 99, which runs along the entire length of the valley, from Bakersfield at the southern end to Sacramento in the north. It seemed to me to be a lifeline, one that would take me out of the valley and into the world.

And so I stepped out, part of a generation of young women eagerly grasping options and opportunities denied our mothers.

We made choices without realizing they might be forever.

We didn't take any crap from anybody.

We pursued careers so successfully that we became like the men our mothers wanted us to marry.

Along the way, we were slipped a bill of goods for some things we didn't even realize we had bought. In that sense, we were, all of us, no matter where we came from, small town girls with big-city dreams.

1989

COMING HOME

"Starfuckers."

Kate McGuire tossed a page from the final edition of the *Los Angeles Times* to the man sitting up in bed next to her.

Glancing at the page, covered with photos from the previous night's Academy Awards show, Alan Field grinned. "I love hearing you swear in that soft, sweet, oh-so-ladylike voice. You look like the girl next door and talk like a sailor."

"I'm right, though. All of them — the actors, agents, power brokers, reporters, photographers, fans, hangers-on." Kate paused for breath, then finished. *"Everyone* who was at the Academy Awards show last night was a starfucker in one way or another."

Tossing the paper aside, Alan said, "But what do you think the beast feeds on? Besides, you were never one of those."

Her soft gray eyes clouded over when she felt the sharp stab of guilt. *Oh, yes, I was, but not anymore.*

Kate's gaze was irresistibly drawn to a small gold statuette that gleamed in the bright, late-morning sun streaming in through huge, uncurtained windows. *A little gold idol,* Alan had called it. It lay on its side on the carpet where she'd dropped it in the early hours of

17

the morning amid a clutter of jewelry and clothes. Her white silk gown and undies were in a jumble with Alan's rumpled tuxedo. Her white satin pumps lay where she'd kicked them off, near his shiny black dress shoes.

Just like old times, leaving a trail of clothes across the polished oak floor in their hurry to get to bed and each other.

Memories, bittersweet and unsettling, came back to her. That was the trouble with getting involved with your ex-husband, she decided. A lot of painful emotional baggage came with the familiar territory.

Now, in the harsh glare of the morning after, she wasn't entirely sure how it had happened. At the ball following the show, Alan came over to congratulate her. The next thing she knew, they were dancing. Then they drank a staggering amount of champagne. Somehow they ended up at her house in the early hours of the morning, and there had been no question of Alan sleeping in the guest room.

Kate felt torn by ambivalence. On the one hand, she felt comfortable with him. After all, they'd spent hundreds of Sunday mornings just like this, lazing in bed, reading the paper, making love. They knew each other far too well to feel awkward or embarrassed, even after being apart for four years.

Still, while their lovemaking had been satisfying physically, it lacked a sense of real emotional intimacy, leaving her feeling vaguely empty somehow. Just like old times, she thought unhappily.

Last night it had seemed only fitting that he share this special triumph with her since he had made her career possible. Now she wondered what on earth she had done. It seemed unreal, but then the whole night had been unreal. Kate remembered the glitzy insanity of it all, the sensory overkill—blazing camera strobes, hands grabbing at people, eager voices entreating the famous and the powerful for a quick word. Thousands

18

of people pouring out of the Shrine Auditorium, pushing, shoving, shouting, laughing, and just beneath the surface exhilaration, *desperation*.

That desperate undercurrent gave the atmosphere an almost tangible sexual charge. The air crackled with it. There were conquests to be made, and there was danger in the seduction. This was a high-stakes game; the buy-in could kill you, and maybe the outcome as well, but there had never been, in all Kate's experience, anything to equal suddenly finding herself a player.

The bedside phone rang. Reaching across Alan to pick up the receiver, she murmured through brief pauses, "Hi . . . yes, it was really something, all right . . . listen, Christie, I've gotta go now, let's talk later . . . no, not this afternoon, maybe tomorrow . . . all right, 'bye."

She met Alan's rueful grin as she hung up.

"Is Christie raring to go?"

Kate stretched tiredly. "Of course. She said we've got to play this hot hand of ours for every nickel it's worth. She said we've got 'em by the 'shorties,' and she's going to demand a million bucks for my next original script."

He raised one dark eyebrow. "So what's wrong with that?"

She faced him. "You know how fleeting this kind of glory is. Eventually, it will all be reduced to a footnote on my agency credits list and a line in a *Variety* obituary."

"But while it lasts, the glory is all that matters."

He really believed that, Kate knew. This was always the most serious difference between them. To Alan, life was a scorecard, and he needed to be ranked right up there at the top. He needed the glory of winning, to the exclusion of everything—and everyone—else.

At this moment she needed it, too, because it announced in no uncertain terms that Kate McGuire

19

was back in town. Back on top of a business that had once nearly destroyed her. It felt so good to prove them wrong, all those people who'd written her off. For a shining moment, she was acknowledged to be the very best at what she did. She knew that whatever else happened to her in life, she would never again experience quite the same sense of triumph.

Alan's grin transformed his nondescript face, giving it a boyish appeal. That quality, rather than physical attraction, had drawn her to him thirteen years earlier; it still caught at her heart.

"Christie's going to make you rich as well as famous. Let's get married again and I'll live off you."

She laughed, grateful for the humor that lightened the subtle tension between them.

Just then the doorbell rang—again.

"Damn," he murmured.

"It's probably more flowers. You get it and I'll take some orange juice out to the patio."

He put on his trousers, and nothing else, to answer the door. She slipped into a gray silk caftan and matching slippers, then padded quietly into the kitchen.

A moment later, Kate stepped out onto the small flagstone patio that overlooked a deep ravine covered by dusky green scrub brush and, in the distance, the Pacific Ocean. Setting the tray that held a pitcher of juice and two glasses on a glass-topped, black wrought-iron table, she leaned against the stone balustrade and took a deep breath. The air was thick not only with the pungent, faintly medicinal scent of eucalyptus that reminded her of the skin cream she'd used as a teenager but also with the salty taste of the breeze off the ocean that gently ruffled her light brown hair.

Malibu was at its most glorious on this spring day. Earlier, morning fog had climbed the chaparral-covered foothills, and the sky had looked leaden, the ocean gray, but the fog had quickly dissipated, and now brilliant sunshine shone on the smooth green hills. Tiny pinpoints of sunlight glistened on the surface of the ocean, and no matter how many times she looked at it, the water was never quite the same color. The constantly shifting light changed it endlessly.

From her hilltop aerie, Kate could see the entire curve of the bay, from Point Dume, a hulking, massive promontory jutting out into the ocean, to the tall white buildings of Santa Monica in the distance, and beyond to the gradual slope of the Palos Verdes Peninsula.

Immediately below her was the Colony, the original Malibu settlement with its smooth stretch of sand and magnificent beach houses where in the 1920s movie stars had built their cottages. A little girl named Irene Mayer (Louis B.'s daughter) had romped on the sand with Dougie Fairbanks, Jr., who later brought his bride, Joan Crawford, there.

Kate hated L.A. but loved Malibu—the pristine beaches, gently rolling hills, tree-lined canyons, and shady valleys, all framed by a towering backdrop of tall, stark mountains.

She loved Malibu in January—when the "grasshopper rain," as the original Mexican settlers called it, came, followed by a warm spring sun that sweated the eggs deposited on the bushes, bringing forth thousands of grasshoppers—and in August—when the green of the towering sycamores turned to russet and falling leaves blanketed the ground—but in the late fall, when the fierce Santa Ana winds blew in from the desert, Kate hated the place and always found an excuse to leave for a few days. The hot, dry winds made her uneasy as their high, keening sound seemed to carry a veiled threat.

The Santa Ana had been blowing the time she left Alan. On that night, she ran from the winds almost as much as from the pain of her shattered marriage; but on this lovely morning, she didn't want to think of that terrible time. It was all in the past, she reassured herself. The only thing that mattered now was the future: a brilliant future full of success and perhaps even a second chance at happiness.

Turning back to the table to pour a glass of orange juice, Kate caught her reflection in the sliding-glass door that opened off the living room onto the patio. Now tall, fine-boned, and with honey-hued skin, she had changed a great deal from the time, twenty years earlier, when she'd left her hometown for L.A., her heart bursting with excitement, her '61 Chevy crammed with all her worldly possessions. No longer a fresh-faced teenager, her expression guileless and naive, she now had an air of chic sophistication. Her maturity complemented her face and figure, lending a soft fullness to her slender frame. She had no doubts about her ability to intrigue a man who attracted her. That was an asset she'd picked up over the course, along with a taste for room service in first-class hotels, the aroma of expensive automobile upholstery, and the front section of jetliners.

All at once she shivered. Incorruptible Kate of Redwood High. Well, not quite, as things turned out.

She felt Alan's arms encircle her waist, his warm breath on the back of her neck. Turning to face him, with her hands resting lightly against his chest, Kate studied her former husband. He had changed profoundly from the endearing young man she'd fallen in love with so long ago. His dark brown hair was flecked with gray, he was heavier, and there were deep lines around his hazel eyes and thin mouth. It wasn't just the inevitable signs of aging that made him so different, she realized, or even the tough, confident air of a powerful producer that had replaced his youthful awkwardness and desperate need to succeed. Somewhere along the line, Alan had sacrificed his dreams for his desires.

Kate knew he didn't regret it. Why should he, when he had everything he'd ever wanted? But she wondered if sometimes, perhaps late at night when he was alone, he felt a gnawing emptiness.

She certainly did.

Reading her mind in the uncanny way he had, Alan said, "You're doing it again, Kate. Don't analyze, just enjoy. You won an Oscar, for Chrissakes."

She laughed. "All right. Let's see who sent the flowers."

Going to the bouquet he'd set on the table, she opened the small envelope and read: "Congratulations. I always knew you could do it."

It was signed *Mark*.

The moment seemed to freeze in time. Kate noticed details: the satiny sheen of the tightly furled rosebuds; the pale cream color of the notepaper; the black, spidery handwriting of some nameless florist's assistant. Then the doorbell rang again and Alan went to answer it, saying, "This place is going to look like a flower shop before the day's over."

Putting the card back in its envelope, she tucked it in the deep pocket of her caftan. Yellow roses. She had once told Mark, long ago, that they were her favorite, and he had remembered. She wasn't surprised. It was so like him.

Last night, when she'd walked up onto the stage to accept the Oscar, she knew friends and family back home were watching, rooting for her; but there had been one tiny, nagging thought. Was Mark watching, too? If so, what did he feel?

Mark.

His memory filled her. It washed over her all at once, a wave she wasn't prepared for, one she couldn't fight. She could only go with it.

Mark, who had needed her so much it had terrified her, touching a need in her that she'd denied for a long, long time.

23

It had been several months since she'd left, and she'd long since convinced herself she didn't miss him.

What a stupid lie.

At the sound of Alan returning, Kate forced her mind to clear, trying hard to look as if absolutely nothing had happened.

Handing her a letter delivered by Federal Express, he said, "It can't be more congratulations. This was sent yesterday before you won."

Kate had a sense of foreboding, though she couldn't have said why. Brushing it aside, she tore open the envelope and took out a single sheet of paper with a few words scrawled by hand across it.

"I need you."

It was signed *Barbara*.

The cryptic message told her nothing concrete, although the words cried urgency, but Kate felt the stirrings within her of something that went beyond her immediate alarm, something long-smouldering and very close to dread.

An old image, unbidden, flashed before her eyes like something from a nightmare: a figure with a startled, uncomprehending expression starkly etched in headlights. The same image had once haunted her dreams, but long ago she had banished it to the deepest recesses of her psyche. With an effort, she willed it back into oblivion.

What could be wrong with Barbara? What could be wrong with someone whose ideal life was the dream little girls are raised on? Kate may have found fortune and glory, but Barbara had the *real* things—a loving husband, a home, family, roots, *security*—all the things Kate had run away from.

Suddenly, she realized her hands were gripping the paper so tightly that her knuckles were white. The surprise she'd felt on first reading the scrawled words had quickly turned to concern, then alarm.

Through twenty-five years of friendship, Barbara

had always been there for her. Barbara was her "safe person," the one she called in the middle of the night when she was scared or broke or torn by conflicting needs and desires. *Should I sell my soul to get this job? Should I have this baby? Should I leave this man?*

Just imagining Barbara's voice, measured and reassuring, calmed her. Barbara was more than merely comforting. Somehow she always had the right answers. She asked the hard questions that Kate tried to shy away from. In being forced to answer them, inevitably Kate came to realize what she should do.

How many times had she said "I need you" to Barbara? Not once had Barbara said those words to her. Until now.

She looked up at Alan. "I have to make a call. I'll be right back."

She hurried to the phone in the living room and dialed Barbara's number.

No answer. She wondered why the answering machine, at least, didn't respond since Barbara never turned it off. It didn't make sense.

Slowly walking back out onto the patio, she focused on the brief message, trying to read some meaning into it. There was none.

There was only one thing to do. Stopping in front of Alan, Kate said, "I have to go back to Visalia."

He was startled. "What—you mean right now?"

She nodded.

"Is it your family? Did something happen?"

"It's Barbara. She needs me."

"Why?"

Her expression was blank. "I don't know, but I have to go."

Alan took her by the shoulders and forced her to look directly at him. "Kate, *this* is where you belong right now." He finished in a gentler tone. "You belong with *me*."

When she didn't respond, he went on in a voice

25

that was strange for him, uncharacteristically hesitant and unsure. "In case you don't realize it, that's a proposal. I've never stopped thinking about you. I think you feel the same way for me. Marry me again. Give me a second chance to show how much I love you."

He finished with a heartbreaking catch in his voice. "Everyone deserves a second chance."

The vulnerability that for one brief moment he allowed himself to show moved Kate deeply. He could always get to her by making her feel somehow responsible for his happiness. Don't do this to me, she wanted to say.

She hadn't expected a proposal, not so soon. Their reconciliation was so new, so fragile, she hadn't entirely come to terms with it. She wasn't sure whether to joke about it or risk taking it seriously. She certainly hadn't thought in terms of forever.

Marriage. Alan. There was a reassuring familiarity in the thought. In a way, it made perfect sense. Make a brand-new start. This time they would have all the wisdom they'd lacked before. This time they wouldn't lacerate each other's very souls.

What had Hemingway written? *Isn't it pretty to think so*.

Failure had always been the most terrifying word in Kate's vocabulary. The failure of her marriage, the most important relationship in her life, had devastated her, shattering her sense of self-worth. Now she could erase the old failure, heal the old scar.

Kate faced him. "We spent one night together. That's all. Just one night when a lot of elements came together to make it seem sort of natural to be with each other again. But a permanent relationship . . ." Shaking her head, she finished in a hoarse whisper, "Oh, Alan, I don't think it's possible."

Determination was etched in every line of his body. "I've had a long time to think about things, about us. It isn't the same with any of the other women I've

26

been involved with. It's more than just a shared history. We got together at the same time that our talents exploded. We brought out the best in each other. We made it together, against all the odds. We can go even farther now. Jesus, Kate, there's nothing we couldn't accomplish now."

"Working together isn't enough, Alan." As she said the words, Kate had an overpowering sense of déjà vu. They had been here before.

"Kate, we built a foundation together that will last us all our lives. We are who we are because of being with each other. Whoever we've been involved with has had to live with what we built together. That's why everyone else always seems like a stranger."

She laid her head against his shoulder. She could hear the beat of his heart. He was right in everything he said. They had spent nearly ten years together, and nothing—certainly not a paper that said *dissolution*—could erase that. Even if they never saw each other again, they would be part of each other forever. She had never stopped caring for Alan, even when she hated him, and she'd always known, without any sense of conceit, that no matter how many other women he loved, he would always compare them to her.

She felt his hand touch her hair. She knew she should say something, but what? Maybe he was right, and it was all so simple. Why not try again? Instead of feeling an eager, tenuous hopefulness at the possibility of maybe, just maybe, this time getting it right, Kate felt an awful, sinking sensation, as if she were once more facing a trap she thought she'd long since managed to escape.

She remained quiet.

There was a time when Alan would have argued until she gave in out of sheer emotional exhaustion, but now he knew better than to try to manipulate her that way. She had gotten a lot tougher since their breakup. *Hard,* one person had said. The accusation had hurt her deeply, conjuring up, as it did, images of a cold bitch who had lost the essential quality of femininity.

Finally, Kate pulled back. "I have to go. We'll talk when I get back."

He finished dressing before she did and watched as she packed a small suitcase. At her car, he leaned in through the open window and kissed her with a tenderness that caught her off-guard. His hazel eyes were alight with excitement. "We could have it all, Kate. Hurry back! There's a great deal waiting for you here."

Alan stepped back from the white Jeep Cherokee, and Kate pulled away slowly. As she headed down the driveway, she saw him in her rearview mirror, standing there, watching her until she was out of sight.

Two hours later, she rounded the final curve of the Tehachapi Mountains and saw the vast San Joaquin Valley, the heartland of California, spread out before her in a patchwork of colors, with Highway 99 running straight up the middle. No matter how many times she saw it, the sudden sight of the valley, vast and flat after an hour of driving through mountains six thousand feet high, was startling. The landscape took on the rural texture of fruit trees covered with masses of pink and white blossoms, golden fields of grain stirring in the breeze, green pastures dotted with horses and cattle.

Her senses were assaulted by all the long-familiar sights and smells and sensations. Something deep within Kate stirred, and her pulse quickened. She felt a rush of relief, and the defense mechanisms that she'd cultivated for survival in L.A. dissolved. Malibu was lovely, but she always felt like a transient there, without roots, a spectator rather than a participant in the rhythm of life.

Now, as she descended into the womblike valley, one feeling overwhelmed all others—the inexplicable pull of a place called home.

In London, Shelly Rashad stood at the tall windows at one end of the richly decorated, wood-paneled boardroom of Rashad Cosmetics, Inc., looking out at the thin, misty rain falling on St. James Park. The soft backdrop was a perfect complement to her ethereal beauty—eyes like drowned violets, white-gold hair falling baby-fine and straight, framing a pale, oval face of china-doll perfection. The only unsettling element in a vision of otherwise pristine perfection was the startlingly sensual, wide, full-lipped mouth made more striking because it was painted a deep red, hinting at a passionate nature kept tightly in check.

As always, Shelly was stunningly dressed, for she had an image to maintain. The president of Rashad Cosmetics, one of the most beautiful women in the world according to *Vogue,* had to look the part. Today that meant a cream-colored wool suit with the unmistakable cut of Chanel, stockings with the sheen of real silk, stiletto heels to emphasize her five-foot, ten-inch height, several strands of heavy gold chains, small gold and pearl antique earrings, and a single ring, a huge emerald-cut diamond, on one finger.

In short, Shelly was a breathtaking vision in white and gold, a contemporary version of a fairy princess.

As a child, she had seen enchanted forests and castles and elves in the billowing white clouds that floated across spring skies. She had pretended she was a princess and that a wicked witch had cast a spell over her, banishing her to a lonely land. A handsome prince would come some day and lift the spell and carry her off to a magnificent castle in the sky, just like in the fairy tales.

29

But the prince never came, and this was no fairy tale.

It was a cutthroat business, and at the moment, Shelly needed all her considerable self-control to keep a rising panic in check. She couldn't afford the luxury of giving in to it. There was too much at stake. To have come this far, to have paid the price she had paid only to see it come to this. . . .

The six middle-aged men and the one woman seated at the conference table behind her — her very proper British board of directors — waited impatiently for her decision.

If Richard were standing beside her, as he had done for so many years, he would face them unflinchingly and force them to back down. Richard, her dearest friend and business partner, was always at his best under fire, and she had learned well from him. He'd told her once that the most scathing indictment that could be made of anyone was to say they were at their best only when the going was easy.

Shelly wanted desperately to live up to his example, to behave with the kind of strength of character that would have made him proud of her, but she was absolutely terrified. More than anything else, she wanted to run and hide. Facing a hostile group alone, with no one on her side, touched her most primal fear. Though she knew where the fear came from, she'd never been able to overcome it.

Taking a deep breath, she plunged in. "Gentlemen, you may tell Terrence Westen I said he can go to hell."

It was the slap in the face she'd intended; they recoiled in anger and dismay. Silver-haired Douglas Massey was instantly on his feet, speaking for all of them. "Westen's offer is a good one, Shelly. Perhaps you don't understand."

"I understand perfectly," she snapped, enjoying Massey's obvious agitation. *So,* the ringleader, she thought, filing the item away for future reference. *If* she had a future with Rashad Cosmetics. "It's a good offer for you. You all stand to gain a considerable profit from unexercised stock options. Not to mention the shares you already hold."

"You'll reap the same profit."

Her eyes narrowed. "True, Douglas, with one small difference — I'll lose my company."

Massey was livid. His aristocratic voice with its crisp Eton/Oxford intonations took on an ominous tone. "Westen is known for getting what he wants, Shelly. If we don't sell willingly, then he'll simply take over the company."

She forced herself to meet his eye. "We can fight him, Douglas."

Another board member, John Fell, finally spoke. "Is it possible you owe us some consideration in this matter, Shelly? It seems to me you're forgetting how this board stood behind you during some very trying times."

"And for that support you've been generously rewarded, Sir John. I told you from the beginning I had no desire to sell this company. I see no reason to change my mind."

She considered Fell's deceptively mild-mannered demeanor for a moment. Sir John was the critical factor. His family connections interlaced with the highest echelons of British government and finance. Shelly was the outsider, the American interloper. True, Rashad was international in scope, with clinics in Paris, Rome, New York, Beverly Hills, and even Riyadh, in Saudi Arabia, but her production facilities, distribution headquarters, and corporate offices were in London and were subject to British rules of commerce. If Sir John was firmly in Massey's corner, it was best to find out now.

"Sir John, if I must fight Westen, shall I have your support?"

Fell spread his palms flat on the polished mahogany

31

table before him and seemed to consider his manicure for a long moment. Finally, he looked up at her. "I would have no choice but to act in the best interests of the stockholders."

Her stomach tightened and her voice was small as she replied, "I see."

Massey, who had leaned forward intently, settled back in his chair, watching her, gloating.

She turned to her last resort, Miriam Leighton, the only female board member. Shelly had fought hard to open up the board to women. If anyone was going to support her, it should be Miriam, a short, plump woman whose grandmotherly facade masked a will of iron.

"Miriam?"

She held her breath, waiting for Miriam's response. It wasn't long in coming.

Miriam answered matter-of-factly. "I'd be a fool to reject Westen's offer, and I'm no fool."

Of course, Shelly thought. It was naive of her to assume Miriam would support her simply because they were both women. It was all she could do to continue facing her hostile board. "In that case, I think it's time we bring this meeting to a close. You have my answer. You may relay it to Mr. Westen at your convenience. Good-day."

With no small measure of satisfaction, she watched their sour expressions as they filed out of the room. They'd expected her to roll over and she hadn't. The Exchequer Club bar—or one of those all-male bastions so necessary to the British gentry—should do a brisk business this afternoon, she judged, wondering if Miriam would resent being excluded.

The last to leave was Massey,—who paused for a final word. "You really have done a marvelous job with Rashad, my dear. Everyone recognizes that. I do, myself. But, as you Americans say, you're playing in the big leagues now. Hardball. I've been told it's no game for a lady."

"It's not, Douglas, but this isn't a game, is it?"

He glared at her, then turned on his heel and strode from the room.

Watching him go, she added to herself, *and I'm no lady.*

When she made her way into her private office, Nora, her newly hired young secretary, handed her a stack of correspondence and phone messages. "One more thing, Mrs. Rashad, Mr. Hunter—"

"Mr. Hunter will have to wait," Shelly responded, striding into her office.

"But—"

Just inside the doorway, Shelly stopped.

Sprawled in a chair, his long jeans-clad legs stretched out before him and his hands clasped behind his head, was Ryan Hunter. Shelly shook her head and smiled, determined not to reveal how shaky she felt. "I might have known."

"You said you wanted the proofs double-quick. They're on the table." His voice still carried a faint hint of a southwestern drawl despite his years of living in Europe. "I didn't think you'd want me loafing out there, distracting Nora."

The years of their association permitted an amiable candor between them. "Very considerate of you, but I'm afraid it's a little too late to start worrying about that, and you know it. The only question is when you're going to pounce."

The corners of his mouth twitched. "Can't imagine what you're talking about, lady."

Still, she could hardly blame Nora for her obvious infatuation with Ryan. In his late forties, his chestnut hair flecked with gray and his brown eyes crinkling at the corners, he was still an immensely attractive man. His features were a little too rough and weather-beaten to be considered handsome, but his easy ir-reverence—uniquely and refreshingly American—was irresistible. Under a deceptively laid-back persona, he radiated intense passion—for life, for his work, and for the opposite sex.

Shelly found that passion disturbing. It slid under her defenses, threatening her equilibrium. Long ago, she'd erected an invisible barrier between them that neither openly acknowledged but both recognized. There was never any physical contact between them, even when he photographed her. During the fifteen years of their friendship, they'd never once danced together or hugged. He'd never taken her hand to help her alight from a car, never lightly touched the small of her back as she preceded him through a doorway; but sometimes during photo sessions, when he stood only a hairbreadth away from her, he seemed to be looking beyond the glossy surface of her appearance to the real flesh-and-blood woman underneath. For an instant, Ryan would clearly hover on the brink of touching her as something indefinable yet electric grew between them. At those moments, Shelly held her breath and retreated within herself. Sensing her withdrawal, he always pulled back.

She occasionally wondered what his touch would be like. She would find herself staring at those large, strong hands that manipulated a camera with such practiced ease, then she would give herself a mental shake and concentrate once more on the business at hand. It was dangerous to think of Ryan as a man, to be curious about him and perhaps even a little beguiled.

She was well aware that other women weren't so reserved. Few of them spent more than five minutes in his presence without wondering what he would be like in bed. Early on, he'd tried to seduce Shelly, but when she proved immune to his charms, he moved on to an endless succession of other women. At one point, when his latest girlfriend had come and gone in record time, she'd asked him what he was looking for that he never seemed to find. The question threw him, and for once he didn't respond in his usual glib manner.

Looking at her intently, he answered, "Maybe I'm looking for something I can never have."

She felt shaken by his words and quickly backed off.

Now, with a rueful sigh, she said, "All right, let's have a look at your stuff before you fall asleep in my favorite chair."

Dropping the correspondence on her desk, she crossed to the table where Ryan's work was spread out. Tripping a mental switch, she put the unsettling board meeting behind her and scanned the photos with an analytical eye. Most of them were of her own face, devoid of makeup and naturally glorious. The simplicity of the shots set off her luminous beauty to perfection. The point of the photos was to show that with Rashad skin care products a woman's skin would be so healthy and youthful she wouldn't need cosmetics.

Shelly was totally objective in analyzing her own face. Her looks were a commodity to her that had nothing to do with how she felt about herself inside. Long ago, she had found no way to escape being a victim of her looks, so she decided to manage her own victimization by convincing herself that being in charge of her exploitation was the same thing as being free of it.

Ryan had crossed to her side and stood looking over her shoulder. He murmured, "You're amazing. I could shoot you with a Brownie and you'd knock people's socks off."

"I'm not interested in knocking anybody's socks off, Ryan. All that matters is selling a product."

He smiled. "It's selling. There isn't a woman in the world who doesn't want to look like you."

She turned away from the display. It always came back to that — the flagship face and body, a lucky

35

accident of the right genes and a savvy mentor.

However, neither the genes nor the mentor had made her president of Rashad. Hard work and a determination born of desperation had earned her the business empire and everything that went with it: the chauffeured Rolls, the river-view condo in Chelsea Harbor, the apartments in Paris and Manhattan, and, most important, the safety that power guaranteed.

Now it was all up for grabs because Terrence Westen was a shrewd operator who knew a good thing when he saw it.

Sounding deceptively casual, Ryan asked, "So, how'd the meeting go?"

She pretended to focus on the photos. "The rats are jumping ship."

"That's what makes them rats. Good riddance." He nodded confidently. "You'll pull through."

Shelly looked up at him. "What makes you so sure?"

"You did it before. You can do it again."

Of course, she knew what he meant. Her husband, Ben, had founded Rashad. In the aftermath of Ben's death, she had nearly lost everything. It was years before Rashad's precarious financial position stabilized, then soared. Against overwhelming odds, the company had survived the tragedy and so had Shelly.

But Richard was here then, she reminded herself. If he hadn't been, Rashad would have gone under and Shelly along with it. She had once come so close to losing the safety and security she had sold her soul to achieve. How could she face that again without Richard?

He was the one man in her life she had trusted completely, the one man who had never tried to use her. He also happened to be homosexual. It was ironic, she thought. Maybe the only men whom women could truly trust were gay because those men

36

were the only ones who didn't want something from them.

Ryan went on in an oddly tentative tone that lacked his usual boundless self-confidence. "You know . . . you don't have to go through this alone."

She looked up at him in surprise and confusion. "What?"

"I'm right here beside you, Shelly. I always have been."

At that moment, she sensed what he was offering, what he'd always offered, but she couldn't accept it. The mere thought terrified her.

Flustered, she replied more curtly than she'd intended. "I can handle this. I've been in tight spots before and survived. I'll survive this."

Ryan's expression was blank, but she sensed that her curt rebuff had cut him to the quick.

After a moment, he replied slowly, as if thinking out loud, "I guess you're right. I tend to think of you as the vulnerable girl you were when we first met, but you haven't been that for a long time, have you? You really don't need anyone, including me."

She felt guilty. "Ryan, I do appreciate your friendship."

Friendship. The word hung between them.

There was a knock at the door and a moment later Nora poked her head around the corner. "Sorry to interrupt, ma'am, but a cablegram just came for you. It's marked urgent and confidential."

Shelly felt relief at the interruption. She wanted to bring this disturbing conversation to an end *now.* "Bring it here, then."

Nora handed it to her then left, closing the door behind her.

"If you'll excuse me," Shelly began, intending to dismiss Ryan, who had assumed his usual disarming grin once more.

"Sure." He strode to the door but stopped and half-turned. "By the way, I wanted to let you know that I'm returning to the States."

Shelly was stunned. "What? When?"

"Soon. In a few days, as a matter of fact." He added in an offhand manner, "I've had enough of Europe. Ever since McDonald's and Kentucky Fried Chicken franchises started popping up all over, it just hasn't been the same."

"But . . . will you still be available?"

" 'Fraid not, but don't worry. There are plenty of other photographers."

"Ryan, this is ridiculous! It's so sudden!"

"Not really. It's been comin' on for a long time. It just took me a while to realize it."

He hesitated, then went on. "You know, when I first became a professional photographer I discovered something. The best pictures come when the photographer falls a little bit in love with his subject. But it has to remain an unrequited love because the photographer must always be searching for something more than the subject is willing to give. That makes for great pictures but lousy relationships."

He finished, "Anyway, I'm sure you'll be just fine."

Then he was gone.

She stood there, the cablegram forgotten, staring after him in amazement. Of all the unexpected, un-businesslike . . . Her outrage rang hollow. She understood perfectly well why he was leaving, and she knew that he was walking out of her life forever. The only confusing thing was her own reaction. Only a moment earlier she'd rejected him. Now she felt bereft and wanted to go after him, to take his hand and say, "Please don't go!"

For the first time in years, Shelly was hungry to be touched. She'd sworn this would never happen again, *never*. It hurt too much when the inevitable betrayal occurred. Passion not only transformed, it destroyed. But she was so tired of the awful loneliness. The shell

38

she had built around her to keep out the world grew harder and harder as time passed. She was terrified that one day she would find the shell had grown so hard she couldn't break through it even if she tried.

Abruptly, she remembered the cablegram clutched in her hand. Face flushed, eyes uncertain, she forced herself to focus on the envelope. Noticing the postmark—Visalia, California, U.S.A.—her dark blue eyes widened and her fingers tightened around the edges of the envelope. All at once, she felt terribly cold.

It's nothing, she told herself, absolutely nothing, just a letter from Barbara; but Barbara never wrote, she always called when she wanted to catch up with Shelly. This was no ordinary letter. It was urgent and confidential.

Tearing open the envelope, she took out the single sheet of paper and, with disbelieving eyes, read the scrawled plea: "I need you. Barbara."

Surely Barbara didn't mean that she wanted Shelly to come to her. She would never ask that. Pushing a button on the intercom, Shelly asked Nora to place a call to Mrs. Barbara Browning, whose number was on file. While Nora placed the call, Shelly turned her chair to face the window overlooking St. James Park. If anything, the weather had worsened, and the view of mist-shrouded, skeletal trees could only be described as bleak.

Barbara. Shelly hadn't seen her in years, hadn't talked to her in months. Their friendship didn't depend on frequent communication. She owed Barbara so much more than she could ever dare to admit.

The intercom buzzed. "There's no answer, ma'am. Shall I keep trying?"

"Yes, please."

Shelly checked her watch. It was 7 A.M. in California. Why would Barbara be out so early, especially when she must be waiting for an answer to her letter?

39

Time passed with agonizing slowness. Nora could raise no one at Barbara's number. Shelly had her try Kate in Malibu and again at her agent's number in Beverly Hills but couldn't track Kate down at either location. There was always Valerie, but what could Shelly tell her? "I just got the strangest letter from Barbara: . . ."?

Besides, Valerie was Valerie. She would be no help.

As the afternoon faded into evening and Nora still couldn't reach Barbara, Shelly's anxiety reached the critical point. She no longer worried about Ryan or Westen's takeover bid. Something much more critical was at stake. She knew what she had to do. Even so, she resisted, terrified of the thought.

It's just a small town, she told herself. It's been twenty years. It's probably changed. What happened belongs to the buried past.

In truth, she knew differently. Small towns never change, not at the core. They remain a window into the living past. In small towns, memories are long and old secrets are never quite forgotten.

Shelly began to feel as if she might drown in her anxiety. She didn't want to go. If it was anyone else asking this of her . . . but it wasn't anyone else. It was Barbara.

Turning back to her desk, she buzzed Nora and asked her to book a seat on the next flight to Los Angeles, with a connecting flight to Visalia.

"Where was that, Mrs. Rashad?"

"Visalia." Her mouth was dry as she added, *"Home . . ."*

In New York, Valerie Simpson stood onstage facing an audience in a small television studio, waiting for the red light to flash on the camera. People were always surprised to see how small she was in real life, barely five-foot-two and weighing less than a hundred

40

pounds. They were also disappointed to find that she was rather plain—freckle-faced and snub-nosed. Only her halo of frizzy, orange-red hair was as flamboyant off camera as on.

When the red light flashed, an incredible transformation took place. Valerie seemed to shine with an intensity that transcended her plainness. It was apparent in her wicked sense of humor, feisty demeanor, razor-sharp intelligence, and the ability to hold her own with the toughest of adversaries.

Now her green eyes glittered like a cat about to pounce on its prey as she began with her signature opening to the show: "I'm Valerie Simpson, and our focus today is . . . *gang rape.*"

Overhead signs flashed APPLAUSE and the audience responded enthusiastically. When their clapping died down, Valerie continued. "This year, two hundred thousand women will be the victims of a violent, brutal crime-gang rape, rape by two or more men. Gang rapes are happening every day in both big cities and small towns and on college campuses. It's a horrendous form of degradation yet is almost impossible to prosecute.

"I'll interview convicted rapists in prison, as well as the victims of those rapists. I'll talk to psychologists, prosecuting attorneys, and defense attorneys, and I'll try to answer the question, 'Is there justice for the victims of this terrible crime?' "

The titles rolled, and when they finished, Valerie went into a voiceover. On-screen, in a dramatization, a young woman walked alone down a dark street, looking fearfully over her shoulder at a group of young men following her. "Because of the unique nature of gang rape, the victim is not likely to report the crime. She is usually convinced she was at fault because she may have known one of her attackers and may have agreed to go with him. Gang rape is a sudden outpouring of group violence, the ultimate expression of male anger at all women directed in force at one woman. . . ."

An hour later, as the television screen faded to credits, Valerie concluded in a voice nearly hoarse from impassioned interrogation of several guests. "Men need to learn that they can't get away with brutalizing a woman in this way. They need to be prosecuted.

"Thanks for watching. See you next time."

A few minutes later, after signing several autographs for members of the audience, she hurried to her office and collapsed on the huge, overstuffed sofa. Thank God, it was over. Valerie hadn't fucking wanted to do gang rape, but her producer, Ellen Delgado, insisted. Since she couldn't give Ellen a good reason—hell, *any* reason—why she shouldn't do such a hot topic, she had no choice.

So she put herself on automatic pilot and did the goddamn show and tried real hard not to think, not to remember, but it got to her—especially when a young female victim whose assailants were never prosecuted tearfully asked, "Why am I the one who has to run scared now?"

Val sighed heavily and closed her eyes. She had done her job, investing it with all the passion and disdain for objectivity that her audience had come to expect of her. Now all she wanted to do was put it behind her. Maybe, she thought, she could get away for the weekend. Her daughter was spending the weekend with a friend. For once, she had time to herself, without the constant demands of single parenthood. A quick trip down to the Bahamas might be nice. Soak up some sun, start planning next season's shows.

Rising, she went to her desk, sat down, and began shuffling through papers. She could just shove the more urgent stuff in her briefcase and get the hell out of there. She'd spent too much time in this office

42

lately; the walls were starting to close in.

Val's office reflected her personality, with bold modern art prints on the walls and furniture upholstered in a vivid shade of purple. Befitting her position as a popular, if controversial, broadcast journalist, the office was a large corner one with windows overlooking Times Square.

She could hear the ceaseless noise coming from far below, the blare of horns, a piercing scream of sirens, the rumble of traffic, but she'd long since grown used to it. In fact, the backdrop of noise, the constantly beating pulse of a city that never quieted down, had become necessary to her, leaving her edgy and ill-tempered if she was away on assignment and absent from the clamor for too long.

A little like booze and drugs, she thought. She'd served a little time on those fronts, as well.

Val needed a caffeine fix. Her secretary had stepped away from her desk, but glancing through the open doorway to the hall, she saw a young man passing by. "I'm dying, Danny. Bring me some coffee before it's too late."

"How do you want it, Val?"

She glanced up at him framed in the doorway, a good-looking kid from the Harlem badlands majoring in broadcast journalism at NYU and working part-time as an intern at the station.

"Just like my men, sweetie."

He grinned. "Hot and—?"

"Fast! First rule of journalism—don't jump to conclusions."

He laughed and moved off.

She chuckled to herself. Everybody got a kick out of Val, and always had. That's how she paid her way, with a laugh, a caustic put-down, a yuk for the gallery, no matter what she was feeling inside. Even against the highly charged background of a television studio, she stood out, with her red hair, loose bright green silk blouse, and tight-fitting designer jeans.

That was a big part of her appeal to her audience. She came across as one of them, unpretentious, down to earth. She didn't wear chic outfits and trendy jewelry.

Val leaned back in her chair, trying to decide what work to take on the trip, but her mind wasn't on it. Her eyes kept going to her phone, subconsciously willing it to ring.

I'm acting like a stupid teenager waiting by the phone, she told herself angrily.

With an effort, she shuffled through the papers again but quickly broke off. Her mind simply wasn't on demographic surveys, Nielsen ratings, lists of potential guests and hot topics. Maybe she should just go to the fucking Bahamas and forget about work entirely for one whole weekend.

Her phone rang.

She let it ring twice before finally answering. "Valerie Simpson."

"Val, it's Ellen." The voice was warm, with a slight accent, the legacy of a childhood spent in the barrio, where she was known as Elena.

There was an expectant pause. It would have amazed anyone who knew Val to see her at a loss for words. Finally, she said, "I got your note. When are you leaving?"

"Tomorrow night."

There was another pause. Their voices were constrained, like strangers talking to one another. Val hated it, after all their years of friendship. They'd been through too much together to be this way with each other. She asked, "Ellen, what are you doing?"

"I'm taking a leave of absence."

She hadn't expected that. A leave of absence implied a long, long time. Val felt something hard pressing against her chest and realized it was panic.

"When will you be back?"

44

"When I've gotten over you."

The raw emotion in Ellen's voice cut through Valerie's defenses and left her feeling helpless. She was incapable of responding to the unarticulated need, of giving voice to her own. It was as though a dizzying chasm had suddenly opened before her feet, terrifying yet beckoning.

Finally, after a silence that seemed to go on forever—a period of helpless desperation suspended between two telephone terminals—Val said, "I don't know what to say. I'll talk to you before you leave."

Abruptly she hung up.

After lighting a cigarette, she took a deep drag, then sat there, her hands shaking. She swore under her breath, a long string of every cussword she could think of, and she could think of plenty. She fought the impulse to bolt from the office and lose herself in the teeming crowd on the street below.

Danny, reappearing with her coffee, pulled up short to stare at her. "Hey, Val, what's wrong?"

"Nothing." She took the coffee, somehow managing not to spill it despite trembling.

Danny stood watching her, frowning with concern.

"I *said* I'm fine."

"Anything you say, mama." Dropping a letter on her desk, he said, "This just came for you. Federal Express." Then he walked away quickly.

Val took a deep breath and pulled herself together. Forcing thoughts of Ellen from her mind, she opened the envelope. At least the letter was a concrete thing, something that could be dealt with rationally.

"I need you."

She stared at the message, her mind trying to grasp the meaning of the three words, but there was nothing to grasp beyond a clear and disturbing outcry. "Shit!" She shook her head. What could be so terrible back there that Barbara couldn't spell it out? Why send a letter instead of calling? Val and Barbara had turned

45

to each other for advice and consolation many times over the years but never in such a way as this.

She lit another cigarette and inhaled deeply. What the hell could be wrong with Barbara, of all people? Sure, she drank too much, but so did most people. From the very beginning—from the first moment Kate had introduced them as freshmen in high school—Val had secretly coveted everything Barbara took so casually for granted. Her beauty. Her idyllic family. Her easy conquest of everyone she met, both male and female. Yet that profound, hopeless desire to be like Barbara hadn't stopped them from being friends. It only added a sharp edge to the relationship.

Only once had the charm failed. Even then, Barbara had handled things far better than Valerie. Val went for months at a time without thinking about Steven Ashe, but, especially today, the memory of their graduation night came washing over her again, smothering her with guilt.

She took several long drags on her cigarette and then reached for her phone and dialed Barbara's number.

No answer.

It didn't fucking make sense. Barbara's life was perfect. She had a perfect husband and a perfect child and a perfect home. It was all perfectly boring as far as Val was concerned, but it was what Barbara wanted.

At least she knows what she wants, Val thought. That's more than I can say.

She could call Barbara's husband, David, at his office and ask him what was going on, but she and David loathed each other. She thought his trust-me-I-know-what's-best bedside manner was patronizing, and he thought she embodied the worst excesses of "women's lib," as he persisted in calling it. Besides, for all she knew, *David* was the problem.

What the hell, she told herself, she could catch the next flight to L.A. or San Francisco, then take a commuter flight to Visalia and be there by midnight.

Apart from Barbara's summons, it would be good to get out of the city, to forget everything for a while. She'd been driving herself hard lately and deserved a break. People had been known to burn out—especially hard-charging investigative journalists and she was one of the best. She owed it to herself to ease up.

Bullshit, Val thought, I'm running away.

But then, she'd been running away for more than twenty years—to Berkeley, to grass and speed and coke and whatever else came to hand, and to men. The men had come closer to killing her than all the rest.

"What the fuck," she murmured, "so I'm running away." She grabbed her purse, checked out with her secretary, and left.

After stopping by her SoHo loft to pick up the small tote bag that was always packed and ready, she was on her way. An hour later, Val was buckling herself into a seat in the first-class section of a plane bound for San Francisco. During the long taxi ride out to the airport, a gnawing sense of panic grew. Now her thoughts flashed from Barbara to Ellen and back again.

Why did Ellen have to take a leave of absence? It wasn't necessary. Val would call her tomorrow, persuade her to wait, then talk to her when she got back to New York.

What the hell was wrong with Barbara? Why did she need Val all of a sudden? Barb had always been closer to Kate.

Val had talked to Barbara just a few weeks earlier. Everything had seemed fine. David's all-consuming ambition had finally gotten him where he badly wanted to be—chief of surgery at Municipal Hospital. Their daughter Allison was busily sending transcripts

47

to the best universities in the country, and Barbara had just been reelected president of the Visalia Medical Auxiliary.

Val had listened to Barbara rattle on with a familiar sense of frustration arising from her own irrational feelings of inadequacy. How could anybody be so convinced she had everything worth having? Despite the bond between them, there were times when she wanted to pull the woman's hair. Finally losing patience, Val had broken in to halt Barbara's account of a ladies' doubles tournament at the tennis club.

"Barb, you need a break from all that stress. I've got an idea—why don't you come to New York for a few days? Do some shopping, take in a couple of plays. I'll set you up with this Asian sex guru who was on my show. He's invented seven new positions. You'll go home cross-eyed."

Without missing a beat, Barbara had replied in a perfectly even voice, "But Val, what on earth would David do while I'm gone?"

They both broke up in laughter. Barbara was so secure that Val couldn't burst her bubble with a red-hot ice pick, and Val had been trying to burst it from day one.

Recalling the conversation now, there didn't seem to be anything wrong on Barbara's end. In short, it was another chapter in the ongoing saga of the quintessential upper-middle-class, small-town American family. Two BMWs in the garage and skeletons kept securely hidden in the closet.

It was a picture totally unlike Val's life as a single parent/career woman who lived and breathed her work. Add "lonely" to that profile, she thought, although she never would have admitted as much to Barbara. Then Ellen had come into her life, challenging everything Val had ever believed about herself.

She put on the headphones and found a hard-rock station to listen to while the plane took off. She turned the music up even higher, hoping the driving beat of "Born in the U.S.A." would drown out her thoughts. The strategy didn't succeed. I can't believe I'm actually going back to that place, she thought. When she'd left twenty years earlier, she had sworn she'd never set foot in it again.

Val shook her head. No matter how hard she tried, or how far she went, she couldn't seem to escape Visalia.

Barbara Browning lay motionless in the bed in the Intensive Care Unit. Her face was ashen yet still retained vestiges of a patrician beauty. Her chestnut hair, normally glossy and expertly styled, lay limp and stringy against the stark white of the pillowcase. Her eyes were closed, but occasionally the lids fluttered nervously as if she were having a bad dream. Her breath came in faint, ragged gasps. According to the machines that were attached to her body by tubes and wires, she was alive.

The attending physician, Albert Garcia, watched David Browning scan his wife's chart. Garcia was young, attractive, ambitious, and very smart, and so he cursed his bad luck at drawing the emergency day shift on the morning that the wife of the hospital's chief of surgery decided to eat the big one.

Browning glanced up sharply. "Dilantin?"

Garcia answered promptly, "There were some initial seizures."

"Incorporate valium." Browning's voice was authoritative, unemotional. He studied the chart a moment longer, then replaced it on the door.

Garcia watched as the older man, tanned and trim with distinguished slashes of silver at his temples, crossed to the bedside. Browning regarded his wife for a moment without expression. He looked every inch the pillar of the local medical establishment—and a

49

good blade man, according to the local book on him — but a cold fish, Garcia thought. Definitely a cold fish.

Browning seemed to have forgotten that Garcia existed. Finally, he expelled a deep breath. "Goddamn it!" he swore with cold fury. The anger didn't seem to mask worry. It was simply anger.

Startled, Garcia didn't say a word. A shrewd intelligence had lifted him out of the Hispanic ghetto of Corona and into his profession. He wasn't about to blow it by saying, "What're you doing, man — that's your *wife* lying there."

Abruptly, Browning turned to him. "Did she say anything?"

Garcia hesitated. When they'd trolleyed her out of the paramedic's van, she'd been semiconscious and muttering incoherently, but enough of it had made sense for Garcia to realize he didn't want to know any more. So he lied.

"No. Nothing."

Browning nodded, then started for the door. "Keep me advised."

Garcia stopped him. "By the way, doctor, admissions has this down as food poisoning."

Browning glanced at Garcia's guileless expression. "Good."

Later in the morning, when Garcia stopped by the room, Barbara's pulse had weakened and her color was worse. He watched the gentle rise and fall of her breast for a moment. At least her respiration had stabilized, but she was showing no signs of regaining consciousness.

He closed the door behind him, very concerned. It wouldn't be in his best interest to have to sign a death certificate on Mrs. David Browning.

Crossing to a corridor phone, he dialed an extension in administration. He wondered whether Dr. Browning would be equally concerned.

* * *

Kate and Val had been sitting for a seemingly endless time in the hospital waiting room when Shelly arrived.

Kate had reached town first and had gone straight to Barbara's sprawling, ranch-style house in the most exclusive part of Visalia. Looking closed and empty, the place seemed to give off an aura of ominous events. The sense of foreboding Kate felt while looking at the empty driveway and blind windows was confirmed when the next-door neighbor told her that Barbara had been rushed to the hospital earlier in the day.

At the hospital, a handsome young Chicano doctor refused to allow her onto the Intensive Care ward and parried her questions. She tried to reach David by phone but was told he wasn't in. Finally, with an intense feeling of frustration, she called Alan to say she wasn't sure when she would be back, then settled onto a small sofa in the waiting room.

Watching the doctor go in and out of Barbara's room several times, she thought how ironic it was. When they were teenagers, Barbara was forbidden to date Chicanos. Now one was trying to save her life.

Hours later, Kate saw a familiar figure cross the waiting room toward her. She shot up in her chair. "Val!"

Val stopped short. "Kate! What the hell—I thought you were in L.A."

"I was, but I got a letter from Barb."

Val stared at her. "You, too?"

Kate nodded as Val sat down beside her.

"What's going on?" Val asked impatiently. "I had to talk to some neighbor to find out she was here."

Kate hesitated, then answered, "All I know is that they're calling it food poisoning."

"Food poisoning! Do you think she fired off those

51

letters because she got hold of some bad quiche?"

"I don't know what to think."

Ignoring the NO SMOKING sign, Val lit a cigarette. "What about David?"

"He wouldn't talk to me. I know he was here when I first arrived because I saw his car in the parking lot, but he hasn't been in to see her since I got here."

"The bastard." Val shook her head. "Well, if he won't talk to you, he sure as hell won't talk to me."

"Constance and Allison are back East. I assume he's notified them, but I don't know."

Constance, Barbara's widowed mother, was a formidable matron who, as the wife of the town's leading physician, had mercilessly dominated Visalia society for years. Kate thought her cold, and Val had been simply petrified of her. Nevertheless, she was unquestionably the source of Barbara's consummate poise and self-confidence. Constance—never Connie—had traveled with her granddaughter to assure herself that such institutions as Harvard and Boston U measured up to her high standards.

"Well, what about her friends?" Val demanded. "That goddamn coven of bitches in her precious auxiliary. Why aren't they here?"

"I don't know. I haven't seen anyone else." Kate sighed wearily. Val's voice had taken on an old familiar edge, reminding Kate how Val could psych herself out in an instant. Inevitably, Val regretted the explosion afterward, but, in the meantime, a lot of damage could be done.

Still, the question was a valid one. It wasn't the only one that had occurred to Kate.

Val puffed furiously on a cigarette, sending up clouds of smoke around the spotless sofa. "Well, someone around here must know something." She turned on Kate, her chin trembling. "I've been on planes for five hours and I want to know what the hell is going on! Now, I don't see an anchor tied to your ass, Katie,

52

so why don't you get off it and *talk* to somebody!"

"*Stop it!*"

No one else could get away with using that tone with Val. She stared at Kate for a moment, then exhaled a long breath. "Sorry. I'm a mess." She collapsed back in the chair without offering further explanation.

Kate eyed her critically. Val was clearly bothered by something more than the mystery surrounding Barbara. She said in a softer tone, "We could talk about it."

"No, we couldn't. This one would put you away."

Kate dropped it. Val was like a string of Mexican firecrackers, ready to start popping at the tiniest provocation, but she was *here* and that simple fact was immensely comforting.

"I got your flowers," she said. "Thank you."

Val managed a brief smile. "We were watching, you know. When they said your name, Michelle and I screamed so loud, the neighbors must've thought we were being murdered. Not that they cared, of course, being New Yorkers."

"How is Michelle?"

"She's hit early adolescence. The mouth doesn't stop. She thinks she's a stand-up comic. Always has a comeback. The awful thing is she's really funny, so I end up laughing instead of coming down hard on her like I should."

"Should you be hard on her?"

"Of course. I don't want her growing up to be like me."

They both laughed. Val stubbed out her cigarette in a potted plant and immediately lit another. "All right, so what do we do now?"

"Wait. We just wait."

In the early hours of the morning, a cab pulled up in front of the hospital entrance and Shelly stepped out. She found Kate and Val curled up on the sofa in the darkened, nearly empty waiting room, dozing fitfully. Unable to find Barbara or David, she had called the hospital out of desperation and learned that Barbara had been admitted.

When they saw her, Kate and Val exclaimed in unison, "Shelly!"

She hugged both women at once. Kate looked tense and exhausted. Val looked like she might fly apart at any moment; that was nothing out of the ordinary.

"I take it we all got letters."

Kate nodded. "The question is, why?"

"Have you seen Barb?"

Val answered with characteristic impatience. "Some tight-lipped nurse shows up every once in a while to say she's still in critical condition, and we go back to sleep."

Kate stared in amazement at Shelly. It hadn't occurred to her that Barbara would ask Shelly to return to Visalia—or that Shelly would come. Kate, of all people, knew what courage it took for Shelly to respond to Barbara's plea. She felt a surge of admiration for her and a deep concern for how Shelly was dealing with being back here.

Look at her, Kate thought. Shelly had flown halfway around the world in a matter of hours yet she looked like she'd just stepped out of a designer's fitting room. Her suit was unwrinkled, her hair and makeup perfect. What contrasts the three of them must present, Kate thought, just as they had done in high school.

Then Shelly had been the quintessential California girl, all long tanned legs and waist-length blond hair. She wore miniskirts and dark eyeliner and pale, pale lipstick in imitation of English supermodel Jean Shrimpton.

Val had been the hippie of the group, in low-slung jeans and tie-dyed T-shirts, her curly hair painstakingly ironed until it was straight. Slightly singed, but straight.

Kate herself had been the middle-of-the-road one, neither as spectacularly beautiful as Shelly nor as flamboyant as Val. Intensely ambitious, she was totally focused on her dream of becoming a successful writer.

Now, facing forty, they were still dramatically different. Shelly was just as beautiful, but a polished sophistication had replaced the youthful prettiness. Val was just as outrageous, but now she was paid vast sums to be that way. Kate—well, her dreams had come true, but they hadn't brought the sense of fulfillment she'd expected.

Despite Shelly's unruffled look, Kate noticed her hands were clenched into white-knuckled fists. Suddenly Kate remembered another night many years past . . . holding Shelly in her arms as Shelly clenched and unclenched those fists, her seventeen-year-old cheeks bruised and tear-stained, her eyes rolling, haunted, terrified.

Val went on. "The weird thing is, it's almost like Barb doesn't exist. Nobody seems to *care*." She dropped back into her chair and stared dully at Shelly.

Christ, still perfect. They hadn't seen each other face to face in perhaps five years, but Shelly was still elegant, composed, remote; an image women in every corner of the globe tried to emulate. I must look like Minnie Mouse compared to her, Val thought with familiar resignation.

She couldn't even begin to imagine what it was like to be Shelly Rashad, but it wasn't envy; Val had gotten over that many years before. It was more in the way of an objective assessment, as one might apply to a work of art. Besides, the woman had paid her dues. They all had.

"For God's sake, what happened?" Shelly demanded.

"She tried to kill herself!" Val exploded, giving way to the pent-up frustration of hours.

"You don't *know* that!" Kate snapped.

"Any idiot could figure it out, and somebody might as well say it out loud. If Barb asked all of us to come, then gave up before we could even get here, something must be very, very wrong."

Kate subsided. Val was right. It was stupid to pretend any longer.

Shelly looked from Kate to Val. Finally she said slowly, "I don't have a clue what could have been wrong with Barbara."

"I don't either," Kate said.

Val merely shrugged. She knew that Barbara's drinking was a clue, but somehow she didn't want to think about that.

Benumbed by weariness, they settled in to continue waiting. Making small talk in a desultory way, they caught up on the bits and pieces of each other's lives.

Kate didn't tell them about Alan. She wasn't sure yet what their night together meant—if anything—and she wasn't prepared to deal with the inevitable critical response. Shelly knew too much of what Kate had gone through at the time of the divorce to be glad that Kate and Alan might get back together, and Val had never wavered from her original scathing assessment of him as "a lightweight."

Kate talked of work and the problems she was having with her latest screenplay, which she'd been working on for months and still hadn't gotten right. Val told gossipy anecdotes about some of the more famous guests who'd appeared on her show recently. Only Shelly seemed reluctant to discuss her career. She talked of redecorating her house and a trip to Ibiza. She'd first visited the island on a modeling assignment years earlier and had loved it so much she'd bought a small vacation cottage there as soon as she could afford it. She invited Kate and Val to come anytime. It

56

would be fun, like an extended slumber party.

As they talked of the demands and the perks of successful, high-powered careers, Kate thought, We've turned into women with designer luggage and name-brand purses. We have accountants, lawyers, personal trainers, and brokers. How did we become these women? Only yesterday we were seventeen and longing desperately for a pair of Capezio shoes, which we couldn't afford.

She thought with wonder of how far they had come, sensing an undercurrent of vaguely defined fear among them. It went beyond Barbara, lying in a bed in this building but as distant and cut off as the moon.

More time passed. Routine traffic continued along the corridor outside the dimly lit waiting room. The bloodied victim of a barroom brawl was hustled along by two police officers, and a pregnant woman in the midst of labor was hurried past in a wheelchair pushed by a chattering nurse. A few others drifted in and out.

It was dawn when a nurse finally appeared in the doorway. Shelly and Val were asleep, so the nurse crossed to Kate and said, "Mrs. Browning has been moved out of Intensive Care and into a private room. She's still unconscious, but Dr. Garcia said you can see her for just a moment."

They stood on one side of the bed, looking down at Barbara's pale face. There were no words between them as each tried in her own way to come to terms with the still figure. It was nearly impossible to reconcile their memories of the vivid girl they'd once known with the pathetic woman lying there.

An image flashed through Kate's mind — Barbara at seventeen, playing tennis with natural grace and skill, radiant with an unshakable self-confidence. And her voice, always tinged with a hint of laughter, "Come on, Katie, let's win this one!"

Barbara had been the candle, and the other three were moths. She was their inspiration, the one they could believe in even when they couldn't believe in themselves. She gave voice to their unarticulated dreams, insisting there was much more to life than Visalia offered, and they could have it for the asking. Always surrounded by a crowd of admirers, always the center of attention, she was vivacious and full of life. They had envied her ability to attract boys and had often chafed under her unwavering assumption of leadership, but they had stayed within her orbit, no more able to break out of it than the earth could escape the sun.

In her mind, Kate had assigned a role to Barbara as the stable center of their group, the one who would always have her life together and who would always be there when needed. Now she knew that Barbara's real life was nothing like what she had assumed.

Reaching down, she picked up one of Barbara's limp hands and held it to her own. It felt cool and nearly lifeless. After a moment, she gently laid it back down on the white sheet.

Shelly said in a ragged whisper, "What are we supposed to do here? Maybe we'd better just go."

"Why are you whispering?" Val asked, her voice sounding unnaturally loud. "She's unconscious. She can't hear."

Kate glanced sharply at Val. Her tough-talk defense was up again, protecting her vulnerable center.

"I think I'll stay" Kate said quietly. "There doesn't seem to be anyone else here."

The other two exchanged a look.

Shelly sighed. "Forget I said anything."

Val nodded. "I guess we're all in this together."

As soon as she'd spoken, she realized the words were an eerie echo of something she'd said once before. The others realized it as well and reacted with stunned silence. In an instant, the years slipped away and they were teenage girls again, trying to grope their way through a tragic and terrifying reality. High school graduation night, a time full of promise, turned out to be the beginning of a downward spiral ending now with Barbara hovering between life and death.

Kate's eyes met Shelly's, then Val's. At that moment, the same awful feeling came over each of them—that the pact they'd made so long ago might be at the core of Barbara's suicide attempt. None spoke, but each shared images and memories like ghosts of a summer twenty years old.

They knew they were finally being summoned to account.

1969-1971

CHOICES

ONE

Kate

Heat seared the San Joaquin Valley. By midafternoon on June 7, 1969, the temperature was 105 degrees and still climbing. The cropland was dry, dusty, and brown, and a silver haze of heat shimmered in waves over Highway 99.

Kate McGuire, wearing only a white cotton slip, lay across her lavender-flowered bedspread, listening to the radio and setting down in her journal her thoughts about high school graduation, *the end of an era*. She was filled with an almost unbearable sense of anticipation that had been building inexorably since the start of her senior year. Momentous events were taking place, and they were all happening elsewhere. She intended to be part of them.

Unlike most of the girls she knew, Kate wasn't going to stay in Visalia and settle for an early marriage to a guy who would manage a gas station or work as an insurance salesman, have a bunch of kids, and maybe, if she was lucky, be accepted in Junior League. She wanted more than that. Much more. She had long since come to the conclusion that greatness happened in big cities, not small towns. Only in a city could big dreams come true, and Kate's dreams were very big, indeed.

Her best friend, Barbara, talked a lot about this thing called women's liberation, constantly quoting people like Gloria Steinem and Betty Friedan. Barbara said that all the rhetoric about feminism being a political movement and not a bedroom war boiled down to one thing—their generation didn't have to repeat their mothers' lives.

Kate, for one, didn't intend to.

Three more months. That was all. Then she would bust out of the hermetically sealed cocoon that was this town. She felt a sense of acceleration as she thought of going away to college in the fall. Until then, she'd be counting the weeks, days, and hours.

The swamp cooler rattled away on the roof, fighting a losing battle with the heat, and Kate could feel her cotton slip sticking to her back. The house was cool in only one spot—the central hallway, where the rush of air from the cooler was ice-cold. The cool air dissipated in the heat of the rest of the house.

She had lived in this same house for every one of her nearly eighteen years. The tiny white stucco cottage was in a marginal area of town—neither "right" nor "wrong." It was part of a subdivision commonly known as "Birdland" because the streets were named after birds. The McGuires lived on Oriole.

All the residents of Birdland were white Christians because the developer, like most men in his position, simply wouldn't sell to blacks or the occasional Jew who might turn up. Recently, an Hispanic family had somehow gotten in. That event caused consternation from Redwing to Meadowlark, and the neighbors refused to let their kids play with the Hispanic children.

Visalia, like the rest of the valley, had been settled by WASPs from the South and the Midwest, as well as successive waves of different ethnic groups. First came the Chinese, who built the railroad; then the Japanese and Filipinos, who came to work in the fields; the Italians, looking for more land than their small native country offered; the Armenians, escaping the holocaust in Turkey during World War I; the Okies during the Great Depression; and the Mexicans, who came as supposedly temporary migrant farm laborers only to stay. Most of these immigrants were people of the soil and were drawn to the valley because of the land.

Kate moved comfortably among friends of many different ethnic backgrounds, but she was aware of an underlying racism that was subtle yet pervasive. Each group had been the victims of bigotry in their time and had treated the next wave of immigrants with the same scorn they themselves had experienced.

Now, the caste system was clear-cut. At the bottom were the Mexicans, who recently had begun insisting on the term *Chicano* as a symbol of greater pride. Next came the poor white trash, descendants of the Okies who had never quite made it, then the Italians and Armenians who had become prosperous ranchers or shopkeepers. They were called Wops and rug merchants and rarely married outside their own groups. Next came the Chinese and Japanese, who were respected for their financial acumen and for the fact that they never got into trouble with the law. They also never married outside their own groups.

Finally, at the very top, looking down on everyone, were the wealthy Anglos. Conservative, religious, with roots in the South, they were mainly ranchers whose fortunes came from owning thousands of acres of the richest agricultural land in the world.

Kate's family was solidly middle class. Her father's job as a policeman didn't provide much money, but it carried a great deal of respect.

She was so absorbed in her journal that she was barely aware of the brief hourly news updates on the radio: a massive civil rights march in South Carolina broken up when the police turned loose dogs and fire hoses on the marchers . . . Warren Burger named Chief Justice of the United States Supreme Court . . . a feminist speakout in San Francisco urging the legalization of abortion . . .

Kate continued to write, staring down at the paper in intense concentration. Her seventh-grade English teacher, a middle-aged Armenian-American spinster named Miss Malkasian, had recognized a raw talent in her bright, ambitious student and had suggested she keep a journal. Miss Malkasian had sacrificed her own dreams and ambitions to the care of an invalid mother, but she told Kate what all small-town kids want to believe: "You don't have to be born to wealth or grow up in a powerful family or a big city to achieve something important in life. You can be anything you want to be."

Now, six years later, Kate was at the end of a thick volume of *The Life of Katharine Eileen McGuire*. Everything went into her journal—awkward attempts at poetry, the beginnings of a couple of novels, interesting quotes from famous people, and her deepest secrets. When she finished writing, she laid down her pencil on a scarred oak nightstand, then skimmed through the journal from the beginning, pausing to read only snatches. As she did so, her life over the past six years played out before her like a film being fast-forwarded, pausing briefly at the high points.

November 22, 1963—Peggy Morrow came into algebra class this afternoon with a note for the teacher, Mr. Feldman. She was crying as she handed it to him. I was embarrassed for her. Mr. Feldman stared at the note for a long time, then looked up, but he didn't seem to be looking at us. He said in a funny voice, "The President has been shot. He's dead, but the world will go on." I couldn't believe it at first, and when I finally did, I couldn't believe Mr. Feldman could be so cold. Maybe the world will go on, but it won't be the same.

May 21, 1967 — Barb borrowed her parents' car and we all went up to Three Rivers to go swimming. She really makes a big deal about being sixteen and having her driver's license while the rest of us are still fifteen. But that's just Barb. If she didn't have something to feel superior about, she'd make it up. While we were lying around, she thought up a game where we each guess what kind of man the others are going to end up marrying. Val said I would marry a professor wearing a tweed jacket and smoking a pipe. I said she'd end up with a hippie who'd make tie-dyed T-shirts for a living. Shelly said Barb would end up marrying a doctor just like her father, and Barb said no way, she was going to *be* a doctor just like her father. She said Shelly would end up marrying an English rock star and moving to a huge estate outside London and having a nanny for her kids. Shelly got that faraway look she gets sometimes and said she wanted to marry a prince. Val said, don't we all?

June 5, 1968 — Robert Kennedy is dead. I can't believe it's all happening again. Why?

October 4, 1968 — I went out with Kenny Ayres last night. He's twenty and goes to State. We went to see a movie called *The Chase*, with a new actor, Robert Redford. God, is he cute. We parked in the orange grove on the other side of Birdland. We talked about movies and books, especially John Fowles's *The Collector*. I said it showed how men think women are prizes to be caught and put on display. Kenny laughed and said, "What are you, a feminist?" I'm not exactly sure what that is so I didn't say anything. He stroked my cheek and said my skin was so soft. He had some pot in his glove compartment. I felt stupid because I didn't know how to smoke it right, but Kenny showed me. We listened to music and made out. When "You've Lost that Lovin' Feeling" came on, I went all mushy inside. Kenny isn't like the boys I've dated. He's so cool, so sophisticated. He isn't awkward and doesn't fumble around. I let him touch me where no one's ever touched me before, then I got scared and made him stop. When I got home, I laid awake in bed for a long, long time, unable to sleep. I feel excited, antsy, strange. I've never felt that way before. He said he would call me again. I can't wait.

October 20, 1968 — Kenny never called. I heard he's dating Sue Montgomery's older sister. Barbara told me what "feminist" means. I am one.

March 1, 1969 — Val says she went all the way

68

with Gregg Hartoonian. He didn't even wear a rubber, and now she's got to sweat out the next two weeks till her period's due. She asked Barb if it's true you can get an abortion by shaking up a Coke and douching with it. Barb told her it would have to be a BIG Coke. Shelly told her it was stupid to take such a risk. Of course, that made Val mad. Even though she won't admit it, I think she's scared. I would be. If you get pregnant, it's all over. When Suzie Hershenson got pregnant last year, she had to leave Redwood and go to continuation school. Her boyfriend, Cal, married her, even though he obviously didn't really want to. She invited all of us over for lunch one day and acted like having a baby and being married was great, but her apartment wasn't very nice, and Cal is gone most of the time, and all I could think of was that she's stuck in Visalia forever now.

March 15, 1969—Val's period started!!! We celebrated by sneaking a bottle of wine out of Barb's house. Barb said she hoped Val learned a lesson. Val said she sure did—from now on she's carrying a rubber in her purse. We all cracked up.

April 17, 1969—Barb asked me to be a pen pal to a friend of her cousin, Larry, who's in Vietnam. He told her a lot of guys over there don't get much mail. So I wrote to this guy, Mike, and I got a letter back from him right away. It was strange, though—right in the middle of it there was a page with HELP! written in big letters, and at the end he asked me how things are in "the world." As if where he is isn't part of the world. Visalia sure isn't.

June 7, 1969—I GRADUATE TONIGHT! Finally, it's over. I thought high school was like reading one of those Russian novels; it was never going to end. I can't wait to start college in the fall. When Dad took me down to L.A. to look over the UCLA campus, I couldn't believe how big it is. An interesting thing happened. While Dad was off somewhere, a real cute black guy tried to pick me up. I had to tell him I was from out of town and was leaving in a few hours. He said he'd look me up in the fall. I hate to think what would happen if he did that here. When I told Barb about it, she freaked. She said I'll never get into a sorority at UCLA if I date blacks. Val says I should go out with him. She says black guys are really hung. I asked her how she knew that, and she just gave me that look that's supposed to mean she's so much more experienced than the rest of us. But I know better. Doing it once with Gregg doesn't make her an expert. . . .

Kate closed her journal and lay back on the bed, staring up at the ceiling. Outside she could hear the sound of her father's brand-new power mower snarling across the backyard grass, but her mind wasn't on her father, stubbornly determined to keep his garden thriving despite the withering heat, or her mother, in the kitchen baking cupcakes for the boys' last-day-of-school parties tomorrow. Her mind certainly wasn't on her little brothers, who were pests, going through her things when she wasn't around, defacing her Beatles poster by drawing horns and

70

glasses on John, Paul, George, and Ringo.

Her body was tense with excitement. Tonight, she thought, I graduate. Next month I'll be eighteen. In September, I'll be at UCLA. Just three more months. Three more months and I'll be free!

When the acceptance letter came, she had opened the long white envelope with shaky hands because inside was her ticket out of Visalia, a ticket to her hopes, her dreams, her entire future. Every once in a while she would take it out of her desk drawer and reread it, only to feel once more the sense of exhilaration. No longer would she languish in the nosiness, narrow-mindedness, and boredom of a small town. Life wouldn't really begin until the moment she left home for college.

Kate knew exactly what she was going to do with her life. She would major in English and become a fine writer, like Eudora Welty or Joan Didion, *not* like Jacqueline Susann, who merely wrote trashy best-sellers. She would live in L.A., or maybe New York. Yeah, New York. Most writers seemed to go there. She would meet interesting, cosmopolitan people and be one of them, accepted, respected. She would travel to Europe and use her high school French while browsing in Left Bank bookshops in Paris.

Her life was going to be very, very different from the way it was now, and she would never, ever live in a small town again!

The ringing telephone, a sweet-sixteen birthday party present from her parents, shattered Kate's fantasy. Reaching out for it, she answered mechanically, "Hello."

"This is your valedictorian speaking. I just wanted to check in with one of the little people who made me what I am today."

Kate laughed. "You're valedictorian because half

71

the teachers are your father's patients. They were afraid to give his daughter anything less than an A minus."

"Jealousy doesn't become you. What are you wearing?"

"That peach blouse and skirt. How about you?"

"I don't know. Maybe some old jeans. My white Wranglers would really look bitchin' with my turquoise T-shirt."

The grad-nite dress code strictly forbade jeans, and Barbara knew it. Kate didn't buy her nonchalant attitude for a second. "You'll never get away with it."

"Of course I will. What are they going to do? Get somebody else to make my speech?"

On second thought, Kate decided, Barbara probably would get away with it. She seemed to get away with almost anything. A pampered only child who was very much aware of her family's lofty position in the local social pecking order, Barbara had limitless audacity. Kate had seen her intimidate people, including adults, on more than one occasion.

"Look, change of plans," Barbara went on. "I've got to go to dinner with my parents afterward. We'll meet at the all-night party in the gym then go over to Foster's, okay?"

"Do I have anything to say about it?"

"No. Call Val and Shelly and let them know. Oops, I've gotta run. 'Bye."

Typical, Kate thought as she hung up. A natural leader, Barbara arranged everyone's life to facilitate her own, and always had. Her friends went along with her because her boundless energy was a little like a roller coaster. All anyone could do was hang on and hope for the best.

It had been that way ever since the four of them had formed their own little clique as freshmen. Initially, they were drawn together for superficial reasons. Kate and Barbara became friends after sitting next to each other in homeroom and realizing they were the two smartest people in the class. Val joined the group by virtue of being Kate's oldest friend, and Shelly became part of it when she and Barbara started talking about the Beatles in drama class one day and discovered they were both madly in love with Paul.

The group solidified as they realized they shared a crucial attitude that most of their classmates lacked — they wanted to get out of Visalia and have interesting, exciting lives. Now, four years later, they were rarely apart.

Kate picked up the phone again and dialed. In a moment, a soft, breathless, shy voice answered.

"Hi, Shelly, it's me. What are you doing?"

"My makeup. Wouldn't you know it, I think I'm getting a zit."

"No way. You've never had a zit in your life. It's disgusting."

There was laughter in Shelly's little-girl voice. "Eat your heart out."

"I just talked to Barb. She wants to meet at the all-night party in the gym, then go over to Foster's."

"Oh? Did she have any more instructions?"

"Probably, but she had to get off the phone."

Shelly sighed with resignation. "Oh, why not? Once I ditch my mom, I don't care what we do."

"Okay, see ya later."

She'd barely hung up when the phone rang again. Picking it up, she said, "Hi, Val."

"How did you know it's me?" Val asked from one block over. She lived in Birdland, too, on Wren.

"I already talked to Barb and Shelly. Who else could it be?"

"Well, it could be Mick Jagger, smart ass."

73

"I am a smart ass, and don't you forget it."

"Listen, I just called Johnny Borba. He said some of the guys are gonna hide beers under their gowns. Isn't that wild?"

"*You* called him? Isn't that a little pushy?"

"Jesus, it's not like I tried to rip his pants off. Although that's not a bad idea. He's one hell of a sexy Portagee. Anyway, I told him to pass one along to us. He said he would."

Kate sighed. "Great. What happens when we get caught?"

"Never happen. Trust me."

"Famous last words."

"Having a cop for a father has really warped your mind. You can be Miss Goody-Two-Shoes if you want, but I'm going over the wall tonight, and if they come after me, they won't take me alive."

Kate couldn't believe Val sometimes. "You are definitely too much."

"Hallelujah, sister."

There was a murderous sarcasm underlying Val's words, but Kate was too familiar with it to pay any attention. "Listen, Barb wants to meet at the all-night party, okay?"

"That's for dorks. Why does she want to go there?"

"We're not gonna stay. As soon as she gets there, we'll go to Foster's."

"But until she decides to show up, it will be boring as hell. I could be out dragging Main in Johnny's 'vette."

"*Val.*"

She gave in grudgingly. "Oh, all right."

"What are you wearing?"

"That new denim skirt and top with all the zippers and pockets and stuff."

Kate rolled her eyes toward the ceiling. "Weird."

"And don't you forget it," Val finished and hung up.

Kate spent the next half hour doing her hair and makeup. She taped a picture of English supermodel Twiggy to her vanity mirror and did her best to copy the look—pale lips, dark-rimmed eyes with lots of black mascara to thicken her lashes, her chin-length hair teased into a bouffant and sprayed within an inch of its life. She dabbed Oh! de London cologne on her wrists and neck and behind her ears.

For years afterward, if she happened to smell that particular perfume, it would all come back to her in a rush of bittersweet memory—the sticky heat of that summer afternoon, her naïveté and optimism and boundless self-confidence, the intoxicating sense of change hovering in the air around her.

When she finished her hair and makeup, she examined her image critically. Her eyes were all right, large, almond-shaped, silvery gray, but she was too thin and, at five-eight, too tall, though not, thank God, as tall as Shelly. Shelly was five-ten in her bare feet, six feet in heels. She towered over a lot of guys.

Of course, Kate reminded herself reassuringly, Twiggy was thin, too, really thin, but her face was so gorgeous it didn't matter. What she wouldn't give for Shelly's curves. If only she were beautiful, she thought with a kind of hopeless wistfulness. Being beautiful made everything easier. She was sure of it. In high school, it was just about all that mattered. She hoped college would be different. Maybe there, intelligence and creativity would be valued more than a flawless complexion and long blond hair. Maybe.

She was ready when her father knocked on the door. Opening it, she hurriedly donned her cap and gown while he stood watching from the doorway.

He grinned proudly. "You look pretty as a picture, Kate. Your mom wants to get some snapshots. Ready?"

"Yeah, Dad, just a minute."

She took one last look at herself in the mirror, frowned, then hurried outside with him. In the front yard, her mother waited with the old Brownie camera. While her father fiddled with it and her mother tried to tell him what to do, Kate stood impatiently, shading her eyes against the sun. Normally, she paid little attention to her parents. Now, for some reason, she found herself staring at them.

Her father was working tonight and so was in uniform. She felt a surge of pride at the imposing figure he made. He stood six-four, weighed two hundred and twenty-five pounds, and was movie-star handsome, with strong, even features and eyes that sparkled with good humor. At family gatherings, Kate heard outrageous stories about what a wild hellion her father had been in his youth, after his stint in the Marine Corps during World War II, but these days, when he was off-duty he came straight home from work to tease his wife and play with his children and work in his garden.

Kate, the firstborn, had always felt especially close to her father. From the time she was a baby, she was "Daddy's girl," his pride and joy. She had his coloring, his gray eyes and soft brown hair, along with his adventurous streak.

That adventurousness nearly got her killed when she was barely five years old. She and her parents had gone to visit relatives who lived on a small farm outside of town. A large German shepherd was shut up in the backyard. Eager to play with the dog, Kate opened the gate, then stood frozen in terror as it came at her, teeth bared, growling viciously, its hackles raised. Kate's mother was nearly nine months pregnant and unable to move quickly, but her father raced over to Kate just as the dog lunged, and beat it off with a rake that had been lying on the ground nearby.

From that moment on, she turned to her father for protection, for reassurance, for guidance. She took her mother for granted but adored her father. He backed her one hundred percent, whatever she undertook, whether it was her disastrous decision to try the clarinet — she proved to be utterly nonmusical — or her ambition to make her way in the world as a writer. His simple credo for her was, "You can do anything you set your mind to, Katie." With her gentle giant of a father behind her, she had a sense of security that never left her.

When she dated a boy, she always compared him to her father. The boys never quite measured up. Often she would come home from a date — always in time to meet her midnight curfew — to find her father sitting up in front of the television, watching the late news. They would sit and talk for a while, sometimes over steaming cups of hot chocolate with a marshmallow floating on top that he made for her.

He never questioned her about her dates beyond a perfunctory, "Did you have a nice time?" He told her often that he trusted her, and she wouldn't dream of abusing that trust. No matter how attracted she was to a boy, she was never tempted to give in. She couldn't imagine going all the way in the backseat of someone's car, or in one of the cheap motels on Mooney Boulevard, then coming home to face her father.

It was her father who encouraged her to apply to a college outside of the valley, while her mother preferred that she go to the state university in the nearby city of Fresno. He had seen something of the world during the war, and he wanted Kate to do the same. He talked of England and France and Germany, of the people and the food and the customs. It was clear that he'd found it fascinating, but when she asked him why he didn't go back, now that the war was long over and he could really enjoy it, he simply shook his head and said, "It costs too much. Maybe someday."

She always sensed that he had wanted to do more with his life but had been tied down by the responsibilities of marriage and parenthood. It scared Kate to think of being held back that way, of sacrificing her life to the needs of people dependent on her. She had no desire to get married for a long, long time, and she wasn't sure she ever wanted to have children.

When she told her mother that, Lea looked shocked and said, "Of course you'll have children! They're the most important thing in a woman's life."

If Kate idolized her father, she felt a vague sense of condescension toward her mother. Lea McGuire was a petite, fading blonde with large, cornflower-blue eyes, the only remarkable feature in an otherwise plain face. Her reserve was the opposite of Harry McGuire's easy, outgoing charm. Rarely surrendering to emotion, she was the family planner, seeing to it that Harry's limited salary as a policeman stretched to cover the needs of a growing family, as well as acting as day-to-day disciplinarian. Harry, conscious of his intimidating physical presence, could never bring himself to punish the kids.

Lea worked every waking minute of the day, cooking meals, baking, cleaning, canning preserves made from fruit grown in Harry's garden, sewing. She had made the bedspread and curtains in Kate's room, copying the patterns from a picture in *Seventeen* magazine. She had an innate sense of design, an unerring sense of what looked good and what didn't, but she could rarely afford to express it.

For weeks after the room was finished, Kate would occasionally find her mother standing in the doorway, staring at it proudly. When she asked her father about this, he told her that before their marriage, Lea had lived in a shack with a plank floor and no running water. Kate realized that her mother must have grown up dreaming about such a room as this; but she couldn't talk to her about it. She could never talk to her mother about anything really personal.

Kate had always carried the vague wish that her mother had been something . . . *more*. More educated, more sophisticated, more interested in the world outside the San Joaquin Valley. Lea sensed that, and it created an underlying tension between mother and daughter.

Now, as she studied her parents, Kate wondered once more what on earth could have brought them together. She had asked her father that question once. He'd merely shaken his head and replied, "I wouldn't be much without her. You'll understand when you fall in love someday."

She considered the possibility that maybe her parents were together because they didn't have much choice. When they were her age, they didn't have the options she did now. When her father married and started a family, he gave up any hope of going to college. As far as Kate could tell, there had never been any question of her mother being anything other than a housewife.

Choices. Options. Opportunities. Kate intended to make the most of hers and never end up like her mother.

"Now, Kate," Lea said. "You and your father stand over there, by the lemon tree."

As Kate and her father took their places in front of the small tree, she winced inwardly. She could al-

79

ready see the squinty-eyed pictures the photo session would produce, to be circulated endlessly at family gatherings. Her brothers, ten-year-old Scottie and twelve-year-old Thomas, stayed clear of the action, watching and giggling from behind their mother.

After several shots, Kate said impatiently, "Mom, we've gotta go! I'll be late!"

"All right, dear, there's just one more thing."

Lea glanced at Harry, who took a small package wrapped in gold foil out of his pocket. He handed it to Kate with a pleased grin. "Can't have a graduation without a present, can we?"

She quickly read the small card that was attached—"To Kate, with all our love, Mom and Dad." Tearing open the package, she found a long, slim, black velvet box. Inside it lay a white-gold watch. The exquisite simplicity of its design reflected her mother's understated taste. Kate knew it must have cost a lot of money, maybe a hundred dollars or more.

She looked at her mother, who controlled the family finances with an iron frugality, and saw the sudden vulnerability in her eyes. For a moment, Kate could barely find her voice. Finally, she managed to whisper, "It's beautiful. Really. Thank you."

Lea McGuire caught her breath and turned away.

Kate's brothers, who had rarely seen their mother speechless, exchanged puzzled looks.

Watching his wife, Harry's eyes seemed to soften.

That moment would stay with Kate always, etched in her memory: the small family gathered on the suburban lawn in the slanting, late-afternoon sunlight, with the sharp smell of lemon blossom leaves on the warm breeze.

For one fleeting moment, she knew a feeling akin to panic at the thought of leaving this safety, this security, this closeness behind, but as quickly as it

came, the feeling left, supplanted by an unquenchable eagerness to begin her life.

An hour later, Kate, along with three hundred
other high school seniors, nervously marched onto
the football field to the ponderous strains of "Pomp
and Circumstance." When Val handed her a beer
that had been surreptitiously passed down from
Johnny Borba, she hesitated, then thought, Why the
hell not? After all, from this night on none of the
old rules applied. Taking a long sip, she choked a
little and then handed it back to Val with a grin.

TWO

Valerie

As twilight set in, a hot breeze came up, rustling the folds of the long blue gowns and sending the gold tassels hanging from the mortarboards swinging gently back and forth. Val looked out into the packed bleachers and saw her parents, Morgan and Bessie, sitting in the very first row.

They had come early to get a good seat. This was an auspicious occasion. Neither of them had graduated from high school, and their two other daughters had both dropped out to get married and have children. Val was the first member of her family to graduate, and with honors, too, as well as a scholarship to the University of California at Berkeley. They had wanted her to attend a college affiliated with their religion, but Valerie had refused.

Looking at them, her nervousness dissipated. After all, what could they do to her now? It was *over*. The control, the restrictions, the incessant harping on the Bible, the arguments when she came in late or did things they disapproved of were all history. She was *free!*

Giddy with abandon, she thought, I fucking own this night. Nobody can tell me what to do anymore.

All her life, she'd heard nothing but the dogma of

the First Southern Baptist Church. "Man is born with a sinful nature," Morgan Simpson would recite in a deep, mournful voice. "Natural functions and appetites must be controlled by putting to death the deeds of the body."

His wife, Bessie, had nothing to add to these stern lectures. A meek, nervous woman, she deferred to her husband in all things, as her religion ordered her to do.

Being a Baptist meant no drinking, no dancing, no smoking, no movies or television or music, except for church hymns. Val had to ask her friends to describe movies to her, scene by scene. When they discussed TV shows, such as "Bonanza" and "American Bandstand," she was left out because her family didn't own a television.

She had to tithe her allowance, memorize Bible verses during meals, and spend every Sunday morning in a segregated Sunday school class—girls in one room, boys next door.

With her family, she went to church twice on Sunday and every Wednesday night. On that night, the children would get up in front of the congregation and practice "sword drills."

The pastor shouted, "Attention!"

The children stood, Bibles in hand.

The pastor commanded, "Draw swords!"

They lifted the Bibles to their chests, clutching them nervously.

The pastor read a passage and shouted, "Charge!"

The children flipped through the Bibles. Whoever found the passage first stepped forward and read it aloud.

Val nearly always won these competitions.

She couldn't care less about the meaning of the passages she read, but she loved being the center of attention, having all eyes on her, seeing the look of envy in the faces of the other children. She might not be as pretty as some of the other little girls, their blond curls pulled back by pink satin ribbons, their organdy dresses all ruffles and lace, but she was smarter than they were. That knowledge was a source of intense gratification. It softened her father's blunt assessment of her—"Not much to look at but smart as a whip."

The only relief she found from the frozen dogma of the church was in books. She would spend hours at a time in the public library, an old adobe building surrounded by towering oak trees, losing herself in worlds far removed from the cold reality of her own. The library was a quiet, serene refuge and also a source of inspiration. There, she learned there was more to life than could be experienced in the narrow confines of a small town.

The intoxication of losing herself in other times and other places swept her into that high, sweet air the Scriptures call "lighter than vanity." In that weightless state, she would imagine that she could be anything she dreamed of being. She could even reinvent herself, as Jay Gatsby had done.

Any identity she could imagine was preferable to the one she was born with, the youngest of three daughters born to Okie migrants who came to California in the late thirties. Her father was too old to serve in World War II, so he got a job in a shipyard in Oakland for the duration of the war. That was the family's ticket out of poverty. For the first time since they were driven out of the Oklahoma dust bowl, they lived in an apartment with indoor plumbing and went to sleep at night without the empty rumble of hunger in their stomachs.

When the war ended, the family moved to Visalia, where Morgan's younger brother arranged for him to work at an appliance factory. Val's mother did ironing for people who would drive up in fancy cars and drop off baskets of wrinkled clothes, then return a few days later to pick up the crisply ironed clothes hanging from a line strung between the kitchen and the living room.

Between Morgan's wages and Bessie's meager but crucial income, they were able to eventually buy a small house in a brand-new tract being built to house the growing families of returning servicemen. Morgan resented it when people started snidely referring to the subdivision as Birdland because of the streets named after birds. To him and Bessie, it was the realization of a longed-for dream. Finally, in their forties, they had a toehold on the edge of middle-class respectability. In a few years, their two daughters would be out of the house and married and things would be easier financially. They could see a time coming when they wouldn't have to count every penny, when they could take a trip back to Oklahoma to visit relatives left behind.

Then, in 1951, shortly after their oldest daughter was married off at seventeen to a young man with a stable job as a mechanic, leaving only one girl at home, Val was born.

Bessie liked the feeling of holding a newborn baby in her arms again, though it meant she wouldn't be able to stop doing other people's ironing for a long time. One of Val's earliest memories was of the line of clothes brushing the top of her head when she ran back and forth under it. While the little girl played, her mother ironed and hummed country and western songs under her breath in a barely audible, furtive way, as if afraid of being caught.

85

Morgan was consumed with bitterness at the birth of another girl. If it had been a boy, it wouldn't have been so bad, but another *girl!* He was livid at the unfairness of it. At church, he offered up angry prayers to God, demanding to know why he'd been saddled with this unexpected and unwanted burden just when things were finally looking up for them.

He had worked hard since he left school at twelve. When they lost their place as tenant farmers in Oklahoma, he swallowed his pride and did whatever backbreaking work was necessary, including farm labor alongside Mexicans up and down the San Joaquin Valley. He kept his family from starving. That was more than a lot of men he knew could say.

Now *this*. Another mouth to feed, and such an ugly little thing, with her carrot-red hair and pasty-white skin. Morgan and Bessie were both blond, as were their other daughters. He didn't know where this little girl got such bright hair, unless maybe it was from his mother, who had been a strawberry blond in her youth.

Valerie was a difficult child, too, always crying. There was a contrariness about her that only got worse as she got older. Unlike the other girls, who'd been docile and obedient, this one seemed to have a mind of her own from the very beginning. She couldn't sit still in church, and half the time Bessie had to take her outside.

Morgan told her to spank the child, that would make her behave, but Bessie could never bring herself to hit any of her children. Her own father had beaten her during alcoholic rages, and she remembered all too vividly the feeling of helpless terror that had engulfed her during his rampages.

86

Morgan had no such compunction. He began by slapping Val's chubby little two-year-old hands when she reached for something forbidden. By the time she was in school, she often found it uncomfortable to sit on the hard wooden seats because of the red welts from being punished with Morgan's thick leather belt. To his intense frustration, these beatings didn't seem to faze her. She would stare back at him, fighting back tears, and he could see defiance written in every line of her rigid little body.

During the hot valley summers, she went to Vacation Bible School, where she saluted the Christian flag alongside the American flag. At some point during the summer, an evangelist would come to hold a tent revival meeting and save souls. Services were held every night for a solid week. Val's family never missed a revival, and as far as she could tell, they had all been saved many times over.

They were supposed to bring friends to be saved. The summer they were fourteen, Val persuaded her best friend, Kate, to come. Kate's family wasn't religious and never attended church, so Kate was a perfect candidate. The two girls spent the entire evening giggling and making fun of the wild-eyed evangelist and his guilty-looking parishioners. They made up outrageous stories about the possible sins the parishioners had committed.

When it was over, a furious Morgan told Val never to invite Kate again.

It didn't matter, though, because that was the last time Val attended a revival meeting. As far back as she could remember, she had questioned what she was taught in church. How could Jesus rise from the dead? Why was it Eve's fault if Adam accepted the apple? How could they be so sure theirs was the only true religion and everyone else would be

87

damned for eternity?

The middle-aged, stern-faced Sunday school teacher would purse her lips and respond, "Valerie Lynn Simpson, you're questioning things you have no right to question! God knows best, and His wisdom is right here in the Bible." When Val responded that men wrote the Bible and men could make mistakes, the teacher made her hold out her hands, palms up, then rapped hard on them with a ruler to teach her not to be impertinent.

Shortly after the revival meeting, Val refused to attend church any longer, declaring that she was an agnostic, a word she had learned from Kate, who had learned it from her father. Morgan started to pull off his belt, determined to beat Val into submission, and for the only time in her life, Bessie stood up to him, placing her short, plump body between her husband and her daughter.

She didn't say a word, but the look on her face stopped Morgan cold. For one tense moment, Val looked from her mother to her father. She didn't know what he would do. She only knew that this time she wouldn't just stand there and take it. Watching him take off his belt, as she'd done so many times before, she felt a rush of rebelliousness, a refusal to let herself be hurt again.

Morgan's face grew red with angry frustration. Abruptly, he threw down his belt and stalked off, shouting over his shoulder, "I'm through trying to save her! She will surely burn in hell, for if ever the devil was in a child, he's in this one!"

All right, Val thought with a fierce determination, if the devil's in me, then I may as well say to hell with everything.

From that moment on, she rebelled against every repressive aspect of her life. She stopped wearing the dowdy clothes her mother sewed for her from cheap, flowered cotton fabric. She got a job at a Dairy Queen so she could afford to buy the kinds of clothes her friends wore — psychedelically patterned minidresses, jeans, halter tops, boots. She started wearing makeup and going to school dances. Smoking. Swearing. Making out with boys. For a while, Val turned her back on school, as well, until Barbara made her see that a college scholarship could be her ticket out of Visalia. Then she buckled down and studied hard with a vengeance, not wanting to end up with the dead-end existence her sisters, Janeen and April, had settled for. Both had married good ol' boys who were blue-collar workers, and had several children each.

On Friday nights, in flagrant violation of her father's orders, she went to movies with Kate, Shelly, and Barbara. Afterward, they dragged Main in Barbara's parents' car, eyeing the boys who were eyeing them. Saturday night was date night, and more often than not she sat at home, surreptitiously reading romance novels that she bought at the Payless Drug Store near the Dairy Queen.

Like many bright young women, Val was a closet romantic. She yearned for the kind of passion and tenderness that she read about in these books and saw in movies and TV. When Warren Beatty kissed Natalie Wood in *Splendor in the Grass*, Valerie felt as if she could die from the unbearable sweetness of it. She longed for a boy to want her the way Warren wanted Natalie. She dreamed of being swept away by an all-consuming passion.

But romance didn't seem to exist in real life, at least not in hers. Her father's blunt assessment of her — not much to look at — was reinforced over and over again as she got older but not prettier. Nobody

89

invited her to the prom. Nobody told her that he liked her. Nobody asked her to go steady or wear his letterman's sweater.

On the rare occasions when a boy did ask her out, she would make out with him on the first date because she was convinced it was the only way to get him to come back for a second. She didn't enjoy the boys' awkward fumbling with her small breasts and their wet, insistent kisses, but for those brief periods, at least, she was held closely, touched, reassured that she was desirable.

In her senior year, she met Gregg Hartoonian, a fullback on the football team, first string, darkly handsome, and big as a young moose, with a hard, muscled physique that left Valerie breathless. He wasn't overly bright, and she knew she could run rings around him intellectually. To make sure she didn't inadvertently do that, she kept her mouth shut when she was around him.

Val stood on the edge of the groups where he was always the center of attention. She laughed at his jokes, smiled at him encouragingly, and every time the Rangers won a game, she told him that he was single-handedly responsible for the victory. When he finally asked her out, she thought she had died and gone to heaven.

If things went well, she thought, maybe Gregg would ask her to the prom. She'd never gone to one, and despite her insistence to her friends that proms were silly and she wouldn't be caught dead at one, she desperately wanted to go. For once in her life, Val wanted to feel like a princess, to wear a gorgeous dress and to be given a corsage to wear, and to feel attractive. As she dressed in her sexiest dress, a bare little wisp of emerald green that barely came to midthigh, she was determined to make her

90

first date with Gregg absolutely perfect so he would call again.

They went to a drive-in theater in Gregg's red GTO. *Butch Cassidy and the Sundance Kid* was playing, but they spent more time making out than watching the movie. Afterward, they parked in an orange grove on the outskirts of town and got into the backseat. Gregg had bought a couple of six-packs of beer using his older brother's I.D. By the time they drank all the beer and got down to some heavy necking, Valerie was feeling a little light-headed. She hadn't eaten all day out of nervousness about the date.

It was cold in the car, and the white leather tuck 'n' roll upholstery felt uncomfortable against the bare skin of her thighs as Gregg pushed up her skirt. With other boys, she'd always told them no at the last minute. This time, she seemed to have lost her voice.

It happened so quickly. Suddenly Gregg was pushing inside her, and though it hurt, Val couldn't protest because he was kissing her so hard. Pressed down on the narrow seat, she felt confused and helpless. She'd fantasized endlessly about what sex would feel like, but she hadn't imagined it would simply be this dull pressure. Instead of being a wonderful, transcendent experience that made the earth move, as it did in books and movies, it was uncomfortable and awkward and embarrassing.

Val thought, How can girls do this more than once?

Then, as abruptly as it began, it ended. Gregg shuddered—she felt his muscles ripple beneath his sweater as she dug her fingers into his shoulders—then he pulled out of her.

When she looked up into his face, she didn't

know what she hoped to see. Not love, certainly, for she wasn't stupid, but maybe some indication of profound feeling. At the very least, a little warmth.

What she saw was a look of blank astonishment.

"You're a virgin!" he blurted out.

Not any more, she wanted to say, but she couldn't let him think she was disappointed or upset. If he felt uncomfortable, if he thought she was criticizing his ability as a lover, he would never ask her out again.

"It's all right," she insisted, in an awkward voice that sounded funny to her own ears.

"Christ, there's blood on my upholstery!" he said in disgust, pulling away from her even more.

He zipped up his jeans, then took a dirty towel out of the trunk and cleaned up the seat as best he could. Val wanted to clean herself off, but there didn't seem to be anything to use. She couldn't bear the thought of using the towel that smelled of stale sweat, so she simply pulled up her panties and pulled down her skirt. Sitting rigidly next to Gregg on the short, silent ride home, she felt dirty and awfully sore. She couldn't wait to soak in a long, hot bath.

He walked her to her door, but instead of kissing her good-night, he mumbled, "I'll call you," then hurried back to his car. Even as he gunned the engine and peeled out, Val knew with heartbreaking certainty that he wouldn't call.

In bed later that night, she realized with a sick sensation that if Gregg had assumed she wasn't a virgin, that meant the other boys at school did, too. She had a reputation! And until tonight she'd done nothing to deserve it.

When she told her friends about going all the way with Gregg, she pretended that it had been exciting. After all, she had an image to maintain as the one who wasn't afraid to break the rules, who had a hell of a lot of fun that the others missed out on because they were afraid to try forbidden things. Val couldn't admit to them that there was something wrong with her because she didn't like sex.

When they brought up the possibility of pregnancy, it was all she could do to appear cool. Inside, she was terrified. What if she was pregnant? It would ruin her entire life. Her parents would kick her out of the house; she would be expelled from school; she would never get that college scholarship; she would never get out of Visalia.

How would she live? How could she possibly support herself and a baby? Val knew that Gregg would deny being the father of the child. He would probably get his friends to claim that they'd all slept with her. She'd heard of boys doing that. Nobody would take her side. It was a girl's responsibility not to get pregnant; if she did, she had no one but herself to blame.

All of Val's religious indoctrination came back to haunt her. Her father had warned her about the sins of the flesh. Maybe he was right and she was being punished for transgressing. She thought about going back to church but knew that instead of finding comfort there she would only encounter condemnation.

For two weeks, she barely slept, couldn't eat, expended every last ounce of energy she possessed in trying to appear unconcerned. When the time came for her period to start, she ran in the bathroom and checked her panties frequently for signs of a telltale red stain.

None appeared.

Her period was one day late, then two, then a

week. Val was a basket case, unable to face her family or her friends. She didn't know which was more terrifying—the thought of trying to give herself an abortion with a bent coat hanger or a knitting needle or telling her parents she was pregnant.

Then one morning she woke up with a bad cramp gripping her lower body. Stumbling to the bathroom, she saw that her period had finally started. Bursting into tears, Val had to turn on the shower to muffle the sound of her own relieved sobs.

Now, listening to the principal call out Gregory Aram Hartoonian and watching Gregg swagger across the stage while his friends and family in the audience hooted and whistled good-naturedly, Val told herself she didn't give a damn about him. For all his good looks and his parents' money, he was boring and not very bright. He would never leave Visalia, never do anything interesting with his life. She had a vision of him, years down the road, fat and balding, repeating tired old stories of his high school victories, saddled with a wife who knew him far too well to be impressed, while Val would be somewhere—anywhere—else, doing exciting things with people who mattered.

The principal called out, "Valerie Lynn Simpson!" Rising, she walked across the stage, head held high, grinning impudently.

THREE

Barbara

A brand-new white '69 Mustang convertible pulled up in front of the Redwood High School gym. White cars were *it*. They were young and sexy. Yves Saint-Laurent drove a gleaming white Volkswagen convertible around Portofino and Sardinia. The girl who drove the Mustang knew this. She made a point of keeping up with the latest trends. That's why she had made it perfectly clear to her parents that the car, her graduation present, had to be white. No other color was acceptable.

After all, she had an image to maintain.

As Barbara Avery stepped out of the car, the ruffles at the hem of her café au lait Young Edwardian chiffon dress swirling at midthigh, she looked rich and classy, and she knew it. She was five-foot-seven, one hundred and twenty-five pounds this morning, slim with aristocratic features and skin the color of honey. Her chestnut hair fell thick and straight past her shoulders. Wispy bangs covered her dark brows and lightly brushed the tips of her long lashes.

Everything about her seemed touched with gold—gold streaks in her hair, a golden sheen to her skin, tiny pinpoints of gold glinting in her almond-shaped brown eyes. She looked like a budding Miss America, fresh and wholesome and pretty and almost impossibly self-confident.

Her confidence, born of her privileged class and her natural beauty, was evident in the imperious way she carried herself when she entered the gym, head held high, a self-satisfied smile playing about her full, wide mouth. Huge banners on the walls proclaimed, "Class of '69!" and multicolored crepe-paper streamers dangled from the ceiling. A local band played "Proud Mary" with more energy than talent, and the dance floor was packed with celebrating graduates. The air crackled with exhilaration.

Val had said once in exasperation, "You always act like you're *entitled,* like you always have a right to be wherever you are. I guess anyone who has two dozen pairs of Capezio shoes, in every color, just naturally walks like she owns the fucking world."

Val, like Kate and Shelly, couldn't afford Capezios.

Barbara had merely smiled in a sweetly tolerant way that she knew would absolutely infuriate Val. "It isn't the shoes, it's the girl wearing them."

Tonight there was an angry edge to her self-assurance. She'd just come from dinner with her parents at their country club, where they'd presented her with the car. She'd barely had time to thank them before her mother started in again with the same complaint she'd had since the beginning of the year when Barbara had applied to several colleges, none of them anywhere near Visalia.

"I don't know why you won't go to Fresno State. You'd only be an hour from home. You could join my old sorority and form friendships with daughters of my old sorority sisters. Those kinds of connections will help later when you want to join the Junior League and other organizations."

Barbara was sick to death of hearing about the sorority and the right connections and Junior League. After eighteen years of her mother's iron control, she felt restless and confined. She wanted only to break out, to lead her own life.

"Fresno State isn't good enough," she insisted.

Constance Avery's face set in the rigid expression Barbara knew so well. "If it was good enough for me, I don't see why it isn't good enough for you."

"Because I want to go to medical school," Barbara explained for the hundredth time, "and it's important that I go to a really good undergraduate school." She turned to her father for support. "Dad, you understand. You went to UCLA."

Andrew Avery hesitated before replying in the thoughtful, sincere way that was so reassuring to his patients. "I do understand, Barbara, but your mother and I are naturally concerned about you going so far from home. You're all we have, sweetheart, and we worry about you."

She noticed that he said nothing about her desire to follow in his footsteps as a doctor. He never did.

Her mother's expression hardened in disapproval. "Let's not argue, shall we? You have an entire summer to reconsider your decision."

Barbara said nothing more, but she had absolutely no intention of changing her mind. Staying in the valley, going to college simply to find the right kind of husband, being a doctor's wife might have been right for her mother but it wasn't for her. She didn't intend to bask in someone else's reflected glory. Barbara was determined to have her own.

Her mother had always insisted that she live up to the highest possible standard of behavior. She was proud of Barbara's achievements and made a point of mentioning them to her friends in the Medical Wives Auxiliary and in the bridge club. Sometimes Barbara would hear her saying to someone, "My daughter's a straight A student, you know" or "My daughter was voted student body vice president."

Then why, Barbara wondered, didn't her mother want her to have a career? After all, she was coming of age in the most exciting time for women in history. Doors were opening everywhere, barriers were coming down right and left. She could do anything, be anything. Why couldn't her mother understand that being a housewife wasn't enough for this generation of women?

A dark little thought, unpleasant to face, had been gnawing at Barbara for months now, since she and her mother began arguing about this. Maybe her mother didn't want her to achieve more than she herself had. Tonight, when Constance said that what was good enough for her should be good enough for her daughter, Barbara had sensed a bitter resentment in her mother. It frightened her because it revealed a crack in her mother's armor of perfection. It also made her feel guilty, somehow, and the guilt made her angry.

Now, as she walked through the crowd, she was aware of heads turning to watch her. She had long since come to take such attention for granted, accepting it as her due. Scanning the room impatiently, she finally found her friends sitting at a table in a corner, looking totally bored. They were her own personal rat pack. She liked having an exclusive little group, and liked knowing that she was the undisputed leader of it. It gave her a sense of control, something she never felt with her mother.

Crossing the room, she asked with a sly grin, "Are we having fun yet?"

Val gave her a weary look. "This place is Geek Central. The only people who are here have no place better to go."

Shelly nodded her head in agreement.

Kate added, "I'm getting real tired of watching Kim Porter dancing with Bruce Brown."

Kim was the head cheerleader; Bruce the captain of the football team. They went steady. Of course.

"It's so *high school*," Kate concluded.

"Well, we're not in high school anymore, are we?" Barbara said. "Come on, kiddies, let's blow this joint."

"Do you have your dad's car?"

"Nope—I have *my* car. I got my graduation present, a Mustang convertible."

Val let out a whoop of delight. "All right, we have wheels! Let's boogie!"

"It must be nice to be rich," Kate murmured as they shouldered their way through the packed crowd.

Barbara smiled at her. "It is."

A fat summer moon hung suspended in the evening sky when the four girls finally hit the crowded streets in Barbara's new Mustang. The fierce heat of the day still radiated from the asphalt, and the breeze blowing fitfully in the open car was warm and dry. The streets were jammed with hot cars; an exciting blur of shiny chrome, powerful exhausts, and squealing tires. Horns and radios blared as young men hung their heads out of car windows to shout at passing carloads of girls.

Besides the staid, strictly supervised grad-night affair in the school gym, there were a dozen parties going on all over town, including one or two pretty wild ones in motels. Val suggested they hit all of them since they'd told their parents they were going to be at the all-night grad party at school and thus didn't have to be home until dawn.

As usual, Barbara was determined to set the agenda. "Let's drive through Mooney Grove first," she said, as they pulled out of Foster's Drive-in on Mooney Boulevard. While "Jumpin' Jack Flash" blasted from the speakers, she took a bottle of vodka, filched from her parents' liquor cabinet, from her large purse and handed it to Kate, who was sitting next to her.

Liberally lacing her own and Barbara's cherry Cokes with vodka before passing the bottle to Shelly and Val in the backseat, Kate said, "All you're gonna see at Mooney Grove are parked cars. No one's gonna party out in the open there."

When they pulled into the park a few minutes later, it was obvious Kate had been right. The narrow roads meandering through the oak-studded park were empty save for an occasional car parked off to the side. From the open windows of the cars, music floated out into the darkness. The gentle melody of "Brown-eyed Girl" mingled with the Stones's "Satisfaction" and Janis Joplin's rasping, heartfelt "Me and Bobby McGee."

"Shit, this town is boring. Let's try the Lamplighter," Val suggested. They pulled back onto Mooney Boulevard.

"Mike Burnett's party?" Kate asked. "I'll bet Mike's best friend, Gregg-you-know-who, will be there—love 'em and leave 'em king of Tulare County."

Barbara and Shelly screeched with delight. All of

them knew they could get to Val by mentioning Gregg.

Val took the bottle of vodka from Shelly and poured more into her Coke. "Yeah? Well, I don't care who's there." She was clearly in too good a mood to launch into her usual tirade about "tall, dark, and stupid Armenians." She went on, "Anyway, if that creep is the love 'em and leave 'em king of Tulare County, I'm the screw 'em and forget 'em *queen* of the San Jo*aquin*."

Shelly squealed and Kate almost choked on a piece of ice.

"Did you hear that?" Barbara said in mock indignation, her eyes roving eagerly over passing cars. "She's so *crude*. I don't know why we put up with her."

"Ignore her. She just wants attention," Kate said, laughing.

Barbara knew they were all secretly in awe of Val. After all, Val knew what it was like to *do* it while the rest of them spent twenty-four hours a day dreaming about it.

Suddenly Barbara became studiously oblivious to the burnished bronze '57 Chevy full of guys that had pulled up alongside them. The driver called out something through his open window.

"Aren't you going to talk to him?" Kate asked with a perfectly straight face. "I think he's in love."

"*Talk* to George? Of course not. He's the Missing Link."

Shelly sighed in mock pity. "Cruel but true."

By now George was pounding on his door.

"I think he's kind of cute," Val said, "in a dwarfish sort of way, of course."

Barbara began to feel the rush of vodka. "I can't stand desperate geeks."

She floored the accelerator. Weaving recklessly in and out of traffic, the Mustang soon left the Chevy behind.

The party at the Lamplighter Motel was just starting to heat up when the girls came in. A band had set up on the poolside patio outside the large banquet room and kids were dancing, but the center of gravity tilted in Barbara's direction as she led the way toward the punch bowl, gathering her usual following.

Responding to some sort of telepathic command from Barbara, Ben Tillet, a tall, handsome basketball letterman on his way to Stanford in the fall, waited with a brimming plastic cup of punch laced with champagne. Ben was one of Barbara's "reserves," boys she knew she could turn to for a date whenever she felt like it. She had any number of them.

Greeting Ben, she took the cup of punch from him while noticing all the young men's eyes turn to Shelly. Even Ben wavered for a moment before remembering that he'd better pay attention to Barbara or she'd find someone else to do so. If Barbara was the most popular girl in school, Shelly was the most desired. They would have been in fierce competition for boys if it weren't for the fact that Shelly rarely dated.

The band swung into another number.

" 'Louie, Louie'!" Val shouted. "I gotta dance!" She grabbed a startled Alan Pinheiro and dragged him toward the patio. "Come on, you sexy Portagee, I've got plans for you!"

Sam Rossini and his cousin Paul moved in on either side of Shelly with cups of punch in hand. The Rossini vineyards were a mini empire, and the huge family was known as the "Muscatel Mafia."

Shelly and Barbara exchanged glances. The two Rossinis were muscular and darkly good-looking but not the brightest members of their clan.

Shelly took a cup from Sam, almost as if she were doing him a favor. She sniffed disdainfully and handed it back. "Fruit punch and cheap champagne."

Barbara laughed.

"Hey," Sam replied indignantly. "That's my ol' man's private label."

"Yeah!" Paul echoed. Paul's conversation tended to be limited to backing up his more verbal cousin.

Just then Barbara noticed someone making his way toward them. Nudging Kate, she whispered, "Guess who's here."

A hand closed lightly over Kate's wrist. She looked up to find Mark Jensen's translucent blue-green eyes roaming over her. Mark was the son of a wealthy West Side rancher, senior class president, and captain of the Rangers' baseball team. With his clean-cut, all-American-boy good looks and easy charm, he was the most popular boy in school.

"Hi, Katie. Let's dance." His voice was sexy and confident.

"I just got here. Maybe later."

He grinned. "This might be your last chance. I could be gone later."

"Oh?" Her tone was cool as she firmly removed her wrist from his grasp. "I'll take that chance."

Shelly put her hands over her mouth to stifle a laugh.

Barbara mentally applauded Kate. Despite her cool response to Mark, Barbara knew that no end of Kate's fantasies had been woven from Mark's ash-blond hair, turquoise eyes, and lean, lithe build.

Just then a busboy arrived with fresh punch, momentarily cutting off Kate and Mark from the others. Only Barbara heard Mark's whispered words to Kate. "There's something about you, Katie. I've watched you in class — you're different. Sometimes it's like you *see* things the rest of us don't. I don't know why, but you get to me."

"Right. Along with Elaine and Carla and Jennifer — and who else was there this year?"

He considered for a moment then said simply, "You don't believe a word I say, do you?"

When Kate didn't respond, his expression hardened. "Forget it."

"Fine. See you around."

Kate started to move toward Barbara, but Mark took her arm once more and turned her sharply to face him.

She snapped, "Let go of me!"

His eyes darkened. "I meant it when I said you get to me. Believe me, I could get to you."

"Don't bet daddy's farm on it." She wrenched her arm free and walked toward the huge sliding-glass doors opening onto the patio.

Handing her cup back to Ben, Barbara said, "Hold this."

She followed Kate to some plastic lounge chairs in a relatively quiet corner far from the band.

"Thinks he's God's gift to women," Kate muttered, leaning back in the chair.

Barbara shrugged. "Well, he is just about the cutest thing going in this whole town, and he wants *you.*"

"*Tonight.*" Without looking at Barbara, Kate went on in a barely audible voice. "He might make love to me in the backseat of his Trans Am, but he wouldn't take me home to meet his family."

Barbara was silent for a long moment. Ever since

she and Kate had become best friends four years earlier, she had blithely ignored the social gulf between them. Now she was acutely aware of Kate's intense self-consciousness. Finally she said slowly, "You know, he's the only guy I ever wanted who I couldn't have."

The admission wasn't easy, and Barbara couldn't quite meet Kate's startled look.

"I didn't know you liked Mark."

"I was intrigued. I thought it would be fun to be the one girl he wanted and couldn't have. It's ironic that it turned out to be you."

"We weren't in competition for him."

"Weren't we? Remember when we saw him for the first time in freshmen English? Mrs. Martin made us each read a poem out loud and he read something by Donne. I forget what it was exactly, but it was so romantic. Some of the kids giggled, but I thought, here's a guy who's so confident he doesn't care if people laugh at him. I thought what a challenge it would be to cut him down, just a little. Then I noticed you watching him, and I could tell — you were crazy about him from that very first minute."

"But he never asked me out. It's not like I had any claim on him. You could have gone out with him."

Barbara shook her head slowly. "Huh-uh. It would have ruined everything between us. Funny, isn't it? No matter how close two girls are, a guy can come between them every time."

"That's stupid high school stuff. It won't be like that in college."

"Won't it?"

Kate started to protest, then stopped.

Barbara stood up. "Come on, let's get Shelly and

105

Val and get out of here. The night is young and we've got a lot of partying to do."

They had to pull a reluctant Val off the dance floor and rescue Shelly from the Rossini cousins before they took off in the Mustang.

After stopping at a drive-in for more Cokes, they drove around aimlessly for a while. Barbara enjoyed the feeling of freedom that came with having her own car at last. She knew she looked good in it, her dark looks contrasting dramatically with the pristine whiteness of the Mustang. She concentrated on that, pushing to the back of her mind the disturbing residue of the argument with her mother.

"This is boring. You drive like a little old lady, Barb. Let's see what this car can do," Val insisted.

Barbara hesitated only for a split second before turning onto Highway 198 and flooring the accelerator. The highway was the main road heading east toward the foothills and Three Rivers, the area where the three forks of the Kaweah River merged.

The hot wind whipped their hair, and the car seemed to skim the surface of the road. Normally, speed made Barbara nervous, but she wasn't about to back down from Val's challenge. She kept the gas pedal floored until they reached the foothills and the road began to twist and turn. The faster and farther she went, the more distance she put between herself and her mother.

On the crest of Rocky Hill, Barbara pulled over onto the edge of the road. The girls sat back, sipping their vodka-laced Cokes, as Visalia lay down below them in the distance, a pathetically small patch of twinkling lights surrounded by blackness.

"It's so *small*," Kate whispered. "I want to go someplace *big*, where people think big and do big things."

"Some place where everyone doesn't know everything about you. Where you can be anything you want to be," Shelly added in a wistful voice.

"Where nothing is predictable and anything can happen," Val finished.

For a moment, there was total silence.

Words like parochial and insular came into Barbara's mind. Visalia was those things, and more. It was dull and narrow-minded and suffocating, and if she had to live out her life there, she would go crazy.

She whispered, "How can people live and die in a town like that? We have to get out, to become *somebody.*"

Shelly frowned. "That's easy for you to say."

Barbara whirled around to face her. "Hey, we're *all* getting out of here! We can do it! We don't have to repeat our mothers' lives!"

"Amen!" Val shouted.

Barbara turned on the ignition. "Like the poster says, today is the first day of the rest of our lives. Let's go for it!"

They were back in town, heading to a party at Nina Manetti's, when a black El Dorado seemed to come out of nowhere, whipping recklessly past them with a blast from the horn. It raced ahead up Noble Avenue.

"Steven Ashe," Barbara said with a frown. "Already half-loaded."

"I'll bet Rick's with him," Kate added. "They're like the Lone Ranger and Tonto. Only Tonto had a bigger vocabulary than Rick."

"Catch him," Shelly said from the backseat.

Her tone caused Barbara and Kate to exchange

puzzled looks. "Why? Talk about bad news."

"Just do it, Barb."

"Okay. Hang on." She hit the gas, and the Mustang surged ahead.

They caught the Cadillac at the Conyer Street light. When Barbara pulled alongside, Steven glanced out his window and flashed the killer grin he was famous for. Mark Jensen might be the cutest boy in school, but Steven was much more than that. He had thick dark hair and six-feet-four inches of hard, muscled body. His green eyes had an intensity that was almost hypnotic.

It wasn't just his looks that drove girls giddy when he moved in, though; his savage temper lent him an aura of danger, and his father's wealth gave him the license to give it free rein. Rumor had it that when a pregnant Sally Sorenson dropped out of school and moved away, it was the Ashe family influence that prevented Steven from being charged with statutory rape.

"What's up?" Steven asked through the open window. He spoke to Barbara but his eye was on Shelly in the backseat.

Shelly returned his look with cool disdain.

"The town's dead. We're going home early," Barbara lied. She could see Rick Paxton, Steven's constant companion, leaning nonchalantly against the passenger-side window. Rick was blond-haired and hazel-eyed. Some people said Steven hung out with him because Rick's pale good looks provided a striking, and very flattering, contrast to Steven's Dark Prince handsomeness.

"Bad mistake. I'm throwing a real party at my dad's place up at Big Rock later." Big Rock was above Three Rivers on the middle fork of the Kaweah River, about half an hour's drive from town.

"He turned the place over to me tonight. You're invited." He glanced at Shelly again. "All of you."

Just then the light changed. "Sorry," Barbara called back as she pulled away on squealing tires. She glanced in the rearview mirror at Shelly. "Satisfied?"

"I just wondered if he'd try."

"Of course he was going to *try*," Kate snapped. "He has his reputation to think about."

"He must still be thinking," Barbara said, "because he's following us."

She sped up, determined to lose him.

When the girls pulled up in front of Nina Manetti's house a moment later, they found cars jamming the driveway and street.

"Ah, *food*," Valerie said. "Let's go."

The Manettis ran one of the two decent restaurants in town. Their youngest daughter, although rather heavy and more than a little obnoxious, could always be guaranteed a big turnout for a party as long as her parents catered it. Kate, Barbara, Shelly, and Val were walking up to the house when they saw Steven Ashe's El Dorado rumble past and turn the corner at the end of the street. Barbara watched Shelly's eyes follow the car until it disappeared. Shelly had never shown any interest in Steven before, and Barbara wished she wasn't doing so now.

"Hey—let's go inside," she said.

Shelly looked as though her thoughts were elsewhere. "Huh? Oh, sure."

Inside the Manettis' sprawling, Spanish-style house, a huge banquet table was covered with rich delicacies. Help from the restaurant carved roast beef and shuttled in and out of the kitchen with platters of spaghetti, ravioli, and cannelloni to keep pace with the horde of hungry teenagers. The Doors blasted from a big stereo console, and the huge, high-ceilinged family room with its hardwood floor had been converted into a dance area.

Barbara and the others gritted their teeth and searched out Nina to pay their respects. "I love your dress," Barbara gushed, embracing Nina briefly. Actually, Nina's voluminous yellow chiffon looked rather like a papier-mâché tent.

As Nina moved on to greet other guests, Barbara saw Steven and Rick come in. She turned to Shelly. "Guess who followed you."

"I don't know why you're looking at me. He was probably invited, too," she said with studied nonchalance, but her face was flushed and her eyes glittered. Barbara knew it wasn't just from the vodka and Cokes.

Before Barbara could say anything further, Gary Wiebel, a lanky, scholarly type who sat next to her in civics, began talking to her. A minute later, he led her over to the banquet table, where they helped themselves to heaping plates of pasta, scampi, and prime rib. Between the food and Gary's enthusiastic description of Berkeley, where he was headed in the fall, Barbara forgot about Shelly and Steven.

When Gary laced her punch with a flask of Southern Comfort and tried to look down her blouse, she got up and moved out onto the dance area. She saw Kate dancing with Benny Sanchez, who proudly wore a letterman's jacket in spite of the heat. Barbara had always found Benny attractive, but she wouldn't dare go out with him. Her parents would have a fit if she dated a Mex, even one who lettered in track and was an honor student. She defied her parents in a lot of ways, but this was one area that was absolutely forbidden.

Just then, Val walked up to her. "I don't believe it. Clyde Redding asked me to go outside and look at his new car. He had some tequila in the glove compartment. After two drinks, he barfed all over his tuck 'n' roll."

"How romantic."

"Barb, it was disgusting." She looked with despair at the banquet table. "I was starving, but I think I lost my appetite." She broke off, staring past Barbara. "Where's Shelly going?"

Glancing in the same direction, Barbara saw Shelly and Steven making their way through the crowd toward the front door. She murmured, "Wait here."

Crossing the family room, Barbara intercepted Shelly and Steven in the foyer, just as they were heading out the door. "Where are you going?"

Shelly didn't meet her look. "We're just going cruising for a while."

Steven's green eyes challenged Barbara. "What's the problem?"

"No problem, but we've got plans for later." The four girls had arranged a slumber party in Barbara's poolside guest house to round off graduation night.

Shelly said quickly, "I'll meet you at your house later."

"You're not going up to Three Rivers, are you?"

Shelly became visibly irritated. "Maybe. I don't know. Anyway, it's *my* business. You're not my mother, damn it!"

Barbara recoiled in surprise. Shelly had never talked to her like that before.

Steven put his arm around Shelly's shoulders. "Come on, let's get out of here."

When Barbara rejoined Val and Kate, who had

finished her dance with Benny, she said, "I'm worried about Shelly."

"She actually left with that jerk?" Val asked.

Kate was startled. "You mean Steven Ashe?"

Barbara nodded. "She seems to think she knows what she's doing. Come on, let's go back to my place."

Threading her way through the crowd, Barbara told herself there was no point in worrying about Shelly. Whatever was going on, they had all just graduated from high school. They were big girls now.

FOUR

Shelly

Highway 198 climbed from Visalia up through the orange and lemon citrus belt into the low foothills above the reservoir that stored water for irrigation. Settling back into the red leather upholstery of the El Dorado, Shelly watched the bright moonlight spill out across the flat table of shimmering water below.

The leather upholstery felt rich and sensuous. Accustomed to her mother's ten-year-old Ford, she'd never ridden in a Cadillac before. Even Barbara's Mustang, with its heady new-car smell, wasn't luxurious like this. When Steven pushed a button and the electric windows silently glided closed, she was startled for an instant.

He gave her a quick, sideways smile. "My ol' man gets a new Cadillac every year. He always gets all the options. Like this." He pushed another button, and she felt the back of her seat tilt back slightly.

She wanted to pretend she was used to all this, that it wasn't new to her, but it was useless to pretend with Steven. There were no secrets in a small town like Visalia. Everyone knew just where everyone else fit into the economic caste system. Her

113

family wasn't on the same social level as Steven's, and they both knew it.

As if reading her mind, he went on, "I hear your ol' lady works at the Hitching Post."

She nodded uncomfortably. How much did he know? She wondered. Did he know that she was illegitimate? A familiar sensation of shame washed over her as she stared rigidly ahead, hoping she wasn't blushing.

"What about your ol' man?" he asked.

She felt a rush of relief. He didn't know everything about her after all.

She knew nothing about her father, not even his name. Her mother always refused to talk about him. Since her mother was brown-haired and hazel-eyed and petite, Shelly assumed she must take after her father. From that meager knowledge, she conjured up an image of a tall, handsome, fair-haired man. She fantasized that he hadn't wanted to leave her but for some mysterious reason he had had no choice.

When she was really little and her classmates talked about their fathers, she made up stories about hers. He was a milkman. A salesman. He was in the army and that's why he was away. As she grew older, she began staring fixedly at tall, fair men in their thirties and forties, wondering, Is *he* my father?

In answer to Steven's question, she finally replied, "I never see my father." She hoped the vague answer would satisfy him.

"Divorced, huh?"

She didn't bother to correct him. Having divorced parents wasn't nearly as shameful as being a bastard.

"My folks are divorced, too," he went on.

114

There was a flash of something dark and un-happy in his expression, and Shelly remembered vague rumors she'd heard of violent arguments between Steven and his parents.

"You're lucky you don't have to bother with your ol' man," he said. "Jesus, parents are a drag. Let's talk about something else."

Shelly leaned back in the seat and relaxed. Thank God she wouldn't have to explain things. It was an unhappy story, one she rarely talked to anyone about save for her closest friends. She didn't even have all the details. During the rare times her mother, Gayleen DeLucca, spoke of her upbringing on a small, struggling ranch outside of town with her father, a widower, it was always with profound bitterness. Shelly suspected that her mother got pregnant at seventeen on purpose as a means of escape. It backfired when the boy who was her ticket out disappeared at the first sign of enforced responsibility.

Gayleen was immediately disowned by her elderly, irascible father, Angelo, who had been born in Italy and had never changed his old world attitudes. He hadn't really cared for his youngest, not having much use for a girl child, especially an unexpected, unwanted change-of-life baby. When he finally relinquished his iron grip on life at ninety-four, he took one parting shot at his disgraced daughter—he left his entire estate, such as it was, to be divided among his three middle-aged sons.

Even in death, Gayleen's father not only didn't forgive her, he took the last possible opportunity to show her how worthless she was to him. She ranted about that posthumous insult for months afterward. Her brothers, all of whom were much older than she, had inherited their father's hard attitude and wanted nothing to do with her. Bitter arguments over the inheritance only served to alienate them further from the sister they were ashamed to acknowledge.

Shelly was aware that she had uncles, aunts, and cousins, but she never saw them. Holidays were spent alone with her mother or in awkward celebration with her mother's latest boyfriend. It was an intensely lonely childhood. She spent endless nights by herself while her mother worked. Occasionally, Shelly woke up in the morning to find a strange man sitting at the breakfast table.

She knew that her mother wanted desperately to get married, but somehow the men she attracted always seemed to be just passing through. Like Shelly's father.

She was fiercely determined not to end up like her mother. That's why, despite her startling beauty, she had a reputation as being an "ice princess" for her standoffish attitude toward boys. Her flawless skin that always seemed to have a sexy glow, the perfect symmetry of her features, and shapely legs that went on forever attracted guys in droves, but Shelly held herself cool and aloof and rarely condescended to date.

Only her closest friends knew the depth of insecurity that lay beneath her cool facade. Kate and Valerie had shown up at her tiny stucco house unannounced one morning to find Shelly and her mother in a screaming argument while a lanky redneck, wearing only a pair of boxer shorts, calmly poured himself a cup of coffee from the pot on the stove.

Shelly left with Kate and Val, in Kate's father's Dodge, and they drove to Foster's Drive-In. Over Cokes and French fries, they pored over the latest issue of *Seventeen* magazine, neither Kate nor Val saying a word about the scene they'd just witnessed. Instead, they avidly discussed an article titled "Can Boys Be Trusted?" and debated about who was more beautiful, Jean Shrimpton, with her huge blue eyes and sensuous mouth, or Jennifer O'Neill, with her fine-boned, patrician beauty.

Shelly chose Jennifer, whom she idolized. Her dream of becoming a model was inspired by the actress, who was obviously not only successful but well-bred. Even her hobby—horseback riding—was classy. She was often photographed putting a jumper through his paces, and she always looked utterly perfect in a close-fitting riding habit and shiny black boots.

Shelly daydreamed about modeling jobs in London and Paris. She saw herself walking through Hyde Park and shopping on the Champs Elysees, maybe taking a class or two at the Sorbonne or Cambridge in her spare time to acquire the patina of sophistication and good breeding that she longed for. During these daydreams, she forgot about the lonely little house on Giddings Street and the increasingly desperate look on her mother's face.

She glanced across now at Steven's perfect profile as he sat drumming his fingers on the steering wheel, keeping time to "Light My Fire." He was just as handsome as Jim Morrison and there was something of Morrison's frank eroticism about him. Turning slightly, he met her look with an absolutely confident smile.

"Cigarette?" he asked, taking one from a pack on the dashboard and offering it to her.

"No, thanks." Her voice wavered tremulously in the upper registers of shyness.

He placed the unfiltered cigarette between his

lips, lit it with the car's lighter, and took a deep, long drag. The Caddy surged powerfully ahead.

"High school was a giant fucking waste of time. I'm glad it's over."

"Me, too," she agreed fervently.

She had hated nearly every minute of it. If it hadn't been for Kate, Val, and Barbara, school would have been unbearable. Shelly didn't have any of the things that were important in high school—money for stylish clothes, enough self-confidence to be outgoing and popular, a nice home where she could invite kids over for parties. Only a fierce sense of self-preservation had enabled her to endure it because she knew a diploma was the crucial first step in her plan to get out of Visalia and make something of herself.

Silence enveloped them once more. They'd hardly spoken since leaving Nina's party, but then words weren't really necessary. She knew her friends wouldn't understand or approve. They had no inkling of what Steven represented to her or of the mysterious and powerful chemistry between them.

She'd thought it might be her imagination, this thing between them that had been building for months. Shelly would feel his eyes on her at unlikely but sharply etched moments, such as when she stuffed books in her locker or sat over a magazine in the library. Once, when she was sitting in senior court, a small area reserved for seniors and bounded by a low brick wall, she felt a shadow pass over her. Looking up, she found Steven watching her with a look of insolence in his green eyes that made her feel at once uncomfortable and fascinated.

At first, it was hard for Shelly to believe he was interested in her. Always taller than most of her classmates, she'd been gangly, skinny as a beanpole, and the object of other children's taunts until she reached high school. She still couldn't entirely believe that her body had suddenly developed incredible curves; that her face, once all planes and angles, had filled out very nicely; and that her height no longer put off boys.

When she became convinced that Steven was playing a game of cat and mouse with her, she decided to play along. She wasn't about to give him the satisfaction of knowing he intimidated her, so Shelly occasionally allowed her gaze to meet his when he was on the football field practicing or during physical ed class, when the boys worked out at one end of the gym while the girls worked out at the other.

During this entire time, there had never been so much as a word between them. Until tonight.

Part of Shelly was drawn to danger, and everything about Steven spelled exactly that. The other young men who pursued her were tame and boring by comparison. Steven came wrapped in the aura of his parents' money and the rumors of his break-all-the-rules behavior.

She'd never breathed a word of her fascination with Steven to her friends. They would only argue with her and say that he was trouble. They were right, of course, but on some profound level, trouble was exactly what she was looking for after all the years of being oh-so-careful.

Half an hour later, she and Steven walked into his father's opulently rustic "cabin." The large, two-story, redwood-and-glass building had been designed by an architect to take full advantage of its dramatic setting on the very edge of a sheer cliff overlooking the river below. Inside, the furniture was covered in deep, hunter-green fabric, there were Indian rugs

119

scattered over the hardwood floor, and a fireplace built of rocks hauled up from the river soared to the top of the two-storied living room. The house was an impressive statement of the power of money to buy anything, even good taste. It was everything Shelly had ever dreamed about in a home.

"It's beautiful," she breathed.

Steven shrugged. "It's okay."

She knew that Steven lived with his mother in Green Acres, the old-money section of Visalia. "Does your father live here?" she asked.

"Yeah, but he's usually away on business." He took her arm. "Come on, let's get something to drink."

He led her through the small crowd of cheerleaders, football players, and other in-group elite who sprawled on the sofas and chairs, smoking cigarettes and drinking, or who danced languidly in the middle of the room to the Temptations. A few others stood out on the flood-lit patio overlooking a narrow granite gorge and the crashing river below. As she walked next to him, Shelly saw darting envy in female eyes and felt a surge of pride at being his chosen date, especially in this powerful group.

The whole gathering carried the easy confidence of privilege, of a class dramatically removed from Shelly's by virtue of present status and future expectation. It was a big part of Steven's appeal to Shelly, an entrée into another world. She had seen this world in *Seventeen;* the pretty girls in their Lanz dresses, the boys wearing attitudes of smug self-confidence because they knew damn good and well they were the chosen.

At Steven's, it was even better than in *Seventeen.* The smell of cigarette smoke in the air, couples making out in dimly lit corners, and others gath-

120

ered around a huge beer keg that seemed to be the centerpiece of the living room charged the atmosphere with a delicious feeling of forbidden adventure.

Rick Paxton, who had gotten a ride with someone else at Nina Manetti's party, came in. He and Steven exchanged a look that Shelly couldn't quite decipher, then he joined them.

"I got it," he said simply.

From a small paper sack he was holding, Rick took out a strainer, rolling papers, a metal roach clip, and a tiny plastic bag of marijuana. Licking two pieces of the sheer white paper together, he made a fold and filled it with marijuana. He rolled it, twisted the ends, and handed the joint to Steven, who took a long drag before passing it to Shelly.

She didn't want to admit that she'd never smoked pot before, so she took the joint from him, holding the roach clip gingerly between her thumb and forefinger, trying to mimic his actions. She'd never been able to inhale cigarettes, and, after the first puff, she started to cough.

Rick laughed. "Looks like you got yourself a real live one here, Steven."

Steven gave him a dark look.

"All right," Rick grumbled, moving off toward the beer keg.

"Here's how you do it," Steven explained, showing Shelly how to take a deep drag, sucking in air along with the smoke and holding it down.

She took several more drags on the joint without experiencing the rush she'd expected.

"It isn't working," she said, feeling somehow like a failure.

"Give it a chance." Steven smiled.

He prepared another joint, and after she'd taken

121

a few puffs, she noticed that the music seemed louder. When "The Tracks of My Tears" began to play, the sound of Johnny River's voice and the emotion of the lyrics touched her as she'd never been touched before, piercing her heart. "Take a good look at my face . . . you know my smile seems out of place . . . if you look closer it's easy to trace . . . the tracks of my tears . . ."

That's so sad, she thought, so sad.

Taking her by the hand, Steven led her out onto the patio where a few couples swayed slowly to the music. Shelly stepped into his arms as if she'd done it a hundred times before. Holding her lightly around her waist, he moved with almost unbearable deliberation, as she clasped her hands around his neck and leaned against him. Her entire body felt so relaxed that if he let go of her she feared she would crumple in a heap onto the stone patio.

A thought floated lazily across her mind. It was wonderful to dance with someone tall enough so that she had to look up at him. Shelly felt small in Steven's arms. Small and helpless, like a little girl. She found herself filled by an indescribable happiness unlike anything she had ever known.

"Steven," she murmured against the cool cotton of his pale blue shirt.

He didn't respond. He didn't have to. All that mattered was the feel of his arms around her, the sensation of closeness, of being surrounded by him.

He's here, she thought, he's right *here*.

As the thought struck her, a fantasy image of her father floated across her mind.

Later, she watched as Steven poured generously from a bottle of cognac into two cut-crystal goblets.

122

They were in a bedroom with floor to ceiling windows overlooking the river and a king-sized bed with a brown velour spread. It was late, and through a peripheral daze made up of music, shifting faces, and her own seemingly disembodied voice, Shelly had a sense of the party winding down and people leaving in a squeal of tires and raucous laughter.

She was higher than she had ever come close to being in her life; a combination of all the vodka she'd drunk earlier, repeated hits on the pot, and now the cognac that shone like liquid fire.

Steven's green eyes, burning with a brilliant light like a multifaceted emerald, watched her.

"So, where are you going to school in the fall?" She knew her voice was thick but hoped she didn't sound too dim.

He crossed from behind the bar with the two glasses and handed her one. "I'm not. I'm going to Europe."

"Europe?"

He shrugged. "Maybe for a year. Maybe longer. Amsterdam. Paris. Then Morocco. Just bum around."

"Must be nice to be able to afford it."

"It is."

She sipped the cognac, her second glass, and was still getting used to the burning sensation as it went down. The reassuring warmth it left behind was nice. Very nice. She felt mellow, relaxed, and at the same time pleasantly tingly inside because of Steven's nearness.

Shelly felt his hand caress her cheek then slip down to unbutton the first button of her pink cotton dress. Thrilled by his desire for her, whatever resistance she had brought with her tonight began to disintegrate. For the first time in her life, Shelly felt eager to be touched.

"Why don't you come with me?" he murmured in her ear.

Stunned, she tried to find her voice. "Go to Europe? With you?" The second button of her dress was undone and she felt his hand slip inside to cup her breast. "Don't—" she whispered.

He ignored her protest. "Why not? My ol' man will write the checks. He'll do anything to get rid of me."

Almost paralyzed with excitement, Shelly felt his fingers slowly massage her breast through the thin silk of her bra. With a smile, he leaned forward to bite at the hollow of her neck. She let her arm slip around him.

"Wouldn't you like to go to Europe with me?" he whispered.

Travel-poster images of the two of them traveling across the world together made her mind soar with dizzying possibilities, but the most heady sensation of all was the thought of being with Steven—walking beside him in romantic places, lying with him at night, being his girl. She felt so lucky.

His hand slipped under the full skirt of her dress and along her thigh, squeezing with hard urgency. Her face buried in his neck and her senses filled with his need of her, she gasped, "I'd love to be with you. God—"

Steven pulled back. "Good." Taking the forgotten goblet from her hand, he set it beside his on a nearby dresser. "We'll make plans later."

She cupped his face in her hands as he maneuvered her gently but firmly onto the bed. After snapping off a bedside lamp, sending the room into a semidarkness softened only by the moonlight pouring in through the windows, he slipped her dress from her shoulders. When he buried his face in her full breasts, she could only tremble and clutch at his shirt.

Somehow her clothes were on the floor, but he remained dressed. Aware she was naked, Shelly stiffened with involuntary resistance until he whispered, "I love you. You know that, don't you?"

She wanted so desperately to believe it.

His clothes were gone then, and she felt his flesh against hers, more intoxicating than the brandy. As he guided her hand to caress him, Shelly felt her last resistance crumble. Her need to be held tightly and loved overwhelmed every other consideration, and there was an even more powerful need — sudden and thrilling as the devilish aura surrounding Steven — a need to behave as wantonly as her mother.

The pain when he entered her in one brutal thrust cut through Shelly's alcoholic fog. She gasped a startled protest, but he was beyond hearing. He thrust into her again and again, his body beaded with sweat. His eyes, inexplicably cold and angry, bore into hers, demanding response.

He needs me, she thought. Shelly repeated this over and over again to herself, like a chant, as she stared at the ceiling. In pain and passion, she arched to meet him, echoing sounds her mother made with her lovers, sounds the young girl had heard through the thin wall separating their bedrooms.

At his climax, Steven shuddered, as if the sexual release had been wrung from him unwillingly. He was utterly still as she lay beneath him, stunned by the abrupt end of their lovemaking. Shelly was intensely relieved that the pain was over, leaving only a throbbing ache deep within her, but she also felt a profound sense of dissatisfaction. Something was missing, but she didn't understand what.

Gasping, he pulled himself off her, stumbled to his feet, and put on his jeans.

Steven didn't say a word, and she didn't know what to say. Her body was sore yet ached with an unfulfilled need. Surely, she thought, this wasn't how it was supposed to feel. It was hard to believe *this* was what her mother had warned her about all those times when she'd said, "Boys only want one thing, and when they get it, they'll drop you like a hot potato."

Shelly didn't ever want to do it again, but she supposed she would have to, for Steven's sake. Maybe after a while it wouldn't hurt and then she wouldn't mind so much. Maybe it would be better when they went to Europe together. Surely over there it would be more romantic and less . . . cold.

Suddenly, she realized the sheet was damp beneath her. Looking down, she saw a patch of red. Blood. Her blood.

At a sound, she looked up, seeing Rick slouching drunkenly in the doorway. Shelly had no idea how long he'd been standing there or how much he'd seen. A sense of humiliation washed over her as she lay exposed to his curious gaze. Desperately, she grabbed the sheet and tried to cover herself.

"Sorry, man," Rick said to Steven. His words were badly slurred.

Something about Steven's expression sent a cold chill through Shelly. It was like a shutter had closed over his eyes; there was no feeling there, nothing.

"You want seconds?"

For an instant, she didn't understand. Then, as the meaning of his words sank in, she tried to

126

speak but no words would come.

Rick hesitated, staring at Steven.

"What's the matter, man, you a homo?" Steven taunted.

That did it. Rick flushed a deep red before lurching toward the bed, unzipping his pants with a clumsy urgency.

Shelly screamed, "No!"

Steven grabbed her wrists tightly, digging his nails into them. She screamed again, and he jammed a fistful of wadded-up sheet into her mouth. Choking, fighting for air, Shelly was overwhelmed by panic.

As Rick forced her legs apart, some other boys came into the room. She stared into their surprised faces, recognizing members of the football team.

Steven said, "That's it! Fuck the bitch, man! She wants it. She's trash. Just like her ol' lady!"

The words struck her like the brutal sting of a whip. *Fuck the bitch, man!*

When Rick drove into her hard, her pain was intense. The uncertain expressions on the faces of the other youths changed to a kind of glittering animal lust. Shelly had seen that same kind of frenzy once when she was a child as she watched a pack of dogs fight over a bitch in heat. She'd never forgotten the terror she'd felt then, watching the male dogs mount the whimpering female. Now she felt that same terror, only it was magnified tremendously.

She kicked at Rick with her legs until two of the boys grabbed and held them down. She was pinned, helpless, unable to move or scream or plead. On the edge of her vision, she could see Steven's flushed face watching as Rick thrust into her again and again.

A feeling of detachment stole over her. It was as

127

if time had stopped, reality was thrown out of kilter. Shelly tried desperately to deal with what was taking place, but she just kept thinking, *This isn't happening.*

Then Rick pulled out of her, and for one precious moment she thought, *It's over*, but someone else got on top of her and gave a loud yell like a war whoop. After a few minutes, he was followed by another, then another. She knew she would never forget the way they smelled—like alcohol and cigarette smoke and sweat.

The whole time, Steven stood right by her head, gripping her wrists so tightly that she thought he would break them, urging on the others, making fun of anyone who hesitated to join in.

Her throat burned from her strangled screams, her breasts were bruised and sore, and her arms and legs were scratched and bleeding. Shelly thought the horror would go on forever. She wished she would die, just die, and get it over with.

She was past struggling then. She just closed her eyes as tightly as she could and tried not to feel, not to hurt, not to think.

She told herself they could only hurt her body, not her mind. It didn't matter what they did to her physically. All that mattered was keeping her essential spirit removed from them. Shelly willed herself to retreat inward to a place where no one could ever touch her again.

FIVE

Kate

Sleeping bags were spread over the tile floor of the small cabana next to the swimming pool at Barbara's house, and Kate, Barbara, and Val, still dressed, sprawled across them, munching on potato chips and chocolate chip cookies. They'd brought Barbara's pink princess phone from her bedroom to call everyone they could think of, waking up a lot of parents in the process.

Exhausted from the long night, the unaccustomed liquor, and the excitement of graduation, the girls talked in low, lazy voices. It was utterly quiet save for the distant click-click-click of a cricket and the soft rustle of the breeze through the magnolia trees that lined the large, parklike backyard. The heady scent of the waxen-white magnolia blossoms hung heavy in the air.

In the peace of the still night, the girls' voices almost seemed disembodied. Conversation ebbed and flowed in alternating currents of excited exclamations and hesitant self-questioning.

Kate lay on her back, her arms folded beneath her head, staring out at the moon and the stars through the open sliding-glass doors of the cabana.

There was no air conditioning in the small room, and the late-night breeze, much cooler than the one that had blown earlier, was a welcome relief from the lingering heat. Even at three in the morning, the temperature was still in the eighties.

Now that high school was officially over and they could start counting the days to their departure for college, Kate was beset by doubts. She'd spent her entire life in the same house in the same small town. She'd gone all the way through school with the same classmates.

The one time she'd been to L.A., she was overwhelmed by its size and fast pace. The girls she'd seen on the UCLA campus had seemed so much more mature and sophisticated than she was. The feeling was just like her first day as a high school freshman when the junior and senior girls had all appeared so much more attractive, better dressed, confident.

She turned to Barbara. "Do you think we'll fit in at UCLA?"

"Of course." There wasn't a hint of doubt in Barbara's tone. "We just won't tell anybody where we're from."

"Right, like we're really going to pass for big-city types."

"It's all a question of attitude. My attitude will simply be that I'm the best thing that's ever hit that campus."

The funny thing was, Kate realized, Barbara meant it. She wondered if Barbara had ever felt even a momentary twinge of self-doubt. Well, if she had, she'd certainly never let it show.

"I wonder what UCLA will be like?" Kate mused.

Barbara replied, "Big. Crowded. Exciting."

"Not as exciting as Berkeley," Val insisted. "That's

130

where *everything* is happening politically. The Free Speech Movement, the Anti-War Movement . . ."

Kate shook her head. "Nope. L.A.'s where it's happening. The Sunset Strip. Hollywood. The beaches . . ."

"The *boys*," Barbara and Val chimed in unison before dissolving into giggles.

At last under control, Barbara went on in a dreamy tone, "Just think of the guys we'll meet. Every single one of them will be blond and blue-eyed and tan and drive a Corvette and have families that live in Beverly Hills."

Val said, "Yeah, but I'll bet the guys at Berkeley all go to Europe during the summer or sail around the Greek islands, and they've read something besides the dirty parts in *Candy*."

Kate made a face. "All you guys ever talk about is boys."

Barbara and Val glanced at each other before picking up their pillows and throwing them at Kate, who ducked so they only hit the back of her head.

"You're so juvenile," she shot back, laughter in her voice.

Val raised one eyebrow as high as it would go. "*Juvenile?* I'm the only one here who isn't still hanging onto her virginity like it was gold."

Kate stared at her. It was true. Val knew something the others didn't. Before Kate could decide how to ask for the details they'd been dying to hear for months, Barbara said in a scathing tone, "You're also the only one who's had to worry about getting knocked up."

Val merely shrugged and lay down on her sleeping bag again. Gazing up at the ceiling, she replied with a sigh, "It was worth it."

"All right," Kate gave in, "tell us what it was like!

131

You know we want to hear all about it."

Val turned onto her side and propped her head on her hand. "Well, to begin with, Gregg was such a good kisser. Not wet or sloppy."

"Did you French kiss?"

Val rolled her eyes. "Of course. Really, that's such a minor point in the scheme of things."

Irritated at being upstaged by Val, Barbara said with studied nonchalance, "I've got a better question. Did you do sixty-nine?"

Kate's eyes opened wide in surprise. She had a pretty good idea what was involved in sixty-nine, but the thought of actually *doing* it. . . .

Val said disdainfully, "I think that's a little too European for Gregg. Anyway, we made out for a while and we were both feeling pretty hot and bothered and then, well, it just happened."

"What did he do?"

"What do you think he did? He stuck his penis in my vagina. By then, it was really big and hard, and it wasn't easy getting it in, but he did it."

"How big was it?"

"I don't know. I didn't have a ruler with me!"

Kate's mental image of a huge appendage growing larger and larger was rather frightening. "Can't you just take a guess?" she pressed.

Val screwed up her face in a thoughtful expression. "Maybe about six or eight inches long."

Reaching into her nearby purse, she pulled out a comb. "About this long." She made a circle with her thumb and finger. "And maybe, oh, this big around."

To Kate, it seemed immense. She couldn't imagine having anything that big *inside* her. She couldn't imagine *wanting* it inside her.

"Then what happened?" Barbara asked, no longer

pretending to be uninterested in Val's revelations.

"We sort of rocked back and forth for a while. That's what you're supposed to do, you know, get a rhythm going. Then he came and that was it."

"Did you come?" Barbara asked bluntly.

Val looked startled. "Well, I mean, sure. Of course."

Kate knew she was lying. She could always tell when Valerie was bullshitting and when she was being straight. She glanced at Barbara and sensed that Barbara didn't believe Val, either. Normally, Barbara would have challenged Val, but this time, for some reason, she didn't say a word.

Kate didn't press the issue, either. The truth was she didn't exactly understand what an orgasm was, and she wasn't about to reveal how truly ignorant she was by asking either Val or Barbara.

Barbara asked, "Did Gregg say anything afterward?"

Val's expression hardened and the brittle edge to her voice sharpened. "No. He isn't exactly the romantic type." She lay back down and fixed her gaze on the ceiling once more. "Let's just say it wasn't like in the movies."

Kate felt a rush of pity for Valerie but had no idea how to express it. Before she could decide what to say, the shrill sound of a ringing telephone shattered the silence.

"It's probably Eric again," Barbara said in a bored tone. She and Eric, one of her many would-be boyfriends, had exchanged several calls over the past couple of hours. "I'm totally bored with him. You answer it, Kate, and tell him I died or something."

This wasn't the first time Barbara had used Kate to do her dirty work for her. Kate resented it but, as usual, couldn't refuse. The phone rang for the fourth time, the sound seeming to grow more insistent.

She picked up the receiver. "Hello."

There was an indistinct, choking sound on the other end of the line. She frowned. "Who is this? Eric, if you think this is funny . . ."

"Kate, come get me. *Please.*"

It took a moment to identify the weak, tremulous voice. "Shelly?"

"Please, Kate, come get me right now!"

She heard rising hysteria in Shelly's voice. Kate's stomach tightened with fear. "Shelly, what is it? What's wrong?"

"I can't talk about it. Just come and get me *now!*"

"Okay, calm down. Where are you?"

"S-Steven's house. Three Rivers."

Kate grabbed her purse and dug in it for a pen and paper. "What's the address?"

"Oh, God, I don't know!"

Shelly sounded as if she might go over the edge into total hysteria at any second. Trying to keep her voice calm and reassuring, Kate asked, "Do you know the name of the road?"

There was silence for a moment. Then, hesitantly, "I think it's Sycamore Road. Somewhere on Sycamore Road. Oh, God, Kate, come *now!*"

"We're coming, Shelly. Don't worry, we'll be there just as quick as we can. Just hold on."

As she hung up, she faced Barbara and Val, who sat upright, staring at her, alarmed. Barbara spoke first. "What's wrong?"

Before Kate could answer, Val asked, "Is Shelly hurt?"

Kate shook her head. "I don't know, but she sounded — oh, God, she sounded awful! We have to get her!"

134

She rose and grabbed her purse, slinging the leather strap over her shoulder.

"But where is she?" Barbara asked as they hurried out to her car.

"At Steven's house, somewhere on Sycamore Road. She didn't know the address."

"Oh, that's great," Val snapped. "I can just see us driving all over Three Rivers in the middle of the night looking for the place."

Kate turned to her. Her voice shook with anger and fear. "We have to find it! Shelly sounded awful. Something is *very* wrong!"

Barbara said irritably, "I *told* her not to go with that jerk."

Sitting in the front seat of the Mustang, Kate peered through the windshield into the darkness. There were no streetlights up here in the foothills, and now that the moon had set, it was pitch black outside. Through the dense stands of pine dimly lit by starlight, she could barely make out the outlines of houses set well back on huge lots along the narrow road.

"Damn it," Barbara muttered in frustration. "How are we supposed to find her?"

Then, with startling abruptness, a figure appeared in the harsh glare of the headlights. Barbara had to slam on the brakes to avoid hitting the figure. In the backseat, Val shouted, "It's Shelly!"

Barbara turned off the ignition and all three girls tumbled out of the car and raced to Shelly. Kate was vaguely aware of the sound of the river in the distance, beyond a large redwood house.

The girls pulled up short when they reached

Shelly. Her hair was a tangled mess and her clothes were thrown on carelessly. Her face, arms, and legs were scratched and bleeding. The expression in Shelly's eyes was unlike anything Kate had ever seen before, desperate, terrified, cowed, like an animal that has been beaten into submission and fears the next beating to come.

"Oh, my God," Kate whispered.

As always, Barbara took charge. She moved quickly to take the sobbing Shelly in her arms. "It's all right, Shelly. We're here. It's okay. You're safe now."

Barbara's voice was measured and soothing; Kate marveled at her control.

Barbara's words and tone, her arms tightly holding Shelly's trembling body, had the desired effect. The sobs that wracked the slender body began to subside.

When she seemed to be calmer, Val asked, "What happened to you? Who did this?"

Shelly didn't reply. She kept her face buried in Barbara's shoulder.

After a moment, Kate said hesitantly, "We have to know. Was it Steven? Did he . . . did he hurt you?" Her throat was tight as she finished.

Still, Shelly didn't speak.

Barbara murmured, "We're here to help you, but you have to tell us what happened."

For a moment, Kate thought Shelly would refuse to speak. Then, haltingly, she began to explain, keeping her eyes averted. "Steven . . . took me to bed. It hurt but . . . he said he loved me. Then . . ."

She stopped.

Kate felt a sick feeling growing within her. She still didn't entirely understand what had happened

136

to Shelly, but instinct told her it was unimaginably horrible.

"How did you get beat up?" Val asked.

"The others came in. The football players. They . . ." Shelly's face dissolved as sobs tore through her once more.

Kate sensed what was coming. She grew rigid with shock and disbelief.

Shelly's voice was a hoarse whisper against Barbara's shoulder. "Steven t-told them to . . . to do it. He said, 'Fuck the bitch.' "

"No," Kate whispered.

Val turned away. Her face had gone pale, and she looked as if she would be sick. "That bastard!"

It took every ounce of strength Kate possessed to speak. "We have to get Shelly to the hospital and then call the police."

Shelly looked up, her now-dark eyes huge and terrified in her pale, tear-stained face. "No!"

Barbara tried to reason with her. "Shelly, you have to go to the hospital, and the police have to be told so they can arrest Steven."

Shelly shook her head fiercely. "I can't face the police! I can't face anyone! He said I was trash, just like my mother! That's what everyone will think, that it was my fault and that I deserved it!"

"No, they won't," Kate began. "My dad will help you."

Val whirled around to face her. "Do you really think the cops—even your father—will get those guys? Hell, no! You know who the football players are. Most of them are from the families that run this town. They belong to the same exclusive little club that Steven's family is in, and Shelly and her mother aren't members!"

137

"My dad will do something about this!" Kate shouted.

"Those guys will get all the sympathy. They'll say that Shelly was asking for it, that they were just having a good time, that it never would have happened if Shelly was a *good* girl! It will be her word against theirs, and you know damn well who the court will believe!"

Shelly's hysterical voice cut between Val and Kate. "Oh, God, stop it! Just get me away from here!"

"All right," Barbara reassured her, "we're getting out of here now."

Kate turned to Barbara for support. "We have to do the right thing. This is important."

Barbara looked away uncomfortably. "Val's right."

"What?"

"She's right! Kate, you don't know those people like I do. They'll band together against Shelly. She'll be the one on trial, not their precious sons. They'll destroy her!"

Kate stood there, stunned, unable to argue with Barbara.

After a moment's hesitation, Barbara bundled Shelly into the backseat of the car and Kate got in beside her, holding her sobbing friend in her arms. Val got in front next to Barbara, who started the engine and carefully turned around in the road.

Val cursed to herself in impotent rage as Barbara headed back toward the highway. "Goddamn bastard . . . thinks he can get away with anything. . . ."

Suddenly Barbara slowed the car. "What's that?"

They saw something they had missed earlier—Steven's black El Dorado nosed over the side of the road into a stand of brush.

"Just keep going," Val ordered, but a few yards

138

farther on, a figure reeled drunkenly into the glare of the headlights. Steven Ashe looked into the light, his expression dazed. For an isolated instant that would live in each of their minds as an eternity, he remained etched there.

Then Shelly screamed, triggering Val's smoldering rage. "Get the sonofabitch!"

Startled, Barbara put her foot down on the accelerator.

In the backseat, Kate's scream, part terror, part fury, joined with Shelly's as the car smashed into Steven's body with a sickening thud and then plowed on past.

Barbara brought the car to a skidding halt a hundred yards down the road. She sat shaking behind the wheel. For a long moment, no one was capable of movement as each tried to gather her senses. Finally, Val flung open her door, yelling, "Come on!"

Without a word, Barbara and Kate followed her back up the road where they found Steven lying on the gravel shoulder, looking like a rag doll that a careless child had dumped on the ground. His body was very still.

They all felt paralyzed as they looked down at him.

Fighting back nausea, Kate knelt at Steven's side and felt for a pulse. There was none. Gently, she lifted his head. In the darkness, she could barely see his empty eyes staring dully back at her, then she felt the moist, sticky warmth on her hand that was cradling his head. Blood.

Slowly, she rose to her feet. Trying to find her voice, she finally managed to whisper, "He's dead."

"What?" Barbara's voice was disbelieving.

"He's dead," Kate repeated.

Barbara shook her head violently. "No! He can't

be! Let's call an ambulance."

Val spoke. "Leave him." Her voice was flat, unemotional.

Kate was stunned by the implication of her words. "We can't do that!"

"The hell we can't! Nobody can do anything for him now. I say we just leave him and get the hell out of here."

"Are you crazy? We *have* to go to the police now!"

"Why? What do you think they'll do? They'll arrest us, that's what!"

"It was an accident," Kate insisted, but she couldn't bring herself to look at Barbara as she spoke.

"The hell it was!" Val exploded.

"I didn't mean to hit him!" Barbara shouted. "I didn't! He walked right in front of the car. You all saw." Her gaze went from Kate to Val, entreating them to agree with her.

"When the police find out what Steven did to Shelly, do you think they'll believe this was an accident?" Val asked, her voice cold. "Barbara will wind up in jail, maybe the rest of us, too, just because Steven got what he deserved."

It was too much for Kate. The night had turned into some kind of surreal nightmare in which everything she'd ever believed—the moral structure her parents had instilled in her—was threatened.

"You're crazy!" she yelled at Val. "What do you want to do? Just pretend none of this happened?"

Kate and Valerie's gaze locked across the deep chasm separating them.

"Yes." It was Barbara's voice, quiet now, and calm, once more in control.

Kate turned on her. "Barbara?"

"Don't say anything. Val's right. This could ruin

140

all of us." She grabbed Kate by the shoulders. *"Think* about it! Do you want to give up college? And your parents—do you really think they'll understand?"

"What about Shelly? Those other guys have to pay for what they did to her!"

"There's no way they're going to pay! Their parents will hire the best lawyers in town, and they won't end up in jail, but *we* will for killing Steven."

She stopped and, against her will, glanced down at Steven's body. "Nobody's going to pay except him."

Kate searched desperately for the right words, but none came.

Suddenly, a light came on in a nearby house.

"That settles it," Val whispered urgently. "Let's get out of here."

Still, Kate hesitated. Val grabbed her arm and pulled. "Come *on!"*

Reluctantly, Kate allowed herself to be pulled back to the car.

Forty-five minutes later, the four girls quietly crept into the cabana. Barbara located a first-aid kit and in the dim light of early dawn tended to her friend's cuts and abrasions. Shelly winced at the sting of the disinfectant but said nothing.

Sitting next to Kate on that silent trip back to town, she had calmed down somewhat, though she didn't speak at all. Now, as Barbara finished, she asked, "What about Steven?"

No one spoke. They didn't look at one another.

Finally, Val answered, "He's dead."

"Oh, my God."

For a second, Kate thought Shelly would crumble. Shelly hung her head and put her arms around her shoulders tightly, holding herself together with a visible effort. "I'm glad," she whispered in a voice so low that for a moment Kate thought she had imagined the words.

Then she looked up, fixing her eyes on Kate as though she were a compass point in a storm. "What are we going to do?"

The question had tormented Kate from the moment she realized Val and Barbara weren't going to call the police, but she didn't have an answer.

Val took over. "We're going to forget everything that happened tonight." Her eyes bore into Shelly's. *"Everything!* Because we're all in this together."

"Val's right," Barbara said. Her voice was firm, but Kate saw her hands tremble in her lap. "We're going to wake up in the morning and pretend nothing happened, and we'll never talk about it again. Not to anybody else. Not even to each other."

Val challenged Kate. "Because *nothing happened!* Right?"

Kate knew how much hinged on her next words. So much was at stake, including the future of each and every one of them. She sensed instinctively that if they made a pact of silence, it would stamp their lives, not just for the moment or the days to come but forever.

How could she simply forget Steven's face etched by Barbara's headlights in that last split-second of his life? Or the look on Shelly's face when they found her?

She couldn't.

She couldn't turn on her friends, either. Val was right. They were in this together.

Finally, she nodded slowly, and, as if listening to someone else, she heard herself say, *"Right."*

When Barbara drove Kate home late the next

142

morning, Kate's father was in the front yard, pulling weeds from a flower bed. As Kate got out of the car, her father walked over.

"Did you girls hear what happened last night?" he asked.

Kate was afraid to look at Barbara. Forcing herself to meet her father's gaze, she asked, "No, what happened?"

"One of your classmates, a boy named Steven Ashe, was a victim of a hit-and-run driver. He was killed."

Kate knew that she must say something, but her throat was so tight she couldn't speak.

"How terrible," Barbara said quickly, her voice sounding amazingly normal.

"Did you girls know him very well?"

"No, not really. Of course, he was on the football team."

Kate's father went on, "He had a party up at Three Rivers. Did you hear anything about it?"

"We heard about it, but we didn't go. We were at Nina Manetti's party, and then we went back to my house."

Listening to Barbara, Kate marveled at her self-assurance. It all sounded so ordinary, so believable.

"We're trying to put together a list of kids who were at the party so we can question them. Somebody may have seen the car that hit him. If you hear of anyone who was at the party, let me know."

"Sure will, Mr. McGuire. Well, I've got to go." Barbara turned to Kate. "I'll call you."

Kate nodded.

Barbara started to shift her car into gear, but Kate's father said abruptly, "Wait a minute!"

Kate and Barbara looked sharply at each other. Kate held her breath as her father bent down to peer at the right front fender. "Looks like you've got a little dent here."

No! Kate froze. They had checked out the car last night with a flashlight and hadn't seen anything. Barbara had even hosed off the front of it, just in case, but it had been dark and they were upset; obviously, they'd missed the tiny dent.

Barbara laughed shakily. "Yeah, I'm still not used to driving this thing and I bumped into one of the trees at my house when I was parking last night. Can you believe it? The first night I got it, too. My dad's really going to be upset. He'll probably ground me for a month."

Kate's father ran his hand lightly over the dent. His expression had turned thoughtful. "It isn't scratched at all, just dented," he murmured, almost to himself.

Kate held herself perfectly rigid. When her father looked up at her, it was all she could do not to lower her gaze.

"Well, I've gotta go," Barbara said again.

Kate's father stood up and backed away as Barbara drove off.

When she was out of sight, Kate said, "I'm going to take a nap. We were up pretty late at Barb's."

Her father reached out to touch her shoulder as she passed him, stopping her cold. When he spoke, his tone was uncharacteristically hesitant. "Katie—is there something we should talk about?"

She couldn't look at him and lie right to his face. She just couldn't. Focusing on the door, she murmured, "No, Daddy," and walked on into the house.

SIX

Shelly

Early that afternoon, Shelly sat at the tiny Formica table in the cramped kitchen of her house. Despite the heat, she wore a long-sleeved cotton blouse and jeans to hide the bruises and scratches on her arms and legs. At her feet was a battered, strawberry-colored suitcase that she'd gotten for her tenth birthday, just before going off to summer camp. It was crammed full of clothes and personal possessions; not that she had all that much. Just a few things from Anita's, a cheap dress shop where Mexican farm laborers and lower-class whites bought poorly made imitations of better clothes.

Once Shelly had saved enough money from her job at a doughnut shop to buy a dress at Ensign's, the most expensive store in town. She had spent two glorious hours trying on everything, luxuriating in the feel of expensive fabric—real silk, soft wool, crisp linen—against her skin.

Finally, she'd settled on a pink dress with lace ruffles cascading down the bodice, exactly the sort of dress Jennifer O'Neill often modeled in *Seventeen*. Shelly always felt special when she wore it, almost as if she were the kind of rich, well-bred girl the dress had been designed for.

On top of the clothes was her alarm clock, radio, and a few paperback books, including her childhood favorite, *A Little Princess*, the story of a little girl whose life changes from one of luxury to one of poverty. She creates a world of fantasy in order to survive, imagining she is a princess, and in the end her fortunes are reversed and happiness restored. Shelly also packed a photograph from Barbara's recent eighteenth birthday party where the four friends stood shoulder to shoulder, Shelly and Kate taller than Barbara and Valerie as they grinned into the camera, their expressions excited and confident.

Shelly slowly sipped a cup of hot, strong tea as she waited for her mother to get up. Gayleen worked until two in the morning and usually slept until noon or later. If she had a date after work, she often wouldn't get home until well after dawn and would then sleep until midafternoon.

It was now three o'clock, and her mother still wasn't up. It didn't appear that she'd brought her date home this time since there was no strange car in the driveway, no telltale glasses smelling of wine or whiskey on the coffee table in the living room. Her mother's bedroom door was slightly ajar instead of being closed and locked, as it was when a man was there.

Immensely relieved she would be facing her mother alone, Shelly knew that today, especially, she couldn't deal with a stranger in the house. When she heard the familiar creak of her mother's bedroom door opening and the soft shuffle of slippers on the hardwood floor, she stiffened. This wasn't going to be easy. She and her mother had never been able to talk comfortably to each other, and this particular conversation was going to be more tense than most.

Gayleen came into the kitchen yawning and running a hand through her curly shoulder-length hair. "Morning," she mumbled to Shelly, not really looking at her daughter. Automatically, she went to the coffeepot and began preparations.

Shelly took in the details of her mother's appearance, committing them to memory because she knew she wouldn't be seeing her again for a long time. At thirty-seven, her mother looked older. Her skin was sallow from so much time spent indoors in a dark, smoke-filled bar. There were bags under her eyes, and without makeup the tiny lines on her forehead and at the corners of her mouth were very apparent.

As the coffee percolated, Gayleen folded her arms and leaned against the counter, eyes closed. Through the blue rayon bathrobe, exhaustion and something more, defeat, were evident in the sagging lines of her thin body. Shelly had seen old photos of her mother and knew that she had been quite pretty once, her cheerleading photos showing a slightly plumper Gayleen with a vivacious smile, her thick dark hair pulled back into a ponytail.

Now, looking at what her mother had become, Shelly felt a rush of pity mingled with disdain. Steven's words reverberated in her mind: *She's trash. Just like her ol' lady!*

I won't end up like her, Shelly vowed with a kind of desperate determination. I *won't!*

When the coffee was ready, Gayleen filled a chipped white mug with "Santa Cruz Boardwalk" written on it, then turned toward the table. Finally she noticed the suitcase at Shelly's feet, her eyes opening wide in surprise. "What's going on?"

Shelly had had plenty of time to rehearse, so her

147

words came quickly, with no hint of the emotion behind them. "I know I told you I was going to move to L.A. at the end of summer, but I decided there's no point in waiting. I'm anxious to pursue my modeling career now. The bus leaves pretty soon, so I'd better get going. I was just waiting to say good-bye."

Gayleen sat down heavily at the opposite end of the table and stared at Shelly. "Wait a minute. You can't just up and leave like this."

"I've got the two hundred dollars I saved from my job. That'll keep me going until I start working down there. I'll call as soon as I get settled and give you my address and phone number."

"Damn it, Shelly, I'm not about to let you run off like this!"

Shelly forced her voice to remain calm. If she let this deteriorate into one of their screaming matches, she wouldn't get anywhere with her mother. "I'm not running off, Mom. I'm just leaving a couple of months ahead of schedule."

"You're not going anywhere without my permission, young lady!"

"I'll be eighteen next week. If you stop me now, I'll just go then. I've made up my mind."

Gayleen blinked back tears. She didn't say anything for a long moment, and Shelly knew she was trying desperately to think of some way to keep her from leaving.

Shelly went on. "Kate and Barbara will be down there in September. I won't be alone." She didn't add that she hadn't told her friends she was leaving. Somehow, she couldn't face them again so soon.

"Why can't you wait until they go?"

Shelly hesitated. Her facade of breezy self-assurance barely held up as she answered, "I need to go *now*. I can't stay here any longer. Don't you understand?"

Gayleen looked away, her expression distant, as if she were remembering something from a long time ago.

Shelly repeated in a whisper, "I can't stay here any longer."

Without looking at her, Gayleen said slowly, "I know."

Shelly felt a wave of relief wash over her. If her mother had forcibly kept her here, she didn't know what she would have done. The thought of spending one more day in this town was intolerable.

She stood up and picked up her suitcase. "I've got to go or I'll miss my bus."

Still not looking at her, Gayleen said in a shaky voice, "I'll get dressed and take you to the station."

Shelly started to protest, but her mother cut her off. "I'll only be a minute. Wait here."

Fifteen minutes later, Shelly boarded a bus bound for L.A. Her mother stood inside the bus terminal, watching her daughter through the windows. They hadn't hugged or touched before Shelly got on the bus, but at the last minute, Gayleen had taken all the cash from her wallet, twenty-five dollars, and insisted that Shelly take it, repeating several times, "Now you call me as soon as you get in, and be careful! Don't trust anybody!"

No, Shelly thought, I won't trust anybody.

The bus was only half full so Shelly sat by herself, clutching the *Seventeen* magazine and candy bar she'd bought at the last minute. When the door closed and the bus began to slowly pull away from

149

the station, she felt a rush of adrenaline, much like a prisoner escaping with his jailers hot on his heels.

She caught the bold headline on the front page of the *Visalia Times-Delta* in a metal newspaper rack outside the station: SON OF LOCAL BUSINESSMAN VICTIM OF HIT-AND-RUN. Nausea rose in Shelly's throat, and it was all she could do to fight it down. Curling up against the window, she closed her eyes, willing the newsprint to disappear.

She stood in the middle of the twenty-by-twenty-foot room and stared in dismay. The ad in the *Los Angeles Times* had said, "Furnished single on Sunset Strip, $100 a month." She'd envisioned something small but cozy, not luxurious but nice. Maybe it would have a view of the lights of L.A., or at least of the glittering Strip itself. After all, a hundred dollars was a lot to pay for a single apartment.

Instead, she found *this* — a threadbare carpet with grease stains; dirty furniture consisting of a sofa bed, a scarred coffee table, and two end tables with tarnished fake brass lamps; a cramped kitchenette with a tiny table and two plastic-seated chairs; a bathroom so disgusting she couldn't imagine actually taking a bath in it; and a view through the single window of a gas station across the street.

The old building itself was three stories tall and in disrepair. Judging by the people she saw in the creaking elevator and in the graffiti-lined hall, the other tenants seemed to be prostitutes, drug addicts, and old people on limited incomes. If this was one hundred dollars a month, she could only imagine what a decent place must cost.

Behind her, the manager, an elderly man with a strong accent that Shelly could not identify, cleared his throat and said, "Well? Do you want it?"

She didn't know what to say. She couldn't possibly live here, yet she didn't have a choice. She'd spent her first night in L.A. in a motel near the bus station. At fifteen dollars a night, she couldn't afford to continue staying there.

Turning toward the manager, she nodded, not trusting herself to speak.

"Okay, it's all yours. First month's rent in advance and a twenty-five-dollar cleaning deposit."

Fumbling in her purse, Shelly took out her wallet and carefully counted out a hundred and twenty-five dollars. As the manager took the wad of bills from her and shoved them deep into his pants pocket, he went on, not unkindly, "You're not like most of the people we get here. New in town?"

"Y-yes. I just got in yesterday."

"Thought so. Well, here's your key. I keep a spare in my apartment, Number 101, in case you ever lock yourself out. Either me or my wife is there most of the time. The laundry's in the basement; the washers and dryers take quarters. Rent's due by the fifth. After that, there's a five-dollar-a-day late charge. Well, that's about it."

He turned to go. At the door, he stopped and looked back at her, concern evident in his watery blue eyes. "A word of advice. Keep the door locked all the time, and don't open it to strangers." Then he was gone.

Shelly stood there for a moment, unable to move. What had she gotten herself into? This apartment was awful. L.A. was awful. After checking into the motel the night before, she'd immediately gone out for a walk to see Hollywood, the place she and her friends had envisioned as being glamorous and exciting. She was shocked to discover that downtown Hollywood was a place of filthy streets, of pushers and pimps, prostitutes and cops.

After only a few minutes, she'd hurried back to her motel room and turned on the TV in an effort to drown out the sounds of police and ambulance sirens, traffic, loud music from a nearby room, and the angry shouts of a woman and a man arguing just outside her window.

Shelly told herself Sunset Boulevard would be different. If ever there was a street of dreams, that must be it. Yet here she was, in this tacky room, feeling even more disappointed than she'd felt in that Hollywood motel room. She had to get out of here or she would suffocate.

She walked for hours up and down the Strip, passing the famous nightclub the Whiskey A Go Go, looking in windows of elegant little boutiques. Exhausted, she sat down at a tiny table at an outdoor cafe and slowly sipped a cup of tea as she watched the parade of people passing by.

Relief rushed over her at finally seeing the Los Angeles of her dreams. The lights of Sunset Strip were every bit as bright as she'd imagined. The people looked every bit as stylish and interesting. Young men with shoulder-length hair walked arm in arm with young women who all seemed to be Cher clones, with long, straight hair, deep bangs, and bell-bottom pants.

It was wonderful and exciting and a million light-years removed from Visalia.

When Shelly went back to her apartment late that night, she told herself it didn't matter that it was so tawdry. She wouldn't have to live there very long. Soon she would be working as a model, making more money than she would know what to do with, and she could move into a nice place. Maybe something with a view of the ocean. She'd always wanted to live on the beach.

On cheap blue stationery that she'd bought from an all-night drugstore on Sunset, she wrote brief notes to Kate, Val, and Barbara, giving them her address and saying how exciting L.A. was. She didn't explain her sudden departure from Visalia. She didn't have to. They would understand.

When she went to bed, she left the light burning in the bathroom and the door open so she wouldn't be in total darkness. Turning the radio on very low, she placed it on the nightstand next to her. The sounds of Janis Joplin and the Who and the Grateful Dead gradually lulled her to sleep.

Shelly refused to think about Visalia or what had happened there only forty-eight hours earlier. She'd been able to survive her ordeal by freezing her pain; it hurt too much to feel. She remained numb inside, but that was okay. This way, no one could hurt her again.

Despite the fact that she'd disconnected from her feelings, Shelly was on edge, compelled to continually monitor her surroundings. When she had been out walking, she had kept a wary eye open for anyone who seemed to get too close. If she passed someone who smelled of alcohol or sweat, she felt a rush of nausea because the smell reminded her of the boys who had raped her. In the apartment, she checked the locks on the door and window several times before finally going to bed, and even then, she was afraid to fall asleep.

The past was dead and buried, she told herself.

All that mattered was the future; but Shelly knew she would forever remain on guard, watching, listening, worrying, and wondering when the next threat would occur. She would never feel safe again, and she would never get over the feeling that somehow she had deserved what had happened to her.

In the middle of the night, she awakened to the sound of someone pounding at her door, a male voice calling out, "Hey, Richie! Open up! It's me, Carlos!"

Shelly froze, her fingers clutching so tightly at the edge of the thin blanket she'd bought at the drugstore that her knuckles were white. She wanted to yell, "Richie doesn't live here anymore! Go away!" but couldn't and didn't realize she was holding her breath until she heard heavy footsteps stomping away. She expelled a long breath.

It was dawn before she finally fell back into a fitful sleep.

Shelly spent the next few days riding buses all over L.A., getting to know the city. She went to Will Rogers State Park and watched smart-looking people playing polo, looking wealthy and aristocratic. Sitting high on the grassy bank of the sunken polo field, she marveled at the sleek horses, the fancy cars, and the exquisitely dressed spectators. They were from a world that she could only dream about, but someday, she told herself, *someday* she would be part of it.

She took the bus out to Malibu and ate at a restaurant on the beach. It wasn't fancy, just a hamburger joint with Formica tables and plastic chairs and a jukebox that played three songs for a quarter, but it was special because it was in Malibu, on the beach. As she drank tea and stared out at the limitless horizon of the ocean, Shelly told herself her own horizon was limitless as well.

On the third day, she scanned the want ads in the *L.A. Times,* where jobs were divided by sex. In the women's section, she saw an ad that read: "Models Wanted, No Experience Necessary," along with the name and address of a modeling agency.

The bus ride from her apartment to the Fairchild Modeling Agency in the mid-Wilshire district took an hour, and when she walked inside, Shelly stood poised uncertainly in the doorway. The small reception area was crowded with young women, all of whom turned to stare at her with expressions of intense competitiveness for a moment before turning back to their fashion magazines or photo portfolios.

Her heart sank. Every single one was far more beautiful than her, she was sure of it. Their clothes were L.A. chic, their makeup perfect, their hair styled in long, tawny manes.

And they were *thin*. Models were supposed to be thin. Jennifer O'Neill might not look as skinny as Twiggy, but she had no obvious curves to mar the perfect slenderness of her figure. Shelly felt extremely self-conscious about her full breasts and round hips.

She wanted to flee, but she'd come too far to turn tail and run. Forcing herself to assume a confidence she didn't feel, she strode over to the bored-looking receptionist and said in a voice that trembled only slightly, "I've come in response to your ad."

The receptionist, who was reading a paperback copy of the latest collection of poems by Rod McKuen, barely glanced at her as she handed her a number and said, "Take a seat. Mr. Fairchild

155

will see you when it's your turn."

There were no empty seats, so Shelly joined several other young women who stood next to the wall. For an hour, she watched as one woman after another was called by a well-dressed, middle-aged man who she assumed was Mr. Fairchild. Some of them reappeared in the reception room after only five minutes, looking angry or disappointed, but most remained with him for a longer time, anywhere from ten to twenty minutes, and when they came out they looked excited. Obviously, those were the ones who Fairchild felt had potential as models.

Shelly had just sat down when her number was called. As she walked through the doorway with Fairchild, she was so nervous she could barely respond when he asked her name, if she had ever modeled before, and if she had a portfolio of her pictures.

It hadn't occurred to her that she would need photographs of herself. When she told him she didn't, to her relief, he didn't escort her back to the reception room. Instead, he led her to a small dressing room. Gesturing to a larger room across the hallway, he said, "Put on one of the bathing suits in there, then come in here. I'll take a couple of snapshots to see how you photograph."

A pile of bathing suits in different sizes lay on a counter in the dressing room. All were bikinis, much briefer than anything Shelly had ever worn. She felt a rush of embarrassment as she contemplated exposing herself in this way before Mr. Fairchild, a complete stranger.

You're being silly, she told herself firmly. Of course he has to see what my body's like. After changing, she went into the other room, where

156

Fairchild sat on a folding chair, waiting impatiently. He took several shots of her from different angles, then said in a voice warm with encouragement, "You definitely have potential. I want to sign you with my agency, but first you've got to get a portfolio of photographs. Every model has one."

Pulling a card from his pocket, he handed it to her. "This is the photographer I prefer to work with. He's good and only charges one hundred and fifty for a complete portfolio. Get that taken care of, then come back. I can put you to work right away."

One hundred and fifty dollars! Shelly couldn't believe it. Where could she get that kind of money?

As she rode the bus back to her apartment, she felt desolate. She had exactly fifty-one dollars in her purse. There was no one she could borrow from. Her mother didn't have that kind of extra money, and even if she did, Shelly wouldn't ask her for it since she was determined to make it on her own.

By the time she got home, she decided to get a job, any job, and save every penny until she had the hundred and fifty. Then she could go back to the Fairchild Modeling Agency to start her career as a model. She spent the rest of that day and the next walking up and down Sunset, looking for HELP WANTED ads in windows of shops and restaurants. She put in several applications but was told over and over, "Experience is necessary."

Finally, Shelly was hired for the graveyard shift at a coffee shop that was open twenty-four hours. The manager, a young man only a few years older than Shelly, thin, with an acne-scarred face and glasses, hired her on the spot, asking her to start immediately. The pay wasn't much, but he assured

157

her she could take home as much as fifteen to twenty dollars a day in tips.

Shelly knew he had hired her because he was attracted to her, which might become a problem in the future, but she didn't care. She would only be there for a couple of weeks, just long enough to get the money for the portfolio.

Two weeks later, she handed the photographer a hundred and fifty dollars in cash and spent the next two hours being photographed in a variety of poses. Shelly was disappointed that he spent so little time with her, seeming bored and anxious to finish, but she realized that he must photograph a lot of models. For him, this was nothing special. For her, it was everything.

She took the portfolio to work with her that night and during brief lulls looked through it with a critical eye. Was she photogenic? It was hard to tell. She didn't have Jean Shrimpton's cheekbones or Twiggy's swanlike neck, but the people she worked with, the other waitresses, busboys, and cooks, told her she looked stunning.

Around three in the morning, a man came in alone and ordered steak and eggs. He looked to be in his late thirties and wore an old, faded leather jacket that looked like it had once been expensive. His long chestnut hair hung past his shoulders, and he had narrow wire-rim glasses like the kind John Lennon wore. His brown eyes crinkled at the edges when he smiled, which was often. He wasn't especially tall, just about her height when she wore flat shoes.

He was cute in a very hip, L.A. kind of way, and Shelly wondered if he might be an actor.

158

Actors and actresses, especially young, struggling ones, often came in late after a night shoot or a party. Shelly loved to listen to their conversations. They were funny, exuberant, full of themselves and their careers. They talked of roles and agents and directors and studios and the latest rock concert they'd attended. She envied them their easy camaraderie, making her miss Barbara, Kate and Val. They had all written to her, but she hadn't written back because she didn't have anything wonderful to tell them yet. She didn't want them to know that she lived in a rat hole and worked as a waitress. When she got her first modeling job, then she would write.

Now, as she gave her leather-jacketed customer his third refill of coffee, he smiled up at her. "You're new here, aren't you?"

There was friendliness in his voice, but nothing more, nothing that hinted of a pickup. She replied with less reserve than usual, "Yes, I just started a couple of weeks ago."

"I thought so. I come in a couple of times a month, after I've had a really late photo session, and I didn't remember seeing you before."

She was immediately intrigued. "Are you a photographer?"

He nodded.

"A fashion photographer?"

His grin was engaging. "Nope. The women I shoot aren't wearing much. I work for *Playboy* magazine."

She sensed a come-on and her smile froze. Shelly had learned a thing or two since coming to L.A.

Reading her thoughts perfectly, the man chuckled. "That isn't some bullshit line. I really do work

159

for *Playboy*." Pulling a card out of his wallet, he handed it to Shelly. It had the *Playboy* logo, complete with rabbit, a phone number and address, and, in smaller print, RYAN HUNTER, PHOTOGRAPHER.

"If you call that number, you'll get the *Playboy* switchboard. They'll confirm that I work for them. I'm telling you all this because I think you might have the potential to be a centerfold, if you're interested. I'd have to take some preliminary shots, but it would be in the office, with other people nearby, so you wouldn't have to be afraid that I'm a phony who just wants to take advantage of you. What do you say?"

Shelly didn't have to think about it for more than a split second. "No, thank you."

He didn't seem to take offense at her curt refusal. He merely shrugged and said, "Fine."

Feeling a little guilty for being so abrupt, Shelly hastened to explain, "I'm going to be a fashion model. I just got my portfolio today."

Hunter's expression altered slightly. "Do you mind if I ask who shot your portfolio?"

"A photographer named Terry Allen."

"I know him." The words were clipped. It didn't sound as if he liked Allen. "Who sent you to him?"

"Mr. Fairchild, of the Fairchild Modeling Agency."

His frown deepened. "Look, this is none of my business, but you obviously don't know your way around this town. The fact is, Fairchild isn't exactly a respected agent. He makes most of his money in kickbacks from the poor, dumb, aspiring models he sends to Allen, who's a real sleazeball. A reputable agency would sign you on without a

160

portfolio. They take care of that kind of thing themselves."

Shelly felt like she'd been hit hard in the chest. She couldn't believe it. She didn't want to believe it.

He said bluntly, "It's a rip-off agency. There are dozens of them in L.A. I'll bet you answered an ad in the paper."

When she didn't correct him, he went on, "A real agency doesn't have to advertise. They have more girls than they can handle."

She stood there, not saying a word.

Hunter dropped a five-dollar bill on top of the check Shelly had placed there earlier, finishing, "I'm sorry. It's just that I see girls like you get taken advantage of all the time by assholes like Fairchild. If you're gonna survive in this town, you've got to develop some street smarts. That means don't trust anybody who wants something from you."

When he left, Shelly handed the money and the check to the cashier then took her portfolio out from under the counter, where the waitresses stashed their coats and purses. Sitting down at an empty table, she looked at the photographs dispassionately, admitting the truth: they looked like pictures taken in a hurry by a mediocre photographer who couldn't even be bothered to get the lighting right.

Her hopes and dreams, as well as what little remained of her trust, were encompassed in this portfolio and what it represented. She wanted desperately to believe that every word Ryan Hunter had said was a lie, but she knew he was right. She could try another agency, but what was the point? She couldn't tell the real ones from the fake ones, and she would probably just end up being taken advantage of again. The only kind of modeling she was probably good for was the kind Hunter had suggested — taking off her clothes and exposing herself before the whole world.

Shelly felt stupid and foolish and wanted to cry, but she was at work, surrounded by people, and she couldn't give way to tears.

Nausea churned in her stomach, and she rushed to the restroom. Afterward, she splashed water on her face and stared at her reflection in the small, scratched mirror. She looked awful — pale and listless, with dark circles under her eyes. Shelly had been getting sick a lot lately, and she hoped she wasn't coming down with the flu. Now that it was clear she wasn't going to have a modeling career, she couldn't afford to lose this job.

SEVEN

Kate

He wasn't like any other boy she'd ever known. To begin with, he wasn't a boy, he was a *man*. He was twenty-two, had just graduated at the end of the summer quarter, and was back on campus visiting his old fraternity before going into the air force. He was leaving in the morning. "This is my last night of freedom," he told her. Much later, Kate realized he'd come on campus looking for one last fling, a one-night stand with no looking back.

His name was John Scarron and his parents were from France, but he had been born and raised in the United States. He was tall and slim and broad-shouldered, so impossibly handsome that he was almost a cliche. Unlike most of the other guys in the fraternity, with their long, unkempt hair and faded jeans, John looked like he'd stepped out of an ad for men's cologne. His glossy black hair was cut short and his tan slacks and loosely woven white cotton sweater were obviously expensive. The deep V neck of the sweater revealed a tanned chest and a soft mat of curling hair. To Kate, he seemed sophistication personified. He had an air of amused tolerance toward his younger frat brothers, who behaved like clods.

Barbara had long since disappeared with some guy, and Kate was about ready to go back to the dorm when she saw John standing alone in a corner. It took all of her courage to walk up to him and ask him to dance. When he said yes, she couldn't believe it, her move had worked!

Afterward, he led her outside, and they sat on the brick wall of a terrace overlooking a street swarming with students making the rounds of the frat houses. Loud music filled the warm summer night. It was the end of the first week of classes, and freshmen were busy pledging the fraternities and sororities.

Not Kate and Barbara. As soon as they arrived on campus and discovered that sororities and fraternities were considered passé by the really sophisticated students, Barbara immediately changed her mind about joining; but that didn't stop them from going to the frat parties. On this first Saturday night of the fall quarter, Fraternity Row on the edge of campus was definitely where the action was.

Kate perched on the brick wall and smiled up at John. "What made you decide to join the air force?"

It wasn't an innocuous question. With the war in Vietnam still raging, despite Nixon's 1968 campaign promise of a "secret plan" to end it, most guys were looking for ways of getting out of being drafted.

John shrugged. "I couldn't stand the thought of settling into a nine-to-five job in some stuffy office. At least, not yet. It seemed like an interesting alternative."

His voice held the slightest hint of an accent, not so much in the way he pronounced words but in the careful, precise modulation of his speech.

"Aren't you worried about being sent to 'Nam?" she pressed.

164

"Nope. Might be interesting to see some action."

Kate was amazed. In Visalia, she hadn't thought that much about the war. It had always been in the background, on the evening TV newscasts that she caught only snatches of between dinner and homework. Bold headlines on the front page of the newspaper told of seemingly endless defeats, but she didn't have time to read the paper and was ignorant of anything save the most general facts about the war.

Since arriving at UCLA, she'd quickly become politicized. Watching nineteen-year-old boys in the dorm agonize over the number they drew in the draft lottery, she realized that their entire future, including life or death, could hinge on whether they were lucky enough to draw a high number or unlucky enough to draw a low one. All because of a war that no one seemed to understand.

Vietnam was on everyone's mind, and sooner or later it became the subject of most conversations. She'd signed her first petition against the war even before signing up for classes. If anyone on campus supported it, they weren't being very vocal, all of which made John's attitude unusual and intriguing. Kate didn't agree with it, but she couldn't help admiring his courage.

"So tell me about yourself," he went on. "Where are you from?"

"The valley."

"Oh, yeah? Where? Encino, Northridge?"

Of course, he assumed she meant the San Fernando Valley. He'd probably never even heard of the San Joaquin Valley, she realized with a sinking sensation. If she explained to him exactly where Visalia was, she'd be labeling herself a hick, and that was the last thing she wanted him to think.

So Kate answered vaguely, "No, further north. No place you've heard of." Before he could pursue the subject, she went on hurriedly, "What did you major in?"

They spent the next few minutes discussing his bachelor of science degree and her confusion over English versus Theater Arts as possible majors. They were interrupted by a raucous group spilling out onto the terrace, so he took her arm. "Let's get out of here."

They walked aimlessly around Westwood, the nearby area of shops, restaurants, and movie theaters, glancing in the windows of chic boutiques and stopping at a sidewalk café for espresso. John had sold his car the day before, in preparation for leaving, so he couldn't drive her down to the ocean. It would have been wonderful, he told her, to walk along the beach together on a night like this, with a full moon hanging low in the sky.

This was the most romantic night of Kate's life, and she wished it would never end. It had all the elements of a really great movie, like *Romeo and Juliet*. A tall, dark, and handsome stranger, romantic dialogue, one night together before he shipped out to fight for his country. She couldn't wait to tell Barbara all about it later.

Kate was relieved that John wanted to talk about himself rather than asking her questions. She had realized from the start that she was way out of her depth with him and only hoped that by listening with eager interest, and saying as little as possible about herself, she could hide her inexperience.

When, some time after midnight, he said he'd better be walking her back to her dorm room, she felt her heart sink. It was over already. Kate couldn't even hope that he would call her because in a few hours he would be in boot camp, or whatever they called basic training in the air force.

In the lobby of her massive ten-story dorm, John said, "Why don't I come up to your room for a while? Unless your roommate's in."

Barbara had been out late every night this week, and Kate knew that tonight would be no different. She smiled at John. "No, she isn't in."

"Good."

As they rode up in the elevator together, Kate fairly tingled with a delicious sense of anticipation. Just think of it—a man in her room! And not some gangly teenager, all elbows and knees and acne, but a man who looked like a movie star and talked like a professor.

The tiny dorm room was barely large enough for the spartan furniture that filled every square inch. There were two of everything—narrow cots that served as sofas during the day when they were pushed back under bolsters mounted against the walls, small dressers, desks, and chairs. Barbara had decorated her side with a pink-and-white quilt from home and some white-framed prints of Expressionist masters, such as Degas and Monet. Kate's side was cheap chic—a madras bedspread and unframed posters saying "Today is the first day of the rest of your life" and "Make love not war."

As John walked over to look at the view through the large window, Kate surreptitiously locked the door behind her. After only a week in the dorm, she'd discovered that girls constantly barged in and out of each other's rooms, often without knocking. She definitely didn't want to be interrupted, especially by one of the older girls who would easily upstage her.

John turned on her small transistor radio sitting

on the desk, and one of her favorite songs, the Beatles' "Here, There and Everywhere," came on.

How utterly perfect, she thought.

When Kate joined John by the window, he put his arm around her and murmured, "Nice view."

All the dorms were on a hill, and this one, Hedrick Hall, was at the very top, overlooking not only the campus below but the millions of twinkling lights of L.A. spread out in the distance. The first time Kate had looked out at this view at night, it made her feel small and helpless and overwhelmed. L.A. was such a massive city, and she was just a small town girl.

When John turned to take her in his arms and bent down to kiss her, she wasn't surprised. She'd been expecting this, waiting eagerly for it, all night, but she wasn't prepared for the intensity of the kiss, his tongue thrusting deep into her mouth and his hands sliding over her hips, pulling her against him.

Jesus, but he's a good kisser, she thought, giving way to the powerful feelings coursing through her. She felt excited, hot, rapidly losing all control. His hands—there was nothing tentative or awkward about their movements as they cupped her behind and pulled her even closer.

Kate was wearing an incredibly short, micromini dress in blue-and-green paisley that she'd bought in Westwood. It barely covered her. Her legs were tanned from long summer days spent swimming up at Three Rivers, so she wasn't wearing nylons. When John slipped his hands underneath her dress, her bare skin quivered at his touch.

Surprised, she pulled back slightly. He smiled down at her then kissed her again, his hands moving higher, lifting her dress. When he reached her

168

white cotton panties, he tugged at them and Kate went absolutely rigid. Things were moving way too fast. She opened her mouth to tell him so, but he said, "You have the softest, sweetest, most kissable mouth, but it's awkward standing here. Not to mention rather public, in front of the window. Let's sit down."

They sat on the bed and he began kissing her again, but Kate didn't respond now. She tried furiously to think of a way to tell John she couldn't do this without sounding like exactly what she was—a silly eighteen-year-old virgin who didn't know how to deal with a mature, sophisticated man.

Sensing her reluctance, he smiled again, and she thought what an absolutely devastating smile it was.

"I know what you need," he whispered.

To her utter amazement, he kneeled down on the floor in front of her, pulled off her panties, opened her legs, and began kissing her intimately. Shock and embarrassment rendered Kate speechless. Then those feelings gave way to sensations unlike anything she'd ever imagined, let alone experienced. Her head went back. She leaned back on the bed, feeling a gradual buildup of almost unbearable tension, as if her body were a spring being coiled tighter and tighter, straining to reach some unknown destination, working harder and harder to get there.

Kate closed her eyes and everything—the tiny dorm room, the view through the window, the music, *everything* was blocked out as she focused completely on her response to John's tongue. It was the most exquisite torture. Please, she begged silently, I can't bear any more, but, oh, don't stop!

She was shaking now, her fingers gripping his shoulders tightly. She was as wound up as a jack-in-the-box and, like the toy, felt as if she were about to burst. Still the sensations kept building in intensity until she at last went over the edge of some deep, dark, deliciously inviting chasm.

Kate slowly opened her eyes, realizing for the first time that she'd been holding her breath, which she now released in a rush.

John moved up to join her on the bed, his expression smug. "It gets even better, babe. Just wait and see."

Then they shed their clothes and she couldn't take her eyes off his body. It was magnificent—hard and lean and muscled and breathtakingly male. She was mesmerized by his penis. It was so different from her little brothers', so big and powerful looking. It was almost frightening in a way, but it was the kind of fear that has a delicious edge to it, like the way she felt when she rode a roller coaster.

What would it feel like to have it inside her? she wondered. Her body trembled with anticipation, and she couldn't wait to find out. She wasn't sure when she'd made the decision to give up her virginity to this man. She only knew that she was ready to do so. There was no doubt, no reluctance, only a breathless eagerness to experience everything that she'd only vaguely imagined until now.

When he wrapped his strong arms around her, pulled her tight against him, and entered her it was unlike any sensation she'd ever known before. Reacting instinctively, she moved with him as he rocked back and forth.

He didn't speak. Instead he concentrated on long, deep, probing kisses. She didn't speak, either. She had no idea what to say. She simply concentrated on the thrilling new sensations coursing through her. Everything about him sent her pulse racing and her head spinning—his tongue teasing hers, his

170

hands massaging her shoulders and back, his taut buttocks moving up and down as her fingers kneaded them.

The rhythm gradually increased until once more she felt that inexorable buildup of tension deep within her. This time the explosion was even more powerful because her entire body was involved. She wanted to scream with exultation, and had to stifle the sound by biting his shoulder.

When she finally came back to earth, she opened her eyes and looked into his, staring down at her. To her intense disappointment, there was nothing there — no warmth, no sense of shared emotion, no communion. Nothing but a look of utter satiation and an air of being thoroughly pleased with himself.

Pulling away from her, he sat up, stretched tiredly, then began dressing.

She felt foolish lying there, so she slipped on her panties and dress, but didn't bother with her shoes. Noticing the telltale stain on the sheet, she stripped it off the bed and tossed it in the clothes hamper at the bottom of the tiny closet.

Then she turned to face John. But before she could think what on earth to say to him, the door handle rattled, then there was a sharp knocking. "Kate! It's me! I forgot my key again."

Barbara.

Looking at John, Kate saw consternation on his face and for some reason felt an overwhelming urge to laugh. Stifling her impulse, she opened the door.

"Lord, what a night!" Barbara exclaimed. Stopping short upon seeing John standing in the middle of the room, she glanced at Kate. Her look clearly asked, "Should I get lost?"

Kate made an instant decision. She didn't want to spend one more minute alone with John.

171

"Barb, this is John Scarron," she said quickly, before Barbara could make a hurried excuse to leave. "John, this is my roommate, Barbara Avery."

As John took Barbara's hand in a rather awkward handshake, Kate went on, "John is leaving in the morning to join the air force. We were just saying good-night."

Barbara's eyes flicked from Kate to John and back again. Are you crazy? her look clearly said. "Nice to meet you, John."

He had obviously been taught perfect manners. "Pleased to meet you," he murmured, *almost* looking as if he meant it. Then, turning to Kate, he said tightly, "I'll be going then. Good-night."

"Good-night."

He left, closing the door firmly behind him.

Barbara grinned. "Where on earth did you find that hunk? And why did you let him go?"

It had always been easy to tell Barbara everything. But for some reason, Kate was ashamed to repeat what had just happened. While they changed into nightgowns, she explained, "We met at the frat party. He's gorgeous but a bore."

She'd spoken in an offhand manner but realized with a start that it was true. He *was* a bore—a conceited ass who had merely been looking for an easy lay, and had picked on an inexperienced little freshman as a likely candidate. She'd viewed their evening together through a romantic haze; he'd viewed it as a one-night stand.

Kate felt like a fool.

Barbara's voice was muffled through the pale blue nightgown she pulled over her head. "Isn't that always the case? 'Gorgeous' and 'jerk' are synonymous. Listen, I've got to tell you about this guy I met tonight . . ."

172

They climbed into their narrow beds and turned out the light, Barbara doing a nonstop monologue on her new beau, David Browning, a third-year med student from Sacramento. He was the oldest of five children, his parents were both teachers, and he had blue eyes like Paul Newman's that crinkled at the edges when he smiled, which wasn't often because he was serious about becoming a doctor. Since his family didn't have much money it was a real struggle financially.

Unlike the other guys she had met so far—and, of course, Barbara had met quite a few—David was *mature*. He knew what he wanted to do with his life. He was ambitious to achieve much more than his parents had. When Barbara casually let it drop that she had been valedictorian of her class, he not only wasn't intimidated, he liked it. He said a really intelligent woman could be a tremendous help to a professional man.

"What did he think of you becoming a doctor, too?" Kate asked.

"Oh, I didn't mention that yet. No point in making him think I'm competitive."

"You might change your mind, anyway," Kate pointed out.

Barbara's voice hardened. "No way. I'm going to be a doctor, and then I'm going to join the Peace Corps or do something else really different for a couple of years before coming back to L.A. and establishing a practice on the West Side. I'm *not* going to change my mind."

Kate didn't argue. She knew better than to contradict Barbara, who talked on about David, his politics (determinedly middle-of-the-road), body (lean and hard—he'd been a track star in high school and college and still got up at the crack of dawn to run five miles a day), and clothes (unimpressive, but then, he had an excuse—he was poor).

Both Kate and Barbara were exhausted by now, barely able to keep their eyes open as Barbara finished, "I can't wait for you to meet him. We're going to study together tomorrow night in the med library. It's real quiet there. I think I'm going to be seeing a lot of him."

Kate was surprised that Barbara would be interested in settling down with one guy so quickly. This was only the first week of school! If she didn't know better, she'd suspect that Barbara was as nervous as she was about this intimidating new environment, with its new experiences, new ideas, new people, and was desperately grabbing for a little security.

"Night," Barbara said with a yawn, turning over to face away from Kate.

Before sleep overtook her, Kate decided that from now on she would look for a boy her own age. Preferably a fellow freshman, who felt just as overwhelmed as she did by the complexity of college life.

She wasn't ready for older men.

A week later, Kate walked up the hill from campus to the cluster of dormitories while talking animatedly to Roger Kowalski, a freshman from New York and a film major who wanted to be the next Roman Polanski, who was his idol. After all, they were both Polish, though Roger was third-generation.

At six-feet-two and a hundred and fifty pounds, he was a gangly beanpole of a boy with shoulder-length brown hair and soft brown eyes. Roger's lopsided smile gave his face a sort of goofy demeanor;

174

however, he was anything but stupid. Bright, articulate, creative, he had captivated Kate from the first moment he tried rather awkwardly to pick her up in the basement stacks at Powell Library.

She had taken *The Virgin and the Gypsy* from a shelf and was idly perusing it when a voice close behind her said, "You don't want to read that. It's Lawrence at his most obvious and self-indulgent. Read *Women in Love*. It's much better."

Roger talked nonstop. "Did you see *Knife in the Water?* You didn't! But you have to! It's the most brilliant movie ever made. The way Polanski kept the sex and violence hovering just below the surface was incredible. I was at Woodstock. Yeah, what a mindblower. Sex, drugs, and rock 'n' roll! Hendrix, Joplin, the Who, but the Grateful Dead were the best. Do you like them? What do you mean, *no!* You've got to like them. Come on over to my room sometime and I'll play all their albums and turn you on to them. . . ."

She found Roger childlike in his enthusiasms, utterly uninterested in any subject that wasn't creative, and flatteringly attracted to her. He assaulted her with a barrage of questions, and while he often disagreed with her fervently, he seemed genuinely interested in her opinions. Every once in a while he would simply shut up and listen to her, really listen.

When Roger told Kate he was from a small farming community in upstate New York, New Paltz, "way out in the boonies," she confessed where she was from. He'd never heard of Visalia, of course, but it didn't matter.

He said, "Isn't it a kick being in a place like this, where so much is happening?"

Before she knew it, they'd been talking for four hours and it was time to go back to the dorm for dinner. Although he lived in Dykstra, the dorm right below Hedrick, he accompanied her all the way up the hill to Hedrick. When he asked if he could take her to a movie the next night, she said yes. Watching him lope away, with all the long-legged awkwardness of a young giraffe, his wavy hair swinging back and forth over his shirt collar, Kate knew that she was going to like Roger very much.

She hurried up to her room to dump her books and meet Barbara so they could go down to dinner together. She couldn't wait to tell her about Roger. Throwing open the door to their room, she began eagerly, "I met a guy . . ."

Kate stopped in midsentence. Shelly sat on the bed beside Barbara, who had an arm around her. Shelly's eyes were red and swollen, her cheeks tear-stained. She was thinner and paler than Kate had ever seen her. She looked awful.

"Shelly," Kate whispered. Nobody had heard from her since that one brief letter at the beginning of summer. Kate had been very worried. Now she flung herself down on the bed and hugged Shelly tightly. "It's so good to see you." Pulling away, she asked in concern, "What is it? What's wrong?"

Shelly's lip trembled. She didn't speak.

Barbara said gently, "She's pregnant."

EIGHT

Valerie

In 1969, Berkeley seemed to Valerie to be the most exciting place in the universe. What a year—Woodstock, the Chicago Seven trial, massive antiwar protests, Chappaquiddick, a man on the moon. Students at Berkeley reacted to all these events and more. Everything that happened was the subject of intense debate or overt demonstration.

Walking down Telegraph Avenue near the university, Val saw posters advertising rock concerts at the Fillmore and the Avalon Ballroom. Hippies lay on the sidewalk or lounged in doorways, dressed colorfully in flowered shirts and headbands, wearing long strands of love beads and leather-fringed vests. They smoked joints and sold hash pipes right out in the open.

When Val read an article in the *Berkeley Barb* that said, "The professors have nothing to teach. We can learn more from any jail than we can from any university," she knew she was in the right place. The rules of middle-class society had no place here, and the world belonged to the young.

The sidewalks, even the streets, were filled with people talking, laughing, arguing, handing out leaflets, and asking everyone passing by to sign petitions. On warm, sunny days, Val sat on the Terrace, the outdoor cafeteria next to the Student Union, looking out at the deep blue water of the bay and San Francisco's breathtaking skyline. People wearing shorts splashed in the fountain on the mall, and the music of individual guitar players, flutists, and drummers mingled together in surprising harmony. The sheer size of the university, the new things waiting around every corner to be discovered, made her feel giddy with excitement and anticipation.

For the first time in her entire eighteen years, Val didn't feel out of place, at odds with her environment. These people were like her, radical, rebellious, smart. *This* was where she belonged. From the first moment she walked on campus, Val felt at home. She'd never really fit in with her family, the church, high school, but she had no qualms about fitting in here.

She sure as hell wasn't going to be homesick and had no intention of ever going back to Visalia again. There was absolutely nothing there for her but criticism and rejection and a deadly repressiveness of the spirit. Val had decided to not even go home for holidays; she would tell her parents she was traveling or staying with new friends or something.

She had signed up to live in a dorm, but during the first week of school, Val answered an ad in the *Barb* to share a house with three other people, a guy and two women. The house was an old Victorian cottage near campus. A previous tenant had decorated it entirely in red, from the red shag carpet covering the hardwood floors to red shades on the windows and red-and-gold flocked wallpaper.

178

Val took one look and termed it "early bordello." Her new roommates, Russ, Carrie, and Myrna, loved the description and added their own touches — a red National Liberation Front flag hung over the fireplace, posters of Che Guevara, Ho Chi Minh, and Margaret Mead.

Russ, a short, stocky redhead with a Beaver Cleaver grin, had been going to school for eight years and still hadn't managed to graduate. He kept changing his major as the whim struck him. At the moment, he was majoring in ethnic studies and was seriously considering taking a trip to various third-world countries on a sort of personal fact-finding mission.

When Val suggested he simply go to Delano and join in the grape strike led by Cesar Chavez, he reacted as if he'd experienced an epiphany. "Of course!" he shouted. "It's third-world politics right here in our own backyard." Then he stopped and asked sheepishly, "Uh — where is Delano?"

Val knew exactly where it was — an hour's drive south of Visalia.

Carrie was a fragile, ethereal-looking blonde who could have played Ophelia. She quoted poetry, especially Blake when she was stoned, which was most of the time. She had flunked out of school a year earlier and now just hung around the periphery of the university, enjoying the atmosphere without actually participating in it.

Her parents back in Iowa didn't know she was no longer a student and continued to support her with monthly checks. Carrie augmented her income by making tie-dyed T-shirts and headbands in soft, pale shades of azure blue and pink and mauve, always using one to hold back her waist-long, straight blond hair. Her clothes were eclectic — long granny

179

dresses, black tights and a black micromini skirt with a scarf wrapped around her chest in lieu of a blouse, and knee-length 1940s dresses from thrift shops.

Myrna was the oldest, in her late thirties, with streaks of gray in her short black hair and an awesome energy glinting in her shrewd blue eyes. She had returned to college after getting a divorce and turning her back on the bland, middle-class housewife life she had lived for so long. Throwing herself wholeheartedly into everything that was happening, she was always one of the leaders in any demonstration that took place on campus. A radical feminist, Myrna had formed one of the first women's encounter groups a few years earlier.

"Women are oppressed," she told Val in her blunt, no-nonsense tone. "Women are treated like blacks, kept down, forced to be subservient."

Val responded instinctively to the idea of women's liberation but felt uncomfortable in Myrna's group. They read Doris Lessing and Sylvia Plath and refused to dress in any way that could be construed as being provocative or appealing to men; that included refusing to shave their underarms or legs while insisting that someday men wouldn't be necessary.

"When sperm banks really get going, men will be obsolete, except as friends," Myrna predicted confidently.

The group met once a week in their living room. The first time Val attended, she was amazed to see the women sprawling over the furniture and floor cushions, legs spread carelessly. She had heard, "Keep your legs crossed, young lady," all her life and knew these women had probably heard the same thing but weren't buying it anymore.

All right, she thought, plopping down on the floor in a comfortable position.

"Now," Myrna said, "let's go around the room and let each person say what's bugging her."

As each woman spoke, it seemed that they were all bugged by the same thing—men.

"I never have orgasms and he doesn't even care. . . ."

"He treats me like a fucking maid. I do his laundry, type his term papers. . . ."

"He says I should work to put him through school because his career is going to support us eventually, but when I ask him what guarantee I have that he'll be around *eventually*, he gets mad at me. . . ."

And on and on.

The talk was so frank, especially about sex, that Val was almost embarrassed. In her wildest moments, she had never talked like this. Even with her closest friends, she had never shared what these women, many of them strangers, were sharing so openly with each other.

They talked about orgasms and the clitoris and vibrators while Val just sat there, silently taking it all in. She was thrilled with the frankness and touched by a sense of sisterhood that she'd never before experienced. Though she'd felt close to Kate, Barbara, and Shelly and had relied heavily on their friendship to get through the dreariness of her life in Visalia, she'd never felt that she could express her deepest feelings. There always lay a reserve, a sense of things unsaid between them while here, in this atmosphere of absolute honesty, there was none of that reticence.

Myrna was amazing, putting it all into a feminist political perspective, answering questions, encouraging women who were afraid to confront the unpleasant truths of their lives; but even while Val stood in awe of her and wanted to be like her in many ways, she wasn't ready to give up men. Especially not now, when she had a whole university full of exciting, attractive men to fuck. She had no intention of letting her miserable experience with Gregg Hartoonian be her only sexual adventure.

No way.

Following the meeting, Val helped Myrna wash up. Afterward, they sat on metal folding chairs at the card table serving as a kitchen table, smoking grass and talking.

"So what did you think of the meeting?" Myrna asked.

"For a bunch of women who say they don't care about men, they sure talk about them a lot."

Myrna laughed. "Yeah, but that's just 'cause men still run things. Comes the revolution, it'll be different. Women have a lot of evolving to do, I admit. We don't think much of ourselves."

"What do you mean?"

"Look at us—we accept that line of bullshit that we're nothing without men. We put our feelings and needs behind theirs. We let them treat us like shit, much worse than they would treat someone they hired to do a job for them, and then we whine and say, *But I love him.*"

"You don't like men very much, do you?"

Myrna nodded. "You got that right."

"Well, I like them," Val said defiantly. "I haven't fucked all the men I want to fuck yet."

"You like being treated like a sex object?"

"Hey, I wish I was treated like a sex object," she joked, but realized that Myrna had a point about the way men viewed women only in terms of possi-

182

ble conquests. For Val, the result of all this was a kind of sex that left her feeling unloved and used.

"I'm not ready to give up on men yet," Val insisted.

"That's just because you still buy into that fantasy that they'll make you happy. Trust me, they won't." Lighting another joint, Myrna took a deep drag and went on. "Look at it objectively—what do you want from men?"

Val thought for a moment. What did she want from men? To be valued by them. To be cherished. To be cared for, respected, appreciated, and maybe even adored.

To be loved. Wholeheartedly and unconditionally.

She felt tears spring to her eyes and had to fight them back, determined not to show such weakness in front of Myrna, who was so strong and independent and together.

Why did the recognition that she needed a man to love her make her feel so vulnerable? she wondered. Maybe because she'd never known such love.

Pulling herself together, Val asked, "But if you dump men, then what's left?"

"Women."

Val started to say something, then stopped. She'd been at Berkeley long enough to know about lesbians. Gay liberation groups joined Vietnam protests under their own banner, and lesbian feminists formed separatist organizations. She wasn't shocked to realize that Myrna was a lesbian, but she was surprised by her own response to this knowledge— she felt uneasy, even threatened.

The silence stretched on awkwardly. Finally, Myrna spoke, sounding understanding and not the least argumentative. "It's all right, Val. I know that some day you'll understand."

"Understand what?" Val asked defensively.

Myrna didn't answer.

On September 15, the four roommates threw a party to celebrate solidarity with the Chicago Seven, whose trial had begun that day. Val felt like Alice in Wonderland falling down the rabbit hole, encountering a strange new world. People came wearing gorgeous, opulent Victorian velvet gowns with white lace ruffles around the throat, African robes, Donald Duck hats and Mickey Mouse ears, Indian war paint. All the windows in the living room had been covered with foil and the room lit only by candles, dozens of them crowded on tables, window ledges, the fireplace mantel. Incense filled the air, and a light show was projected on one wall.

Everyone was smoking joints, and when one was passed to Val, she sucked in her breath deeply then made a soft *shooing* sound as she exhaled. She lay on the floor on huge, paisley-patterned cushions, with people lying all around her. There, nestled with strangers, listening to sitar music on the stereo, and puffing on joints, she felt a sense of belonging unlike anything she'd ever known.

This was heaven.

Carrie, wearing white tights, a pink ballerina tutu, and a white feather boa, lay down next to her and held a little blue tab gingerly between two fingers. Holding out her hand, she said, "Put it under your tongue."

Val didn't have to ask what it was. She had never tried LSD but was intensely curious. Was it as marvelous, as transforming, as dangerous as people said?

Well, there was only one way to find out. She

184

slipped it under her tongue and waited expectantly.

First came a buzzing in her head, then Val felt stabs of pain like pins and needles all over her body. She couldn't move and for one terrifying moment thought she was paralyzed and might even die. Then the world began to come alive. "Tune in, turn on, and drop out," Timothy Leary had said. Oh, *yeah*, she thought.

Val no longer knew what was real and what was a hallucination. The light show on the wall seemed to have gone insane, the shapes distorted, the colors more vivid. Objects—the furniture, candles—wavered, going in and out of focus. Everything seemed out of control and unpredictable, and she began to be afraid of what she might see next.

It wasn't fun anymore, and Val began to cry, soft little whimpers, almost like tiny hiccups. Closing her eyes, she saw Steven Ashe's face in Barbara's headlights. An image buried deep in her subconscious, now it forced its way to the surface, terrifying her. Val screamed, and Russ raced to her, helping her up. He led her to his bedroom, where he shut and locked the door and put her in his bed. He lay down beside Val, stroking her hair, murmuring words of gentle reassurance, nursing her through the bad trip.

"It's all right," he kept repeating, like a litany. "It's all right."

At some point, Val fell asleep but awoke while it was still dark. The quiet told her the party must have wound down. Russ lay beside her, asleep, his face barely visible in the pale moonlight filtering through the open window. It was a sweet face, gentle and innocent as a little boy's.

She thought, anyone with a face like that could never possibly hurt me. After a moment, he stirred.

As his eyes slowly opened, Russ smiled at her. "Are you all right now?"

She nodded. When she spoke, her mouth felt dry. "Thank you."

"No problem."

Val was aware of how close they were, their bodies touching, their breath warm on each other's faces. Cupping her face in his hands, Russ kissed her gently. The exquisite tenderness got to her, making her feel warm and relaxed. She kissed him back with an eagerness she would have been embarrassed to show before, and he responded. He undressed her slowly, carefully, and for once Val felt so comfortable that she didn't worry about whether or not she was attractive.

Russ's lovemaking was easy, unhurried, pleasant. Val loved it, loved being held gently and caressed. She didn't feel especially passionate but felt a need to be close and wanted it to go on forever. When he came a short while later, a sharp jolt of disappointment ran through her.

"I'm sorry," he whispered. "You didn't come, did you?"

She rushed to reassure him. "It's okay. It was lovely. I enjoyed it. You were wonderful."

He yawned tiredly. "Good." Cradling her in his arms, he immediately fell into a deep sleep while Val lay awake for a long time, watching the light filtering through the window turn from gray to pink to white. She wished she could have had an orgasm. She felt incomplete and dissatisfied, but she told herself that it wasn't *that* important. All that really mattered was being held in Russ's arms.

The next time they made love, she was sure, it would be better.

Late that morning, Val awoke to find Russ gone. Yawning and stretching happily in the big bed, she thought how considerate it was of him not to wake her when he got up. She dressed quickly then hurried into the kitchen, eager to see him and kiss him good morning.

She didn't have any classes and if he was free, too, maybe they could go down to the beach or browse through bookstores. She didn't really care what they did, she just wanted to be with him.

Carrie was alone in the kitchen, brewing herb tea and chanting *om* over and over again.

"Where's Russ?" Val asked.

"Om . . . with Paula . . . *om."*

"Paula?"

Carrie stopped chanting and looked at Val. "Yeah, you know, his girlfriend. Oh, that's right, you haven't met her yet. She couldn't come to the party last night. Had to work or something. Anyway, they went down to Big Sur for a couple of days."

Val went cold inside. Carrie rattled on about Big Sur, but she wasn't listening. Of course, she told herself, there would be another girl. Probably lots of other girls. After all, this was Berkeley. Free love and grass and politics. What had she expected, anyway? That Russ had fallen in love with her?

Get real.

Val went into her room, turned on the Jefferson Airplane, and lit a joint. There were a lot of other guys around, she told herself, but an irritating little voice inside responded that she didn't want a lot of guys. She just wanted one.

187

NINE

Kate

She never knew exactly how the arrangements were made for the abortion. She only knew that Barbara left to talk to David, who apparently talked to someone else. When Barbara came back to the dorm room late that night, she had the name and address of a bar in Tijuana along with a figure: five hundred dollars.

It might as well have been five thousand as far as Shelly was concerned. Even if she sold everything she owned, she still couldn't come up with anywhere near that amount. The three sat in silence for a long, unhappy moment. Through the closed door, Kate could hear the muffled sounds of music from stereos, talk, laughter; students with their entire lives ahead of them and nothing more serious to worry about than mid-terms and finals and term papers.

"How far along are you?" Barbara asked Shelly, who sat quietly, her expression hopeless.

Kate knew what Barbara was getting at—was the pregnancy the result of the gang rape? When Shelly looked down and murmured, "Four months," Kate knew it was true. It was all so horrible. Shelly couldn't even know which boy was the father of the baby.

Dear God, she thought, what could they possibly do to help her?

"There are homes for unwed mothers," Barbara began tentatively. "You could have the baby then . . ."

"I won't have this baby!" Shelly burst out. Her stricken eyes met Kate's. "I *can't!*"

Grabbing her purse, she rose to leave.

"We'll help you." Barbara's voice was calm and reassuring, with the steely undercurrent of determination that Kate recognized so well.

Shelly turned to face Barbara, hope glistening in her tear-filled eyes. "How?"

"I can raise the five hundred."

"But where will you get that kind of money? If you ask your parents . . ."

"I don't have to ask my parents. I'll hock my jewelry."

Barbara had inherited some valuable pieces from her maternal grandmother. Although most of the gems were locked away in a safety deposit box in Visalia, her mother had reluctantly allowed Barbara to bring a few pieces with her to college. There was a large, square-cut emerald ring, her birthstone, that she often wore when she went out at night; lovely, old-fashioned amethyst earrings; and a small, heart-shaped diamond pendant on a thin platinum chain.

"I can't let you do that," Shelly argued.

"Don't be silly. I have plenty more jewelry at home."

"If your parents ask about those pieces . . ."

"I'll say they were stolen and I didn't want to tell them because I knew they'd be mad."

Mad was an understatement, Kate thought. Barbara's mother would be livid.

Barbara went on. "It's all settled. Kate and I will

189

drive you down to Tijuana. We'll stay with you through the whole thing." She looked at Kate. "Won't we?"

There was only one answer. "Of course."

She turned back to Shelly. "Come back in the morning around ten thirty. That'll give me time to go to a pawnshop. There must be one somewhere in Westwood."

"Don't you have classes tomorrow?"

"We can miss one day of classes. Now, I'd better take you home. You shouldn't ride the bus this late at night, and you need to try to get some sleep. We have a long drive ahead of us tomorrow."

For the first time all evening, Shelly looked as if there might be some hope in her dark pit of despair. "I . . . I don't know what to say."

"You don't have to say anything. It's going to be all right."

As Kate watched her two friends leave the room, a suspicion nagged at her. Was Barbara helping Shelly out of friendship or was her motivation guilt over the role she'd played in the events on graduation night?

It didn't really matter, she told herself. All that mattered was helping Shelly, but Kate was scared about Tijuana. Would the abortionist be a real doctor? How could David be sure? Would it be safe? Everyone had heard horror stories about girls killed by back-alley butchers. Surely David wouldn't have recommended someone who wasn't safe. He was practically a doctor. He *must* know what he was doing.

It occurred to Kate that she'd have to get hold of Roger and postpone their date. She had more urgent business to do tomorrow than see a movie.

El Palomino was the filthiest, most dangerous

place Kate had ever been in, full of mean-looking men and garishly dressed women of the prostitute persuasion. When the three college girls walked in, the patrons looked them over briefly then dismissed them, turning back to their drinks and desultory conversation.

David had told Barbara that they were to sit in a particular booth and wait. That was all. Just wait. As the minutes dragged into hours, Kate tried to hide her nervousness. Shelly looked scared enough as it was, with dark circles under her eyes and trembling hands.

As usual, Barbara was the only one who appeared calm and collected. She had brought a textbook with her, *British Poetry of the Nineteenth Century,* and seemed to be completely immersed in it, though when she would look up and meet Kate's eyes, there was a flicker of uncertainty in them.

She's just as nervous as we are, Kate realized. She just hides it better.

When they'd been sitting there for almost three hours, a middle-aged Mexican appeared, his overalls stained with oil, his long hair unkempt, and his skin badly pockmarked.

"Shelly DeLucca?" he asked.

Shelly nodded, unable to speak.

"Come."

He didn't introduce himself, but they followed him anyway out to a battered cab and climbed into the backseat. His silence continued as he drove them down side streets and narrow, garbage-strewn alleys.

"Where is he taking us?" Shelly whispered hoarsely to Kate.

"It's all right," Kate reassured her, but she was terrified. Where *was* he taking them?

Fifteen minutes later, the cab stopped on a dan-

191

gerous-looking street in front of a cement-block house with narrow windows that had black wrought-iron bars over them, resembling a jail.

The silent man gestured to the girls to go inside, and as they left the cab, Kate whispered to Barbara, "Do you really think we should go in there?"

"We don't have any choice." Barbara took Shelly's hand and led her toward the door.

There was a small group of people watching a tiny black-and-white TV in the living room. An elderly couple glanced up as the three entered but immediately returned their attention to the television.

Within moments, a man came out and asked in heavily accented English, "Which one of you is Miss DeLucca?"

Shelly took a deep breath and stepped forward.

"Come with me."

As Kate and Barbara started to follow, he said, "No, just Miss DeLucca. You wait here."

Shelly gave them a pleading look.

"We want to go with her," Kate insisted.

The man frowned. "She has to come alone. Otherwise, we no do business."

Barbara started to argue but Shelly interrupted. "No, it's all right. I can handle it. Just . . . just wait here." She followed the man out of the room.

There were no empty chairs in the nearly barren room, so Kate and Barbara stood in a corner together, worrying. The house was a stinking cesspool with mingled odors of urine, sweat, and bugs. This so-called doctor wasn't dressed like a doctor; his hands were dirty, especially his fingernails. What was he doing to Shelly in that other room? Was she lying on dirty sheets? Was there any anesthetic?

Suddenly they heard a low moan before a cry of pain came through the closed door. Kate and Barbara jumped, looking at each other in fear and confusion.

"What do we do?" Kate asked shakily.

"I don't know." The words caught in Barbara's throat. "Oh, God. I don't know!"

Kate walked over to the door and tried the handle.

Locked.

A young man looked up at her. *"Su amiga está bien."*

Kate's high school Spanish was barely enough to interpret his words—Her friend was okay—but the cries were still audible. Desperately, she tried to think of the right words. *"Qué . . . qué pasa allí?"* she asked haltingly. Instead of answering her question—What's happening in there?—he merely repeated, *"Su amiga está bien."*

Returning to Barbara's side, Kate asked, "Do you think we should pound on the door or something?"

Barbara shook her head. "Shelly isn't calling for us. If we interrupt now, who knows what would happen."

It was all Kate could do to stand there listening to the sounds of Shelly's pain, able to do nothing. Though it seemed much longer, it was only half an hour before the door opened. Shelly stumbled out, her face white and her entire body trembling. There was a blood stain on the back of her yellow cotton sundress.

Nausea rose within Kate as she realized Shelly hadn't even been undressed for the operation.

She and Barbara hurried to their friend's side, uncertain what to do.

"Adiós," the young man said with a smile.

The "doctor" was nowhere in sight.

They helped Shelly outside, where they found the cab still waiting. Thank God, Kate thought, with a

193

feeling of intense relief. The driver took them back to the bar, and once they were safely in Barbara's car, Kate asked Shelly, "What happened?"

She was lying down in the backseat with her eyes closed, using a sweater of Barbara's as a pillow. Without opening her eyes, she whispered, "There wasn't any anesthetic. He said it was too risky. It . . . hurt. A lot. There were bugs crawling up the wall, and I kept watching them, trying to concentrate on them, but it didn't work. And then . . . when it was over . . . he said, 'Get your shoes on and get out!' That was all."

Barbara, sitting behind the steering wheel and staring rigidly ahead at the road, uttered a low cry. Tears filled Kate's eyes. How could they have put Shelly through this? Kate dampened a handkerchief from a thermos of water they'd brought along and gently wiped Shelly's forehead. The car was stifling and Shelly was sweating profusely, but when Kate felt her forehead, she was startled to discover that it was burning hot.

Shelly kept moaning low in her throat, obviously in pain.

"I think we'd better take her to a hospital," Kate told Barbara.

"Are you crazy? They'll find out what she did."

Looking back, Kate saw a patch of blood spreading on Shelly's sundress.

"She's bleeding," Kate whispered to Barbara, hoping Shelly couldn't hear.

"That's . . . that's probably only natural," Barbara insisted, but her voice lacked conviction.

As they headed into Los Angeles, the bleeding grew worse and at Kate's insistence they ended up in a waiting room outside an emergency ward while a doctor examined Shelly.

Barbara called David, who made the forty-five-minute trip in half an hour. When he arrived, she threw herself in his arms, sobbing, "Oh, David. Thank God, you're here! The doctor said she was hemorrhaging when we brought her in."

"Calm down," he insisted. "Getting hysterical won't help."

This was Kate's first look at David. She was surprised by her immediate negative reaction to him. How could he be so cold at a time like this? How could Barbara like him so much? He was very attractive, in a conservative, buttoned-down sort of way, but there was absolutely no warmth in those ice-blue eyes.

Forcing herself to sound as polite as possible, Kate introduced herself to David, then explained what had happened in Tijuana. Barbara said nothing, merely clung to David, as if to a life raft. When Kate had finished, David frowned.

"That isn't how it was supposed to be. I was told the man was a certified doctor. However, I can understand why he wouldn't use an anesthetic. It can be very dangerous."

"The whole thing was certainly very dangerous for Shelly," Kate snapped.

"I'm sorry." David sighed. "I didn't know it would be like that." He added in a matter-of-fact tone, "But even if we'd known, there wasn't an alternative unless you have a great deal of money."

No, Kate thought, there wasn't an alternative.

David excused himself and spoke to the receptionist in a low voice. A moment later, she opened the door and he stepped into the emergency room, leaving Kate and Barbara sitting there, exhausted, their concern mounting by the minute. When he returned, his expression was even more sober than before.

"How is she?" Barbara and Kate asked in unison.

"I spoke to the doctor. They're admitting her to the hospital for a few days. You can't see her tonight. They've given her a sedative and some pain medication. She lost quite a bit of blood and needed a transfusion. If you hadn't brought her in as quickly as you did . . ."

His voice trailed off, but Kate felt herself go cold at the implication. Shelly could have ended up dead, all because of what had happened to her on graduation night.

David went on, "She should be all right."

Barbara whispered, "Thank God." Hugging David, she finished confidently, "Oh, I just knew she would be okay."

For the first time, Kate found herself questioning Barbara's attitude of self-assurance. Was it a sham? The word *denial* flashed into Kate's mind. Barbara was denying the harsh reality of what they'd just experienced, the same as she'd done on graduation night, when she'd so quickly fallen in with Val's plan to pretend nothing had happened.

Kate knew that all the denial in the world wouldn't change the terrible truth of what they'd gone through on this day or on that night months earlier. She herself had managed to thrust the memory of graduation night and Steven Ashe to the recesses of her mind. Days went by when she didn't even think of it, and the nightmares she'd suffered for weeks afterward had finally disappeared altogether.

Nevertheless, Kate had the horrible feeling that it would never end; the tragedy would go on haunting them, threatening them, forever.

TEN

Valerie

Myrna started an underground newspaper, *The Voice of the People,* which operated out of a small office over the shop that printed it in Berkeley. The paper's philosophy was pure far left, espousing everything from radical feminism ("Why Men Are the Enemy") to the usual antiwar line ("Pull Out, Dick, Like Your Father Should Have").

Myrna, as publisher, editor, main reporter, and the entire circulation department, would stand on a street corner near the university once a week selling copies at a quarter each. When she found out that Val was a journalism major, she immediately enlisted her help.

From the first moment Val stepped inside the office, she was hooked. She loved it—the smell of fresh ink, newsprint stains on her fingers, the freedom of being able to write anything she wanted without censorship, unlike the situation on the fucking college newspaper, where faculty advisers controlled *everything.* Val had started calling them "thought police" after they had squelched an article she wanted to write about sexism in the university's hiring practices.

She and Myrna were kindred souls, radical and

outrageous and determined never to be under anyone's thumb again. Sometimes they would sit in the office late at night, smoking joints and drinking cheap wine, while Myrna talked about her years as a housewife in suburbia.

"It's Ken and Barbie land," she said with a wicked grin. "All the little Ken dolls get in their big cars every morning and drive into the city to their offices to make money and fuck their secretaries, and all the little Barbie dolls do housework and join the PTA and brag about how much money their husbands are making."

"How did you ever get into that scene?" Val asked in amazement.

"I was twenty when I got married. You're really stupid when you're twenty. You don't know how much you don't know. You know?"

She shook her head. "Anyway, I dropped out of school to work and put Jim through graduate school. Then he became a financial planner, making big bucks telling rich people how to get out of paying taxes. Right now, the government's going after Joan Baez because she doesn't want to pay for fucking missiles, but they let millionaires get off without paying a cent."

"What made you finally get out of there?"

Myrna was uncharacteristically thoughtful for a moment. Without quite looking at Val, she said, "One day, I was cleaning the bathroom and Jim called to tell me about a big deal he'd just pulled off. He was so damn proud. He told me to start looking for a bigger house in a nicer neighborhood. He reassured me that he couldn't have done it without my help and support. When I hung up and went back to cleaning the bathroom, I thought about what he'd said about my support making him such a success. I realized that for twelve years all my energy had gone into making *his* dreams come true — *his* career, having the kind of house *he* wanted, leading the kind of life-style *he* wanted — and I began to wonder what I could have done with my life if I'd put that energy into achieving my own dreams. I had been pretty smart in school and had goals, plans, things I wanted to do with my life. What if I hadn't shoved all that aside for Jim?"

She finished with a touch of irony. "I wondered if I could have been a contender."

"So what happened?"

"I told him I was going back to school and was going to figure out what the hell I wanted to do with my life. He was absolutely floored. That wasn't part of the picture, you see. What was supposed to happen next was that we would finally have kids, which he'd been wanting and I'd been putting off. I told him I couldn't have kids and go to school, so we'd have to forget about the kids for a while."

"Did you want kids?"

"Nope." There was absolutely no hesitation in Myrna's voice. "I knew if I did, I'd be trapped in that life forever. I'd never get out. It was an either/or proposition. I mean, have you ever met any women who are wives and mothers and yet manage to lead their own lives and have successful careers? Damn few."

"So you got a divorce."

"So I got a divorce. And went back to school. And got involved in the feminist movement. And discovered that there were a lot of other women who felt like I did. You want to hear something wild? I thought my mother would freak when I told her about all this. Instead, she just said that she wished she could have gotten away with doing the same thing when she was my age."

Myrna shook her head. "Can you believe it? She

was past seventy, and she told me to go for it."

Thinking about her own mother, Val wondered if she'd ever resented her subservient life. When she had been young, did she have dreams of doing something more than washing and ironing and sleeping every night beside a man who was rigid and uncompromising?

For an instant, Val had a vision of her mother as a child, innocent and wide-eyed, delightful and exuberant. Full of hopes and dreams. Then she grew up and got married and had babies. There was no way out for her.

Val shuddered. She would never, ever let herself end up in that situation.

By the spring quarter of 1970, Val was spending most of her time working at the paper and living off the small salary Myrna was able to pay her. She went to classes as little as possible and did only the bare minimum required to keep from flunking out. In the beginning, she had been so excited to get to the university. Now she felt strongly that all the really important things were happening off-campus, and she intended to be part of every one of them.

After her night with Russ, Val had drifted in and out of several relationships, mostly with guys involved in the radical political scene, a few antiwar activists, a member of the Weather Underground who came and went in a flash. None of the men seemed to hang around for long, but Val didn't let it bother her. That's just the way it is, she told herself.

It did bother her that she had never had an orgasm. It bothered her a lot! She felt like a failure, somehow. After all, it must be *her* fault. All the guys she'd slept with couldn't be wrong. What's wrong with me? she kept asking herself as she heard other women talk openly about multiple orgasms and read sex scenes in books and saw them in movies. The whole world seemed to be having a great time in bed.

Val didn't confide in anyone, even Myrna, who was now her closest friend. It was just too humiliating to admit that radical, uninhibited, try-anything-once Val, who was so hyper and wired that anyone would assume she was hell on wheels in bed, might actually be frigid. It certainly wasn't like she didn't want sex. She went to bed with anyone who asked, including some wildly attractive guys, but somehow it was never quite satisfying.

She didn't want to think about it, so she threw herself into her work on the paper and felt enormously proud when Myrna told her she was really coming along as a writer.

"Your style reminds me of Hunter S. Thompson, but without the macho bullshit," Myrna said. "From now on, you do all the writing and I'll handle the business end and do some editorials, just to keep my hand in. Don't worry. I'll give you a raise."

Val wasn't worried about a raise. She loved what she was doing and would have done it for nothing. She was thrilled to think that Myrna would turn over the entire editorial content of the paper to her, and she had visions of turning the paper into a viable money-making proposition and, more important, a respected voice of the far left.

Then, in May, all hell broke loose.

A bunch of street people who hung out around Telegraph Avenue started building a makeshift park in an empty lot owned by the university. The lot was muddy and strewn with garbage and junk, so the people cleaned it up, hauling off the junk and laying down sod. As they worked, they drank lemonade and passed around joints and sang. There were no leaders to tell everyone what to do. Everyone was equal and pitched in wherever needed. It was total anarchy, and it worked.

When the park was finished, they celebrated by bringing in a rock band and roasting a suckling pig. Everyone ate, got stoned, sang, and danced. Someone put up a flagpole and nailed a sign to it: "People's Park. Power to the People."

Mothers brought their children to the park, now that it was filled with flowers and trees, slides, swings, a dance platform, a barbecue pit, and a set of giant letters for kids to crawl through; but the university wanted to build a soccer field, and it owned the lot.

Val wrote "An Open Letter to the University" that said, "You ripped off the land from the Indians a long time ago. Your land is covered with blood. If you want it back, you'll have to fight for it again. We are the people!"

On the morning of May 15, Val was sound asleep when Russ came bursting into her bedroom. "Cops are putting up a fence at People's Park!" he shouted. "Everyone's heading down there. C'mon, let's check it out!"

She jumped out of bed, hurriedly pulled on jeans, a T-shirt, and sandals, and grabbed her pen and notebook. At the park, she found police wearing gas masks and carrying shotguns standing guard while construction workers installed a cyclone fence. More and more people gathered to watch in dismay as their park was taken away from them. Telegraph Avenue was cordoned off to traffic while police with telescopic rifles knelt on the roofs of nearby stores. The crowd, three thousand strong now — and angry — moved onto the campus where a rally was held to protest the university's action.

As Val moved with the crowd, she wrote furiously in her notebook, stopping occasionally to interview the protesters, who were more than eager to share their outrage. The stony-faced police refused to talk.

After the rally, Val followed the crowd back to the park. Along the way, people hurled rocks through the Bank of America windows and kicked in doors. There was a sense of something inexorable building, building, reaching the breaking point. Val had never felt so excited. As the song said, "Something's happening now." When the crowd reached the cyclone fence, some people began throwing rocks at the police and shouting insults. Suddenly, seemingly from out of nowhere, there were shots. Smoke. The protesters began running in all directions, some with blood on their faces and clothing.

It wasn't exciting anymore. It was terrifying.

The National Guard was called in, and for the next nine days, Val wrote continually about the battles raging in the streets. On the first day, a young man, apparently just a bystander, was shot and killed. Hundreds were hospitalized. Groups of determined protesters fought the guard with Mace, bats, rocks, anything handy. All the while, helicopters whirred overhead as tanks rumbled heavily down Shattuck Avenue.

Val wondered, Is this what it's like in Vietnam?

She worked for forty-eight hours straight, then continued to work for hours on end, taking catnaps whenever she got a chance. *The Voice of the People* came out every day, with Val's updates on the conflict and interviews with the participants filling the small paper.

She was so on top of the situation, and so connected to many of the leaders of the protest, that members of the national news media covering the event turned to her as a source of information. One man, whom Val had grown up watching on network news, said to her, "You're a hell of a reporter, young lady. Wild and undisciplined, but a hell of a reporter."

It was terrible and thrilling, and when the conflict ended, Val felt as much disappointment as relief.

On Memorial Day, a beautiful, clear, early summer day, there was a rally at People's Park 2, which had recently been built on public land. Val had never seen such a diverse group of people—women wearing "Mothers for Peace" buttons wheeling babies in strollers, Hell's Angels on motorcycles, students, hippies, professors, old people, young people, blacks, whites. Thirty thousand people took part in one helluva party, with everything from Frisbees to joints.

At the end, some of the leaders of the protest spoke, reluctantly admitting defeat, and that was the end of the conflict.

Back at the office of *The Voice of the People*, Val wrote her final story on the battle for People's Park. When Myrna read it, she looked up at Val and grinned. "I can't wait to get this out on the street. This is better than any of that establishment cant the *Chronicle* is printing!"

Val was thrilled. "You really mean it?"

There was laughter in Myrna's voice. "Don't I always mean what I say? You're fucking brilliant!"

Impulsively, Val threw her arms around Myrna and hugged her tightly. Myrna responded. As Val pulled back to smile, suddenly and unexpectedly Myrna bent forward and kissed her cheek. It was the lightest, most innocent contact, yet it affected Val like a sudden shock. At that instant, as she and Myrna touched, she felt profoundly drawn to this woman, to her softness, her warmth, her love.

The feeling was unlike anything Val had ever felt

before, and it frightened her badly. Abruptly, she pulled back and looked away, focusing on the small, cluttered room, the view of the street through the window, *anything* but Myrna.

The silence between the two women was intense. Then, as suddenly as it had come, it ended.

"Why don't you go home and crash for a couple of days," Myrna said easily. "You've got finals coming up soon."

Val was deeply grateful for the return to a normal tone. She said, "I'm not going to take them."

"What?"

"Why bother? Now that I've tasted a slice of real life, I'm not about to remain in the womb of the university. Besides, I know exactly what I want to do — I'm going to be the best counterculture journalist in this country. I don't need a fucking degree for that."

Myrna eyed her thoughtfully. Finally she said, "What the hell. You're right. Be here at eight in the morning. We've got a lot of work to do. Tom Hayden's gonna be on campus and all the media will be after him. I want you to get an interview with him, if you can."

"I'll get it," Val assured her.

Myrna grinned. "I'll bet you will."

ELEVEN

Shelly

One day in the late spring of 1970, Shelly came to the UCLA campus to meet Kate and Barbara for lunch. It was as beautiful a day as L.A. ever sees— no smog, clear skies, the temperature a perfect seventy-five. Students with books tucked under their arms passed her, chattering happily. Other students lay on the rolling green lawn of the sunken sculpture garden, reading, napping, talking lazily with each other.

Shelly walked along slowly, enjoying the lovely day and the pleasant surroundings. She was early and in no hurry. This was such a welcome change from her tiny apartment and the coffee shop, the two places where she spent most of her hours. For the first time in months, she felt lighthearted. Finally, after the terrible autumn when she'd been so ill and the dreary winter when she'd done nothing but drag herself to work each night, then sleep all day of sheer depression, Shelly actually felt as if life might be all right after all. Maybe not wonderful, certainly not what she'd hoped it would be, but bearable.

As she watched the students around her, she

thought about going to college; both Kate and Barbara had been encouraging her to do so. The problem was Shelly had never been a scholar like Kate and Barbara and Val, who all seemed to get good grades effortlessly while she had worked her ass off in high school to make unexceptional Bs.

Kate, especially, had been urging her to go to one of the local junior colleges, get her required courses out of the way, then transfer to a university, maybe even UCLA. Kate was getting through on a combination scholarship, part-time job, and what little money her parents could contribute. Shelly could do the same, Kate insisted, substituting a student loan for a scholarship.

"You can do it," Kate kept saying, and Shelly knew she was right—but why bother going to all that effort when she had absolutely no idea what to do with her life now that she had given up on her dream of a modeling career.

Kate and Barbara were so sure of what they wanted. After getting involved with Roger, Kate had switched from English to film as a major and was completely immersed in eating, breathing, and living movies twenty-four hours a day. When Roger wasn't available, Kate dragged Shelly off to esoteric foreign films that Shelly had no interest in seeing, except for the French films, especially the romantic comedies, where the scenes of Paris invariably took her out of herself and her dull life. She would give anything to be able to go to Paris.

As for Barbara, well, she'd always planned on becoming a doctor. Nothing would change that. Someday Barbara would have her own practice while Shelly would still be waiting tables.

She didn't resent Kate and Barbara's single-minded determination. But she hated her job, her

207

lack of money, and her apartment. Although her friends had helped her paint the walls a soft yellow and hang some bright posters, it was still a shabby little room in a decrepit building where frightening people argued loudly in the hallway at night. Her job was physically exhausting and she lived on her tips, agonizing over how she would pay her rent when tips were low. Shelly had been in L.A. for nearly a year and would soon be nineteen. Time was slipping away.

She had to *do* something! Maybe Kate and Barbara were right. Maybe she should at least try college for a while.

"Hey! How're ya doin'?"

Shelly turned to face a vaguely familiar man smiling at her. Ryan Hunter, the *Playboy* photographer! He was sitting on a bench, a camera slung around his neck and a worn leather camera bag propped up next to him. His skin was still tanned a deep bronze, and his dark hair was even longer and shaggier than she'd remembered.

Shelly smiled hesitantly, shyness overcoming her so that she could not quite meet his look.

"It's been a while. You still working at the same place?" She nodded as he went on, "I was out of the country for a few months, bumming around Morocco and some other places. Got some far-out shots. So, are you going to school here?"

"No . . . no, just visiting friends. Are you . . . um, working?"

Ryan smiled. "Yeah, in a way. Every once in a while *Playboy* has me hit the local campuses looking for likely prospects. It's actually a good place to find the kind of girls they want — young girl-next-door types who can look real sexy with the right makeup and lighting."

He stood up and faced her. "Girls like you, actually. I don't suppose you'd consider changing your mind about posing?"

When he'd asked her before, Shelly had immediately turned Ryan down; but a lot had happened in the meantime. Now . . .

Sensing her hesitation, Ryan pressed. "If you're picked to be a centerfold, you get five thousand dollars and a chance to join the Playboy Modeling Agency." Before she could ask, he answered her unspoken question, "It *is* a legitimate agency. The only nude modeling is for the magazine. The agency handles fashion, cosmetic advertising, the usual modeling jobs."

He eyed her speculatively. "I'd say you're tall enough to be a high-fashion model, and you've got great bones."

Shelly couldn't believe it. Five thousand dollars! She could get a nice apartment in a decent area; buy a car and stop taking buses everywhere; go shopping in those boutiques she passed on Sunset every day; and pay back Barbara. Though Barbara never mentioned it, Shelly felt weighed down by her debt, and felt she needed to clear it up before she could put the abortion behind her.

But even more . . . a chance of becoming a model! The possibility that her dream might not be dead after all sent a rush of excitement through her.

Still . . .

"I'm not perfect," she said.

His grin was impudent. "Nobody is. Lights, shadows, camera angles can help. A little bit of deception goes a long way. So, Shelly, what do you say? Wanna go for it?"

Yes. She desperately wanted to go for it.

"All right!" she said, surprising herself.

"Great! I think you'll find that it's a lot more painless than you might imagine."

Taking a card from his camera case, he scribbled something on it. "Be at that address at that time. I'll take some preliminary shots and we'll see what happens."

Shelly took the card. "Thank you," she said shyly.

"Hey, it's my job. See you tomorrow."

As she walked away, she felt extremely nervous at the prospect of posing nude — but she reminded herself that the chance to sign with a modeling agency was all that mattered.

"*Playboy!*" Barbara exclaimed. "You *can't* be serious! It's so demeaning!"

Kate didn't say a word. Her gray eyes narrowed thoughtfully as she looked at Shelly in that disconcerting way she had of seeming to see right through people, right down to what they were really feeling inside.

Shelly knew her friends would react negatively, so she'd waited until they had finished lunch and were strolling around Westwood before casually dropping in a "by the way."

Now Kate and Barbara stood facing her, inquisition style, while people walked around them.

"I may not even get picked," Shelly pointed out.

"That isn't the point," Barbara insisted. "Why would you even consider doing something like that?"

"Because it's a chance to be a model. I told you, the Playboy Modeling Agency . . ."

"Yes, you told us. So what? That's no way to become a model."

"Then what is?" Shelly exploded. All the frustration and unhappiness of these long, terrible months

210

came boiling to the surface. "I tried the only other way I know and it didn't work! I got taken! At least this way, *they'll* be paying *me*. I won't be paying them the way I did with that crooked photographer. And Ryan seems really nice."

"Sure." Barbara's tone was scathing.

"He gave me some good advice once, and he didn't have to bother. He certainly didn't ask for anything in return."

"Now he's asking you to take your clothes off while he takes pictures of you."

"In the Playboy office, not in some apartment somewhere. It's all perfectly legitimate."

"But if they do pick you for the magazine, you'll be exposing yourself to millions of men. Think about that."

For an instant, Shelly thought of how she'd been exposed to a half dozen young men at Steven Ashe's party on graduation night. They'd done far more than simply look at her. A familiar rush of nausea and terror threatened to overtake her, and Shelly fought for control. In comparison, the idea of men staring at her picture in a magazine didn't seem all that bad.

She turned to Kate. "You haven't said anything."

Kate, looking intensely uncomfortable, didn't speak for a moment. Then she said slowly, "I think I understand how much the chance at a modeling career means to you."

"I don't think you do," Shelly broke in. "You've got what you wanted. Both of you. You're going to college. You know what you want to do with your lives. You've got boyfriends. All I hear is how great Roger and David are and how exciting your classes are and what you're going to do when you graduate. What do I have? *Nothing!*"

"I just think there must be another way," Kate insisted.

"If there is, I don't know it."

All three were silent. For the first time, Shelly felt estranged from her friends. She hated it but didn't know what to do about it. There was simply no way they could understand the desperation and urgency she felt to get her modeling career off the ground.

Finally Kate said, "Would you like us to go with you tomorrow? You know, for moral support?"

"Yeah," Barbara added with a rueful grin, "just to make sure these people aren't white slavers or anything."

Shelly was filled with gratitude. She felt a rush of love and wanted to hug them but held back because they were in the middle of a crowded sidewalk. "That's okay. I'll be all right."

As they resumed walking, Shelly asked, "By the way, have you heard from Val lately? I got a card at Christmas, but it didn't say much. How is she?"

"Oh, you know Val," Barbara said. "Crazy as ever. She decided to drop out of Berkeley and write for some little rag. She sent us copies, and it was so radical, you wouldn't believe it."

The three friends continued talking, their conversation punctuated by occasional laughter, as they walked down the sidewalk side by side.

Shelly slipped on the short white terrycloth robe that hung in the changing room and hesitated before opening the door into the photography studio.

It's nothing, she told herself, just a few pictures. Ryan's a nice man. It will be all right.

She was so nervous that she wished she hadn't

turned down his offer of a glass of white wine earlier, but since graduation night, Shelly hadn't been able to drink or even consider smoking grass or doing any of the drugs that floated around so freely in L.A. The thought of losing control again was terrifying; remaining stone-cold sober at all times was essential.

Now, she took a deep breath, opened the door, and stepped into the spartan, white-walled studio, where Ryan stood in the center, adjusting a camera mounted on a tripod. In front of him, a long cushion covered by a white fur rug lay on the floor. Behind it was a pale blue backdrop.

Looking up, Ryan smiled. "I'm just about ready. Why don't you lie down there and I'll take a few preliminary shots. You can keep the robe on for now."

She felt a rush of relief.

"Is there any particular music you like?" he asked.

At her look of surprise, Ryan gestured toward a stereo sitting on the floor in a corner. "I've got a lot of different records. Sometimes listening to music helps a model relax. What would you like to hear?"

Shelly used to like Johnny Rivers, but ever since graduation night, she couldn't bear to listen to any of his songs, especially "Tracks of My Tears."

"Do you have anything by the Beach Boys?"

"Hey, my personal favorites! I've got all their stuff at home. Talk about feel-good music." He went over to the stereo and began flipping through a stack of albums. "Let's see what we've got here." After a moment he said, "All right, here we go."

A moment later, "Surfer Girl" began to play. Ryan turned down the volume so it was merely soft background music and returned to his cameras.

"All right, Shelly, now what I want you to do is

213

lie on your left side, facing me, and look into the camera." She did as she was told, secure in the robe, and Ryan smiled encouragingly. "Great. You're a natural." As he took several shots, he murmured, "The camera's gonna worship you."

Shelly began to relax. He was right. This was pretty painless, after all. She enjoyed posing for the camera, trying out a variety of facial expressions. "Pout a little for me, honey," Ryan directed. Then, "Smile with your eyes. Chin up."

"Okay. That's it for the prelims," he said abruptly. "Let's get down to the real thing. Why don't you just slip off that robe and toss it behind you."

Shelly froze. As she tried to speak, her face flushed with embarrassment. What must he think of her? To her amazement, he put down his camera and knelt next to her. "It's all right, Shelly. I do this all the time," he said in a gentle voice. "I see girls without their clothes on and it doesn't mean a thing to me. Just think of me as a doctor or something, 'cause that's how I'm gonna look at you, professionally, objectively, not with any sense of personal interest. I'm not trying to invade your space, and I don't want you to do anything you don't want to do. Okay?"

She nodded, still unable to speak.

Ryan returned to his tripod and waited expectantly as Shelly weighed the option of getting dressed and walking out against the thought of turning her back for the last time on her dream of being a model. Inside her, something closed off. All thought. All feeling. Shelly slipped off the robe and let it fall behind her, unaware of anything except Ryan's eyes opening wide in appreciation as he murmured, "The camera's gonna worship you."

He gave directions and she did as she was told, looking up, looking down, staring straight into the camera, lying on her side, her stomach, her back, but it was almost as if someone else was doing all this. Shelly had gone away. It wasn't until she stepped off the bus two hours later that she was suddenly acutely aware of her surroundings, the noisy traffic, the awful exhaust fumes of the bus as it pulled away, the warm sun beating down. Gazing around in startled wonder, Shelly felt empty inside; but that was okay. Empty was safe.

She was at work one week later when Ryan came in. Instead of sitting down, he came directly to her, grinning broadly. "You got it!" he said. "You're gonna be Miss September! I wanted to tell you myself. Judging by the competition so far this year, I'd bet you have a shot at being Playmate of the Year. I knew when I was taking the pictures that you had a lock on being a centerfold, but I didn't want to raise your hopes in case it didn't work out somehow."

Shelly simply looked at him.

Taking her speechlessness in stride, he went on, "We'll have to set up a time for you to come in next week to do the actual shoot. We'll do some stuff in the studio and go out to the beach at Malibu for the rest. Don't worry. We'll pick a real private spot. No onlookers. When you come in, your check will be ready. Oh, yeah. The people from the modeling agency will be calling to set up an appointment, too."

When she still didn't say anything, Ryan stopped and asked, "Hey, are you okay? I mean, this is supposed to be good news, you know."

215

"Oh, it is," she assured him. "I'm just . . . surprised."

"You shouldn't be. I've seen a lot of girls, kiddo, and you're one of the best. You're going places. This is just the beginning."

The beginning. Shelly couldn't believe it. Finally, after all the months of nothing working out, she was on her way.

"How does it feel to be on the brink of fame and fortune?" Ryan asked.

"It feels great!" she answered, her voice filled with relief rather than excitement. Thinking about the shoot bothered her, though, until she remembered that she could always just tune out if it got to be too much. Shutting down inside could get her through anything.

"You don't need this job now," Ryan pointed out. "Why don't you just say to hell with it and walk out. I'll take you out to dinner to celebrate. Afterward, we can go to Hefner's place. He's having a party and would like to meet you. He went crazy over your shots."

Shelly's smile dissolved in an instant. Were Kate and Barbara right? Was Ryan handing her a bill and expecting immediate payment? As if reading her mind, he shook his head slowly. "It's not what you're thinking, kiddo. I don't get personally involved with the models. I don't mix my business and personal lives on this job. Despite what you might think, I *am* a professional."

"I'm sorry. It's just . . ."

"Hey, no apologies necessary. You're about to join the big leagues, and it can be rough. You're smart to be a little suspicious. Now, why don't you tell your boss to shove this job, and I'll take you home to change."

216

"But I don't have anything to wear to a fancy party."

Ryan threw back his head and laughed. "No one's gonna care what you're wearing."

The party at Hugh Hefner's Holmby Hills estate was like something out of an X-rated fantasy. Shelly and Ryan passed through a guarded gate and drove up the winding drive to the opulent mansion. The downstairs rooms were filled with successful-looking men and beautiful young women wearing sexy gowns. The glittering crowd spilled out through open French doors onto the patio and the elaborately landscaped grounds at the rear.

Some people were swimming in the huge pool, and in the center was an island. Beneath it, Ryan explained, was a grotto where swimsuits tended to be discarded.

The atmosphere reeked of hedonism, money, sophistication. Shelly felt completely out of her depth and clung to Ryan's side, intensely relieved he didn't abandon her for one of the many gorgeous women wandering around. He sensed her discomfort and was kind enough to stay with her.

To her surprise, Hefner made only a brief appearance, dressed incongruously in gray silk pajamas and robe. When Ryan introduced her, Hefner said, "Glad you could make it, my dear. I'm thrilled to have you in the magazine. Your pictures are fabulous."

Shelly murmured indistinct words of gratitude and relaxed only after Hef, as he asked her to call him, ended the conversation with an open invitation for her to visit anytime. Then he went back upstairs, presumably to his bedroom where, Ryan explained, he had a closed-circuit television monitoring every room in the mansion.

Watching her expression, Ryan teased, "You expected him to try to seduce you on the spot, didn't you?"

"Well, sort of, I guess."

"I won't pretend he isn't interested, but he won't force himself on you. All you're required to do is the layout for the magazine."

The layout. Shelly felt a surge of nervousness at the thought of once more posing nude, only this time in front of a group of people, including Ryan's assistant, a makeup artist, a hairstylist, and a wardrobe mistress.

She told herself it would be all right. She would get through it. Then she would go on to the modeling career she so desperately wanted.

Two weeks later, the centerfold layout was shot and Shelly had signed with the Playboy Modeling Agency. Her days were now filled with tests, shoots, and training in "go-sees," or how to make the rounds of the magazines and designers' studios. She got assignments quickly and was soon booked for weeks in advance. With her classically beautiful face, Shelly was especially in demand for cosmetics ads.

Out of the first money she earned, she paid back Barbara despite Barbara's resistance; only Kate's intervention persuaded Barbara not to tear up Shelly's check. Next, Shelly sent her mother a generous amount of money on her birthday with a scribbled note saying, "Buy yourself something nice at Ensign's."

Her rattrap apartment gave way to a nicer one in

Westwood, where she could now see Kate and Barbara more often. She bought her first car, a little red Fiat convertible that she drove out to the beach on weekends. Although she sometimes felt like a billboard, peddling everything from lingerie to shaving cream, Shelly told herself the money, the exciting milieu, the sense of endless possibilities made it all worthwhile.

She was constantly on the run, partly because she was so much in demand and partly because she didn't want to stop and think about things. Deep inside, Shelly knew that the role she was playing now was the same one she'd always played—the ice princess, lovely and desirable to look at but forbidden to touch. She worked hard every day and went to bed early every night so she would look fresh for the camera. Without a moment's hesitation, she turned down the many invitations from a wide variety of men, everyone from designers and male models to actors and other celebrities. No one could penetrate her defenses.

Inside, Shelly still felt like the daughter of a small-town whore. To combat that feeling, she would make an inventory of all her possessions, looking through the stunning clothes in her closet, running her fingers through the gold necklaces and earrings in her jewelry case, admiring the tasteful, limited-edition prints that covered the walls of her sunny, cozy apartment.

I've made it, she told herself. I've left Visalia behind—but no matter how fervently she said the words, she didn't quite believe them.

Shelly had run away to L.A., but it wasn't far enough. She needed to put even more distance between herself and Visalia. When the opportunity came for an assignment in Paris, she grabbed it, her most cherished fantasy coming true!

In Paris, Shelly told herself, she would be happy. She would be safe. She would finally put the past behind her.

All the same, in some deep part, Shelly knew neither happiness nor safety could be found in a place. Beyond the beckoning dream of the city of lights, there would be new and different dangers.

TWELVE

Barbara

Darkness. She lay on a narrow bed with sagging springs in a tiny cubicle of a room, waiting for it to be over. She and David had come close to going all the way so many times before, and she'd been so turned on and so frustrated when he would pull away. "We shouldn't do this until we're married," he always said.

Barbara had wanted to shake him and say, "It's nineteen seventy! We've been going together for a year! It's all right!"—but she didn't because his basic conservatism was one of the things she liked about him. Unlike so many of the other guys she'd dated, David was a rock. He was steady and reliable. He was . . . just like her father.

That thought was disturbing, and Barbara pushed it from her mind while she tried desperately to think of something else, anything else, to distract her from the dull throb of pain deep within. Who would have thought it would hurt this much? She'd wanted it so much. She had actually seduced David, seeing to it that he was so aroused that this time there would be no pulling back.

Now she hated it and wished it were over.

When David finally shuddered and collapsed

against her, Barbara felt relief. All she wanted to do now was get the hell out of David's shabby little rented room over an elderly couple's garage, go back to the dorm, and take a long, hot shower.

David raised his head and looked down at her. "Oh, Barbara, I'm sorry. I just couldn't stop this time."

"It's all right," she replied dully.

"Did I hurt you?"

Yes, you idiot! "No, not much."

The lie came easily. It was so important not to hurt his feelings, not to damage his ego. She didn't question why his feelings were more important than her own; Barbara just assumed automatically that they were.

"I know it wasn't too great for you, but it'll be better next time. I promise."

Next time? No way was there going to be a next time. If this was what sex was all about, this discomfort, this disappointing dull ache, then she wanted no part of it. Then again, she supposed she'd have to do it for David's sake. He probably wouldn't want to stop now that they'd started. She would just have to grit her teeth and do her duty, as she'd heard her mother say once about sleeping with her father.

Suddenly David exclaimed, "Oh, shit!"

"What is it? What's wrong?"

He sat up and stared at her in dismay. "I forgot to use protection. Some doctor I'm going to be! I can't even remember to use a goddamn rubber."

Barbara had never heard David swear before, not once. He must really be upset, so she hurried to reassure him. "It's all right. I'm not gonna get pregnant the first time."

"Famous last words."

222

She forced herself to smile. "Don't be crazy. To-morrow I'll go down to the med center and go on the Pill or something."

"That's a good idea. I couldn't face your folks if I got you pregnant. They'd be so disappointed in me."

Anger flared within Barbara at the idea that he cared more about what her parents thought than he cared about her. Ever since he'd visited her in Visa-lia over the summer, he'd been in awe of her par-ents, especially her father. It was now October, she'd been back in school for a month, and David still couldn't stop talking about how much he admired Dr. Avery.

"He has everything I ever wanted," David would say. "A successful practice, a beautiful home, a wife who's a big asset to his career. When he let me go on rounds with him, you should have seen the way the other doctors deferred to him."

Barbara didn't want to spend what little free time they had together talking about her parents, espe-cially now that they'd stopped being merely boy-friend and girlfriend and had become lovers.

Lovers. The word sounded so romantic, so ma-ture, yet she felt anything but romantic or mature at the moment. She wished she could talk to David, tell him she really didn't like sex and was bothered by the fact that she didn't want to do it again. Did that mean she had some kind of sexual hang-up? Maybe she was even frigid.

Barbara recoiled at the thought.

She wished David would simply hold her and re-assure her that it would be all right, that she would like sex eventually and that he wouldn't pressure her to do it again until she was ready—but she knew he couldn't talk to her like that any more than she could tell him how she honestly felt.

It was embarrassing enough having sex for the first time. Talking about it, actually putting their needs and desires into words, would be intensely awkward because no matter how much people talked about a new era of free love, sex before marriage still carried a stigma of being bad and dirty and shameful.

Barbara sat up and straightened her disheveled clothes. "I'd better get back to the dorm. I've got a midterm tomorrow."

"I'll drive you back."

David hesitated, then asked, "Are you . . . that is, are you okay?"

She tried to keep her tone light. "Sure."

In her room, Barbara undressed quietly so as not to wake Kate, then took her desired long, hot shower. Afterward, she lay in bed, unable to sleep. What if she *never* liked sex? What would she do? Would she become one of those hard-faced, unattractive, middle-aged women like her high school gym teacher, Miss Hennessy?

She finally fell asleep, just before dawn, with images of herself staring in a mirror, watching her face growing more and more plain and rigid.

As she went from class to class the next day, Barbara couldn't stop thinking about their lovemaking. The memory of the discomfort had faded, and she began to feel more intrigued. So much so, in fact, that she went to Powell Library and skimmed passages from the Masters and Johnson study of sex that everyone seemed to be reading. Now she understood why. Barbara had never dreamed there could be such variety in sex. She'd always assumed that the woman just lay there and let the man do whatever it was he did, but this book suggested all kinds of erotic possibilities.

She started to feel a little twitchy and decided that maybe she would see David tonight after all, even though she'd told him she would probably have to study.

That night they made love again, and didn't forget the condom. Although Barbara didn't like the feel of the condom, she did like the feel of having David inside her. This time, when he moved, she moved with him. When he came, leaving her at a fever pitch of excitement, she felt that she couldn't bear it. Without stopping to think, she took his hand and pressed it against her, her meaning unmistakable. David hesitated, but when she writhed against him, he began to massage her with tentative, awkward movements.

It didn't matter that he lacked both expertise and exuberance. Barbara came in a flash. When her body finally settled down from the waves of delicious sensations that had rocked her to her very core, she knew with relief that she wasn't frigid.

She spent the night with David, and in the morning they made love again; this time she came just as he did. She felt like a kid who had just been given a brand-new toy and couldn't get enough of playing with it.

When Barbara returned to the dorm that night, she knew Kate would ask where she'd been. She felt awkward about confessing that she was no longer a virgin. It had been such an important issue in high school. When Val had had sex with Gregg, they'd all talked about her behind her back, saying how foolish she was to do something like that with a guy who wasn't even her boyfriend, let alone her husband. Plus, there was always the danger of getting pregnant. Still, this wasn't high school, and birth-control devices were available at the med center for practically nothing.

When Barbara walked into the room, she found Kate sprawled on her bed, reading. Kate immediately put down her book and asked, "Where were you? I was so worried when I woke up and saw that your bed hadn't been slept in."

"I'm sorry. I should have called, but I didn't know I was gonna be out all night."

Kate smiled. "Hey, I'm not your mother. I was just kinda worried."

Sitting down on her bed, Barbara kicked off her shoes and curled her feet up under her before saying, "I, uh, spent the night with David."

To her surprise, Kate whooped with delight. "I knew it! You guys are sleeping together, huh?"

Barbara nodded, then laughed in embarrassment. "So, what do you think?"

"I think it's about time. I've been sleeping with Roger ever since we got back to school in September."

Barbara was stunned. "You're kidding! But you never stay all night with him."

"Of course not. His dork of a roommate never spends one single night away, and I didn't want to risk doing it here and having you walk in, so we have to grab an hour now and then, whenever we can."

Barbara hugged her pillow to her chest. "I can't believe we waited so long to find out what sex is all about."

"I know. What a waste. Think of all the fun we could have been having."

"Yeah, but we couldn't do it with just anyone. I mean, it's okay because we're serious about David and Roger, but we couldn't do it with someone we were just casually dating."

Kate got a funny look in her eyes. "I don't know. Remember that cute guy I went out with the first week we were here last year?"

"John something?"

"Yeah. We made love."

"Kate! You only went out with him once! What must he have thought of you?"

"I'm not sure I care."

Barbara tossed the pillow at her playfully. "You little slut."

Kate laughed.

Barbara went on. "So tell me about it. How did it happen the first time with Roger?"

"We went to see a revival of this really romantic French film, *A Man and a Woman*. Roger splurged and took me out to dinner at Mario's afterward, and there was candlelight and everything. It was just a wonderful, perfect evening, and Roger didn't even talk too much, for a change. We went back to his room, and he told me that his roommate was visiting relatives in Pasadena and wouldn't be back until real late. He lit a candle and some incense and turned out the lights and put on the Righteous Brothers. You know what 'You've Lost that Lovin' Feeling' does to me. Anyway, we started kissing and then one thing led to another . . ."

She stopped and giggled.

"So how was it?" Barbara pressed.

"Nice. Very . . . *nice*."

"The first time?"

"Yeah. You know, Roger's kind of clumsy, kind of like a puppy who's always tripping over his own feet, so I didn't expect him to be real great at love-making, but he was so gentle and sweet, really concerned about me and my feelings and whether or not I was enjoying it."

Barbara felt a twinge of jealousy. If Roger, who was so young and unsophisticated, could be so sensitive, why couldn't David, who was much older and presumably more experienced?

"And the funny part is," Kate continued, "I think it was probably his first time, only he would never admit it because it wouldn't be macho."

Barbara wondered if this had been David's first time. No, it couldn't be. He was twenty-seven, for heaven's sake, and an intern. He was so attractive. There must have been other women. Probably plenty of them. She wondered if it had been better with the other women, if maybe she was at fault for the initial awkwardness and her lingering feeling of dissatisfaction.

"So, have you been to the med center to get the Pill?" Kate asked.

"I have an appointment next week to get an IUD. I'm afraid my mom would find the pills when I go home, and you know she would hit the roof."

Kate's expression sobered. "Be careful, Barb. You don't want to get pregnant."

Barbara looked at her and knew exactly what she meant. Shelly's experience had deeply affected them both.

"Of course, I'm careful," she snapped irritably, but her anger was more at herself than Kate because she hadn't used any protection the first time she and David made love. Since then, they'd only used a condom, which she knew couldn't be as safe as the Pill or IUD.

A faint sense of danger nagged at the back of Barbara's mind, but she told herself she was just being silly. She wouldn't get pregnant this fast. Once she was using an IUD, there would be nothing at all to worry about.

A month later, Barbara was riding an escalator at Bullock's department store in Westwood when she suddenly felt dizzy. Stepping off at the top, she leaned against a nearby jewelry counter and waited for the wave of dizziness to pass. In a moment it was gone and she felt perfectly fine.

It's just the IUD, she told herself. It had been extremely painful to insert, and she'd had problems with it ever since, with cramping, a little bleeding, then a missed period. If the problems didn't get better soon, she'd have it taken out and go on the Pill, as Kate had done. She'd just have to be real careful about where she kept the tiny pastel-colored dispenser when she went home on holidays.

It was a cold, dreary day in mid-December. Finals were over, and Kate was packing to go home for Christmas vacation when Barbara came into the room after being gone all morning.

"We'll have to hurry if we want to make it down to the cafeteria for lunch," she said, but Barbara stood at the window, her back to Kate, staring out at the gray, overcast day. Five stories below, she saw students scurrying to get to the last of their finals. Others were returning to the dorms to get ready for vacation. There was an air of excitement, of endings and beginnings. As Kate chattered away in the background about how much she would miss Roger, all Barbara could think of was that her life was over.

Finally Kate realized that Barbara was being awfully quiet. Walking over to her, she asked, "Is something wrong?"

Barbara couldn't look at her friend. She said in a voice so low it was barely audible, "I'm pregnant."

There was a shocked silence before Kate asked slowly, "Are you sure? Everyone misses a period now and then."

"I went to the med center this morning. I'm eight weeks pregnant. I probably got pregnant the first time David and I made love."

She turned to face Kate, her face crumpling. "Oh, God! What am I going to do?"

She felt Kate's arms encircle her in a fierce hug, and she leaned against her, sobbing uncontrollably. Barbara felt utterly devastated as panic overwhelmed her. What could she do? How could she get out of this mess? She had no answers and knew Kate didn't either. When she finally pulled herself together, they sat on the bed as Kate asked, "Do you want to have this baby?"

"Of course I don't want it!" Barbara shouted. "It's ruining everything!"

"Then . . . then maybe you should have an abortion."

Barbara looked at Kate. Both were thinking the same thing. Shelly. Agony. Terror. She shook her head. "No." The word was small and soft and helpless.

"Maybe you could go away somewhere and have it and give it up for adoption."

"My parents would never let me do that."

There was a helpless silence, then Kate said, "Remember this summer when we went up to San Francisco to visit Val and she told us about all the women she knows who are raising children on their own?"

"I'm not one of Val's stupid hippie friends who carry their brats around in backpacks and sell drugs for a living! Can't you just see my mother showing off the baby to her bridge club—*and this is my bastard grandchild.* How would I stay in school? How would I support a baby? My parents sure as hell wouldn't help!"

She stopped. "Oh, God, Kate. I'm sorry. I'm just so damn scared."

"I know, I know."

Barbara took a tissue from a nearby box and wiped her wet face.

"Have you told David?"

"Yeah. I saw him after I went to the med center."

"How did he take it?"

"He just kept saying, 'Oh, my God. What are your parents going to say?' Can you believe it? I think he's more worried about facing them than I am."

"Will he talk to them with you?"

"Oh, yes, he'll do the right thing. He won't make me face the music alone. He even said he'd marry me."

"Well, at least that's something."

Barbara turned an anguished face to Kate. "You know what that means! We'll get married, I'll drop out of school, and that's it! My life is over!"

"Not necessarily. You could go back to school after you have the baby."

"Sure. I'd fit right in."

"Barb, this doesn't have to be the end. I'll babysit for you. I know about babies. I helped with my little brothers. You could take a class or two, and then when David's through with his residency and you have more money, you can hire a full-time sitter and finish school just a year or two behind."

For a moment, Barbara felt a fragile hope. Kate made it all sound so possible. If David did his residency in L.A., maybe she could continue going to UCLA. She could go during the winter quarter, then take off during spring and summer. By next fall, she could do as Kate suggested, take at least one class or maybe two, and when David's residency was over and he was working, there'd be enough money for her to return to school full-time. By the time she got to med school herself, the child would be four or five years old and in school part of the time. She could hire a nanny. . . .

Her mind raced with ideas. It could work. If her parents helped out financially. If David was willing. . . .

If.

Two days later, Barbara and David sat on the sofa in her parents' formal living room, facing the two who sat in high-backed Queen Anne chairs opposite them, expressions as cold and grim as she'd expected. She felt like a little kid who had done something wrong, but this time she knew she faced far more than a scolding.

"Your mother and I need to discuss this alone," her father said tersely, so they got up and went into his study, closing the door firmly behind them.

Barbara and David waited nervously until her parents finally returned fifteen minutes later. As always, her father spoke for both himself and her mother. "We realize that anger isn't going to solve the problem. We simply have to deal with the situation. This is how it will be handled."

Not "How do you want to handle it?" but "This is how it will be handled." Of course, Barbara

232

thought with a sinking sensation.

Her father went on. "Your mother thinks a small, informal ceremony in Los Angeles would be best. Possibly in a chapel in one of the churches near the university. Only immediate family and friends will be invited, and, needless to say, we'll have to arrange this as soon as possible. It wouldn't look seemly if your pregnancy were apparent."

Barbara resented her mother deciding all the details of her wedding without even asking her what she wanted; but she knew better than to protest.

Her father looked at David and his anger subsided an infinitesimal degree. "I must say I'm glad to see David accepting his responsibility toward you so enthusiastically. It says a lot for him."

David looked immensely relieved. "I love Barbara very much, Dr. Avery. I want to take care of her."

Barbara wanted to scream that she didn't need anyone to take care of her, but she kept her mouth shut. None of this really mattered. The important thing was arranging things so she could finish her education and go on to medical school.

"We'll help you out financially until David finishes his internship in June. After all, you'll need a decent apartment. Then I'll pull a few strings and arrange for him to serve his residency here in Visalia at Community Hospital."

Barbara froze. "What?"

"That will solve several problems. You and David can stay here during that year since you won't have enough money to live on your own, and your mother can help with the baby. At the end of his residency, he can join my practice. He'll save a great deal of money not having to set up an office of his own, and of course there's the financial ad-

233

vantage of aligning himself with a highly lucrative practice."

David fairly glowed. "That's a generous offer, Dr. Avery! I don't know how to thank you."

"You can thank me by making me proud of you. I have the most respected practice in town. Don't lower my reputation. The town's growing; new people are moving in all the time. We've gone from a population of fifteen thousand to more than thirty thousand in the last few years alone. Eventually, you can do very well for yourself, if you work hard and don't make any more mistakes."

"Yes, sir."

"But I want to stay in L.A.," Barbara insisted. "I can't come back here."

"Why on earth not?" her father demanded.

"I want to stay in school . . ."

Her mother snapped, "Don't be ridiculous, Barbara. You'll have a baby to care for. That changes everything."

David took her hand. "Your parents are right. This will solve everything."

She pulled her hand away from him. "I want to finish school! I want to be a doctor someday. Don't you understand?"

Her mother's frown deepened. "You'd better stop thinking about yourself, Barbara, and start thinking about the family you're about to have."

Barbara stood up and shouted hysterically. "I won't come back here! I won't!"

"You have no choice." Her mother's tone was even, controlled, absolutely rigid.

Barbara burst into tears and ran from the room. In her bedroom, she slammed the door shut, then locked it and threw herself on her bed. As tears covered her face, she told herself she *did* have a choice. She *didn't* have to do what they said. It was *her* life, damn it, not theirs!

They were so busy arranging everything so that it suited them without even asking her what she wanted or needed. Even David—she couldn't believe how quickly he acquiesced to her parents' plans. When her father mentioned what a successful practice David could have here, his expression had altered profoundly. She could almost hear him thinking that maybe this pregnancy was a blessing in disguise because it had motivated her father to help him.

Barbara knew, without even asking him, that David would insist they do as her father wanted. After all, it made everything so easy for him. Her mind raced, trying to come up with some way out of this. She could simply refuse to do what they wanted, but she knew what would happen then. David would walk out on her. Her parents would cut her off financially, leaving her with no way of supporting herself and a child.

If she went to a home for unwed mothers and gave up the child for adoption, her parents would disown her. She might be able to get through college without their financial help, but medical school? No way. It would be too damn hard, and she wasn't used to having to do things the hard way. All her life, Barbara had had everything she'd wanted. Things came easily because she was smart and pretty and rich.

The one time she'd faced disaster, on graduation night, even then she'd managed to avoid dealing with unpleasant consequences. It was ironic, she realized, that in this situation her family's wealth and social position not only didn't help, they made things worse. If she'd been poor, she would have had nothing to lose, but she had everything to lose, including a comfortable way of life that she'd always taken for granted.

She'd never had to find any real courage within herself, and she couldn't do so now. The longer Barbara thought, the more trapped and hopeless she felt.

There was no way out.

Barbara sat quietly in a tiny anteroom off a small chapel that was part of the University Presbyterian Church near the UCLA campus. It was January 15, 1971, her wedding day. In the chapel waited a handful of guests—David's parents, looking as if they still hadn't quite taken it all in; Barbara's parents, putting the best possible face on a shameful situation; and two of David's friends from medical school.

Barbara's dress was a simple knee-length silk chemise in a soft cream color. Her bouquet consisted of one peach-colored rose surrounded by baby's breath. It was all very tasteful and understated, exactly as her mother had planned.

Afterward, there was to be a dinner at Mario's, one of the most expensive restaurants in Westwood, then the guests would leave and Barbara and David would return to the apartment her parents had rented for them not far from campus.

There was no time for a honeymoon. David couldn't spend more than a few hours away from his work, and Barbara had classes as well. Despite her parents' insistence that it was a waste of time, she had signed up for the winter quarter. When the time came, she would sign up for the spring quarter as well. She was determined

236

to stay in school until the last possible moment.

Behind her, Barbara heard Kate, Valerie, and Shelly talking animatedly. They had so much to catch up on. Val had arrived that morning, looking outrageous in low-slung jeans and a purple paisley blouse, and Shelly had flown in the night before from Europe, where she was modeling.

"I've had assignments for *Elle, Marie Claire, French Vogue,* and a bunch of other European fashion magazines," Shelly was saying.

"Sounds like you're doing great!" Kate exclaimed.

Shelly shrugged. "There isn't as much money in it as you might think, but it gives me a chance to stay over there. Paris is so gorgeous. You guys have to get over there sometime. You could stay with me. My place is just a studio, but it's got the most fabulous view of the Paris rooftops."

"You don't want to come back?" Val asked.

"No!"

"So, is there a cute Frenchman in your life?" Val teased.

"No. Is there a cute hippie in yours?"

Val laughed. "Yeah, dozens, and a couple of writers and artists and musicians and even a biker, but no one in particular. Not like Kate and Barb, who've settled down already."

"Wait a minute," Kate argued, "I'm not about to marry Roger."

Val looked at Barbara. "You never know. I mean, look at Barb. All of a sudden she decided to be an old married lady."

Barbara waited for Val to add something about her also being a mother shortly. Val knew she was pregnant. She had told both Shelly and Val at the same time she called to ask them to come to the wedding. She had tried to make it sound like a

237

happy event, but Barbara wasn't at all sure she'd pulled it off. After all, these were her closest friends. They knew her.

To her surprise, Val went on in a careful voice. "David seems very nice."

Everyone looked at Barbara, waiting for her response. Finally she said in a determinedly light voice, "He is very nice, and he's going to be a terrific doctor. He absolutely adores me. Even my parents approve of him. What more could I ask?"

No one said anything.

Barbara knew that despite her forced cheerfulness, Val and Shelly weren't sure what to make of this hasty wedding. Was a wild celebration in order? Or commiseration? Even if they suspected the truth, she was determined to put up a good front. They'd always looked up to her, envied her, and she wasn't about to exchange that adulation for pity.

The idea that Val, of all people — Val, who had always been so crazy and was getting even crazier as she got older — might be in a position to feel smugly superior to her was unbearable.

Only Kate knew how desperately unhappy Barbara was about this baby and this forced wedding. Kate wouldn't betray her confidence, though, even to Val and Shelly.

Through the closed door leading into the chapel, Barbara heard the slow, formal strains of the wedding march begin to play. She felt her throat constrict and for a moment couldn't catch her breath. This must be what claustrophobia feels like, she thought. This awful panic that everything's closing in around you and you can't get out.

Someone knocked on the door. Kate opened it and Barbara saw her father standing outside, looking distinguished in his best suit, ready to give away his daughter.

"You girls had better take your seats," he said. "It's time."

Val and Shelly filed out, flashing encouraging smiles at Barbara. Val pointedly ignored Dr. Avery, who was staring at her casual attire in obvious disapproval.

As Kate left, she paused to hug Barbara tightly. "Are you all right?" she asked.

Barbara couldn't speak. She nodded, fighting back tears.

"Barb, you don't have to go through with it," Kate said hastily.

Barbara looked at her for a long moment. "Oh, but I do," she whispered.

Kate started to say something more, then stopped.

After all, Barbara thought helplessly, what was left to say?

When Kate was gone, Barbara's father took her arm and led her into the chapel. They walked up the short aisle, her arm in his. She saw Kate, Val, and Shelly sitting together off to one side, slightly apart from the others. They smiled at her and Val, irrepressible as always, flashed a peace sign; but there was a bittersweet quality to their expressions, and Barbara felt another rush of panic.

At the altar, David waited, looking stiff and uncomfortable in his rented white tux. He watched Barbara's slow, deliberate progress, his eyes bright with expectation. She'd never seen him look happier.

1973-1979

CONSEQUENCES

ONE

Shelly

She had modeled in Rome and Munich and Paris, in the formal gardens of French châteaus and in the lush English woodlands, and on runways for haute couture collections, but none of those glamorous, exciting places could compare to Ibiza. From the moment Shelly arrived with three other models and a makeup and wardrobe crew, she fell in love with the island off the coast of Spain.

Undiscovered by tourists until recently, it was still lovely and unspoiled: low, rolling hills; sleepy villages of whitewashed houses and churches; farms where goats and cows grazed in small, stone-walled fields; groves of olive trees, umbrella pines, almond trees.

When Shelly arrived at the airport on a flight from Paris, she was driven to a first-class hotel. In her instruction sheet, she found her wakeup time and a description of the assignment, so she went to bed early, as usual, because she couldn't afford to look tired. She had long since learned that loneliness and boredom were as intrinsic to modeling as the surface glamor.

In the morning, Shelly went to the assignment with clean hair and no makeup. She and the other models,

243

along with the crew, left behind the bustling streets and shops of the town to go into the countryside, where they were to shoot the fashion layout. She responded to the simple pastoral beauty of the island with a depth of emotion that caught her offguard. This place reminded her of the San Joaquin Valley. It had an air of quiet and peacefulness, a profound connection to the land. After living for four years in big cities, Shelly had grown used to the noise, the frantic pace, and the squalor; here, the slower pace and simpler values brought on a wave of homesickness, though she knew she could never go back to Visalia.

When the photographer arrived, Shelly watched as he hopped from his rented Jeep and walked toward them, two cameras slung around his neck. There was something about him that looked vaguely familiar—chestnut hair glinting with golden highlights in the bright sunshine, skin bronzed from a great deal of time spent outdoors. She couldn't see his eyes through the dark sunglasses, but somehow she knew they were brown.

Ryan. Ryan Hunter.

It all came back to her in a vivid flash of memory. Posing nude for *Playboy*, feeling vulnerable and exposed. Only Ryan's kindness—and an ability to simply shut off inside—had enabled her to get through it.

He stopped in front of her and she saw the familiar grin. "Shelly! What a surprise. I didn't know you were going to be here."

"I wasn't supposed to be here. Another model got sick at the last minute and I took her place."

"It's nice to see you again. I heard the agency had sent you to Europe, but that was a while back. Are you living over here now?"

"Yes. In Paris. I prefer it," she said succinctly.

"I'm living there, too. How about that. Small world, eh?"

"What brought you over here?"

"I got burned out on photographing giggling nymphets through gauze-covered lenses. I had a chance to do some work in Paris for a few weeks. That was two years ago and I'm still not sure when I'm going back."

Noticing the crew looking impatient and the other models looking bored, he finished, "I guess we'd better get to work. We'll have to do some catching up later."

"Okay," Shelly agreed.

But as they worked that day she wasn't at all sure she was glad to see Ryan again. He was a reminder of something she preferred to forget—not just the nude pictorial but her early days in L.A. working at the dingy coffee shop. Her new life in Paris allowed her an anonymity that was reassuring. Ryan didn't know her well, but he knew her better than she found comfortable.

During the warm, sunny days she posed against backdrops of cottages with red tile roofs and white walls with vivid magenta bougainvillea cascading down. At night, she and the others returned to the hotel, where they drank the local wines and ate delicious, massive paellas made of rice, meat, seafood and vegetables.

She watched as, one by one, the people in her little group paired off, either with each other, with the locals, or with other guests in the hotel. It was the early seventies, and sexual experimentation was de rigueur. Marie-Christine, a dark-haired, black-eyed French model, met a blond Scandinavian student staying at the hotel and after the first night with him declared herself wildly in love. Ursula and

245

Liv, the other two models, made the rounds of the local clubs, bringing home different men each night. Hans, the German makeup artist, and his new assistant, Gunther, decided to do more than just work together, and Maggie, the little Cockney photographer's assistant, was swept off her feet by a strikingly handsome young waiter in the hotel's restaurant.

Françoise, the plain, middle-aged wardrobe mistress, was the only one, aside from Shelly, who went to bed early—and alone—each night.

Shelly was used to the randy comings and goings so common in the fashion world. Whenever she participated in an extended shoot, especially if it was in a remote, romantic place like Ibiza, she saw people drawn to each other. Usually the affairs lasted only as long as the shoot did; there were rarely any hurt feelings when it was over, just a few sad sighs as the lovers boarded separate planes for home.

It never happened to Shelly. At first she had been awkward in her rebuffs of men, and the occasional woman, who tried to seduce her. Gradually, she developed her standard response: "I'm sorry but I'm not free. I live with someone and I'm totally committed to him." It usually worked quite well, and her would-be seducers moved on to the next beauty.

Tonight, as she sat alone in the patio restaurant of the hotel, she felt tired but happy. This had been the last day of shooting and tomorrow they would return to Paris. She couldn't wait to get back to her little apartment on the Rue du Petit Pont on the Left Bank. In a few weeks, Kate would be coming over for three whole weeks after graduating from UCLA and Shelly was eagerly looking forward to showing her around Paris, just the two of them browsing through the flea markets, sipping espresso at sidewalk cafés, gossiping and giggling late into the night.

She had only seen Kate briefly over the last two years when she returned to the States for modeling assignments. It had been hard for Shelly to make friends in Paris, especially with the other models, because of the competition between them.

She had become friendly with two other American girls who, like her, felt lonely and out of place. But they didn't have that shared history that made complete understanding possible. With Kate, Shelly never had to fill in the blanks or explain herself.

"All alone on our last night?"

Shelly looked up to see Ryan smiling down at her.

"I'm just relaxing," she replied. "It was a long day." Actually, she had been pleasantly surprised at how easy it was working with Ryan. He was genial and easygoing, unlike so many of the European photographers she worked with, who could be neurotic and domineering. "You're a slave driver," she teased.

He assumed an angelically innocent expression. *"Moi,* a slave driver?"

Both laughed, then he asked, "Mind if I join you?"

Shelly felt herself tense inside but tried to sound nonchalant as she replied, "No, of course not."

All week, Ryan had been watching her with a special interest he hadn't shown in Marie-Christine, Ursula, Liv, Maggie, or any of the single women staying at the hotel. She knew what was coming now— "It's our last night here. Let's spend it together"—and mentally she prepared her speech.

He ordered wine from the waiter, who looked

profoundly unhappy because he had to work on Maggie's last night in his country. For a long moment, Ryan simply stared at Shelly, who began to feel uncomfortable under his scrutiny. That perceptive, critical photographer's eye was disconcerting.

"It's been a while since I met you in that dive on Sunset Strip," he said.

"Yes."

"You've changed a lot."

She tried to keep her tone light. "I hope so."

"I don't just mean that you're thinner and have a model's grace and self-assurance. You've changed inside. You're even more remote." He added softly, "Untouchable."

The conversation had taken a disturbingly personal turn. Trying to steer it back onto safer subjects, she said with a laugh, "Well, you've certainly changed, too. Your hair barely covers your shirt collar now."

"Yeah, I decided it was time to end my hippie phase. I hated like hell to cut my hair and replace the wire-rim glasses with contacts, but we've all gotta grow up sometime."

Before she could respond, he asked unexpectedly, "Where are you from? Originally, I mean."

"No place you would have heard of. A little town in central California. Then L.A. Now Paris."

"Aah, a small town girl. You've come a long way from Podunk Corners, or whatever it's called."

She met his look. "Yes, I have."

He waited for her to ask, "And what about you? Where are you from? Let's learn a little about each other before getting on to the real business of sleeping together."—but she said nothing.

"What brought you to Paris?" Ryan asked.

"I used to fantasize about it when I was a little

girl."

"I know what you mean. I grew up in a small town in the middle of nowhere, too. In that kind of situation there's nothing to do but get out and go as far away as possible."

She didn't say anything, hoping the silence that stretched out between them would discourage him. It didn't.

"How old are you, Shelly?"

"Twenty-two."

"How long have you been modeling now? Three, four years?"

"Three years. Why?"

"I just wondered if you were experienced enough in the business to take what I'm about to say without getting hurt or mad."

Despite herself, Shelly was intrigued. "Why don't you just go ahead and say it."

"Okay, here goes. It's time you thought about getting out of modeling."

She was stunned. "If you're not happy with the job I've done this week. . . ."

"Don't get in a snit. It isn't that at all. You're a beautiful girl, one of the most beautiful I've ever seen, and I've seen a few. You're a good model— not a great one, because you hold back too much— but a good one. The grim reality is that you're just about over the hill."

"At twenty-two?"

"I saw your portfolio, and it didn't include any recent magazine covers. There was just one TV commercial, and that was three years ago. You haven't made it to the next level up, and at this age, you're not going to make it. Your last job was a month ago. It'll probably be a while before your next one. The time between jobs will stretch out longer and longer because there are all those fresh-faced seventeen- and eighteen-year-olds out there just waiting to take your place."

Shelly had sat in rigid silence while Ryan delivered this blunt assessment of her career. "Is there a point to all this or did you simply want to insult me?" she asked coldly.

There was compassion in his voice. "No, I didn't want to insult you. Like I said, I've been watching you, and I'm concerned. I don't think you're tough enough to deal with the harsh realities of this business, especially when it gets down to the bitter end. For what it's worth, I wanted to advise you to think about getting out, doing something else to earn a living."

"I'm tougher than you think, and I can take care of myself."

She remembered all the Christmas eves she spent alone while her mother worked; all the mornings she'd gotten herself ready for school, from kindergarten on, because her mother was sleeping; all the dinners eaten alone in front of a TV set.

"I've been taking care of myself for quite a while now," she finished.

Ryan was too good-natured to argue. "Okay. You know what they say about free advice. It's only worth what you pay for it."

Her mouth curved in the barest hint of a smile as she realized Ryan meant well. He was disturbingly accurate in his assessment of her career, though she didn't want to think about that just now.

"How about some more wine?" he suggested.

She shook her head. "No, thanks. I'm going to turn in soon."

"How boring. You can't waste your last night in this gorgeous place going to bed early." He reached out to take her hand. "At least not alone."

His grin was infectious, but Shelly wasn't having any. She took her hand from his. "I live with someone," she began, glibly repeating her old excuse, "and I'm not available."

The look he gave her was so shrewd, she felt herself grow intensely uncomfortable.

"I don't buy that," Ryan said.

"What?"

"I can't see you being that involved with anyone."

Shelly didn't know what to say. It was hard to summon up righteous indignation since he was absolutely right. Realizing that she was no match for him verbally, she took refuge in retreat.

Standing up, she said firmly, "Good-night, Ryan," but he didn't give up easily. "I'll walk you to your door." At her look of suspicion, he hurried on, "Just to your door, I promise. I'm down the hall from you. I think I'll be virtuous for once and turn in early, too."

When they reached the door to her room less than a minute later, she unlocked it, then turned to face him. "Good-*night*, Ryan." It was clearly a dismissal.

His eyes watched her thoughtfully. "You're a fascinating enigma, Shelly DeLucca."

She shook her head. "No, I'm just a simple, small town girl. Remember?"

"You're anything but simple." He leaned against the door frame and crossed his arms over his broad chest. "You don't photograph as many women as I have without getting to know a lot about them. I've seen women who were beautiful and smart, women who were beautiful but empty inside, and women who were beautiful victims, but I've never met one who intrigued me the way you do."

"That's a clever line, Ryan, but I'm not buying it. Why don't you try it on Maggie? She's probably kind of lonely tonight."

Once more, he assumed that innocent expression. "Shelly, I'm hurt. I really am. You don't take anything I say seriously."

She simply smiled.

"First of all," he went on, "Maggie and I have an understanding. After losing my last three assistants to unfortunate emotional disagreements, I've sworn not to get personally involved with her. As for my comment that you're an enigma. . . ."

He paused, then leaned toward her. "I meant it. You are a lovely riddle, one I would dearly love to solve."

"Good-night, Ryan."

He cocked his head to one side. "Do you ever let anyone — any man — get close to you?"

"Not a man who's simply looking for a one-night stand."

He shook his head slowly. "No, I don't think it's just that. You keep your distance, emotionally as well as physically, from everyone, but especially men. Why? It isn't that you prefer girls. I'd know it if that was the case."

Irritated, Shelly replied, "If you're so damn smart, go figure it out for yourself."

With that, she stepped into her room and closed the door in his face.

The next morning, Ryan made a point of sitting next to Shelly on the plane that would take them to Valencia, Spain, then on to Paris. She tried to ignore him, but Ryan wasn't the kind of guy to let himself be ignored. He talked cheerfully about the

252

in-flight movie, the food, the terrific shots he'd gotten on Ibiza, his desire to return there for a vacation some time. When Shelly didn't respond, he said, "C'mon. You're not still mad because I hit on you? I would have been enormously disappointed in myself if I hadn't tried. It's bad enough that I got nowhere. It'll take several new conquests to restore my self-confidence."

In spite of herself, she couldn't help laughing. "You're terrible."

He sighed. "I know, but what can I do? Maybe you could redeem my tattered character."

"The pope couldn't accomplish that."

"All right, we'll leave my character just the way it is. How about having dinner with me sometime when we get back to Paris?"

Before she could utter a tart response, he went on quickly, "Okay, how about breakfast instead? That's safe enough."

She still didn't say anything.

"Can I at least call you sometime?"

"Ryan . . ."

"Just to talk. *Honest.* I won't even try anything kinky over the phone."

She laughed. "You are irrepressible."

"I know, but I make you laugh, and I'd say that's something you don't do often enough."

In spite of herself, Shelly was drawn to Ryan. Although he was clearly the kind of charmer who never made a commitment, she was beginning to like him. It would be nice to have someone to laugh with, and he was right—she hadn't laughed very much for a long time.

"Okay. You can call me sometime."

"All right! Now all I have to do is work on your puzzling resistance to my usually foolproof charisma."

Shelly simply shook her head. He was hopeless.

During the three weeks that Kate stayed with her, Shelly didn't think much about getting another modeling assignment. They were too busy having a ball, doing all the things she'd planned and more. Kate and Ryan got along famously. He treated them to expensive dinners in four-star restaurants and drove them around the city and into the nearby countryside in his Jeep, a surprisingly utilitarian choice for someone in the fashion industry.

"You're crazy not to be involved with him," Kate said when Shelly made it clear that she and Ryan were just friends.

"I'd be crazy to get involved with him," Shelly replied. "He's a womanizer."

"I don't think so. Oh, sure, he flirts a lot, but that's just because he knows it's expected of him. Women must have been falling all over themselves to get to him from the time he was in the cradle."

"Kate, I don't need that kind of guy."

"That's just it. I don't think he *is* that kind of guy. I bet there's a lot more to him than that."

"Then *you* get involved with him."

"I'm perfectly satisfied with Roger. Besides, you're the one he's interested in. Haven't you noticed the way he looks at you?"

"The same way he looks at all attractive women between thirteen and sixty."

Kate shook her head. "Huh-uh. He cares about you."

"Sure."

"I wish you'd give him a chance." At Shelly's stubborn look, Kate went on, "All right, if not Ryan,

254

then someone else. Anyone else. It isn't good to go on being so isolated."

The conversation was veering perilously close to the reason why Shelly kept to herself, so she abruptly changed the subject to a discussion of their sightseeing plans for the next day and, to her relief, Kate didn't press the issue, although she looked at Shelly with an expression of mingled concern and compassion.

The next afternoon, Shelly had to run an errand and returned to find Ryan deep in conversation with Kate. They seemed startled by her appearance, and if Shelly hadn't known how much Kate loved Roger, she would have assumed she'd interrupted a romantic tête-à-tête.

"I just stopped by to invite you two to a cocktail party inaugurating a Manet exhibition tonight. Lots of free champagne and high-flown rhetoric. How about it? I'll even throw in dinner afterward at my favorite restaurant."

Ryan's attitude was as casually charming as ever, but Shelly sensed a subtle difference now. Throughout the evening, she caught him watching her, his expression disconcerting because it was far more serious than usual. Later, when she and Kate were alone in her apartment, she asked what Kate and Ryan had talked about before Shelly's return.

"Nothing in particular," Kate answered.

Shelly noticed that Kate didn't quite meet her look, but before she could press the issue, Kate yawned tiredly and said, "Boy, am I exhausted. All I want to do right now is crash."

Shelly decided to let it drop. Kate wouldn't lie to her and Ryan was probably having girlfriend trouble.

When Kate's money finally ran out, she flew back

to Los Angeles. Beneath the sadness of saying good-bye to her friend, Shelly felt a growing panic. Her agent hadn't called the entire time of Kate's visit. Back in her apartment, she spent days busying herself with long-neglected housework, mending, and grocery shopping, but finally she couldn't take it any more and called the Agency Internationale, asking for Hugo Darcy, her agent.

After a few minutes of the usual "Darling, how have you been? It's been insane around here," Shelly asked, "Any assignments for me, Hugo?" After an awkward silence, Hugo replied, "Let me see now . . . ah, yes, there was a possible offer from French *Vogue*, but that fell through. They're skewing younger nowadays, I believe."

"What about runway work? When I did Dior's fall collection last year, they were very pleased with me. They said they'd love to have me back."

When Hugo didn't respond, Shelly forced herself to go on, even though she knew it was futile. "Maybe you could call them."

"Darling, if we have to call them, it makes us both look desperate, and there's nothing worse. Besides, all the designers are into ethnic models nowadays. It's the new rage. I'm afraid your blond, California girl look is passé."

Shelly twisted the phone cord in her fingers, feeling her stomach tighten. The truth was, she was rapidly running out of money. She had never earned the big money that top models make, and it was extremely expensive living in Paris. As Shelly had worked less and less this year, she had used up most of what little money she had managed to save. If she didn't work again soon, she would have to give up this apartment and move to something cheaper and shabbier, like her first apartment in

L.A. The thought of doing that was intolerable.

"The thing is, Hugo, I really need to work." She tried hard to keep from sounding as if she were begging, though both of them knew that she was.

After another awkward silence, Hugo said slowly, "There is one possibility—a job on a yacht anchored off Cannes. Not bad money, a thousand for the weekend, Friday night through Sunday afternoon."

Shelly felt weak with relief. "Oh, that sounds marvelous! Who's the photographer? Anyone I've worked with before?"

"Well, actually, there won't be a photographer."

"You mean it's runway work on a yacht?"

"No, not really."

"Then . . . what am I supposed to do?"

"Be nice."

She gripped the receiver in her hand. Shelly was neither naive nor inexperienced and had a pretty good idea what sort of job this was. What did surprise her was that a reputable agency like Hugo's would deal in that sort of thing; but she wasn't in a position to be self-righteous.

"When is it?" she asked in a voice that was far from collected.

"This weekend. If you take it, there'll be a round-trip plane ticket, first class, waiting for you at Orly. Someone will pick you and some other girls up at the airport in Cannes and take you to the yacht. You should pack a couple of evening gowns as well as more casual clothes."

He talked as if of course she would accept the job.

The terrible thing was, he was right.

"Okay," she whispered.

"Good. Well, I must run, Shelly. Great talking to you. We must have lunch some day soon. I'll give you a call just as soon as this madness subsides around here and I have a free moment. Ciao, bellina."

When she hung up, Hugo's phony Italian ringing in her ears, Shelly felt sick inside. Maybe it won't be so bad, she told herself. But she knew better.

Through the windows of the helicopter, Shelly saw the Mediterranean glistening a brilliant turquoise on this hot, cloudless day. Next to her, an English model named Alexis, whom Shelly had worked with once or twice before, was happily chattering away.

"Hamdan al Fassi throws the most fabulous parties. They last all weekend, and all sorts of wealthy and famous people come. Last time, I met an American film star and a shipping tycoon. The tycoon bought me an emerald bracelet, to match my eyes, he said. Can you imagine? Not bad for a grocer's daughter from Manchester."

She gave Shelly a worried look. "Oh, but don't tell Hamdan that's my background. I rather gave the impression that my people are County. He likes that, you know. Well-bred, glamorous young women to languish on the silk-covered sofas and slither along the chamois walls of his seventy-million-dollar yacht. So clean up your history, if you must. Invent a Wall Street tycoon in your family tree. He'll love it."

"Tell me about Mr. al Fassi. What's he like?"

Alexis smiled. "Oh, just your basic Arab middleman who makes a fortune brokering deals between Arab royalty and the outside world."

"Is he nice?"

Alexis shrugged. "Nice doesn't really enter into it,

does it, when you have as much money as he does. I mean, he can buy the finest caviar and champagne, so he figures why not buy the best women as well."

At Shelly's look of dismay, Alexis went on, "You should be flattered, really. Recruitment standards for his party favors are strict."

"Party favors?"

"Us. Anyway, he only takes girls between eighteen and twenty-four, preferably closer to eighteen, so you and I barely squeaked in under the wire. They have to be classy and elegant and capable of making fairly interesting conversation. Not to mention very clean, with just the right combination of innocence and sexiness. No blowsy tarts for Hamdan."

"Have you . . . worked for him a lot?"

"Several times. His parties are a great way to meet the right type of man, if you know what I mean. The sort who can take care of a girl. Well, I mean, we won't be in demand as models forever, will we? We have to think of our future."

Just then the helicopter landed on the yacht's own heliport. As Shelly and Alexis stepped out, they were greeted by a deckhand, whom Alexis seemed to know well.

"You have your usual cabin, miss," he said, as he led them below deck. "And Miss DeLucca is right next to you. Everyone's at the stern, having cocktails. As soon as you've changed and freshened up, I'll show you there."

In her tiny but luxuriously furnished cabin, Shelly stood in the center of the room. What had she gotten herself into? Was there any way out? Maybe she could find Mr. al Fassi and tell him she was ill and had to leave. She wouldn't be paid, of course, but hopefully he would let her use the return ticket to Paris.

And then what? a voice inside her asked. She had no job on the horizon and in less than a month would have no money. She would have to return to L.A., where she would have to start her modeling career all over again from scratch. That thought was unbearably depressing.

There was a knock at her door and a moment later Alexis poked her head in. She wore a flamboyant flowered silk dress that clung to her curves and was cut scandalously low.

"Hey, you're not even dressed! Here, let me help. You'd better hurry. The most fabulous party of your life is waiting."

Shelly dressed in a simple, elegant silver sheath and a pair of silver pumps, telling herself that if necessary she would simply disappear inside herself as she had done for the *Playboy* shoots. Instead, she spent the weekend moving from deck to deck on the opulent yacht sipping champagne and dining on duck and venison; dancing in the yacht's own disco, bathed in clouds of artificially generated mist; sunbathing by the small pool; and taking the launch into town to window-shop at the exclusive boutiques along the strand.

Al Fassi was nothing like she expected. Tall and slim, he wore an impeccably tailored tux and spoke flawless English, learned while a student at Cambridge. Only his black hair and swarthy complexion hinted at his heritage. When Alexis had introduced Shelly to him, he had said graciously, "Welcome to my little boat. It's a pleasure to have you as a guest. I hope you thoroughly enjoy your stay."

"I'm sure I will," Shelly murmured politely.

Several men, most of them middle-aged and prosperous looking with an air of supreme self-confidence, talked to her, danced with her, swam with her. One, an American arms merchant, laid subtle but unmistakable claim to her, and when he suggested they have a nightcap in his stateroom, she didn't demur. After all, that's what she was there for.

His lovemaking was smooth and assured, and he didn't seem to notice that she had gone away.

When Shelly returned to Paris on Sunday evening, she was a thousand dollars richer. She paid her rent, busied herself unpacking and doing her laundry, and fixed an herb omelette, but as soon as she took the first bite, she felt nausea well up. Rushing to the bathroom, she threw up repeatedly.

When the violent retching finally subsided, Shelly stood on shaky legs and stared into the mirror over the sink. It almost seemed to her that she saw her mother's reflection looking back.

TWO

Kate

When she returned from visiting Shelly in Paris in July 1973, Kate officially moved into the apartment in Santa Monica that Roger had rented at the start of their senior year. She'd actually been spending most of her time there, rarely setting foot in the dorm room where her parents thought she was living. She knew they would be upset to learn about the living arrangement, but they would just have to accept it. It was the seventies, for heaven's sake, not the fifties, and *everyone* was living together.

The small, unfurnished apartment was in an old Spanish-style building. Kate had turned the barren room into a home for the two of them by simply placing bright cotton rugs on the hardwood floor, tacking rock posters to the white walls, and filling wine bottles with flowers from the lush beds surrounding the building.

When they weren't in school or working, the two spent their time studying and making love, so that the room became a refuge for Kate. When she graduated, she was eager to leave college behind to begin a career, but she never wanted to leave that room where she had felt such peace and love.

Then late one night, she was awakened from

a deep sleep by the ringing of the bedside phone.

"Kate, honey. I'm sorry to wake you up at this time of night," her maternal grandmother began, "but I'm afraid I have some very bad news."

Kate went cold inside. Her widowed grandmother struggled to survive on Social Security and the pathetically small savings of a lifetime. She *never* made long-distance phone calls. Kate knew this was going to be very, very bad.

"What is it?"

She heard tears in her grandmother's voice. "Oh, dear, there's just no way to break it to you gently. You see, your father . . ." Her voice broke and stopped. After a moment, she pulled herself together and went on, "Your father was shot while trying to stop a robbery at a liquor store. They took him to the hospital right away, but it was no use. He died almost immediately. Katie, honey, I'm so sorry."

He died almost immediately.

It was unreal, like a surrealistic scene from *Zabriskie Point* or one of the other avant-garde movies Roger loved and she found tedious. For an instant, Kate almost believed she was dreaming. Roger sat up beside her, yawning and asking, "What's wrong?" and she knew it was no dream.

"Katie, I am so sorry to have to tell you this."

He died almost immediately.

When Kate didn't respond, her grandmother went on, "Your mother is in a very bad state. She just couldn't call. Your aunts and uncles are on their way over. I'm going to stay here tonight. The boys are very upset, of course, and they need someone. Oh, dear, I wish your grandfather were here."

Kate still couldn't quite take it in. Her big, strong father *dead?* It was impossible. Nothing could hurt him, and as long as he was around, nothing could really hurt her.

"Kate, how soon can you get here?"

"I . . ." She stopped, her throat too dry to speak. After swallowing twice, she managed to whisper, "I'll be there in three hours."

"Be careful, honey. Maybe you should take the bus. You shouldn't drive at a time like this. Someone could pick you up at the bus station."

Kate looked at Roger, who had realized that something terrible had happened and had taken her free hand in his.

"It's all right, Grandma. I'll ask a friend to drive me."

"Good. We'll see you in a few hours, then. Take care, Katie. I love you."

"I . . . I love you, too, Grandma."

She hung up the phone, her hand fumbling with the receiver. The silence that ensued was utterly empty. Looking at Roger, Kate tried to tell him what had happened but no words would come. Tears streamed down her cheeks and she began to shake violently.

Roger held her close, murmuring indistinct words of comfort, still having no idea what had happened. To Kate's intense relief, he didn't question her as she gave way to the feelings of shock and loss and anger and unhappiness coursing through her. The most devastating feeling of all was the knowledge that her father was gone forever and that she would never have a chance to make things right between them. As far as she knew, her father had never said anything to anyone about his suspicions regarding the dent in Barbara's car. That silence, which had gone against everything he believed in, had driven a wedge between father and daughter. Ever since she'd lied to him about graduation night, and he'd realized she'd lied, nothing had been quite the same. That special bond of trust and closeness they had once shared had been shattered.

Kate told herself that somehow, someday, she would repair the damage, reestablish the bond that no other relationship could replace. Now, his sudden, unexpected, senseless death deprived her forever of the chance to make it right. She would have to spend the rest of her life knowing she had let him down and knowing she would never be able to redeem herself in his eyes.

Terrified, she held onto Roger even tighter.

"It's okay," he said. "I'm here. I'll always be here."

Kate clutched at him as if he were a lifeline and she were drowning. He was all she had now. She didn't know what she would have done without him.

All through the funeral service and the gathering of friends and family at their small house afterward, Kate kept half-expecting her father to show up and say, "It was all a terrible misunderstanding." He didn't, of course. She leaned on Roger, who had driven her to Visalia and stayed with her throughout the ordeal. With his long hair and scruffy clothes, he looked out of place among the conservatively attired Visalians.

She watched her mother being stoic, as always. Only her red-rimmed eyes revealed that she must have cried at some point when no one was around. Lea McGuire politely accepted the condolences of the crowd of people who came to the wake but otherwise said nothing, so that even now, when both women had lost the man they loved most, they could find no way to reach out to each other. Their only physical contact was a brief hug when the funeral service was over.

Kate's younger brothers were devastated. Thomas, at sixteen, tried hard to look like he could handle being the man of the house now, but he couldn't stop the tears from rolling down his cheeks as they lowered his father's coffin into the ground. Her younger brother, Scottie, only fourteen, was frightened and confused. He had always been especially close to Kate, who had read him bedtime stories and watched horror movies with him so he wouldn't be too scared. Now he clung to her, never leaving her side.

Barbara and Val came to the funeral. Val's presence was immensely comforting, but Kate felt awkward around Barbara and avoided her because every time she looked at her friend, she was filled with the vivid, painful memory of the morning following the graduation tragedy. She could still see her father's concerned expression as his hands explored the dent in Barbara's car . . . the suspicion in his voice when he questioned Barbara . . . and, finally, the fear in his eyes when he asked Kate if she needed to talk to him.

She was relieved when Barbara left the wake early to get back to her baby, Allison, and she avoided Barbara for the remainder of her stay.

When she and Roger returned to L.A. after a few days, she felt guilty knowing her brothers needed her. But Roger had a job to get back to and Kate, who was broke, had to find a job as quickly as possible. She felt closer than ever to Roger, who was sweet and supportive and patient. When she would suddenly burst into tears for no apparent reason, he would simply take her in his arms and hold her until the crying stopped. At other times when she would lash out in fury at the smallest thing, he wouldn't even try to argue back.

Roger hadn't been able to visit Paris with Kate because he had gotten a job as a script reader at an independent production company immediately upon graduation. "It's my big break!" he had told her excitedly. "I'll make all the right connections, show my student film to some people, and before you know it, I'll be an assistant director! I'll work as an A.D. on a couple of films, just to get the feel of things, then I'll direct something low budget but impressive. After that, it's the big time!"

Kate kept her mouth shut. The truth was, his student film, the culmination of his four years in UCLA's vaunted film school, hadn't impressed anyone. Intended as a humorous look at dorm life as seen through the eyes of a dorky freshman, Roger's male friends had told him it was wonderful but Kate had found the humor, which was on an adolescent male level, banal. When she'd tried to suggest some improvements to his script, he had informed her that she didn't know what she was talking about since she was merely a writer. *He* was a director and knew what would play.

Hurt and angry, Kate backed off and let Roger do exactly as he pleased. On the night before graduation, when all the student films were shown to an audience that included industry professionals, Roger basked in his friends' praise but refused to acknowledge the fact that not one of the professionals said a word to him, though they spoke to many of the other budding directors.

Now Kate hoped that the job as a reader would, indeed, be an entrée to the directing career that Roger wanted so badly, but she was very much afraid that he would find the real world much harsher in its judgment of his talent than his friends in college had been.

After returning to L.A. from her father's funeral, Kate spent weeks looking for a job similar to Roger's that could open a door for her to the film industry. She had always been intensely ambitious, especially once Barbara started encouraging her to get out of Visalia and achieve success on a large scale. After her father's death, however, Kate was even more fiercely driven than before. The knowledge that she had let him down haunted her, and she felt compelled to be successful in order to erase that feeling of failure.

As the weeks passed and she grew more dependent financially on Roger, Kate suffered discouragement until she finally landed an entry-level position as an editorial assistant on a local film magazine. The pay was terrible and the hours even worse. Roger called it a shit job and told her she deserved better, but Kate didn't care. Like him, she now had her foot in the door.

As the months passed, both were too excited and too busy to care that they had very little money and were treated like slaves at their jobs. They were utterly powerless in a business where power was everything, but they were confident that would change. It was just a matter of showing people what they could do.

At first, Kate's job consisted entirely of the grunt work that no one else on the small staff of *Cinema* wanted to do. Gradually, she was allowed to write short items and to occasionally fill in for sick or vacationing staffers. Her first byline came with an interview of an empty-headed, coke-snorting rising starlet. Her second came with an interview of a hot new director who had spent the entire time trying to get her into bed.

Kate would never have gotten that plum assignment if a flu epidemic hadn't decimated the staff. She made the most of the opportunity, writing a brilliant article about the director that gave keen insights into his work yet not mentioning his attempted seduction. Afterward, she was promoted to junior editor.

She and Roger celebrated her promotion and her much-needed raise in salary by having dinner at an expensive beachfront restaurant in Malibu. Kate was ecstatic that finally, after nearly a year at the magazine, she seemed to be getting somewhere. Roger was uncharacteristically quiet. Belatedly, it occurred to Kate that he might be feeling a little jealous since his script reading job didn't seem to be leading anywhere and the only person at the production company who had been willing to look at his student film had dismissed it as derivative and juvenile.

She didn't know what to say. Downplaying her growing success wouldn't improve Roger's situation; besides, she resented the idea that in order to protect his ego she shouldn't really enjoy something she had worked so hard to achieve.

The previous Christmas, Val had sent her a subscription to a new magazine, *Ms,* that frequently published Val's articles. It had changed Kate's perspective, and she had started challenging Roger about his refusal to do his share of the work around their little apartment. After all, they both had full-time jobs. Kate didn't see why she should be the one to come home and do all the housework, cooking, shopping, and laundry. Despite her irritation with Roger over these issues, she was still deeply in love with him. He had been there for her when she had needed him most, and she would forever be grateful. Tonight, sensing Roger's insecurity, she tried to focus attention away from herself and onto him.

"So, tell me what's happening at work. Read anything interesting?"

"Of course not. They only give me the shit scripts submitted by agencies that they don't really want to do business with."

That didn't leave much room to continue a conversation, so Kate relapsed into silence.

When dessert was served, Roger commented tersely that it was good and Kate agreed with more enthusiasm than was really called for, but they were like two people on a first date, awkwardly trying to make conversation. In the five years Kate had known Roger, this was the first time she had felt uncomfortable with him.

When dinner was over, they lingered over coffee, Roger silent, staring out at the moonlit ocean, seemingly oblivious to Kate.

"Roger, is there something bothering you? Something we should talk about?"

Finally he looked at her. "You remember me telling you about my Uncle Max? My cousin Steve's dad?"

"Was Steve the one who died in Vietnam a few years ago?"

He nodded. "Uncle Max owns a sporting goods store in Queens. He always planned on turning it over to Steve someday, but . . . well, anyway, he hasn't been in real good health lately. My Aunt Lillian has persuaded him that it's time for them to retire down in Florida, the way they always planned."

Kate had no idea what point there was—if any—to this family saga, but she waited patiently.

Roger went on. "They just have the two girls, my cousins Irene and Betty, and both of them are married and living in upstate New York. Neither of them wants to take over the business." He paused, then finished hurriedly. "Oh, hell. The thing is, Uncle Max has offered to turn the business over to me."

Kate couldn't believe it. "But . . . you're not really thinking about going back?"

"It's a *great* deal. I'd work with him for a year or two, until I know the business well enough to take over by myself. How many guys do you know who own their own business before they're even thirty? And it's a prosperous one, too. Uncle Max told me he nets about fifty thousand a year. That's more than my father and mother earn together."

"But, Roger, you'd have to move back to New York, give up your career!"

He snorted disdainfully. "What career? Writing coverage on scripts that no one's interested in? Look, Kate. I didn't say anything to you, but there's talk about cutting back in the story department, and I've already been told that I'd be the first one fired. The ax could fall any day now."

Seeing how scared he was, Kate immediately went on the offensive. "Well, it's a rotten job, anyway. You'll get a better one. You're so talented. . . ."

He interrupted angrily. "I started out with three other guys in the story department, and all three of them have gone on to bigger things. One's a second A.D. on a Mark Rydell film, another's writing a script for Paramount, and the other guy was made an assistant to a top development executive. I'm still in the story department with a bunch of new people who will probably go on to bigger and better things

271

while I'm still reading scripts for a living."

"You're just feeling down right now, but you'll get over it. That's no reason to go running back to New York, to give up what you've dreamed about and worked so hard for."

Roger looked at her without saying anything. Motioning to the waiter, he asked for the check, and when it was paid, he led Kate out of the restaurant.

All the way home in his battered VW bug, Kate kept trying to think of encouraging things she could say to Roger, things that would build up his self-confidence, but when they entered the apartment, he threw himself down on the secondhand sofa bed and said, "I know you're trying to help, but you just don't understand. All I ever wanted to do was be a director. I spent my whole childhood in the neighborhood theater. I didn't even care what was playing, I just loved being there. In the darkness, watching those actors looking larger than life, I didn't feel poor or clumsy or unattractive. I felt like I could do anything, be anything."

Kate sat down beside him and leaned her head on his shoulder. "I understand."

He put his arm around her and kissed the top of her head. "I know you do. That's why I love you so much."

She looked up at him. "I love you, too. I can't bear to see you accepting defeat like this, without a fight."

"But I have fought. I just haven't won."

Before she could respond, Roger went on. "I think, deep inside, I always knew I wasn't really that good."

"But you *are!*"

"I don't think so anymore, and even if I am good, what does it matter? One thing I've learned over the past year is that talent doesn't necessarily have anything to do with whether or not you succeed in this business. You've got to have the right connections or be tough as hell."

His smile was bittersweet. "Well, I don't have any connections, and I'm not all that tough."

Kate didn't argue anymore. At some point during the conversation, she realized that he'd made up his mind. He had given up, and there was nothing she could say to change that; but the thought of losing him was almost more than she could bear. They had spent five years together, had in many ways grown up together. They had been there for each other in the good times and the bad. They had taught each other about sex and learned to live on macaroni and cheese. No matter what happened, they knew they could count on each other.

What would she do without him?

Roger said in a tentative voice, "Kate . . . come with me."

"What?"

"Let's get married." He hurried on, his enthusiasm building. "I'll be able to support you very well. You wouldn't even have to work, or maybe you could work part-time in the store with me until we have kids. You'd like Queens. It's real nice. My family would be just as crazy about you as I am."

"What about my writing?"

"You can do that anywhere."

"But I want to be a screenwriter. The movie business is *here* in L.A. Not in Queens!"

Impatience showed in his sour expression. "You've written two scripts that haven't sold and haven't even gotten you an agent. Give up."

"No!"

A lifetime of striving for something more, something better, went into that single syllable. Unlike Roger, she wasn't about to give up.

"But I love you!" he repeated in the tone of a very small child insisting, "It's not fair!"

A profound sense of loss washed over Kate. "I love you, too."

Roger left almost immediately. They assured each other that they would call and write and that Kate would go back to New York to visit just as soon as she could get away, but she knew it was over. They wouldn't see each other again. It would hurt too much.

Just like one of her own screenplays, she could see their story unfolding over the years. Roger would be successful and prosperous, his life well-ordered. Maybe it would be boring and would lack the excitement of his attempt at a career as a director, but if the highs weren't as high, at least the lows wouldn't be as low. He would cut his shoulder-length hair because it just wouldn't fit the image of a businessman, and he would start wearing something a little more formal than jeans and T-shirts. He would fall in love with a nice girl who wanted to be a housewife. They would get married and have children. She would be a very lucky girl because he would make a terrific husband and father. The rest of his life would be laid out before him with utter predictability. If he was fortunate, he would die a very old man surrounded by his children and grandchildren after having lived in comfort and financial security.

As for Kate herself, she was afraid of what might lie in store for her. What if, like Roger, her dream never came true? What if she simply continued working for *Cinema* or some other magazine like it, eking out a living on low pay in a city that was becoming more and more expensive every day?

Roger was special. What if she never met another man as terrific as he? Would she find herself a lonely, bitter, middle-aged woman regretting the chance at love and security that she threw away when she was young and foolish?

Those were terrifying *ifs,* but even more terrifying was the thought of giving up her dream and spending the rest of her life wondering if she could have made it if she'd just persevered.

In letting Roger go despite her love for him, Kate knew she was putting her ambition ahead of her personal happiness. She had an awful suspicion that she was making a terrible mistake, but she had no choice. She had to make it big, to erase the sense of failure that haunted her.

So Kate threw herself into her work, putting in even longer hours at the office and spending all her free time in front of her typewriter at home, turning out yet another spec script. She went out occasionally, but never with the same man twice. She always compared them to Roger, and they never measured up.

Then one glorious spring day in May 1976, Kate McGuire fell in love for the second time.

THREE

Shelly

She sat in the backseat of a taxi driving down the Champs Elysées. It was night, and the famous boulevard was brightly lit with the lights of countless thousands of cars streaming beneath the golden glow of the floodlit Arc de Triomphe. In the darkness, the ghostly gray form of the Eiffel Tower rose high above the jagged Paris rooftops. In the gentle illumination of the nearby fountains, the tower looked like lacy filigree instead of steel girders.

Shelly had enjoyed this lovely sight hundreds of times but never grew tired of it. After living in Paris for four years, she still couldn't quite believe this city of fantasy was her home.

The familiar sharp stab of panic returned. If she wasn't careful, it wouldn't be home much longer. Her money was just about gone and this taxi ride was an inexcusable luxury, but Shelly couldn't face the lengthy ride on the Metro from her small apartment on the Left Bank to the exclusive address on the Place des Vosges on the Right Bank. Besides, the woman who had called her earlier that day had talked of a job, "a highly lucrative one." Maybe she would be able to afford the taxi after all.

It had certainly been an odd call. A patrician

voice had said in heavily accented English, "Mademoiselle DeLucca? I am Madame Justine Valois. I should like to discuss an employment opportunity with you. A highly lucrative one. Tonight at eight o'clock would be convenient for me. My address is Thirteen Place des Vosges, apartment seven. Shall we meet then?"

Thoroughly intimidated by the imperious Madame Valois, Shelly agreed without thinking to ask what the assignment would be. Now, as she stepped out of the taxi and gazed up at the imposing facade of the posh apartment building, she felt a twinge of doubt. Maybe she should have asked a few questions first. She had never heard of a Madame Valois. How had Madame Valois heard of her?

It was too late for second thoughts. Shelly had squandered precious francs on the taxi. She was here. She badly needed a job.

Apartment seven was on the fourth floor. Shelly rang the doorbell, and almost immediately a prim-looking, middle-aged maid wearing a starched white uniform answered the door.

"Mademoiselle DeLucca?"

"*Oui.*"

"This way, please," she said in English, and led Shelly into an exquisitely furnished sitting room. "Madame will be with you in a moment."

She closed the door behind her.

It was a supremely elegant room furnished with gorgeous antiques from the Louis XV and XVI periods. Graceful porcelain figurines graced the gray marble mantel above the large fireplace, where logs snapped in the grate, taking the chill off the winter evening. The walls were painted a deep, rich red and covered with an impressive variety of original artwork, including some fine examples of Impressionist art. An Oriental carpet in deep shades of red, blue, and black covered the hardwood floor.

Shelly's attention was particularly caught by several objects and pictures from the period when Colette was a young woman at the turn of the century. A bust of the famous French writer stood on a table near the door. Since coming to Paris, Shelly had read English translations of Colette's romantic novels and was an admirer. She would dearly love to be able to one day afford even a small one of these objects that were mementos of a more graceful, elegant time.

Walking over to a long window, she looked out at the view of the south side of the Palais Royal, where the French Revolution had begun in the brothels and cafés beneath the colonnades. At the sound of a door opening, she turned.

The woman who entered was tall and elegantly slim. Her silver hair was cut in a French *coupe,* and behind black-rimmed glasses her dark eyes were shrewd and calculating. Her thin, wide mouth didn't smile as she returned Shelly's look. She wore a black suit and white silk blouse, with several long strands of pearls and smart black pumps. A large gold bracelet seemed to weigh on one frail wrist.

Madame Valois sat down in a chair with her back to the fire and appraised Shelly silently. Finally, as if reaching approval, she nodded slowly and said, "You may sit down, Mademoiselle DeLucca."

Shelly sat down on a silk-upholstered chair across from her and began, "Madame Valois?"

"Yes, but you may call me Madame Justine, or, when we are better acquainted, *tantine,* aunt. All my employees do."

The maid returned, bringing a tray of tea and coffee, then retired.

"Which would you prefer?" Madame Justine asked as she bent over the heavy silver tray.

"Coffee, please."

Her lips curved in what might have passed for a smile. "Of course. You Americans and your coffee. Actually, I prefer it myself. Tea is a rather weak beverage in comparison. How do you take it?"

"Black, thank you."

Madame Justine poured coffee into a delicate porcelain cup, placed it on a matching saucer, and handed it to Shelly. After pouring a cup for herself, she leaned back in the chair and slowly sipped it, all the while watching Shelly with a disconcertingly frank expression.

"You mentioned a job," Shelly began, anxious to get to the crux of the matter. She needed money too badly to sit here making small talk over coffee.

"Yes, but first I would like to ask you a few questions about your background, education, and so forth."

No one had ever questioned her background before when offering her a modeling job. Shelly wondered if perhaps this was something else—a position as sales clerk in an exclusive salon, perhaps. Many former models ended up doing that kind of work because they looked good in the clothes that the salons sold. Whatever the job was, she was in no position to reject it.

"I graduated from high school in California, began modeling in Los Angeles, then came to Paris. I've worked all over Europe for a variety of magazines and designers .

"I am familiar with your professional resumé," Madame Justine cut in. "I spoke with your agent, Monsieur Darcy. I am interested in your personal resumé. So, you have no university education? And

279

no professional experience as anything other than a model?"

Shelly's heart sank. Did this mean she wouldn't get the job? "That's correct," she admitted reluctantly.

"No matter," the older woman said with a dismissive wave of her hand. "I can teach you what you need to know."

Thank God, Shelly thought, breathing an audible sigh of relief.

"May I see your purse, please?"

Shelly wasn't sure she'd heard correctly. "My purse?"

"It is a shortcut to a character reference. I can tell a great deal about a woman by the contents and condition of her handbag."

Feeling more than a little ill at ease, Shelly handed her bag to Madame Justine.

"Good quality," the older woman murmured. "It must have been difficult to afford on a model's salary."

"I did some ads for the company and was given the model's discount. Even so, it was rather expensive and I had to save up for it. I'd rather have one nice thing than a dozen cheap ones." As she spoke, Shelly remembered the single dress she'd been able to buy at Ensign's, Visalia's best dress shop, long ago.

Madame Justine nodded approval, then quickly looked through the contents. There was very little—an appointment book with distressingly blank pages, the key to her apartment, a tortoiseshell comb and matching mirror, a tube of lipstick, tissues, a matching wallet with a few francs and the only credit card she possessed, and a small paperback guide to the Metro, the Paris subway.

Handing the purse back to Shelly, Madame Justine said, "There is an admirable lack of clutter, Mademoiselle. I approve. Now then, let's get down to business, shall we? I think you might just do, though of course there will have to be a physical inspection. Unpleasant but necessary."

Physical inspection? Shelly had never heard of such a thing. Suspicion rose within her. "May I ask what sort of job you're offering me?"

Madame Justine's dark eyes narrowed. "I thought you would have heard of me. No matter. I will explain. I heard of you through a *rabatteurs*—how do you say it?—like a beater in a pheasant shoot. He felt you might be a valuable addition to my stable of girls. I run an escort service of the very highest exclusivity. I may say there is no one in Europe—actually, no one in the world—on my level."

Shelly felt sick. "You mean prostitutes."

Madame Justine's eyes flared in anger. *"No!* I merely offer a service, introducing beautiful, cultivated young women to my charming, important, wealthy friends. For this service, the young women receive one thousand dollars a day minus a thirty percent commission for myself."

Despite herself, Shelly was impressed by the figure. At that rate, one day's work would pay her rent and support her for an entire month, if she lived very frugally; but she wasn't a prostitute, she told herself furiously. That weekend on Hamdan al Fassi's yacht had been a onetime affair done out of desperation. She had no intention of doing it again. When Hugo had called recently with a similar job, she had turned him down in no uncertain terms.

Putting down her cup of coffee, Shelly rose. "I'm not interested in your offer, Madame Valois. I'll be going now."

To her surprise, the woman didn't look particularly taken aback. She merely said, "Think about it, Mademoiselle DeLucca. I think you could earn a great deal of money for very little work. Work, might I add, that would actually be quite pleasant. Weekends at English country houses, parties in Rome, state dinners with diplomats. This is not some tawdry little business. My friends include presidents, tycoons, even kings. Think about it."

She pressed a buzzer in the wall, and a moment later the maid returned. "Show Mademoiselle DeLucca out, Jeanne."

As Shelly left, she felt Madame Justine's eyes following her.

A few days later, she had an aperitif with Ryan at a bistro near her apartment. Since the shoot on Ibiza, they had seen each other often, but always in casual situations such as this. Shelly had no intention of getting involved with him. Though he never stopped trying to seduce her, he was always able to joke about it and keep it light. She found she could talk to him as she had never been able to talk to any man—as a friend.

Looking at her now, Ryan said, "You've lost weight. You're not eating properly, are you?"

If it had been anyone else, she would have insisted that she was dieting because of her modeling career, but Ryan knew she hadn't worked in a while and he knew when she was lying.

When Shelly didn't say anything, he went on in a gentle voice, "I can't get you modeling assignments. If I could, I would have done so before now, but I might be able to help you get a job as a receptionist at a magazine or as a salesgirl in a boutique. I know a few people . . ."

"Thanks," Shelly cut in abruptly, "but I don't think so. If nothing works out, I'll go back to L.A. Kate has offered to let me share her apartment. I could get a part-time job and go to college."

"You don't sound real thrilled with that plan."

"No. I'd rather stay in Paris."

"Look, if things get really tough, you can stay at my place for a while." Before she could protest, he said, "On the couch, of course. No hanky-panky." He grinned. "Well, maybe just a little hanky-panky."

Shelly couldn't help smiling. "That's a generous offer, Ryan, but I think I would cramp your style. What would all those girls think who go in and out of your bedroom?"

"I'd tell them you're my sister. What the hell. We're both Americans."

There had been something on her mind ever since she first greeted Ryan this afternoon, so she said slowly, "Have you ever heard of a Madame Justine Valois?"

He raised one eyebrow quizzically. *"The* Madame Justine?"

Shelly nodded.

"She's supposed to be the most famous, or I guess I should say infamous, madame in Europe. Supposedly, she's politically powerful as well as wealthy. To hear people talk, she's just about an extension of the French government. She supplies call girls to visiting diplomats. I've even heard it rumored that she supplied President Kennedy with a girl when he visited Paris in the early sixties."

He eyed her thoughtfully. "Why?"

"Oh, nothing. I just met her recently and found her kind of fascinating in a way."

There wasn't a hint of humor in his expression

283

now. "Shelly, did she ask you to join her stable?"

She just looked at him. She didn't have to answer.

"Don't do it!"

Shelly was surprised at the vehemence in Ryan's tone and reacted defensively. "I turned her down."

"Then why are you asking me about her?"

"Because I was curious. I don't know why you're so upset. Prostitution is legal in France."

"But procuring isn't, and that's exactly what she is—a pimp!"

"I *said* I turned her down, all right?"

"But you're thinking about it, aren't you? I'll bet she laid it on thick, the money, the jet-set life."

It was true that since their meeting, Shelly had found herself fantasizing about all the things she could do with that kind of money, especially as her food was running low and only this morning her landlord had asked when he could expect the rent. Poverty was frightening and humiliating.

"Don't let yourself get sucked in," Ryan went on. "You don't know what it would be like. How degrading it would be."

Don't I, though, Shelly thought bitterly, remembering the weekend on Hamdan al Fassi's yacht.

Ryan looked at her intently. "I tried to tell you to get out of modeling, but you wouldn't listen to me. *Please,* listen to me now! *Don't do this!*"

"It's *my* life, Ryan. Why should you care what I do with it?"

His voice was uncharacteristically sober. "Because I care about you."

Shelly was more touched than she could possibly admit. At that moment, she felt an urge to talk to Ryan, to open up to him, but she couldn't. How could she say the words aloud? *I was gang raped by a*

284

*group of boys who said I was trash, just like my mother,
and I think they were right! That's what I am, trash!*

When she didn't speak, Ryan said slowly, "Shelly,
when Kate was here, I asked her what had happened to make you so frightened of men."

She stared at him in dismay. "She didn't . . ."
Shelly stopped, unable to continue.

"She was reluctant to talk about it. It took a lot
of talking on my part to convince her how much I
care about you. Finally, she told me that you were
raped once."

How much had Kate revealed? Shelly wondered
anxiously. Had she told Ryan everything, including
the facts about Steven Ashe's death and her abortion?

In answer to her unspoken question, Ryan said,
"She didn't go into detail. I think she felt guilty, as
if she were betraying a confidence. I tried to make
her understand that I had already guessed as much.
It was so apparent—the way you flinch when any
man, even a model you're working with, touches
you. Kate's reluctant admission that you'd been
raped just confirmed my suspicions."

The awareness that Ryan knew even part of her
secret made Shelly feel intensely vulnerable and naked, as if all her defenses had been stripped away.
She reacted in anger. "How dare you cross-examine
my friends! Prying into my life! Getting into areas
that are none of your business!"

He reached out to take her hand, but she pulled
it away from him. "Shelly, listen to me. It wasn't a
question of prurient curiosity."

"No? Then what was it? A way to develop a new
line since your old ones haven't gotten me into
bed?"

There was compassion in his voice. "It has noth-

285

ing to do with getting you into bed. I wanted to understand . . ."

"Bullshit!" Shelly rarely swore, so the epithet had even more force than it normally would.

"Listen to me! You can be as mad at me as you want. I can take it. But don't let what happened to you in the past put you in Madame Justine's hands."

Shelly rose stiffly. "I have to go," she said, avoiding Ryan's look. "I have an appointment to talk to Hugo."

Ryan stood up and faced her. "Shelly, I meant what I said. You can stay at my place if you need to. No strings attached."

"Good-bye, Ryan."

Shelly hurried out of the bistro, afraid that she might break down in tears in front of him.

She hadn't lied about an appointment with Hugo Darcy, her agent. He was a suave young Frenchman who spoke several languages fluently, a necessity in a business where models came from all over the world. He was also clearly gay, which made Shelly feel comfortable with him. Until today. As Shelly sat in his stylish gray and white office, she felt anything but comfortable. He hadn't wanted to meet with her, but she had insisted. She hated letting him see how desperately she needed work, but she was long past the point when her pride could be salvaged.

"As I told you over the telephone, Shelly, there simply isn't anything at the moment."

"*At the moment?* Hugo, there hasn't been anything for weeks. There must be something you can do. I'll take anything."

286

"You turned down the last job offered to you," he pointed out with a sniff of disapproval.

"They didn't want a model, they wanted a prostitute, and you know it."

His eyes narrowed. "Nevertheless, it was a job. The only one I could find. I can't force people to hire you."

"I was in demand when I first came here. I worked constantly."

"That was nearly five years ago. You are no longer fresh, and fresh faces are everything in this business."

"But some models continue working well into their thirties!"

"They are the exception, and you know it. How many of the girls you worked with five years ago are still working? A handful, no more."

"Hugo, I'm not even twenty-five yet . . ."

"You will be soon," he interrupted curtly. "Careers are short in this business, Shelly. You are not stupid. You must know that. Your career is over. Accept it and go on."

"Go on to what?"

"I have no idea. That is your affair. Now, if you don't mind, I am quite busy."

"You're not going to find any work for me, are you?" she asked in a hopeless voice.

Hugo glanced at her, then looked down at his desk calendar, pretending to be engrossed in it.

Slowly, Shelly got up and walked out, knowing she would never talk to him again.

"I'm sorry about this unpleasantness, but I have to ask you to undress," Madame Justine said in a businesslike tone. "It is nothing personal. I don't

287

care for *les dames horizontales.*"

Rigid with embarrassment, Shelly removed her clothes and stood there in the elegant sitting room with the brightly crackling fire warming her bare skin.

Madame Justine's dark eyes examined her critically for a few agonizing seconds before she said, "Very well. You may put your clothes back on."

When Shelly was dressed again, Madame Justine went on. "I am glad to say that it will not be necessary to subject you to cosmetic surgery. Some of my girls have a flaw that must be corrected, but you are quite perfect."

Briefly she explained the details of the business—she charged her clients three hundred dollars for an afternoon, six hundred for an evening (8 P.M. to 2 A.M.), and one thousand for an entire day. Weekends were negotiable. Her commission was thirty percent.

"We must get right to work for we have much to do. Right now you are a pretty girl. I will make you over into a stunning woman."

Shelly listened in silence.

"When I first came to Paris, a long time ago, I was a lonely young woman from the provinces, set apart by my ugliness. I set out to change myself, to become chic and attractive, if not actually beautiful. I succeeded tremendously. I learned that my talent lies in making young women the very best they can be, then matching the girls of my creation with my clients. I can do a great deal with you."

Shelly forced herself to ask, "What will happen?"

"First, I will inspect your flat to see if it is appropriate. There may be times when a client will want to meet you there."

"I . . . I'm behind in my rent," Shelly admitted.

288

"My landlord has asked me to move."

Madame Justine shrugged. "No matter. If the flat meets my requirements, I will pay the rent; if it doesn't, I will find another for you. Next, I will send you to a particular boutique that I do business with. They have very sophisticated clothes, nothing cheap or obvious. I will buy you a set of luggage, which you will need because you will be doing much traveling. By the way, always keep a bag packed and ready. You may have to leave at a moment's notice. I will send you to my coiffeur to have your hair redone. Platinum, I think, would be more striking than the muted gold of your hair now. Finally, you will see a doctor every week for medical inspections."

Shelly noted her choice of words—inspections—as if she were a piece of meat being inspected by the health department.

Madame Justine continued in a haughty tone. "I will teach you everything you need to know. I will play the role of Pygmalion. You are not a creature of dreams and fantasies now, but you will be. I will teach you how to dress, how to have graceful gestures and the very best manners. I will teach you how to behave in society, for there will be official dinners, weekends at fabulous châteaus, manors, and villas. You must be able to converse, so I will tell you which books to read, which films to watch."

"I'm not stupid," Shelly interrupted angrily.

"No, but I am very demanding, and right now you do not live up to my standards. When I am through, you will be able to walk into Maxim's or the Crillon or the Dorchester and look as if you belong there. When you find yourself in the company of a king, a prince, a foreign minister, or a business tycoon, you will not be an embarrassment to me."

Madame Justine finished slowly, underscoring each word. "Many of my clients are exceptional and fascinating men. I will turn you into an exceptional and fascinating woman."

Over the next three weeks, she worked with Shelly for hours each day, teaching her how to walk, dress, talk, behave in high society. Under her iron tutelage, Shelly did, indeed, learn how to walk into Maxim's without looking ill at ease, how to converse with a diplomat, and how to make love skillfully through the books Madame Justine gave her on sexuality, everything from the *Kama Sutra* to *The Joy of Sex*.

She was transformed from an extremely pretty but unsophisticated girl into a stunning young lady with real presence. Looking at her reflection in an oversized triple mirror at the dress shop where Madame Justine had arranged for her to buy a new wardrobe, Shelly was amazed. She didn't look like the same person. Her long, golden blond hair was swept back in a sleek platinum bob. Her makeup was more subtle than she was used to wearing as a model but also more effective. She looked supremely self-confident, and even if she didn't entirely feel that way, she hid it well.

Her first client was an American diplomat who often used Madame Justine's service when in Paris. He was sixtyish, sophisticated, intelligent, and didn't bother removing his wedding ring when he arrived at Shelly's apartment to take her out to dinner. They ate at a small but chic restaurant overlooking the Seine and made small talk about everything from the current political scene in America to the man's hobby, raising orchids.

Afterward, he asked her to stop by his room at the Plaza Athenee for a drink. Shelly had no illusions about the euphemism. The hardest part was undressing in front of him. He watched intently as she shed her clothes, then asked her to help him undress. At some point, she retreated within herself, hardly noticing what his body was like and only dimly aware that his lovemaking was fast and impersonal.

She concentrated instead on the white ormolu clock on the mantel, praying for 2 A.M. to come. The moment it did, she slipped out of bed, dressed quickly, accepted the money he gave her for a taxi, and left.

Back in her apartment, Shelly took a long, hot bath and told herself it hadn't been so bad—but she had a hard time falling asleep.

Shelly quickly became one of Madame Justine's most popular girls and was off on a jet-set lifestyle—weekends at English country estates and Roman villas, nights at palatial mansions outside Paris. She made more money than she had ever dreamed of, and her life was a fantasy beyond her wildest imagination: shopping in the private showrooms of top designers, eating in the most elegant restaurants in different European capitals, moving into a luxurious Right Bank apartment.

She quickly learned how to perform with enough sexual technique to please her clients and yet at the same time to simply shut off inside. Her life was exciting and glamorous, she told Kate and Barbara and Val during many trans-Atlantic phone calls. Traveling by private jet, sipping champagne at midnight in chic private clubs, hobnobbing with the famous and wealthy.

Shelly didn't tell them she was working as a call

girl. She simply made it sound like this was all part of her modeling career. Ryan was the only one who knew the truth, and his concern for her grew. When he questioned her transformation from a sweet, shy, vulnerable girl into a brittle woman, she told him she was doing just fine, thank you, and pointed out that considering the number of women he went through, he was in no position to throw stones.

If she could find no escape from feeling the victim, then she would become the manager of her own victimization. Being in charge of her own exploitation, she told herself, was the same as being free of it.

FOUR

Valerie

Regine's is hot tonight, Val thought, gazing around the packed, noisy room. It was New Year's Eve 1976, and everyone who was anyone was at the exclusive club in New York. She saw Andy Warhol chatting with Warren Beatty and Jack Nicholson, who had gained weight since Val had interviewed him for *Rolling Stone*. Anjelica Huston and Apolonia, a model, were making girl-talk in a corner. Catherine Deneuve still looked more gorgeous than any woman Val had ever seen, with the possible exception of Shelly.

Val had seen Shelly in Paris a few months earlier when she had made a quick trip over to interview a French rock star who was the rage for about thirty seconds. Shelly looked so different that Val hadn't recognized her at Orly. Come to think of it, Shelly now bore an uncanny resemblance to Deneuve, with the same silver-blond hair and air of cool self-possession—not to mention a fabulous apartment on the chic Place Dauphine and a closet stuffed with designer clothes.

Val knew that top models made a small fortune, but she'd never realized Shelly had been that successful. If she didn't know better, she'd assume there

293

must be a rich man in the background, but Shelly had told her she wasn't dating anyone in particular and Val believed her.

The woman lived like a nun. When they went out on the town, Shelly rejected overtures from several very attractive men. She packed it in early, going home alone, while Val went off with the sexiest little French sax player she found playing in a band in a Montmartre club. He was short but, boy, could he blow.

Now, as Val watched Beatty, who was with Iman, the magnificent black model, she sighed heavily. Models had it fucking made.

Val didn't make as much money as Shelly obviously did, but she did okay. Ever since an editor at *Rolling Stone* had seen her stuff in *The Voice of the People* and had given her that first assignment three years earlier, she hadn't looked back. She had felt a pang of guilt about leaving the paper, but Myrna told her to go for it. "Grab all the gold and the glory you can get," she had urged, and Val did.

The truth was, the left-wing revolution that the paper so enthusiastically anticipated had never happened. "You say you want a revolution," the Beatles sang, but apparently not that many people really wanted one. When the war in Vietnam ended, the air seemed to go out of all those radical balloons. As they got further into the seventies, people started calling it the "me" decade, now more concerned with making money and living well than with fostering massive political change.

When Jimmy Carter was elected president the preceding November, that did it for Val's involvement in politics. From now on, she would just write scathing articles about politics and stop actually participating. If a fucking born-again Christian could run the country, delivering pious lectures just like the holierthan-thou preachers Val had listened to at the First Southern Baptist Church, then what was the point? Besides, it was really getting to be a drag living on no money and left-wing ideals. She wanted to own a car. She wanted to buy clothes from someplace other than army surplus and thrift shops. She wanted to eat at some of the expensive little restaurants that were popping up in Berkeley instead of subsisting on a fucking macrobiotic diet.

So she wrote her ass off for *Rolling Stone* and Andy Warhol's *Interview* and the other hip new magazines that began calling her. When she wrote a controversial, much-discussed article for *Ms* on faking orgasms ("Oscar-Winning Performances in Bed"), she became a celebrity herself. Warhol was right, she decided. Someday everyone would be famous for fifteen minutes.

Outrageous and irreverent, Val held nothing back, whether she was interviewing someone or was the subject of an interview herself. Her flamboyant, gutsy personality, as much as her colorful, often insightful writing style, propelled her to the top of the funky, glitzy milieu of rock music, film, and counterculture politics. She was seen with Jagger, Pacino, and others from Liverpool to the Village to the Roxy.

Despite her dismay at the conservative turn in American politics, Val's outspoken articles never stopped challenging the Establishment. Whenever she ran across hypocrisy or pompousness, she felt an irresistible urge to strip it bare and reveal it in all its ludicrousness.

All of which had led to her being at Regine's tonight with the Beautiful People. Maybe she wasn't one of them, in the sense of being beautiful, but, nevertheless, she was Someone! It felt good, being part of this tight little clique. There was a delicious irony in it. In high school, Val definitely hadn't been part of the "in crowd" despite her friendship with Barbara. That pitiful little group of teenage snobs, who were so proud of being big fish in the small pond of Visalia, paled in comparison to the "in crowd" that Val was part of now.

If they could see me now, she thought, enjoying a sense of amusement and satisfaction.

Val eavesdropped on a small knot of people standing next to her. An older man she didn't recognize was introducing his daughter, who couldn't have been more than sixteen or seventeen, to the group, including a well-known actress and a few celebrity wives. Val could tell that the girl made the women nervous because she outshone them. She was so young and sweet and transparently innocent.

In comparison, the older women had hard faces and pencil-thin bodies; they didn't just look old, they looked used up, having seen a few too many midnights while snorting too much coke and sleeping with too many men—or women.

It would make a great anecdote in an article she was writing about celebrity wives ("Reflected Glory"). Val took out the imitation-leather notebook that she'd bought in a dime store and jotted down some brief observations.

"Spying on us, as usual?"

She looked up to find a delicious-looking young man smiling at her sardonically. Matt Latimer, aka Needle, was one of the new wave of androgynous rock stars who wore makeup with more panache than most women and who kept their sexual persuasion a subject of mystery and rampant gossip. Tonight he looked surprisingly normal—his almost-too-handsome face was scrubbed clean, his pale blon____ ___r was cut short and slicked back, and he ___ _____itional black tux. Only the diamond stud ___ ___ and the skinny black cigarette dangling from a corner of his mouth gave any hint that he could be outrageous.

Val had met Needle briefly at a party in L.A. recently, but she was surprised that he would remember her since he'd been stoned at the time.

"Of course I'm spying on you. That's my job," she responded.

"How come you haven't interviewed me?"

"Your publicist said you weren't doing interviews for a while."

"He's right, but I might make an exception for you."

Val immediately became alert. An interview with Needle would make the cover of any magazine she chose to sell it to.

"I liked that thing you did on Elton," he went on. "You actually managed to give him some substance. Think you could do the same for me?"

"That depends on whether you're smart or stupid. I'm only as good as the material I have to work with."

Needle threw back his blond head and laughed. "You've got an attitude problem, don't you?"

"I try."

Gesturing around them, he said, "This place is a drag. All these Hollywood types trying to figure out if the party's really an A-list affair because if it isn't they're going to leave, and all the pathetic little hangers-on and the smug rich bitches and assholes. Let's blow this joint!"

Val knew exactly what he was getting at. Making an instant decision, she responded, "Okay. Let's go."

In the backseat of his rented limo, they drank champagne and kissed breathlessly, and Needle asked her to take him in her mouth. Val had engaged in oral sex plenty of times before but never in a limo cruising along Central Park West. She hesitated, then thought what the hell since the driver couldn't see them through the tinted glass.

When he came, messing up her new burgundy velvet dress, she was irritated, but he told her she could clean up at his place, which turned out to be a huge, rambling loft in SoHo, all black-leather furniture, glass-and-chrome tables, and a giant portrait of Needle by Warhol. Val cleaned off her dress in the bathroom and came out to find Needle sitting on the floor. On a low table in front of him was a mirror and a razor blade; he was laying out a couple of lines of coke.

Val had known Needle would have coke. That was half the reason she'd come with him. From the first moment she'd been introduced to the stuff by another rock singer she had profiled for *Rolling Stone*, Val had carried on a love affair with the pristine white powder. As far as she was concerned, it was another angle of feminist catch-up time. If men could do drugs, so could women.

This drug was so ladylike. No unsightly needle marks, no scuzzy smells. It could even be carried around in a cosmetics case just like a tube of lipstick.

Unlike heroin, which she'd tried once then abandoned, coke didn't make her nod off. It made her feel energetic, creative, stimulated—the way she'd always wanted to feel her whole life: free, happy, and just as good as everyone else. Val actually felt attractive and confident when she was flying high on coke. Now she sat down happily next to Needle, folding her legs in front of her. Even the act of using it was sexy in a ritualistic way. She watched Needle tap a razor edge against mirrored glass to smooth the powder . . . the loving motion of carefully cutting portions into lines . . . the precise rolling of a hundred-dollar bill. . . . As chemical foreplay, it was incredibly seductive.

Needle handed her the bill and she bent over to sniff. The white powder flew up her nose. Val leaned back, pinching her nose shut.

Needle did the same. Then, wetting his index finger, he cleaned the surface of the mirror and ran his fingertip across Val's gums, slowly moving his finger in and out of her mouth as she sucked on it. The gesture was intensely erotic.

"C'mon," he said, leading her to his bed, a king-size mattress lying on the floor. They fucked wildly. His body was incredibly sexy and hard and more muscled than she had expected. Val liked the way he felt, but she hated the taste of him, a sour combination of liquor and cigarettes and drugs.

As always, she didn't come. If he noticed, he didn't care. She told herself she didn't care, either. It didn't matter that she never had an orgasm. All that mattered was being in bed with a famous man whom millions of women would give anything to be with. She was no longer a nobody from Nowheresville. Plain little Valerie Lynn Simpson from Visalia had arrived with a vengeance.

Afterward, as they lay in bed propped up against several huge pillows, she took her notebook from her nearby purse and began, "Okay, tell me about yourself. Forget the usual bullshit about where you were born and how you got in the business. Tell me something you've never told anyone in your life." Needle stared at Val for a moment in complete amazement. He threw back his head and laughed in that immensely appealing way he had.

"You're some piece of work, Valerie Simpson."

Looking her in the eye, he said, "All right. How's this—whenever I sing a love song, I fantasize that I'm singing to a man, not a woman."

* * *

Back in San Francisco, Val worked around the clock to finish the Needle interview in time for *Rolling Stone*'s next issue. When she turned it in, only hours before press time, she told the editor she didn't want to hear from anyone for the next forty-eight hours. She was going straight back to her apartment on Telegraph Hill and crash.

"There's just one thing," he said as she was walking out the door. Val turned and glared at him. "How would you like to interview the biggest marijuana smuggler in California?"

Michael Parano, who had been a philosophy major dealing his way through Berkeley, had started as a five-dollar-a-bag man in the mid sixties. Now a different kind of seventies entrepreneur, he used his organizational genius and itch for adventure to build the biggest, most sophisticated smuggling operation in history.

Rolling Stone had been trying to interview him for years, and he had finally agreed, under two conditions—first, that his real name not be used, in order to protect his cover as a winery owner in Napa Valley; second, that Valerie Simpson write his story. He was a big fan of hers.

As Val drove her red Corvette convertible up to the million-dollar fortresslike estate on two hundred and fifty acres, she wondered what she'd gotten herself into. Would Parano turn out to be a publicity-hungry mobster? Or merely another boring pothead who had smoked a little too much weed and killed a few too many brain cells?

A decorative wooden bridge arching over a pond stocked with koi led to the entrance of the two-story, redwood-and-glass mansion. In the distance was a stone building with PARANO WINERY emblazoned over the arched doorway. Beyond that was the vineyard itself, acre upon rolling acre.

When Val pulled to a stop, the massive double doors opened and a man stood on the threshold. Short, not much taller than her, and built like a young bull, with broad shoulders and a barrel chest, Parano wore his black hair unfashionably long, curling past the collar of his blue workshirt. His jeans were old and faded.

For an instant, Val felt as though she was having a flashback to her year at Berkeley. This guy looked as if he had never left the sixties! Caught off-guard by the warm smile that softened his darkly handsome face and crinkled the corners of his brown eyes, Val hadn't expected him to look so . . . *nice*—and she hadn't expected the immediate physical attraction she felt toward him.

Despite the fact that she'd hopped in the sack with so many men that she'd lost count after fifty or so, Val did it more out of a determination to maintain her reputation as a hell-raiser than out of irresistible desire. Now she felt an attraction toward Parano that was unlike anything she had felt since Gregg Hartoonian in high school. She was thoroughly shaken by this unaccustomed feeling because it made her feel vulnerable.

Fear of that vulnerability made her voice even sharper than usual. "So. Are you the big-time dealer?"

His smile didn't waver. "Yeah. Are you the big-time writer?"

She couldn't help it. She laughed. "Valerie Simpson," she said, extending her hand.

"Michael Parano," he responded, taking her hand in his. "I'm very glad to meet you."

He took her on a tour of the house and grounds, pointing out the sixteen camera monitors equipped

301

with infrared night vision atop the high stone walls, a bullet-proof central command post just off the master bedroom, and a forty-five-kilowatt generator.

"This is a cross between country chic and Hitler's bunker," Val commented.

Michael laughed. "That was the point. I spent more than a million making this place safe."

"Safe from whom?"

He gave her a wry glance. "The bad guys, of course."

There was an electrified metal staircase leading to the second story, an electric grid in the floor upstairs, a subsonic noise machine that could emit sound waves to upset an intruder's sense of balance and make him nauseous, and closed-circuit TV monitors in the ceiling of the master bedroom.

As they stood in the center of the bedroom, its stained-glass windows giving it an oddly churchlike atmosphere, Val said, "I thought you'd be surrounded by bodyguards."

"Oh, they're around somewhere. I told them to make themselves scarce for a while. I just didn't want you to feel intimidated." He smiled. "I should have known better. I'll bet nothing intimidates you."

The way my body responds to you intimidates the hell out of me, she thought.

He glanced at his plain watch and said, "Right on time for lunch. You can interview me while we eat. I hope you're hungry. I made this myself."

"I'm starved."

Over a meal of shrimp salad and cannelloni ("My mother's recipe," he pointed out) and a selection from his own winery, Val asked her questions. Why did he suddenly decide to grant an interview? Wasn't he worried about the authorities?

"It's because of the authorities that I decided to give an interview. I want to thumb my nose at them, to say, 'Hey, you dumb shmucks. You haven't been able to catch me after ten years! Now the whole world will know I'm smarter than you are!" As for being afraid of them, the only thing I'm afraid of is getting bad dope and accidentally putting it out on the streets."

"How much business do you do?"

"I smuggle in hundreds of thousands of pounds of pot a year. Ninety percent of the Colombian pot that comes to the West Coast comes to me." There was an unmistakable note of pride in his voice as well as a matter-of-factness that might have come from a businessman talking about electric can openers.

Crossing his arms, Parano leaned forward on the glass table and went on. "There's one thing I want to make clear. I'm just a product of the hippie generation, the last hippie drug smuggler on a big-time level because coke, guns, and violence have taken over everywhere else."

"So you're just a modern outlaw in a harmless way."

"Yeah. Hell, my hero is Butch Cassidy. He never killed anybody while he was robbing banks and trains. I'm not hurting anyone, either. There's no violence in my operation, and I don't deal in hard drugs."

Val was skeptical. "You mean, with your Colombian connection, you don't deal coke?"

Parano shook his head, his gaze as straightforward and innocent as a choirboy's. "No way. I don't think marijuana is any more harmful than alcohol. It should be legalized. As for other drugs, they're just flat dangerous and I don't want to have anything to do with them."

"Wouldn't the people you do business with in Colombia like you to deal coke as well?"

"If they do, that's their problem."

"How much money do you make?"

"Net or gross?" he asked with a grin.

"Net."

"Oh, anywhere from one to two million dollars a year, depending on various factors."

Val was amazed. She knew there must be a lot of money in this operation, but a couple of million a year? *Net?* "What do you do with it besides buy every security device ever made?"

"One branch of the operation launders it through offshore banks. You know, the kind of banks that charge a hefty fee for accepting large cash deposits. I pay my employees very well, contribute to causes I believe in, like Greenpeace and the Sierra Club, and the rest goes into the winery."

There was just one question—the most intriguing one—remaining. Putting down her notebook and pen, Val leveled a steady gaze at Parano and asked, "Why?"

"Why do I do this for a living?"

"Yeah. Why take the risk? At least, why continue to take it? By now, you must have enough money to retire."

He had a killer grin tinged with a recklessness that did something funny to Val's insides. "Define *enough.*"

"I'm serious. Why do you do it?"

"Someday, when the winery is self-supporting, I'll quit. Until then, I'm having a ball."

"What is it about smuggling that makes the risk of getting caught or even killed worth it?"

He hesitated for a long moment, then said abruptly, "Come with me tonight and I'll show you."

"You mean—watch the pot being delivered?"

He nodded. "What do you say? If you're afraid, just say so. It's okay."

"Of course I'm afraid!" she snapped. "I may be

MORE PASSION AND ADVENTURE AWAIT... YOUR TRIP TO A BIG ADVENTUROUS WORLD BEGINS WHEN YOU ACCEPT YOUR FIRST 4 NOVELS ABSOLUTELY *FREE*
(AN $18.00 VALUE)

Accept your Free gift and start to experience more of the passion and adventure you like in a historical romance novel. Each Zebra novel is filled with proud men, spirited women and tempestuous love that you'll remember long after you turn the last page.

Zebra Historical Romances are the finest novels of their kind. They are written by authors who really know how to weave tales of romance and adventure in the historical settings you love. You'll feel like you've actually gone back in time with the thrilling stories that each Zebra novel offers.

GET YOUR FREE GIFT WITH THE START OF YOUR HOME SUBSCRIPTION

Our readers tell us that these books sell out very fast in book stores and often they miss the newest titles. So Zebra has made arrangements for you to receive the four newest novels published each month.

You'll be guaranteed that you'll never miss a title, and home delivery is so convenient. And to show you just how easy it is to get Zebra Historical Romances, we'll send you your first 4 books absolutely FREE! Our gift to you just for trying our home subscription service.

BIG SAVINGS AND FREE HOME DELIVERY

Each month, you'll receive the four newest titles as soon as they are published. You'll probably receive them even before the bookstores do. What's more, you may preview these exciting novels free for 10 days. If you like them as much as we think you will, just pay the low preferred subscriber's price of just $3.75 each. *You'll save $3.00 each month off the publisher's price.* AND, your savings are even greater because there are never any shipping, handling or other hidden charges—FREE Home Delivery. Of course you can return any shipment within 10 days for full credit, no questions asked. There is no minimum number of books you must buy.

crazy, but I'm not stupid. What if the authorities show up?"

"Won't happen. They never get close to me."

"You're proud of that, aren't you? Proud of outsmarting everyone."

"Sure. Aren't you?"

At that instant, Val realized they were very much alike, and she realized that she wanted to go to bed with him. If he'd led her back upstairs to his bedroom right that minute, she wouldn't have resisted. She wondered if he could tell that she was turned on by him. How could he not tell? she thought. It must be embarrassingly obvious.

If he noticed, he didn't say anything.

They agreed on a meeting place and time. As she drove away a few minutes later, Val thought, of course he's not attracted to me. He's probably used to flashy women, not snub-nosed, freckle-faced, skinny, flat-chested *dogs* like me.

She would just have to make a point of keeping as much distance as possible from him. Remembering how humiliated she'd felt by men in the past, when she'd actually let herself fall for them, she was determined not to feel that way with Michael Parano.

It was midnight — the perfect time, he said with a grin, for committing high crimes and misdemeanors. From a hilltop command post in a luxuriously appointed motor home overlooking San Francisco Bay, he used large maps to assign positions for unloading the boats. An armada of dope-laden fishing boats made runs with military precision into the bay, right under the noses of drug enforcement agents. Michael's father had been a colonel in the army, and Michael had learned well from him.

305

Watching this man, Val saw that his senses were keyed. She shared the same sense of heightened awareness. Her hearing was more acute; she could see better. The undeniable air of danger gave everything a sharper edge. Val had never felt so excited, so frightened, so *alive!*

"There are ninety-four boats," Michael said as Val hurriedly scribbled notes, "including a ninety-foot trawler, twenty-nine barges, assorted houseboats, a dozen large fishing boats, and speedboats."

As he explained the operation to her, he paused occasionally to communicate with his people at various locations by walkie-talkie or radio.

"Where are they?" Val asked.

"One group is on the hill watching the Richmond Bay patrol, another is at the Golden Gate Bridge, and another is in a radio communications yacht on the bay."

"What happens now that the boats are entering the bay?"

"It takes exactly forty-five minutes for each boat to reach the dock, then the dock crews take over, unloading anywhere from twenty-five to thirty thousand pounds of grass in just a few minutes."

He was back on the radio, handing out orders in a brisk, no-nonsense tone. For several hours, until just before dawn, it went on, boats arriving in the bay, reaching the dock, being unloaded, leaving. At any second, Val half-expected cops to come bursting in, guns drawn, or at the very least to hear the sound of a distant bust coming over the radio.

When dawn came and the last boat had been unloaded and departed, Michael and Val sat on a blanket spread on the ground in front of the motor home, watching the sunrise. The gray of early morning turned to streaks of peach and lavender with the gold of the rising sun. In the distance, the tallest bronze spires of Golden Gate Bridge poked through the clouds.

It was cold out here, with the brisk ocean breeze blowing in, and Val huddled in her down-filled jacket. Wisps of hair blew across her cheeks as she turned to look at Michael. He was distinctly attractive; smart, funny, with a frank sensuality that was refreshing after all the gay and bisexual men she had met, not to mention the smarmy philanderers who assumed all women were available for their amusement. In an odd way, Michael had his priorities straighter than most of the glitzy people she had interviewed and partied with. She couldn't imagine him at Regine's.

"You're not in it for the money, are you?" she asked. "Even to support the winery."

"Nope. I'm into the challenge and excitement. Damn, it's fun!" There was an appealing mischievousness about him, and she thought what an absolutely adorable little boy he must have been. Val could easily picture him charming his way out of scrape after scrape, the same way he was charming his way right into her heart.

"I'm convinced I'm right, you know," he went on in a more serious voice. "It's all corrupt politics. The alcohol industry has financial clout, so alcohol's legal. The government doesn't have the right to tell me what I can and cannot put into my own body. I like to think of this as my personal protest against unfair laws."

"Like the Boston Tea Party," Val quipped.

He laughed. "Yeah. I'm a patriot." Michael continued. "When I think I'm right, I don't back down. Not for anybody. My father taught me that."

"Does he know what you do?"

"Nope. We didn't see much of each other once I left home to go to college. He's dead now."

307

"I'm sorry."

"It's okay. We fought a lot of battles with each other, especially when I told him that if they drafted me I was going to Canada. Turned out I got a medical discharge for a minor hearing problem, anyway. The point is, I didn't think it was right, killing anybody, and I wasn't going to do it."

"My father and I never saw eye to eye either," Val admitted. As soon as the words were out, she couldn't believe she'd said them. She never talked about her family to anyone except Kate, Barbara, and Shelly.

"My dad and I reached an understanding at the end, just before he died," Michael said. "He actually admitted that he was proud of me for having the guts to stand up to him. That was the only time in my whole life he said he was proud of me."

Val said pensively, "My father never said that. As far as he was concerned, I was worthless."

Michael's brown eyes were warm with compassion. "It hurts, doesn't it?"

For once, Val didn't put up a front. "Yeah," she admitted in a shaky voice. "It hurts."

She rarely cried, and never in front of anyone else, even her closest friends. Now she blinked back the tears that stung her eyes. Val couldn't believe she was letting herself get all weepy around someone who was a complete stranger, someone she really didn't know at all.

Except she felt that she did know him, because he was, in some primal way, just like her.

To her amazement, Michael reached over and hugged her. He didn't kiss her or try to feel her up. He just hugged her with all the tenderness he would show to a puppy or a kitten—or a wounded human being. It was the best feeling she had ever known, and it melted her defenses as nothing else possibly could.

When she finally looked up at him, he smiled down at her and lightly brushed her lips with his. It was the most gentle, most innocent of kisses, yet it was more erotic than any kiss she'd ever experienced.

When he drew back, Michael said, "Let's do this right. I'll pick you up at eight. We'll have dinner at a little place I like in Sausalito, and we'll get to know each other."

They lingered over dinner, in no hurry to leave. The anticipation building between them was so wonderful, Val was afraid that the actual lovemaking would be a letdown. It always had been before.

Michael, however, wasn't like those other men, and when they finally went back to his house and his bed, their lovemaking wasn't like the other times. Val felt loved, not used, and when he made certain that she came before he allowed himself to do so, it was easy and natural and she wondered why on earth it had never happened before.

So this was what it was like to have an orgasm with a man instead of through masturbation. It was completely different, infinitely more fulfilling. Val felt like a virgin, as if this was the first time and she was completely innocent.

It was wonderful and terrifying and she didn't know whether to laugh or cry. Val had never imagined that sex could be like this. Whether it was made more exciting by the sharp edge of danger inherent in his clandestine life-style or by the sheer tenderness of his touch or both, she neither knew nor cared. All that mattered was that for the first time in her life, Val was glad she was a woman.

As she lay there beside him, absorbing these

strange new feelings, she decided that she should leave. Val was used to other men sending her on her way when they were through with her, but she couldn't bear it if Michael did that. It would shatter this perfect, fragile experience.

She got up and reached for her clothes.

Propping himself up on one elbow, Michael asked in surprise, "What are you doing?"

"I'll call a cab," she said quickly. "No need for you to drive me all the way into the city and then come back here."

He reached out, closed one strong hand around her wrist, and pulled her down beside him.

"I don't want you to go, and I don't think you want to go."

She was afraid to believe what she was hearing. "But—"

"No *buts!* I want you to stay. Forever."

Val put into words a feeling she had never dared to share with anyone. "But I'm ugly. How could you possibly want me?"

For one long moment, Michael simply stared at her in amazement, then he said slowly, choosing his words with infinite care, "You are a vibrant, sensuous woman. I love the fact that you're my match in every way. I love that you're smart. You've got guts. *I love you!* And in case you're wondering, I haven't said those words to a woman in a long, long time."

Her defenses dissolved in a flood of emotion so overpowering Val could hardly bear it. She couldn't respond that she loved him, too. She could only lie there, burying her face against his hard chest, letting tears flow freely down her cheeks.

Loving Michael was dangerous, she knew, but then Val had never been one to calculate the odds.

FIVE

Kate

She sat in the garden patio of the Paramount commissary beneath the plant-covered trellis roof, sipping ice tea and going over her list of questions to ask rising young actress Lisa Boyes, this year's blonde. God help us, she thought irritably. What questions could she possibly ask this bimbette that would elicit answers that were even vaguely interesting?

The interview was due to take place right here, right now, but if she knew actresses (and after three years at *Cinema* magazine, she did), Lisa would be fashionably late. She would come breezing in, talking a mile a minute about tests and meetings and dropping names like crazy—Steven (Spielberg), Jack (Nicholson), Barbra (Streisand) . . .

The male writers at *Cinema* always seemed to get the substantial interviews with the top studio executives, brilliant directors, and hot stars while Kate got airheads like Lisa, whose main claim to fame so far was the highly erotic nude scene she'd done in a recent big box office success. In that scene, she'd performed a slow, seductive striptease in front of her bedroom window, knowing that a male neighbor was watching her every movement.

Kate was thoroughly frustrated with doing these fluff pieces, but she knew it wouldn't do any good to complain. The male editor in chief, or chief SOB, as he liked to refer to himself, would simply suggest that if she wasn't happy, she could leave. His favorite saying was, "Writers are a dime a dozen." In a sense, he wasn't far wrong. There were any number of people just dying to get Kate's job because it would give them an entrée to the film business that might lead to their big break.

Kate had had the same fantasy when she first went to work at the magazine. She dreamed of showing a spec script to one of the producers, actors, directors, or studio executives that she interviewed; it would sell for a solid six figures and she could tell her editor in chief to shove it.

Unfortunately, so far that scenario remained a fantasy. After writing three spec scripts, Kate had found only one person (a low-level assistant to a development executive) to read one of them, and his response had been lukewarm. "Interesting but not commercial," was his terse comment, followed by a crude pass at her.

She mailed her scripts to agent after agent, but they were always returned, usually without having been read.

While Kate endured one rejection after another, she watched Val's career skyrocket. Scarcely a month went by without at least one major magazine featuring her interview with a popular celebrity or an article on the latest controversial topic. Kate was happy for Val, but she would have been even happier if her own writing career was flourishing as well.

It was hard not to feel jealous as hell. There had always been an element of competition in their friendship because both wanted to do the same thing—write—and each was convinced she was better

312

than the other. In high school and college, Kate had always been the more successful simply because she had her act together in a way that the wildly rebellious Val never did. It seemed only logical that Kate would be the first to achieve success as a professional writer. She was big enough to hope that Val, too, would be successful. She just hadn't expected Val to get there first.

In her regular weekly phone calls to Barbara, Kate's frustration boiled over into endless complaints about her stalled career, but whenever she threatened to give up and become a teacher, a secretary, *anything* other than a glorified lackey, Barbara always encouraged her to keep at it. "Don't give up your dream," she would insist.

Though she always told Kate that her life with David and their daughter Allison was perfectly happy, Kate wondered if Barbara regretted giving up her dream of being a doctor. She *must* regret it on some level, but if she did, she wouldn't admit it. She talked about the stunning new house that she had helped the architect to design. She talked about David's success and Allison's precociousness. She talked about her busy schedule of Medical Wives Auxiliary meetings, chauffeuring Allison to school and to lessons, entertaining David's colleagues — but she never talked about the dream she had given up.

Maybe, Kate thought, Barbara honestly didn't mind. Maybe she had a life that was infinitely more satisfying. It certainly looked that way. Especially when Kate compared her own life to Barbara's. She came home every night to the tiny apartment she had once shared with Roger. It had seemed warm and cozy then. Now it merely seemed cramped and lonely. She drove the same aging Chevy that had been her eighteenth birthday gift from her parents. She struggled financially, barely able to make ends meet. Worst of all, she didn't seem to be getting anywhere as a screenwriter.

None of that could compare with the security and love and clear-cut sense of purpose that filled Barbara's life.

Kate's unhappy thoughts were interrupted by Lisa Boyes's arrival amid a flurry of breathless explanations. As Kate expected, Lisa explained that she was late because she'd gotten hung up on a screen test for *Steven's* new film starring *Dustin*.

Stifling an almost irresistible urge to ask dumbly, "Steven and Dustin who?" Kate suggested they order lunch and begin the interview.

Like most actresses, Lisa was on a constant diet. She grazed on a plain green salad enlivened by a few sprouts and some bean shoots and worried aloud that she might balloon from a size four to a six if she wasn't careful.

It took Kate a fast fifteen minutes to go through her list of questions. Lisa's answers were pretty much confined to a monosyllabic, "Yes," "No," and an occasional, "Gee, I don't know. I never thought about it."

The only time she strung more than a few words together was when Kate asked if she had read any interesting books lately. Lisa's chocolate brown eyes opened wide and she answered enthusiastically, "Ooh, yes! I just finished the most *fabulous* book. It's called *The Total Woman* by Marabel Morgan. Have you heard of it?"

Kate nodded, suppressing a groan.

Lisa went on animatedly. "Well, it's just *marvelous*. I learned so much from it. Especially the part where she says, um . . ." Lisa screwed up her face, trying hard to remember the exact words. "Something like, 'A total woman caters to her man's special quirks, whether they're in salads, sex, or sports.'"

She smiled at Kate. "Isn't that something? I mean,

it really tells you how to have a successful relationship."

Kate simply stared at her, incapable of responding.

She knew that, unlike Lisa, there were plenty of intelligent, interesting actresses in Hollywood, but they tended to be older (as in older than forty) and by definition on their way down, not up. *Cinema* wasn't interested in them any more than casting agents were.

Now Kate struggled to think of a question that would add some spark to the interview. She asked herself what Val would do in this situation and immediately got an outrageous idea.

Leaning forward, she said brightly, "So, Lisa, how often have the love scenes you've done on film translated into real-life love scenes with your costars?"

Lisa blinked nervously, obviously unsure how to answer the question. She wasn't straightforward enough to simply say, "It's none of your damn business." She clearly struggled with wanting to be seen as likable and cooperative, but at the same time she worried about revealing some embarrassing situations since most of her costars had been married.

Kate felt a twinge of pity for Lisa and immediately regretted the question. It really wasn't fair. Unlike Val, she couldn't go for the jugular, no matter how interesting it might make the interview.

"I'm sorry," she said. "Forget it."

Closing her notebook, Kate finished. "I think that about does it. Thanks for your time."

She had no idea how she would stretch this thin material into the requisite length for the magazine, but she would worry about that when she got back to the office. Maybe the art director could flesh it out with a *lot* of pictures.

Lisa left, trailing the strong scent of her perfume after her.

Kate remained behind to pay the bill.

"You shouldn't have let her off the hook."

Kate turned to look over her left shoulder. At the table immediately behind her, a young man sat alone. He must have come in after her because she hadn't noticed him earlier. Not that he was particularly noticeable anyway. He had nondescript brown hair, hazel eyes that were overshadowed by rather unattractive glasses, and unprepossessing features. Though he was sitting down, she could tell that he was rather short, probably no taller than her, with a thin, wiry frame.

"Didn't your mother ever teach you that it's rude to eavesdrop?" Kate responded.

"If I didn't do any of the things my mother told me not to do, life wouldn't be worth living."

He grinned, and abruptly Kate decided he wasn't so unattractive after all. There was something intensely appealing about him when he smiled. It touched her emotionally in a way she didn't quite understand.

Suddenly, she realized what it was. When he grinned in that funny, lopsided way, it made him look kind of boyish; it reminded her of her little brothers, especially Scottie.

He held out his hand. "I'm Alan Fields."

"Kate McGuire."

"You write for *Cinema*, don't you?"

"Unfortunately, yes. Do you read it?"

"Yeah, it's part of my job. I'm an assistant to a vice president here. I have to read and summarize the important articles in all the trade rags for him because he's too busy trying to establish a power base to waste his precious time reading. Actually, I'm not entirely sure he *can* read. At least, not without moving his lips. Mind if I join you?"

Kate had no intention of being picked up. She

started to say that she was just leaving, then thought, Oh, what the hell. She was in no hurry to return to the office and begin working on the article about Lisa. Besides, if Alan worked for the studio, maybe he could do something with one of her scripts.

They talked for a few minutes about their respective jobs. It immediately became clear that neither was happy. Alan wanted to be a producer. He joked, "You know, drive a black Ferrari, get the best table in the best restaurants, have Paul Newman return my calls immediately."

"You don't want much."

"Hey, there are a lot of guys in this town who have all those things who aren't nearly as smart as I am."

"Does being smart have anything to do with it?"

"No, I guess not. So, what would you really like to do?" he asked, folding his arms in front of him on the table and leaning toward Kate as if he was truly interested in what she had to say.

Her smile was rueful. "What every bartender, waiter, and parking valet in town would like to do."

"Act?"

"No, write screenplays."

"That would have been my second guess. Have you written any?"

"Three. I can proudly state that they've been rejected by the top people in town."

"Judging by your articles, you know how to write, and you're obviously bright. You're just doing something wrong."

"No kidding?"

"Cook me dinner tonight and I'll read one of them and give you my opinion." He grinned. "You don't even have to meet me at the door wearing Saran Wrap, as Marabel Morgan suggests in her silly book. Although I wouldn't object if you did."

"I see you've read *Total Woman*."

317

"Only the dirty parts. So what do you say about dinner?"

"Why should I care about your opinion?"

"Because I read all the scripts that get submitted to my boss and tell him which ones to buy and which to reject, and he listens to me."

"Good reason. So tell me, do you like roast beef?"

"I *love* it."

Unlike her mother, Kate was a lousy cook. She had no natural aptitude for it, no interest in it, and most of the time preferred to grab a hamburger and onion rings at a fast-food joint near her apartment. If Alan had said he hated roast beef, she wasn't sure what she would have done. Sticking a roast in a pan and covering it with onions, potatoes, and carrots was the best she could do in the way of home cooking.

Kate didn't bother putting candles and fresh flowers on the table, as she normally would have done for a date, or running around doing a quick cleanup job in the tiny, cluttered apartment. This wasn't a date, she told herself; she wasn't sexually attracted to Alan and she didn't care what he thought of the apartment or of her, for that matter.

He was a contact. This was networking. Period. All she cared about was what he thought of her screenplay. Kate picked the one that she felt was her best, most professional work, a subtle, sensitive story of a girl's coming of age in a small town not unlike Visalia. It was sitting on the coffee table when Alan arrived promptly at eight.

She had timed dinner to be ready almost immediately so they could get it out of the way and he could get right down to the business of reading her script. After offering him a glass of wine, which he accepted, she said, "Dinner's ready. Let's eat."

Over dinner, Alan talked about the movies the studio was doing, especially those his boss was supervising.

"They don't sound very interesting," Kate commented honestly.

"They're not supposed to be interesting. They're supposed to make money, and most of them will. The execs at Paramount, hell, at every studio, worry a lot more about their profit margin than winning Oscars or pleasing critics."

"That's why they turn out such bad movies."

Alan cocked his head to one side and eyed her quizzically. "You're a film school graduate aren't you?"

"Yes. What are you getting at?"

"Just that you're full of that film as art crap. It isn't art, it's craft, and if you're good at the craft, you can make an obscene amount of money."

"Now we're back to your theory that all that matters is how much money a movie makes."

"Yup. That's pretty much it."

"You'll make a successful producer." Her tone was dry.

He didn't look at all offended. "I hope so."

"So you can drive a black Ferrari, et cetera et cetera?"

Alan's grin dissolved as he became serious. "No. So I can be somebody."

The cockiness was gone, and there was a vulnerability in his voice that tugged at Kate's heart.

"Why don't you think you're somebody now?" she asked gently.

"Because until you have clout, you're nobody in this business. I don't have clout but I will!"

There was more bravado in his voice than real conviction. It made Kate want to reassure him as

319

she had reassured her brother Scottie when he had been unhappy or scared.

Before she could say anything, Alan quickly changed the subject. "So, where's this famous script you want me to read?"

"You don't have to read it."

"I want to. If you can take criticism."

Irritation flared within her. "I can take it."

"Okay, then let's get to it."

He settled comfortably on the sofa with the script and a glass of wine while Kate busied herself clearing off the table and washing the dishes, which unfortunately didn't take long. When she was finished, she curled up in a chair with a manuscript that needed editing and tried to focus on it, but it was no use. Her mind wasn't on the manuscript. It was on Alan and his reaction to her script. Kate kept glancing at him surreptitiously, trying to gauge his reaction by the expression on his face, which remained noncommittal. She couldn't tell if he loved it or hated it.

By the time Alan put down the script an hour later and took off his glasses to wipe them with a handkerchief, Kate was sitting on the edge of her seat, dying to know what he thought. "Well?"

He looked at her, blinked, then put the glasses back on. "I'll say this for you, you *can* write, but this will never sell."

"Why not?" she demanded angrily.

"It's too serious. There isn't enough humor, and there's no sex."

"But Allie yearns for Tom . . ."

"Yeah," Alan interrupted, "that's all she does. *Yearns.* She's passive and he's a wimp." His tone was scathing. "There's no energy, no fun, no action. No one to root for."

His words stung! Kate was determined, however,

not to show it. She'd told him she could take criticism, so she would just have to take this without getting defensive. She knew all too well that defensiveness was the mark of the amateur writer.

"Thanks for taking the time to read it," she forced herself to say through clenched teeth. As she started to take the script from him, Alan said, "Wait a minute. I'm not through."

There was no way she could take any more critical battering. "Oh, I think you've said enough."

"I know how you can fix it."

"What?" The conceit of the man! Insulting her, then calmly insisting that he could fix what he felt she'd screwed up.

Ignoring the anger in her tone and her rigid body, Alan went on eagerly. "Instead of taking thirty pages to get down to introducing Tom, open up with Allie watching him and telling her best friend how much she likes him."

"But there's no best friend in this story."

"I know. There needs to be. Allie needs someone to talk to instead of constantly looking like a lovesick cow. Novels are about introspection. Movies are about *action*."

Despite her anger, Kate had to admit he had a point. Actually, she had worried that the Allie character didn't *do* enough.

Alan went on, his enthusiasm growing. "And they could make love and it's Allie's first sexual experience, her awakening as a woman."

"But they're just seventeen."

"I hate to break this to you, but seventeen-year-olds have sex nowadays."

"I know they do, but . . ."

"No *buts*. What you have right now in this script is a fairy tale that bears no resemblance to the

321

reality of most teenagers' lives. Weren't you having sex at seventeen?"

"No!" she snapped.

He grinned. "Neither was I, but only because I couldn't find a willing girl. I didn't get lucky until I was a freshman in college."

Kate wasn't about to admit to him that it had taken her until she was a sophomore.

"If they make love," he went on, "that deepens the relationship and puts more at stake. Then you're dealing with something of substance."

Her last ounce of resistance died. He was absolutely right.

"The whole point of the story can be whether they stay together instead of will they ever get together," she said slowly, thinking out loud.

"Exactly. The audience will care about that in a way that they couldn't possibly care now."

Kate sat down next to Alan on the sofa and, taking the script from him, began flipping through the pages. "You think the story should begin here, around page thirty?"

"Yup."

Picking up a pen from a nearby table, she began scribbling notes on the script. "When should the love scene occur?"

Alan moved closer to her and skimmed through the pages. "Let's see . . ."

He stayed until one o'clock in the morning working on the script with Kate. Her initial resistance had turned to enthusiasm when she began to realize just how good his ideas were. She was sorry when he finally said he had to go. At the door, Alan said, "Thanks for dinner."

"Thanks for the help."

"Want to do some more work on it tomorrow night?"

"Sure."

"I'll bring a pizza over. You don't strike me as the domestic type who likes to cook every night."

She laughed. "No."

"What kind of pizza do you like?"

"Pepperoni."

"Me, too. It's astounding how compatible we are."

"Because we like the same pizza?"

"Yeah. Similar taste in pizza is important in a relationship."

Her voice was just a little unsteady. "I didn't realize we had a relationship."

"Of course we do. Didn't you notice?"

He leaned toward her and his lips lightly brushed hers. The tentative nature of the kiss betrayed the insecurity beneath his bravado. He whispered, "Goodnight, Kate."

"Good-night, Alan."

As she watched him walk down the sidewalk toward his car, she realized that she hadn't felt quite this lighthearted since Roger had left.

Every night for a month they worked on the script, either at her apartment or at his larger, more comfortable one on the outskirts of Beverly Hills. As they got to know each other, Kate realized that Alan's smart-aleck attitude masked a tremendous inferiority complex. Born and raised in a small town in Oklahoma, Alan was the oldest of five children. His father worked at the local oil refinery and his mother was a housewife. They had never made it through high school and wanted nothing more for Alan than a steady job at the refinery and an early marriage to a nice girl who would give them lots of grandchildren.

He wasn't particularly attractive, was hopeless at sports, and was poor. Only his intellect set Alan apart. Among the good ol' boy redneck population of Enid, Oklahoma, in the sixties, that wasn't considered of much value. Like Kate, once he got a scholarship to the University of Southern California, he never looked back.

Alan was now thirty years old and he had a plan—to be a film producer by thirty-five and a millionaire by forty. He wanted this with a hunger that bordered on desperation. Kate hoped he achieved his goals because she realized that he would never be happy settling for less.

Considering how different their views on movies were, it was amazing how well they meshed as collaborators. Kate finally decided they were similar to Lennon and McCartney of the Beatles: like Paul McCartney, she tended to write in a soft, sensitive style; like John Lennon, Alan tended to be sharper, more acerbic. Together, they hit a happy medium, neither too maudlin nor too hard.

Late one night during that month, Kate suggested to Alan that he might as well stay at her place since it was so late. Her meaning was unmistakable. She knew that if she waited for him to make the first move, they would never make love. Despite his glib humor and cocky air, Alan wouldn't put his fragile ego on the line and risk rejection.

That night, they indeed became lovers. As they sat next to each other on the sofa, she put her arms around his neck and drew him into a long kiss. Kate felt open, ready, eager to be loved again as she hadn't been loved since she let Roger walk out of her life forever. All of her—her body, her soul—waited for the fulfillment she was sure Alan could provide.

She'd had two very brief, unsatisfying relationships

324

since Roger had left. This, she was certain, would be different. Since that first night, she'd felt a bond with Alan, a bond that grew stronger the more they came to know each other. They came from the same background, shared the same ambition to be enormously successful. Both needed to be loved. Surely that was enough.

Kate was surprised and dismayed to learn that it wasn't.

She lay there afterward, wondering what had gone wrong. On the surface, everything went smoothly. She even had an orgasm, eventually, but inside . . . *nothing*. There was none of the warmth she'd known with Roger. Making love to him had been so easy, despite their inexperience. Making love to Alan had been work. Not entirely successful work.

She told herself it would get better. Naturally, no relationship could recapture the special feelings of first love. She and Alan would gradually develop an even better relationship than she'd known with Roger. It wasn't Alan's fault that she'd been less than swept away. She just needed to try harder.

Already she had begun to need him, and needing him caused her to make excuses for him.

The night they finished the rewrite of the script, they celebrated and got very drunk. Alan proposed. Kate accepted. The next thing they knew, they were on a red-eye flight to Las Vegas, drinking more champagne and giggling like a couple of teenagers. They didn't think about inviting friends or relatives. They didn't think about anything except how exciting it was to run off together like this.

Even the tacky pink decor of the god-awful Chapel of Everlasting Love on the glittering Vegas strip couldn't dampen their exuberance. On the flight back, Alan talked about what they would do when the script sold—he was totally confident it would—

while Kate started thinking about a new story they could write together.

Back in Alan's bed, they snuggled together and fantasized about what they would do when they were rich and famous.

"A place at the beach," Kate said.

"A new car," Alan said.

Both were filled with a boundless optimism. They were starting out at the bottom together, and together they would make it to the top. Struggling toward success, against overwhelming odds, would strengthen the powerful bond between them. Kate was certain of it.

As she fell asleep with Alan's arm around her, she felt, for the first time since her estrangement from her father, that she had a man in her life who would always be there for her.

Kate would never be afraid or lonely again.

SIX

Shelly

She sat on a hard bench seat on the Metro, trying to decipher the guidebook. Shelly was completely lost. No matter how many times she took the subway, she never felt entirely comfortable with it. When the train stopped at a station, she got out and entered the next train, hoping it was the right one.

She sat there, eyes downcast, not looking at anyone. After six years in Paris, Shelly knew it could be dangerous making eye contact with strangers. Out of the corner of her eye, she noticed a strikingly handsome young man watching her. He appeared to be about her age, in his mid-twenties. He had black hair, ice-blue eyes, and chiseled features that hinted at generations of well-bred ancestors.

He gazed at her with those piercing blue eyes, and she found herself wishing she had dressed in something more attractive than jeans and a turquoise T-shirt. As was her habit on days when she wasn't working, Shelly wore no makeup and her hair was pulled back in a ponytail.

When the man caught her looking at him, he smiled, a warm, kind smile completely devoid of the arrogance and conceit she would have expected from someone that spectacularly good-looking. She broke the rules and smiled back.

Just then the train pulled into another station. Realizing where she was, Shelly was no longer lost and changed trains, at last headed in the right direction. When she walked through the door of the next Metro car, she was surprised to see the young man again.

They both laughed at the coincidence, and he began to speak to her in French. Although she could speak the language somewhat, she still had difficulty understanding when it was spoken rapidly, so Shelly asked the young man to please speak more slowly. He asked, in flawless English, if she were American.

"Yes. How did you know?"

"You look like an *Americaine*. Tall, healthy, with a sweet naturalness that few Frenchwomen, especially *Parisiennes*, have."

She had no idea how to respond. "Sweet" and "natural" were no longer words that she would have used to describe herself.

The man introduced himself with an endearing air of formality. "I am Philippe de Pretevel, at your service, mademoiselle."

"Shelly DeLucca," she replied, taking his outstretched hand.

He raised her hand to his lips and kissed it lightly, just as she had seen Charles Boyer do in old movies on late-night TV. Other Frenchmen had done the same thing, but Shelly had never found it as affecting as it was now.

She was leading a *Belle de Jour* existence. Like the character Catherine Deneuve played, a proper housewife who assumes a different persona moonlighting at a brothel, Shelly felt like two completely different people. She even used a pseudonym at work—Jennifer Neal, inspired by her admiration for the model-turned-actress, Jennifer O'Neill.

When she worked, she had an air of complete confidence instilled in her by Madame Justine. In bed, she had become a consummate actress—clients asked for her over and over again—but outside of work, she was still the same shy, insecure young woman she had always been.

Now, with this young man, her shyness was even more intense.

He had no such problem as he talked easily, explaining that he took the Metro because it was the quickest way to get around Paris, where the traffic situation had become unbearable. He asked simple, straightforward questions. How long had she lived in Paris? Where was she from? What did she do?

Without saying very much, Shelly managed to give the impression she was from a comfortable background and had decided to model in Paris as a lark. She wasn't surprised when he got out with her when the train reached her destination, though she doubted very much that it was his destination as well. On the street outside, she told him she had an appointment at a nearby beauty salon and so must take her leave of him.

He asked, "May I see you again?"

There were any number of polite rebuffs she could have made. To her surprise, she simply spoke the truth. "Yes, I'd like to see you again."

They settled on dinner that night. Once more taking her hand gently in his and kissing it ever so lightly, Philippe de Pretevel turned and went back down into the subway.

Later, sitting in the chair at the salon while the stylist chattered away, Shelly was startled to realize what had just happened. She had opened the door to her heart—just a little.

* * *

Lassere, an elegant and expensive restaurant, was one of the few in Paris where Shelly hadn't dined with a client. She was glad. It made everything seem nicer, somehow, untainted by association with her work. When the doorman greeted Philippe by name, she realized he must come here quite often and thus that he must be fairly well-off, as his silver Jaguar also attested to, but it didn't really matter to her if Philippe had money or not.

The dining room was filled with elegantly dressed patrons. In the soft light of glittering crystal chandeliers, multicolored jewels sparkled among the silk and satin gowns of the wealthy. In contrast, Shelly was almost primly dressed in the first thing she had bought when she arrived in Paris, a demure gown of white gossamer silk threaded with silver. High-necked, long-sleeved, with a tight bodice that flared into a full skirt that nearly reached her ankles, the dress reminded her of Cinderella. In it, she felt innocent again, and almost happy.

When Philippe saw her, he said softly, "You look like moonlight."

Shelly rarely drank, out of fear of losing control, but she felt so relaxed with Philippe that she allowed herself to enjoy the warmth of the wine he chose. As they ate a five-course meal that began with a light whitefish from Australia and ended with a dessert of raspberry cream, she listened, entranced, as he talked of his background, his family, his work. He was the eldest son of a marquess, and his family had a townhouse in Paris and an ancestral estate southeast of the city. Descendants of the aristocratic Bourbons, they were prominent bankers. Philippe had gone to work in his father's bank right after graduating from the Sorbonne with a degree in international economics.

"I want to work in our branches throughout the world," he said eagerly. "London, New York, Hong Kong. It would be so exciting to see the world, but of course eventually I will return to Paris to raise my children."

She smiled at him. "You're not even married and already you talk of children."

"Of course. Business is necessary. One must work hard, be responsible. That has been instilled in me for as long as I can remember. But marriage, children, *family* — those are the most important things in life."

"You must come from a close, happy family," Shelly said with just a hint of wistfulness.

"Of course. Don't you?"

She hesitated. "My father . . . died when I was very young. I never knew him. My mother never remarried. It was rather lonely at times."

Philippe took her hand reassuringly. *"Pauvre enfant.* You had not my advantages — lots of brothers and sisters to play with, a mother and father who adored us, many happy memories of holidays when we gathered together with aunts, uncles, and cousins."

Listening to him, to the sheer joy in his voice, Shelly felt acutely what she had missed: love and closeness and happiness. Suddenly Philippe stopped talking, his blue eyes softening with concern. "You look so sad, Shelly. What is it? What's wrong?"

She shook her head. "Nothing. Go on. Tell me more about your family."

Instead of resuming his narrative, he looked at her intently, as if trying very hard to understand her. "You remind me of the fairy tales my mother used to read to me when I was very young. There was always a beautiful princess under a terrible spell, waiting for a prince to save her."

This isn't a fairy tale, Shelly thought. I'm not Cinderella, and even though you are unbelievably wonderful, you are no prince. If you knew the truth about me, we wouldn't be here right now. We would be in bed somewhere, and you would be extracting every last franc's worth of pleasure from me.

Philippe went on. "Do you know the very first thing I noticed about you?"

She shook her head.

"How utterly perfect you are. Your beauty is so natural, without need of artifice or camouflage. Do you know what the second thing was?"

Again, she shook her head.

"How vulnerable you are. It made me want to protect you, and here I don't even know what I must protect you from!"

Shelly blinked back tears. He was making her feel emotions she didn't want to feel. Before she could put a safe distance between them, Philippe said, "Let's leave now, shall we?"

"Yes. I . . . I have to get up early tomorrow. I'm working," she lied. Her job wasn't until the next night, when she was scheduled to attend a state dinner with a visiting American diplomat who only wanted to be seen with her to hide his homosexuality.

Instead of taking her straight home, Philippe drove to the river, where they walked along the Quai de Bethune, which was deserted this late at night but not dark. Floodlights turned the huge poplar trees black and silver; trees, the stone facades, and the towers on the nearby bridges were all transformed by the artificial light into objects that didn't look quite real. In the distance, Shelly could see the spires of Notre Dame soaring majestically into the star-studded night sky.

The river was especially beautiful on this warm

spring night. By day, it was a dark, shining ribbon, but at night, it became a thing of mystery, laced with silver and gold. Looking out at the Pont Marie, arching gracefully over the river, and at the moonlight casting paths that glistened like diamonds, Shelly whispered, "It's like a fantasy. It isn't real at all."

"*You* are the fantasy," Philippe responded, a catch in his voice.

She smiled.

"Do you believe in love at first sight?" he asked.

Her smile faded. "No."

"I do. Do you know what Richard de Fournival said in the thirteenth century?"

She shook her head.

"He said, 'Love is a folly of the mind, an unquenchable fire, a hunger without surfeit.' That is how I feel about you, Shelly, and I haven't even kissed you yet."

He drew her to him gently, his arms encircling her. Bending his head, his mouth found hers. For once, Shelly didn't stiffen and withdraw. She let herself taste his lips, feel the slight pressure of his hands splayed against her back. The question that had hovered at the back of her mind since that first moment was answered. Was this a man with whom she could lower her defenses and let herself feel the attraction between a man and a woman?

Yes. Oh, yes.

It was the sweetest kiss Shelly had ever known or imagined. She sensed that Philippe was making a tremendous effort to control his desire for her; therefore, she needn't fear that he would demand more than just the feel of her lips on his.

She felt that she'd stepped out of the sordid reality of her day-to-day life into a wonderland of magic and beauty and love. At that moment, Shelly knew that for the first time in her life she was falling in love.

When he finally pulled away, neither spoke. Philippe took her hand as they walked back along the river toward the car. "I'll take you home now," he said.

She nodded.

At her apartment, she unlocked the door before turning to face Philippe. Her heart was so full, there was so much she wanted to say, but she couldn't find the words.

"How soon may I see you again?"

She longed to say, "Tomorrow," but couldn't because of her lie about work. "The day after tomorrow."

"Is ten o'clock in the morning too early?"

"No, but don't you have to work?"

The corners of his mouth turned up in a slow, provocative smile. "I'll take the day off. Play hooky, I think you Americans call it. I've never done that before, but this . . . this is important."

He kissed her again, and this time it was the most fleeting, tantalizing of kisses. Then he whispered, "Good-night," and left.

Later, as Shelly lay in bed unable to sleep, she thought, This is what Sleeping Beauty must have felt like when she was awakened from that long, long sleep.

They saw each other nearly every day for two weeks. She turned down jobs from Madame Justine, taking only those she was already committed to. It was especially difficult now going to bed with clients because Shelly was finding it harder and harder to simply remove herself emotionally while they used her sexually.

Though Philippe's kisses became more ardent, he never pressed for more, taking her shyness and reserve for inexperience. Desire built within her, growing stronger each time she was with him. For the first time since Steven Ashe, Shelly *wanted* to make love, to feel a man's touch on her skin, to lie beside him and open herself to him, but she held back, afraid of seeming too forward and therefore shattering his illusion of her innocence.

At the end of their second week, Philippe invited her to meet his parents, who were spending the weekend at their country estate. She changed clothes a dozen times before finally settling on a pale blue linen suit with a white silk blouse. As always with Philippe, she wore little makeup and pulled her hair back with a ribbon.

The château was fifty miles southeast of Paris in the Île-de-France, the green belt surrounding the city. "This area has been painted by all the great ones — Renoir, Monet, Cézanne," Philippe explained as they drove down narrow lanes shaded by the gracefully arching canopies of trees.

"It's so beautiful."

"It's the heart of France. There are Romanesque ruins from Caesar's army, Gothic cathedrals, castles, forests, quaint villages. Ah, here we are."

He turned up a long, forested drive, the thick foliage obscuring the château itself for several minutes.

"You'll see the house in a moment."

When the Château de Pretevel finally came into view, she knew she would never forget that first breathless vision. It was magnificent! Built of cream-colored brick, it was three stories tall in the center, with flanking two-story wings. Tall windows with slate blue shutters looked out on a wide sweep of lawn. A stone terrace ran the length of the house, with broad steps leading down to the lawns and, in the distance, a small artificial lake.

"Philippe, it's lovely!"

"Yes." He smiled at her. "But not as lovely as you."

They pulled to a stop near the front steps, and Shelly saw the marquess, Roland, and his wife, Cecile, waiting to greet them. The marquess was an older version of Philippe, tall and handsome with gray flecks in his black hair. His wife was a petite blonde with a warm smile.

While Philippe greeted his father, his mother took Shelly's hands and said in English, "Welcome to our home, Mademoiselle DeLucca. Our son has told us so much about you."

Her husband added gallantly, "But his words did not do justice to your beauty. You are everything he said, and more."

Shelly was speechless in the face of such a warm welcome. She murmured a soft, breathless, "Thank you," then Philippe was at her side, his arm around her reassuringly.

"All the family is here," his mother said as they walked into the house. "I hope, my dear, that you do not feel overwhelmed by so many de Pretevels. The twins, especially, can be little pests, but then, they are only twelve, a difficult age for boys. The girls, Eleanore and Lysette, are dying to ask you about being a model. They will probably pester you even more than the boys."

"I don't mind," Shelly replied honestly. As they entered the hallway, lined with marble columns, she went on, "Your home is so beautiful. Has it always been in your family?"

"Amazingly enough, yes. Fifteen generations of de Pretevels have been born and died here since Louis XIV gave the land to Arnaud de Pretevel in the mid-sixteen hundreds. Come, let me show you around the house while the men settle themselves in

336

the sitting room and start talking business."

The sitting room that opened off the entryway was a large, high-ceilinged room made sunny and cheerful by several French doors opening onto the terrace. A massive fireplace, with a gray marble mantel, dominated the room while tall vases and round, fat bronze bowls stuffed nearly to overflowing with fresh flowers added color. The polished oak floor was covered with several small area rugs in soft shades of peach and cream and blue.

"And this is the *chambre du Roi*," Cecile explained, leading Shelly into a spacious, richly decorated room. "During the reign of Louis XVI, every château was required to have a room in which he could be received at any time."

With its ornately carved ceiling and walls covered with peach-colored silk wallpaper and matching velvet drapes, the room was impressive, indeed. Shelly had been in many grand houses, but she had never seen a room to match this.

"We don't really use it," Cecile explained. "It's too formal to be comfortable. With so many children, it is nicer to be more casual."

They went through many other rooms, all of them filled with photographs, paintings, and mementos of the long de Pretevel line. Shelly had expected the château to be impressive, but she wasn't prepared for the atmosphere of warmth and comfort. This was no cold showplace but a home full of love and laughter.

Glancing at her watch, Cecile said, "Oh, dear. We'd better hurry out to the terrace. Luncheon is being served outside on this beautiful day, and I'm afraid we're a bit late."

The terrace was plain, save for the traditional French boxed orange trees, but the view of the gardens was breathtaking on this perfect spring day, when all the flowers were in bloom. There seemed to be thousands of flowers of every conceivable color and variety. Beyond them, weeping willows and red-and-pink rhododendron bushes lined the small lake. A narrow wooden bridge spanned part of the lake and led to a tiny island with a white gazebo. It was an incredibly romantic setting; Shelly hoped Philippe would take her for a walk out to the gazebo later.

The entire de Pretevel clan was seated around the table when Shelly and Cecile arrived. The marquess introduced his daughters, two lovely, dark-haired girls, and his twin sons. The girls were as pretty as their mother, the boys as handsome as their father. They were all clearly fascinated to meet her, the boys especially staring intently at her, then whispering between themselves and giggling.

The marquess ordered them to behave, but Shelly didn't mind. They were just being little boys, after all. As Cecile had predicted, Philippe's sisters questioned her about modeling, and during lunch, the marquess asked a few discreet questions concerning Shelly's background in such a way that he didn't seem to be checking her out. The longer she was there, the more comfortable she felt, and her shyness gradually left her.

It was all so perfect. The loving, happy family chattering animatedly among themselves, making a point of including her in the conversation. The lovely setting. And Philippe, sitting next to her. Every once in a while, he reached under the table to give her hand a reassuring squeeze.

He took advantage of a particularly loud exchange between his little brothers to whisper to Shelly, "I knew they would adore you as I do."

Afterward, as if reading her mind, he suggested a walk down to the gazebo. When his brothers wanted to come along, he told them "No" in a firm, no-nonsense tone they clearly recognized, as they didn't

338

press the issue. Philippe led Shelly away.

In the gazebo, they sat on a cushion-covered bench and looked out at the lake.

"What do you think of my home, my family?" Philippe asked.

"They're . . . absolutely perfect."

"I'm very glad you feel that way. It means a great deal to me." He hesitated, and when he finally spoke again, his voice was uncharacteristically nervous. "Shelly, I have something for you. I wanted to give it to you here, in this place that is very special."

Taking a small gold-wrapped box from the inside pocket of his white blazer, Philippe handed it to her.

She knew what it was before she opened it. Even so, Shelly was awed by the magnificence of the ring.

"The diamond is from the crown of Napoléon," Philippe explained. "The sapphires surrounding it are from Josephine's jeweled choker."

She looked at him, her violet eyes glistening with tears.

"This is where my father proposed to my mother. I wanted to give you this ring here because I am asking you to marry me. We will celebrate our marriage here. My home, like my heart, is yours."

He kissed her.

Shelly gave in to everything she was feeling—the sweetness of his lips on hers, the love she felt for him. She let herself glory in it all. When the kiss ended, Philippe looked at her long and searchingly, waiting for her answer.

There was no question that Shelly wanted to share this idyllic life with Philippe; oh, how she wanted to become part of this family. But what if he found out that she worked for Madame Justine? She had been with so many men, several of them in the highest echelons of French politics and business. What if they should happen to meet and one told Philippe of her secret?

Philippe had said he wanted to work overseas. Maybe if she could persuade him to leave soon, maybe if they didn't return to France for several years, surely by then her clients would have forgotten her.

It was a terrible risk, but Shelly had to take it.

Back in Paris, she went to Madame Justine and told her she was quitting to get married. Shelly hadn't known what to expect—cold anger or terrifying fury—but she knew without a doubt there would be a response, a formidable one. Shelly had made a great deal of money for her, and Madame Justine wasn't the sort of businesswoman to willingly relinquish a profitable situation.

As she faced the older woman in the sitting room of her exquisite apartment, Shelly waited, hands clenched in her lap, heart beating rapidly with nervousness.

For a long moment, Madame Justine didn't speak but merely looked at Shelly in a manner that suggested profound disappointment. When she finally spoke, her words were as sharp as knives. "Do you expect me to wish you well? Perhaps to buy you a wedding present?"

"No." Shelly's voice shook. She took a moment to compose herself. She had to be strong. "I love him and he loves me."

"How touching."

"Please let me go."

"But how can I stop you? You are perfectly free."

Hope leapt within her. "Then . . . you won't tell him?"

"Of course not. Why should I do that?"

It was all Shelly could do to keep from bursting

into tears of relief, but she knew she mustn't fall apart in front of this woman. "Thank you," she murmured, rising to leave.

Madame Justine said, "There is just one final thing. A matter of business."

Shelly froze.

"You have some commitments."

"But . . ."

"You understand, my reputation is at stake. I must meet my commitments, and I expect you to meet yours."

The thought of being with other men now, after having fallen in love with Philippe, was abhorrent, but she had no choice. If she refused, Madame Justine would destroy her. Shelly had heard stories of the woman's wrath when crossed.

Meeting Madame Justine's look, Shelly said, "Very well. I will meet my current commitments, but no more."

Madame Justine's smile was triumphant.

For the next month, Shelly juggled assignations with clients along with preparations for her wedding. It was horrible being with those men, but every time she left a client, she told herself she was that much closer to spending the rest of her life with Philippe.

When Shelly was with him, she felt consumed with guilt over her subterfuge. Despite their engagement, he still treated her with perfect respect, and she promised herself that she would make this up to him by being the very best wife he could possibly want.

Two weeks before the wedding, Shelly finished with her last client. At Madame Justine's to collect her pay, she said in relief, "That's it, then. I'm finished."

"Not exactly. You have one more client."

"No!" Shelly exploded. "Last night was the last one!"

Madame Justine remained unmoved. "One more client. Your last, I promise you. Judging by the person who referred him to me, he must be from a very influential family. Were I to disappoint him, others in his social circle would hear of it and it would adversely affect my business. Naturally, I cannot allow that."

"Is this someone I know?" Shelly asked, thinking that perhaps she could talk to the man and excuse herself.

"No, it's a new client."

"I can't do this," she whispered.

"You can and you will, or I shall see to it that you regret it bitterly for the rest of your life. No one crosses me, Shelly. *No one!*"

Shelly's voice was so small and soft that the words were barely audible. "Very well."

"Good."

Madame Justine handed her a slip of paper with the address of the Hotel Meurice. "His name is Monsieur Hugo, a *nom de guerre,* I am certain. He will be waiting in the lobby at three o'clock this afternoon."

Her dark eyes narrowed. "Don't be late, Shelly. Clients don't like to be kept waiting."

Shortly before three o'clock, Shelly stepped out of a taxi in front of the hotel on the Rue de Rivoli. The lobby was lined with marble and gold and mahogany mirrors; even the ceiling was mirrored.

Walking up to the receptionist behind the front desk, she asked for Monsieur Hugo. The woman pointed toward a young man sitting in a chair at the far corner of the lobby, engrossed in a newspaper.

He was impeccably dressed in a well-tailored suit and had black hair. Though his eyes were downcast, Shelly knew what color they were — sapphire.

For a second, she simply stood there, unable to move, to breathe, to think, then she bolted outside, flagged down a passing taxi, and collapsed into the backseat. A few minutes later, she was shown into Madame Justine's sitting room.

"What are you doing here? You'll be late for Monsieur Hugo!"

"His name is Philippe de Pretevel, and he's my fiancé!" Shelly sobbed, "I couldn't go through with it. Surely you understand. I *couldn't!* We haven't even slept together yet."

Madame Justine's lips curved in a humorless smile. "So. You have denied him your charms until your wedding night, and he, being a normal, healthy young man, has turned to my service. How ironic. Colette would have found it amusing, I am sure."

"I can't go back there. You'll have to send someone else."

"No one else is available at such short notice. You will go back."

"But he'll know what I've done, what I am."

"That is your problem, not mine. Go now. You have kept him waiting long enough."

"I can't!"

"You can and you will, or I will tell him myself. I will tell him exactly how many men you have been with. How do you think he would take that?"

Shelly felt nausea well up within her. There was no way out. No way. Maybe it was only right, after all, she realized unhappily. Lying to Philippe, abusing his touching trust in her, had been wrong. How could she have considered marrying him without being honest?

Without saying another word to Madame Justine,

Shelly turned and walked out of the apartment. Back at the hotel, she stood for a moment, staring at the back of Philippe's head. He was still reading the paper, but occasionally he glanced at his watch impatiently.

Even though she knew that telling him the truth was the right thing to do, Shelly would have given anything in the world—even her life—not to have to confront him. The moment she did, all his lovely illusions about her would be shattered forever.

Gathering every ounce of courage she possessed, she walked over and stopped directly in front of him.

Philippe looked up, an expectant half-smile on his lips. The moment he saw her, the smile dissolved into stunned amazement. He stood up. "Shelly! What on earth are you doing here?"

It was a moment before any words would come out. "I believe . . . you're expecting me."

Understanding dawned, and with it came revulsion. "No! No!"

"Please let me explain, Philippe."

His expression was so devastated, so hurt beyond description that the explanation died on her lips. What could she possibly say that would make it all right? Nothing. Even if she pointed out to him that his use of an escort service compromised him as much as her work for that service, it wouldn't matter. The double standard was alive and well.

He turned on his heel, not unlike a military pivot, strode out of the lobby, and climbed into a taxi waiting by the entrance. Shelly watched as the taxi drove off. Philippe did not look back.

That night, she put her engagement ring in a box and enclosed a note that said simply, "I am more sorry than you will ever know." She wrapped it and mailed it.

The next day, Shelly packed her clothes, cleared out her checking account, notified her landlord that she was leaving, and caught the first flight she could get out of Paris. She didn't care where it was going.

SEVEN

Kate

Kate and Alan sat in the darkened theater, listening to the laughter of the people surrounding them. Kate couldn't believe it. They were only a few minutes into the movie and already *Cutting Loose* had the sweet smell of success. She could sense it in the way the audience laughed heartily at the funniest lines; the way they sat alertly, their entire attention focused on the screen instead of murmuring to each other and rustling in their seats out of boredom.

This was no ordinary crowd, either. The premiere screening on the Paramount Studio lot played only to top employees of the studio and other industry insiders. It was a tough crowd, both knowledgeable and critical. To Kate and Alan's intense relief, these people actually seemed to love *Cutting Loose*.

The script they'd worked so hard on had sold with surprising quickness to Paramount. Alan promptly quit his job there, Kate quit hers at *Cinema*, and they began working on a second script that was much like the first, a raunchy teen sex comedy.

Now, as they sat here watching their first produced movie, Kate felt on top of the world. It was the most incredible high, watching something she'd written come to life on a screen! She remembered going to the Fox Theater in Visalia as a kid, watching Marilyn Monroe, Elvis Presley, and Dean Martin and Jerry Lewis, losing herself completely in a larger-than-life world that she was sure she could never, ever participate in. After all, movies weren't real, and people like her, kids from small towns in the middle of nowhere, could never hope to be part of their glamour and fantasy.

Yet here she sat, watching a movie that *she* had written. The actors spoke *her* words. Kate was on the inside looking out, and the view was everything she'd ever imagined it to be! What exhilaration she felt! Being represented by one of the top agencies in town. Having lunch at expensive Beverly Hills restaurants. Talking deals. Signing six-figure contracts.

It would have been absolutely perfect if only her original vision of the film hadn't ended up being compromised so drastically. The changes that Alan made were considerable; then the studio wanted a rewrite to make it even more commercial. The director and leading actor and actress had suggestions. By the time the process was finished, her sweet, lyrical, coming-of-age story had evolved into an outrageous, sexy romp.

When Kate occasionally voiced regret over the qualities of sensitivity and substance that had been lost along the way, Alan reminded her that this script had sold for a hundred thousand dollars. She was now driving a new Mustang and helping her brothers with their expenses at Fresno State University, the closest major college to Visalia. Unlike her, they hadn't wanted to go too far from home.

Even more important than the money was the fact that the script made it to the screen. A lot of screenplays were purchased but were often shelved.

Not only did *Cutting Loose* get made, it looked like it was going to be a big box-office hit.

Alan leaned over and whispered in a voice tight with barely suppressed excitement. "We did it, babe! We'll get two hundred and fifty grand for the next one!"

She knew enough about the business to realize he was right. If *Cutting Loose* did as well when it opened as it was doing with this preview audience, they would be able to raise their price considerably. Their ambitious young agent, Russ Carlisle, who was at least as hungry for success as they were, would see to that.

Kate couldn't even imagine that much money. It was more than her father had earned in twenty years as a small town cop; more than her mother would probably earn over the rest of her life in her job as a seamstress. No matter how often she reassured herself she had worked hard for this and deserved it, on some deep level Kate was uncomfortable. Why should she have so much more than her parents, her grandparents, *anyone* else in her family? They had worked hard, too, at back-breaking manual labor, and they hadn't been rewarded like this.

Along with Kate's exhilaration came fear. Until now, failure had been her worst nightmare. To her surprise, as she sensed the thrilling possibility of success growing stronger with each scene in the movie, she felt the first faint suspicion that success might be more complicated than she'd ever realized. Like failure, it might have its own price. She had no idea yet what that price might be, but she had an uneasy sense it would be high.

Kate's thoughts were interrupted by the sound of rousing applause as the final scene in *Cutting Loose* faded to black and the end credits rolled. Alan leaned over and gave her a big hug that left her breathless. "All right!" he shouted. His rather plain face was transformed by triumph. Kate felt her own face flush with excitement.

Nevertheless, even as they gloried in the success they'd achieved together, a bittersweet thought struck her forcefully: No matter what happens in the future, we'll never be quite this close and happy again.

As they moved with the flow of the dense crowd toward the commissary, where a party was to be held, Kate listened with eager curiosity to the comments of the people around her.

"What a good movie . . ."

"A lot of fun . . ."

"I can't believe that scene in the bathroom . . ."

"I nearly died laughing . . ."

"Wild, really wild . . ."

"Great script . . ."

Turning to Alan, she said, "Did you hear that? *Great script!*"

He grinned in that adorable way that melted her heart. "Damn right it's a great script, and there are gonna be a lot more just like it!"

"Our second one is just like it. Let's try something different next time. I have an idea for a drama . . ."

Busy surveying the crowd making its way into the commissary, Alan barely paid attention to her. Without looking, he said distractedly, "What? Don't be silly. We've got to give them what they want, another teen sex comedy." Before she could respond, he went on, "Look, there's the producer, Hank Quinn. Let's talk to him."

They had met Quinn only once, shortly after he

349

had agreed to produce the movie for Paramount. Following that brief initial meeting, his assistant had passed on Quinn's notes on changes in the script. Kate and Alan had religiously incorporated those notes into the rewrite. They knew if they didn't do exactly as Quinn wanted, he would simply fire them and hire another writer.

Quinn's disdain for writers was no worse than most, just like the other producers, directors, and studio and network executives. Kate knew it had always been that way and always would be. If she had any sense, she wouldn't let it get to her. "Take the money and run," Alan liked to say. Deep inside, she couldn't entirely suppress a feeling of resentment at being at the mercy of these people, who were almost always men and were usually assholes — or worse, stupid.

Shaking her head, she said, "I don't think he wants to talk to us, and I know I don't want to talk to him. I get intimidated just looking at him."

"You can't let 'em intimidate you! Just remember, they can kill you but they can't eat you."

Kate grinned. "I'm not so sure about that."

"I don't intend to spend the rest of my career sucking up to guys like Quinn. I want to *be* Quinn! But for now, I've got to play the game and do some schmoozing. Be right back."

She watched Alan walk up to Quinn and begin talking to him. All around her, people were engaged in intense conversations. She knew deals were being made or broken. No one was talking about politics, the weather, religion, or any of the subjects that people normally discussed at parties. They were all talking business, *film* business.

It was 1978, Carter was president, the Mideast could ignite at any moment. Oil prices were skyrocketing, a lot was happening outside the tight-knit community known as Hollywood, but you couldn't tell it by these people. Their concerns were limited: evaluating who was on the way up and who was on the way down; comparing the latest grosses of the big studio releases; debating whether the upstart little independent production companies really posed a threat to the studios and whether cable would ever pose a threat to the networks.

Kate didn't know how to talk to these people. The few women in the room looked tough and far more sophisticated than her, and the men all looked like they wouldn't want to bother with her. Despite having lived in L.A. for nine years, and having finally broken into the film business after working on the periphery of it for five, she still didn't feel part of it.

Maybe she would eventually, Kate told herself. Maybe it was just a matter of time before she would feel comfortable in these surroundings and would be able to talk to these people as easily as she could talk to Barbara or Val or Shelly.

After all, this was her world now. She had no choice but to learn how to function in it. If she had to swim with the sharks, she'd better figure out how to do it without getting eaten.

She had lost sight of Alan in the crowd and was relieved when he finally returned. His eyes glittered with excitement and he was even higher than he'd been before.

"Quinn thinks we've got a big hit on our hands. The studio brass are already talking about increasing the promotion budget and the number of theaters it's gonna open in! Can you fucking believe it?"

She grinned. "No."

Alan went on quickly. "I told him about the new script and he's dying to read it. Says if it's as good as this one, he'll not only buy it, he'll let me co-produce and give me an office to work out of here on the lot!"

No wonder he looked so thrilled, Kate realized. A chance to produce meant everything to Alan.

"Honey, that's wonderful! I'll bet Russ will just love negotiating a co-producer deal for you."

Alan grinned. "Yeah, I can't wait to tell him. Forget piddly little screenplay fees. Now we're talkin' *real* money!"

As they drove home, he went on and on about the deal, how much he might get, where he would go from there. Kate had never seen Alan like this, so hyper and euphoric. She figured that he'd probably had a little too much to drink, but he wasn't slurring his words or walking awkwardly, so she hadn't argued when he had insisted on driving.

When they first sold *Cutting Loose,* he had bought a black BMW. People were saying that Bimmers were even better than Mercedes, and they were quickly becoming the status car of choice among successful young adults. Alan loved driving it so much he never let Kate take the wheel.

When they got home, she discovered it wasn't the excitement of the evening or a few drinks that had made Alan so high. It was a fine white powder in a plastic Baggie that he pulled from the inside pocket of his jacket.

"Quinn gave me some in the bathroom at the commissary," he explained as Kate stared at him wide-eyed. "Come on, try it. They say it makes sex great!"

Like most of the people she'd gone to college with, Kate had smoked a little grass, but coke . . .

that was something else again. When she'd interviewed people who were obviously using it, she'd thought they were rather pathetic in their false euphoria; but this was Alan, her husband, her collaborator! He was happy, and he wanted her to be happy with him. Kate didn't want to put him down, to appear rigid and self-righteous, but she couldn't stop thinking about her father and what he would think of her if he were still alive.

"We don't need that stuff to have great sex," she said with a forced laugh. Putting her arms around Alan, she coaxed. "Come on, I'll prove it."

To her relief, he didn't resist. Alan dropped the Baggie on a nearby table and followed her to the bedroom.

Later, as Alan slept soundly beside her, Kate lay wide awake. For the first time in their relationship, sex had been so bad she couldn't pretend otherwise. She'd finally faked an orgasm just to get it over with. She couldn't understand what was wrong. This should have been the happiest night of their life. They should have been closer than ever.

So why, she wondered unhappily, did she feel they were a million miles apart?

It wasn't just the coke, she knew, it was everything it represented — a drastic change in life-style, a seductive glimpse at limitless horizons. *Success.* She had wanted success badly, convinced it would redeem her and erase the soul-wrenching guilt she felt every time she thought of her father. Now that she was *this* close to achieving it, she had the awful feeling she might have been wrong.

One thing was certain. Nothing would ever again be quite the same.

* * *

Moving to Malibu in 1977 was Kate's idea, but Alan chose the house. Their second script, *Fast Track,* a teen comedy similar to their first, sold for only a few thousand less than the quarter million he had predicted. They could finally afford the real home that Kate had longed for. More important, she wanted all that it represented, including, at some point in the not-too-distant future, children.

She was godmother to Barbara's daughter, Allison, and loved buying her frilly little girl dresses and taking her out for ice cream when she visited Barbara in Visalia. She and six-year-old Allison had a special closeness uncomplicated by the deeper conflicts of a mother-daughter relationship. Allison called her "Auntie Katie" and idolized her in a way that she could never do to the mother she took for granted.

Her relationship with Allison, special as it was, however, wasn't enough. Kate wanted children of her own. She and Alan had never talked about children. She had simply assumed that, like her, of course he would want them. Until they had children, they weren't truly a family.

She had started looking at Cape Cod-style houses in the Point Dume area of Malibu, a family-oriented enclave on a peninsula off the Pacific Coast Highway. When Alan had showed her the ultramodern redwood-and-glass A-frame on a sheer cliff overlooking Trancas Beach, she had felt a stab of disappointment. It was far from the cozy, traditional home she had envisioned; but Alan wanted it.

Trancas, located just north of Malibu, was even trendier than that glitzy beach community. Many of the new young hotshot filmmakers who were taking over the film industry in the late seventies were moving out there. As always, Alan was determined to be part of whatever was "in."

So Kate gave in, telling herself that somehow she would make this a cozy home: a little paint, some wallpaper, a bouquet of fresh flowers, and it would be wonderful. When the kids came along, they would love playing on the beach.

They moved in, bringing along modern leather furniture and some very expensive limited-edition prints in a stark modern art style that Kate hated. Alan bought them anyway, insisting they were good investments.

Despite her determination to make the best of their first real home, she still felt less than happy. It was a major step up from the apartment they'd shared since their marriage and a complete change of life-style from the tiny apartment she'd lived in before that, but somehow that unpretentious apartment had seemed more like home than this imposing new house did.

The first night they were there, Kate and Alan sat on the living room floor, surrounded by unpacked boxes and empty rooms, as the furniture hadn't yet been delivered. They toasted each other with wine in plastic cups.

"This is just the beginning," Alan said. "Someday soon we'll get a house right on the beach. Russ told me a lot of deals are made by socializing with neighbors jogging on the beach and having cookouts."

Kate felt a sinking sensation. In spite of her dislike for this house, she didn't want to move again for a long, long time. She also didn't want to socialize with people just to make deals. Lately, when Alan talked about people, it was always in terms of

355

what they could do for him, how he could use them to get ahead. It bothered Kate, but she didn't know how to talk to him about it. It would sound like criticism, and she knew that despite everything, Alan remained, at heart, extremely insecure and easily hurt.

She'd known from the beginning that on an emotional level she was the strong one in the relationship, despite appearances to the contrary. Kate felt responsible for Alan's happiness. If he was down, she felt it was her job to bring him up; if he was beset by self-doubts, she reassured him he was one hell of a writer/producer. So now she swallowed her concern and told herself it would get better once he was an established producer and had gained a little more self-confidence.

Still, as they settled into life at the beach, her concern mounted. She despised the industry crowd Alan liked to party with, coke-sniffing party animals who talked only of making it big and who were in vicious competition with each other. Most important, she felt unfulfilled by the blatantly commercial, lightweight films Alan insisted they continue to make. He refused to take a chance and risk failure on serious projects. Despite their success, he was torn by the nagging suspicion that he wasn't completely accepted by the high-powered producers, directors, and studio executives of the new-generation Hollywood.

During one especially bitter argument with Kate, he had admitted that he was haunted by the sense that if they wrote one failure, he would once more be on the outside looking in, unacceptable in a business where you're either an insider or you're nothing.

In high school and college, Alan had been the

classic geek—short, slight, unathletic; the kind of boy the more athletic boys made fun of. Now he made up for that sense of failure with a vengeance, glorying in his newfound power and position.

Kate knew that women came on to him, especially when he moved from merely writing to producing as well, but she was confident that Alan would never hurt her by being unfaithful. The bond between them—the bond of two people who had come from nothing and together had achieved their wildest dreams—was too strong.

Until one day in the early spring of 1979.

Kate hadn't been feeling well for the past month so she went into town to see the doctor. Afterward, literally glowing with happiness, she decided to drop in at Alan's office unexpectedly and surprise him. Telling his secretary not to bother buzzing him, she hurried into his private office.

The young woman leaning across his desk was extremely pretty in a dark-haired, dark-eyed gamine sort of way reminiscent of the young Leslie Caron. When Kate entered, both the woman and Alan looked up sharply. They weren't doing anything— they weren't even touching—but Kate *knew*. It was all too evident in the guilty look that flashed between them in that first stunned moment.

Kate's heart sank.

"Kate!" Alan said in a determinedly cheerful voice. "What a surprise!" Turning back to the woman, he said in a tone that was all business, "I'll call your agent about that part, Mandy."

"Thanks," she replied in a nervous little voice.

She isn't a very good actress, Kate thought dully as the young woman brushed past her.

As if suddenly remembering his manners, Alan rose and crossed over to where Kate still stood in mute humiliation. Kissing her on the cheek, he asked, "So what brings you into town?"

She looked into those guileless eyes, no longer framed by glasses since he'd started wearing contacts.

"She isn't the first, is she?" Her voice was amazingly calm, as if she were someone else, someone detached and objective and uninvolved.

To his credit, Alan didn't pretend that he didn't understand the question or insist that he was innocent. There was one drawn-out moment of awkward silence before he simply said, "It doesn't mean anything. *You* are the only woman who matters to me. What we have together is the most important thing in the world to me."

"You think that saying it doesn't mean anything makes it all right? Don't you see how insulting that is? If it meant something, if you were in love with her and couldn't help yourself, then I could understand. But if it doesn't mean anything, then why do it?"

"You don't understand."

"No!"

Kate couldn't stay there, couldn't face him, couldn't say one more word to him or listen to him say one more word to her. Whirling around, she raced from the office.

Alan didn't follow.

She drove north up the Pacific Coast Highway, far past their house, nearly to Santa Barbara. As she drove, she cried. She tried to think, to come to a decision, to put things in some kind of order, but she couldn't do it. She couldn't make sense of any of it.

They had worked so hard together, had come so far. How could he do something that would threaten the life they'd built?

Finally, when it was very late and she was exhausted, Kate went home. She didn't know where else to go.

Alan sat in the living room, a book open beside him, but he didn't look as if he'd been reading. Exhaustion and worry were etched in the creases of his face and in the poignant expression in his eyes. When Kate came in, he rushed over to her and took her in his arms. She didn't respond. She simply stood there as he hugged her tightly and told her how much she meant to him. She was aware that he didn't say that he regretted the affair or that it would never happen again.

They sat down on the sofa. Kate said without preamble, "I'm pregnant. That's why I came to your office today. To tell you."

Alan looked absolutely stunned. She realized that a baby was something he hadn't for one moment considered.

Finally, he asked tentatively, "What do you want to do?"

Not, "I'm so happy. I want this child."

Not, "This is just what we need. It will pull us together again.

Kate realized, as clearly as if he'd said the words, that he wanted her to have an abortion but was afraid to suggest it. She knew that whether she had the baby or had an abortion, her marriage was over. It couldn't survive either decision.

The thought terrified her even more than the discovery of Alan's infidelity.

What was she without him? *Nothing!* She hadn't become successful until she met him. Without his support, her career would be finished. Within the film business, Alan was given almost total credit for the success of their movies. After all, he was not only the co-writer but the producer. She was merely his little wife, with whom he generously shared writing credit.

Until now, Kate hadn't realized how much their success meant to her. She saw that it was like a drug: a hard habit to kick.

When she remained silent, Alan said tiredly, "It's late. Let's go to bed and talk in the morning. Everything will look better then."

She rose and allowed herself to be led to the bedroom.

A week later, Kate sat at an outdoor café in Beverly Hills having lunch with Valerie. They hadn't seen each other in months, since the last time Val was in town to do a celebrity interview. Normally, Kate would have been excited to see her friend again and would have planned a whole day of shopping, lunch, and catching up on the latest developments in each other's lives. Now she sat in silence at the small table, fiddling aimlessly with the straw in her glass of iced tea.

Folding her arms in front of her, Val leaned across the table and looked Kate straight in the eyes. "Okay, what is it?"

"What do you mean?"

"Don't bullshit me, Kate. I know you too well. What's wrong? Either things are fucked up with Alan or they're fucked up with your career. Which is it?"

Kate looked away. "I'm pregnant."

Slowly, Val unfolded her arms and leaned back in her chair. "I see. How far along are you?"

"About seven weeks."

After a moment, Val asked, "Do you want to have it?"

"I can't."

Val didn't ask why.

"Will your doctor do an abortion?"

Kate shook her head no.

After a moment, Val said, "I had an abortion last year."

At Kate's look of amazement, she explained in an offhand tone, "It's no big deal. I mean, they're legal and everything now."

"But . . . who was the father?"

Val looked away. "I don't know."

There was an awkward pause, then Kate asked gently, "Why didn't you say anything?"

"There was nothing to say." She looked intensely uncomfortable. Finally, she admitted, "I wasn't sure how you'd feel about it. Anyway, the point is, it's not very painful, not like for Shelly, and it's easy to arrange. Would you like me to help?"

Kate nodded.

"Okay. I've got some contacts I can use to find out the best place. We'll go back to my hotel and I'll make a few calls."

An hour later, it was all arranged. Kate would go to a women's health clinic in Venice Beach the next evening at seven o'clock, take a pregnancy test, purely as a matter of form, and they would immediately perform the abortion.

Val insisted on going with her even though Kate said she was sure she could handle it by herself. Val waited in the reception area while Kate went into an examination room. It was so different from Shelly's nightmare experience in Tijuana. The clinic was modern and antiseptically clean; the nurses and doctors, all of whom were women, were efficient

361

and reassuring.

As she knew it would, her test came back positive. Dr. Oliver, who wasn't much older than Kate herself, sat down and talked to her for a few minutes, explaining the procedure and the minimal aftereffects.

"Are you sure you would like to terminate your pregnancy?" Dr. Oliver asked in a kind voice.

"Yes." Kate's voice wavered just a little.

It went very smoothly and very quickly. She was given an anesthetic before being wheeled into an operating room. The last thing she remembered was Dr. Oliver bending over her, smiling reassuringly, saying, "Don't worry, Mrs. Fields, you'll be just fine."

Some time later, she woke up in a room with a handful of other recuperating women. A nurse told Kate to rest for a few minutes until the nausea and light-headedness passed. After half an hour, she got up, got dressed, and went out to the reception room.

Val immediately put down the copy of *Ms* she had been reading and came over to Kate, taking her arm. She led her outside to the parking lot, where Kate, suddenly violently sick, vomited on the ground next to the car, one hand on the fender to steady herself.

Putting her arms around Kate's shoulders, Val said in a soft voice, "It's all right. Don't be scared. It's just a nervous reaction. I did the same thing."

When she finally raised her head, Kate looked at Val and burst into tears. Val held her tight, whispering over and over again, "I understand . . . I understand . . ."

Sadly, Kate knew that she did.

EIGHT

Barbara

A banner across one wall of the gym read RED-
WOOD HIGH SCHOOL CLASS OF 1969. Looking at it,
Barbara Browning felt bemused. Had it really been
ten years since she'd last set foot in here? It certainly didn't seem that long. The years had passed
quickly and had been full, almost too full, with raising a child, building a showplace home, running
the Medical Wives Auxiliary, entertaining often and
lavishly.

She was well aware that most people envied her;
but then, they always had. At twenty-eight, Barbara
was more beautiful than she'd been at eighteen, still
slender, her chestnut hair long and glossy, though
now it brushed the top of her shoulders instead of
falling to the middle of her back. There was nothing of the innocent young girl about her now. The
years had laid a subtle yet unmistakable aura of sophistication over her patrician beauty. There was a
new determination in the set of Barbara's small,
round chin, and the full mouth could purse tightly
in displeasure when someone failed to meet her expectations.

People commented that as she grew older she
looked more like her mother, Constance. It was

meant as a compliment, but Barbara felt a knot tighten deep in her stomach every time she heard it. Following her marriage and the birth of her daughter, Barbara had settled into an uneasy truce with her mother, interrupted by frequent arguments over who should be in control of her life.

It got better once Barbara and David moved into their own place after he completed his residency. At least she had her own home and could do as she pleased in it. Constance was far too well-mannered to simply drop in whenever she felt like it. She always called first. When Barbara didn't feel like seeing her, she could simply say that it was a bad time for a visit, Allison was fussy, the place was a mess, or she was expecting friends from the Auxiliary.

Then Barbara's father died suddenly and unexpectedly of a massive heart attack. Without her husband's career and social position to focus her considerable energy on, Constance turned all her attention to her daughter and granddaughter, trying to tell Barbara how to handle herself socially, which school to send Allison to, which contractor to use in building her house.

Barbara alternated between ignoring her mother and arguing furiously with her. It was especially galling that David usually took her mother's side. He was the complete opposite of the stereotypical son-in-law who hates his mother-in-law. He remained deeply grateful to his in-laws for their help, especially in terms of his career. When Barbara's father died, he left David in charge of a highly lucrative and well-respected practice. David had everything he'd ever dreamed of having while still a comparatively young man.

He encouraged Barbara to be just like her mother, a social force in the community. Barbara went along with his ambitions because she had nothing better to do with her time, but during those rare moments when she paused in her whirlwind schedule long enough to realize just how precisely she was repeating her mother's life, she felt intensely frustrated and angry.

The problem was, she had no idea what to do about it. Going back to college would be difficult; going on to medical school was out of the question. There was no point in getting a job. She didn't need to work for financial reasons, and besides, there weren't any jobs in Visalia she was particularly interested in doing.

Barbara began to drink much more than she'd done in the past, but when David accused her of becoming an alcoholic, she furiously denied it. She didn't have a problem, she insisted, unlike Marcy Walters, whose drunken behavior had become such an embarrassment that some of the members of the Medical Wives Auxiliary had asked Barbara to demand Marcy's resignation. Not long afterward, Marcy's husband had divorced her, to no one's surprise.

Barbara hadn't seen Marcy after that. She tried not to think about her, to wonder what had become of her. Marcy's story was too depressing. She also denied the emptiness and lack of fulfillment at the core of her life. She told herself the anger that seemed to constantly burn just below the smooth surface of her perfect existence was purely in response to her mother's domineering ways and David's workaholism. Eventually, her mother would realize she couldn't control her, David would cut back on the long hours he put in, and things would settle down.

In the meantime, Barbara kept her life as busy as

possible, with the Auxiliary, the tennis league at the local country club, the PTA, and frequent trips to Los Angeles and San Francisco to shop and to visit Val and Kate. She entertained often, focusing all her free time on decorating her house with exquisite perfection. *Anything* to fill her time and keep her mind distracted.

The reunion was just the latest in a long line of things she'd thrown herself into, devoting her considerable energy to its success. She had organized it, planning everything down to the most minute detail, from the blown-up graduation photos of successful alumni (including Kate and Val) to the local band energetically playing sixties tunes. Overhead, multicolored lights flickered off and on and gay blue-and-gold crepe paper streamers hung from the ceiling. Excitement and nostalgia filled the air, and the crowd that grew larger with each passing minute was clearly having a great time.

As Barbara moved through the packed gym, checking on things, she saw vaguely familiar faces that she couldn't connect names to. There was a stunning redhead wearing what Barbara recognized as a designer original gown that must have cost thousands of dollars. Finally she realized who the woman was: Carol Bradshaw, the class frump. Carol's fundamentalist parents had kept her in dowdy, long-sleeved, high-collared dresses when everyone else was wearing miniskirts and tank tops with plunging necklines. Clearly, Carol had changed in a big way, escaping her parents' control.

Flirting with Carol was a blond-haired young man who also looked vaguely familiar. Barbara strained to place him. That strong profile and arrogant attitude struck a chord in her memory. What was his name? Mick? Dick?

366

Rick.
Rick Paxton!

The reunion, carrying with it, as it did, strong reminders of graduation, had brought back memories of that night, but Barbara had firmly pushed them aside, dulling them with alcohol when nothing else would work. Now, staring at Rick across the room, she remembered him sitting beside Steven Ashe in the black El Dorado. She remembered Steven and Shelly leaving Nina's party, and she remembered Steven's face in that instant before she ran him down.

Barbara shuddered. No, she insisted, she would *not* think of it. She needed a drink. There was no alcohol at the party since it was being held on school grounds, but she had taken precautions. Hurrying out to the parking lot, she unlocked the glove compartment of her car and took out a small flask, drinking deeply of the vodka mixture she'd poured into it before leaving the house that night. Vodka was marvelous. It left no telltale smell.

She drank most of it, leaving a little for the drive home, and felt its reassuring sensation as it slid down her throat and began to dull the panic that had engulfed her. It was all right now. Everything was all right.

Returning to the gym, Barbara saw, to her intense relief, that Rick seemed to have left along with Carol. The other familiar faces she ran into were harmless enough. Looking at them, she realized that only a few had left Visalia after graduation, and most of those had returned, inexorably pulled back by what writer Joan Didion called the fatal lure of the valley. Of Barbara's friends in high school, only Kate, Val, and Shelly had managed to make new lives elsewhere.

367

As if on cue, Barbara saw Kate and Val sitting at a table in a corner, happily gossiping away. Shelly, of course, hadn't come to the reunion. No one expected her to do so. The three women had enjoyed a brief get-together earlier, but Barbara had been so busy overseeing the last-minute details of the reunion that they hadn't had much chance to talk. She'd felt uneasy listening to them catch up with each other's career successes and was glad of an excuse to cut short the visit.

Now she joined Kate and Val at their table, sitting down with a huge sigh. "Thank God! It seems to be going all right. I can kick back and relax."

As the band played "Twist and Shout," Val looked out at the crowd on the dance floor and said, "I can't believe I came back here. I swore these people would never see me again for my dust."

"Have you seen your parents?" Kate asked.

"Yes, for about ten minutes. My father and I got in an argument, my mother cried, and I left. Before you start telling me how I should be less confrontational, may I ask how your visit with your mother went?"

Kate's expression sobered. "The same as usual. I offered to help her financially. She refused. We made polite conversation for what seemed like hours, but was only thirty minutes, then I left."

"I rest my case."

Barbara said, "I can't believe we're pushing thirty and still fighting with our parents."

"I can't believe the way these people look," Val responded. "The women are wearing midis instead of minis, but they look like they still get their hair done at the same place, and I swear the guys haven't changed one bit, except for a little less hair and a lot more belly."

Kate glanced at the small groups scattered throughout the gym. "They're still gathering in the same little cliques they belonged to in high school."

"So are we," Barbara pointed out.

They looked at each other and burst into laughter.

Kate said thoughtfully, "You know, every time I come back here, I feel like I'm caught between two worlds. The small town, working-class values I grew up with and my high style of life in L.A. Sometimes I feel like I don't fit in either place."

"You can take the girl out of the country . . ." Val quipped.

"I'm serious. I'm just beginning to appreciate the values my parents tried to teach me, but at the same time I want to taste some of the good things life has to offer. Every time I buy an expensive dress, I feel guilty because I know how hard my mother has to work to make her money."

Val nodded agreement. "The problem is we're both part of the first generation to achieve more than our parents did. We come from families who never bought new cars, who clipped coupons, and ate bologna sandwiches on white bread. Our families thought there would be just barely enough, never more than enough."

She downed the last of her Coke and grimaced. "Can you believe it? There's no fucking liquor here."

"That's because we're on school premises," Barbara explained.

"Whose stupid idea was it to hold the reunion here?"

"Mine."

Val rolled her eyes. "Shit-piss-fuck. I haven't gone this long without a drink or a smoke since, well, since high school. Excuse me while I go to the john and sneak a cigarette. God, déjà vu."

When she was gone, Kate and Barbara exchanged a wry that's-Val-for-you look.

"Have you talked to Shelly lately?" Barbara asked.

"Yeah, a couple of weeks ago. She's fine. She just moved into a new apartment in Chelsea and we're all invited to come stay with her."

"That would be fun. Taking in some West End plays, shopping at Harrods." Barbara sighed heavily. "What am I saying? I can't get away. David wouldn't know what to do with Allison for a week or two, and there's no way I would want to take her."

"I know. I can't get away either. Our next movie is about to go into production and I have a rewrite to finish."

"Listen, before Val gets back, tell me about this mysterious boyfriend of hers. She won't tell me anything about him, and when I visit her in the city, she never suggests I meet him."

"I met him once by accident. He was leaving her place just as I was arriving for a visit. He's incredibly cute and seems real pleasant, unlike some of the yahoos she's dated, and she's crazy enough about him."

"What does he do?"

Kate shook her head. "Who knows? Val won't say, which probably means he deal drugs or something else illegal or immoral."

"Why am I not surprised?"

"The funny thing is, in a strange way he seems to be good for her. She isn't doing coke anymore. I didn't want to ask too many questions that are none of my business, but I got the impression that he helped her get off the stuff. Anyway, the point is, she's happy. Maybe that's all that really matters."

Barbara didn't say anything but she caught the bittersweet tone in Kate's voice. She knew about Alan's affairs. Every time Kate discovered a new one, she would call Barbara in tears, agonizing over what to do about it. Barbara listened sympathetically but couldn't help feeling a twinge of smug superiority. *Her* husband would *never* be unfaithful. She was absolutely confident of that. Even when they argued about her drinking, David always ended up telling her how much he loved her and how important she was to him.

Just then Val returned, smelling of nicotine and looking more relaxed.

"This town is truly in a time warp," she said. "Nothing's changed. Nobody's changed. They still don't realize there's a whole other world outside the Visalia city limits." She turned to Barbara. "How can you stand it?"

Barbara assumed a complacent expression. "I have a highly successful husband who adores me, a child who is absolutely perfect, and the house of my dreams."

In one sentence, she had just reeled off all the things that Val and Kate didn't have, and Barbara knew it. She watched as they exchanged a look of undisguised envy. Nevertheless, Val wasn't about to give up. "The valedictorian of the Class of '69 should be doing something more meaningful than serving as president of the fucking Medical Wives Auxiliary, a stupid little group of no-brain, no-talent women who snared doctors so they wouldn't have to work and support themselves. *You* were the one who told us to get out, to make something of ourselves. *You* were the one who said you couldn't live and die in a place like this. You let everyone down, including yourself. Face it, Barbara. You sold out."

Barbara went pale with anger. "What gives you the right to criticize? You have a boyfriend you're ashamed to introduce to us and you write profiles of semi-literate, druggie rock stars and other airheads for a living! If anyone sold out, it's *you!*"

"Stop it! Both of you!" Kate snapped. She went on in a tired voice. "Maybe we all sold out, in one way or another. Maybe that's what being grown up is all about, selling out and learning to live with it. The point is, life is a hell of a lot more complicated now than it was when we were in high school and all we had to worry about was being invited to the prom."

Val and Barbara were silent until Val said sheepishly, "You know, not being invited to the prom made me feel more like a failure than anything else that's ever happened to me. No matter what I do, I'll go to my grave feeling worthless because some acne-faced boy didn't like me enough to rent a tux and buy me a stupid fucking carnation corsage."

"Hey, don't feel bad," Barbara said in a voice no longer defensive. "I didn't go either."

"Why didn't you?" Val asked.

"What do you mean?"

"When I got here tonight and saw all your ex-boyfriends and would-be boyfriends, I realized something I should have guessed ten years ago. You could have gone to the prom if you wanted to. You must've had a dozen invitations. So why didn't you go?"

Barbara shrugged. "None of you were going. It wouldn't have been any fun without you guys."

Kate looked at her in amazement. "You mean, you didn't go because you didn't want to show us up?"

Barbara shook her head. "I just didn't want to go.

372

Period."

Val grinned. "Huh-uh. Kate's right. You didn't go because you didn't want to show us up. You always manage to come out looking good somehow. How on earth do you do it?"

"Natural superiority?" Barbara suggested with a laugh.

"Maybe," Val agreed.

Kate turned to Barbara. "So how's Allison? Did you get the teacher you were hoping for?"

For the next hour, the conversation stayed safely on innocuous subjects, such as school and fashion and the hopelessly retro appearances of most of their classmates. When they parted, after agreeing to meet at Barbara's house for brunch the next morning, there was no trace of the tension that had flared up so suddenly between them.

It had always been like that, Barbara thought as she drove home. Their very closeness made their arguments more furious than they would have been if they hadn't cared so much for each other. Still, the rapprochement couldn't erase the lingering sense of gut-wrenching envy she felt toward Kate and Val. No matter how much she told herself—and them—that her life was perfect, so well-ordered and meaningful and secure compared to theirs, the truth was just the opposite. Barbara felt as though she was drowning in a sea of meaningless trivia.

Kate and Val had careers. They had identities of their own. Barbara was defined by the people she served—she was David's wife and Allison's mother. It was especially bitter because, as Val had reminded her so forcefully, *she* was the one who had inspired them to get out, to make something of their lives.

At a stoplight, Barbara bent over to open the

glove compartment and take out the flask. She furtively finished the last of the drink, wishing there were more. At home, she checked on Allison, still amazed at times that she had an eight-year-old daughter. Seeing Allison's angelic face as she slept, Barbara felt guilty for ever having resented her, and kissed her tenderly on the forehead.

In her bedroom, she found David sound asleep as well. She really wanted to wake him, to talk to him about the disturbing emotions churning within her, those violently conflicting feelings of love and resentment, but he had an early surgery, she knew, and he would be angry at being disturbed. Since it would never occur to David that maybe, just once, her needs should come before his professional obligations, she tiptoed silently out of the bedroom.

In her high-ceilinged living room, Barbara went over to the elaborately carved oak bar and took out a bottle of wine. She didn't check to see what vintage it was. It didn't matter. Opening it, she took the bottle and a glass out to the patio, where she curled up in a chaise longue and drank until there wasn't a drop left.

Above her, the millions of stars in the clear summer sky seemed symbolic of limitless horizons, endless possibilities—but not for her.

NINE

Kate

She was the last of the three to leave the reunion, remaining behind to listen to the band play the classic Paul McCartney song, "Yesterday."

The poignant lyrics seemed especially appropriate. Graduation night might have been ten years ago, but it seemed like only yesterday. The four of them — Kate, Val, Barbara, and Shelly — had been so full of optimism and great expectations. They had been absolutely convinced that life couldn't be anything but wonderful. After all, they were coming of age at the most exciting time for women in history. The barriers were coming down, they could do anything, be anything, and no one could stop them. They didn't have to repeat their mothers' boring, restrictive lives.

In the ten years since, they had learned of harsh realities and disillusionment. Even though they'd all done well, it wasn't as satisfying as they'd expected. It wasn't enough. Then, too, was the dark, ugly memory of what had happened on graduation night. Even tonight, when Kate knew that Barbara and Val must be thinking about it, no one had said a word.

"It never happened," Val had said at the time,

and they had all agreed. Ten years later, they were still denying it had ever happened.

The song drew to a close, and Kate shook herself out of her reverie. It was time to go. She wished she hadn't come. It had been a mistake. Aside from Val and Barbara, she hadn't really cared about seeing any of the people she'd gone to school with.

Well, maybe *one* person, but he hadn't come.

The memory of Mark Jensen's brilliant blue-green eyes was as vivid as if Kate were looking into them at that very moment. With a start, she realized she *was!* The man in her mind was standing only a few feet away, his eyes locked with her slowly focusing eyes as the band began playing "Brown-Eyed Girl."

Kate blushed. After ten years, he was still able to make her feel acutely self-conscious. In the dim light, Mark looked startlingly the same. Tall, lean, all-American-boy handsome. His eyes were as translucent as she remembered, his hair as gold. As he came closer, Kate realized with dismay that he was far from being the same. Mark wasn't just lean, he was gaunt. His white shirt hung loosely on his thin frame, and his gray slacks bunched slightly at the waist where he'd had to cinch his belt tighter than should have been necessary. There were dark shadows under his eyes, which bore a haunted expression. Mark was a ghost of his former cocky self.

As he stopped in front of her, Kate felt an emotion she'd never expected to feel toward Mark Jensen — compassion.

When he spoke, his voice was deeper, huskier than she remembered.

"Hello, Katie."

His tone was devoid of the overweening arrogance he'd displayed in high school. Something about the way he said her name — *Katie* — with a catch in his voice tugged at her heart.

"Hello, Mark." How strange to think that this time she sounded so much more confident than he did.

"As I recall, you refused to dance with me in high school."

"Yes."

His smile was a pale imitation of the devilish grin that had once sent her pulse racing. "I think you owe me one. How about it?"

She wanted to say no. Somehow, she couldn't. Kate found herself nodding silently.

Mark took her in his arms, and they held each other for the first time. The years dissolved and they were seventeen again, back in the same gym where she had once watched him from afar, yearning hopelessly for his touch.

Kate's head came to Mark's shoulder; her cheek touched the cool cotton of his shirt. Her breasts lightly, tantalizingly brushed his chest. As he held her, their bodies swaying to the music, she was reminded of the heady physical sensations he'd once elicited in her, sensations no other man, not Roger, not Alan, had ever provoked.

Neither spoke as they danced, but Kate felt as if some long-dormant part of her was slowly coming to life again, like a budding flower blooming under a warm spring rain.

When the song ended, they stood still for a moment until Kate stepped back.

"Can I get you something to drink?" Mark asked in a tentative voice, seeming half afraid she would turn him down.

Although she wasn't thirsty, she didn't want this contact to end.

"Sure," she said lightly.

They took their drinks to an empty table in a corner far from the band where they could talk without having to shout.

"I hear you're living in L.A. now," he began conventionally.

"Yeah, and you?"

"I took over the ranch when my dad passed away last year."

"I'm sorry. My father died a few years ago, too."

"I know. I'm sorry."

There was an awkward silence. Kate tried desperately to think of something to say, but her mind went blank.

Then Mark asked, "So, how do you like L.A.?"

Another conventional question, but at least it gave her something to respond to.

"It's a whole different world. I'm not sure Visalia and L.A. are on the same planet."

"How do you mean?"

"Haven't you been there?"

"Once, right after graduation, when a bunch of us went to Disneyland. That's about all I know of L.A."

"Actually, Disneyland and L.A. have a lot in common, but Disneyland's cleaner. Both places aren't quite real, somehow."

"Tell me about L.A."

"The days are almost always warm and the nights are cool, especially out at the beach, where I live. A lot of the buildings are pastel and there are yogurt shops everywhere."

"Yogurt?"

Kate smiled. "I guess it hasn't made it to Visalia yet, but take it from me, it's about to replace ice cream."

"What's it like working in show business?"

Show business. Kate hadn't heard it referred to in that way for a long time. Everyone she knew simply called it "the business," as if there were no other, and as far as most of them were concerned, there wasn't.

She answered dryly, "I pass TV detectives in the halls when I go to the networks to talk about series. I ride in elevators with famous newscasters whose faces I grew up watching on TV. I almost get run over on the movie studio lots by big stars. That's what it's like."

"Do you like it?"

She considered the question. It wasn't nearly as easy to answer now as it would have been a few years earlier. "When I first got down there, I thought I was in heaven. All I'd thought about throughout high school was getting out of Visalia and going to L.A. I wanted to be there so bad."

"And now?"

"Now . . . well, maybe I've come to understand the city too well. The sunsets are spectacular because of the smog. The ocean's so polluted you can get sick from swimming in it. There are no seasons like there are here in the valley, just an endless summer interrupted occasionally by a cold, rainy day. Because it's always the same, there's no sense of time. It's hard to remember what month it is or even what year. Sometimes I feel like my life is passing in a blur of eternal summer days that have absolutely no meaning."

Kate stopped, embarrassed. She hadn't meant to reveal so much.

"But you stay there," Mark said.

"Yes. I stay there. My career is there, and my husband," she added in a guilty afterthought.

"You're married?" he asked in surprise.

Kate knew what prompted his surprise. She wasn't wearing a ring. She'd stopped wearing it a few months earlier. Initially, she had told herself that since Alan had never worn one, there was no reason for her to do so, but the truth was, she no longer felt married. Anxious to stave off any questions about the state of her marriage, she asked, "How about you? Married?"

Mark shook his head. "No."

Just then, an announcement was made that the band was about to play its last song. Glancing at her watch, Kate was amazed to see that it was one o'clock in the morning.

She looked at Mark, unsure how to say good-bye.

He said, "Look, you wouldn't . . . I mean, would you like to go for a drive somewhere? I'd like to talk to you some more."

Kate hesitated. She felt it was dangerous to prolong her contact with Mark. It would be best to end things now.

Instead, she said, "Yes. I'd like that."

They drove through town in a blue-and-white Chevy pickup. Although it had been scrupulously cleaned, it still retained the faint, unmistakable smell of the ranch. The night was like all the summer nights she remembered from the valley, warm, clear, seductive. The air blowing through the open windows of the pickup was tinged with the heady aroma of magnolia blossoms and other, more subtle scents.

As they reached the fork in the road where Main Street merged into Mooney Boulevard, Kate saw something she hadn't noticed before on her rare trips to Visalia.

"What is that?" she asked, pointing at a small, triangular-shaped stone monument.

"It's a memorial to local guys who died in Vietnam. They just put it up recently."

"Can we stop? I'd like to take a look at it."

Mark clearly didn't want to stop, but he did so anyway, pulling the pickup over to the side of the road. They got out and walked over to the monument. Engraved on the smooth granite surface were about twenty names, most of them Hispanic.

Among them was Benny Sanchez.

Kate felt a sharp jolt of shock. She remembered Benny so clearly: dancing with him at Nina Manetti's party on graduation night; seeing how proud he looked in his letterman's sweater; listening to him talk about going to the local junior college and then, if he could get a scholarship or a loan, going on to a university. He wanted to be a lawyer, to help poor people, especially *his* people, the Chicanos, fight for their rights.

He would have done it, too, Kate was sure. He was bright and determined and hadn't let the pervasive racism in the valley keep him down. All that potential had been wasted on a bloody battlefield in a part of the world that no one even cared about. He had died and Kate hadn't even known. Somehow, she felt horribly guilty, not just because she hadn't known of his death or because she had been busy demonstrating against the very war that he was off fighting and dying in. Her guilt came from the terrible unfairness of life. She was alive and could fulfill her dreams while Benny had never had a chance.

Watching her reaction, Mark said gently, "You knew Benny, didn't you."

381

She nodded.

"He was a hero. Not that it mattered." He shook his head. "What a fucking waste."

There was a cold bitterness in his voice.

Surprised, Kate said, "I didn't realize you knew him that well."

"I didn't. We just flew over on the same plane."

She was completely taken aback. It never would have occurred to her that Mark would have gone to Vietnam. Even if he was drafted, surely he could have gotten out on a college deferment.

"You were there?"

"Yeah. I was there, but I came back twelve months later and Benny didn't."

Kate didn't know what to say. She knew plenty of people who had demonstrated against the war, but she'd never actually known someone who had fought in it.

Mark went on. "I read a statistic once. Hispanics make up ten percent of this country's population, but they accounted for twenty percent of the casualties. Around here, it was even worse. In some towns, they made up seventy to eighty percent of the casualties."

He shook his head. "What a way to finally come out ahead of us Anglos."

Kate was amazed at the grim numbers. "But why?"

"They weren't in college and couldn't get deferments, and they were generally the least-educated guys over there and were given grunt assignments." At her look of confusion, he explained, "Dangerous positions."

"You mean the powers-that-be felt they were expendable?"

"Exactly. I heard a sergeant say once that they

weren't going to amount to anything anyway so who cared."

Kate said carefully, "I hope you don't take this wrong, but, well, I don't remember you being so sensitive toward Hispanics."

There was no real humor in Mark's thin smile. "I grew up watching them work on the ranch, listening to my dad call them dumb Mexicans. I went to school with them, but I never really knew one, as a human being just like me, until I went to 'Nam. When you have to depend on someone to help you survive, you stop worrying about their race."

"But I heard there were a lot of racial conflicts."

"Yeah, there were a lot of problems, but in spite of that, there were also a lot of close friendships that had nothing to do with race."

Kate said softly, "Knowing Benny, I'll bet he thought he had to prove something to his country. To be a man of honor. Gaining respect meant so much to him . ."

She broke off, unable to continue.

Mark gently took her arm. "Let's go."

They drove aimlessly down Mooney Boulevard, just like they would have done on a date in high school. It was so late that no restaurants or drive-ins were open, not even the bars. Finally, after the silence had stretched out for an interminable period, Mark asked, "Would you like to come back to my place for some coffee?"

Kate knew there was nothing sexual in the invitation. There was literally no place else to go, and neither wanted to part yet.

She looked at him. "All right."

She had heard about the vast Jensen Ranch located a few miles from town, but she'd never seen it before. Kate couldn't see much in the night, just a long winding drive bordered by a white fence; beyond the fence, pastures stretched into the darkness. The house was a fairly modern adobe hacienda with massive double doors made of oak. It was large, and she thought how lonely it must be for Mark living there alone.

He led her through the terrazzo-floored entry past a huge living room and into the kitchen. It was immaculate, and Kate realized there must be a housekeeper or at least a cleaning lady who came in regularly.

Mark made the coffee. In his own home, he was much more at ease than he'd been in the school gym, and that made Kate feel less nervous. When the coffee was ready, they adjourned to the study, which was lined with floor-to-ceiling bookcases and had a small adobe fireplace in one corner. The furniture looked surprisingly old and worn but comfortable.

"This is the only really cozy room in the house," Mark explained. "It was my father's office. He did all the paperwork for the ranch here. As far back as I can remember, I used to come in here and curl up on the sofa, just like you are now, waiting for him to finish so we could talk."

"You were very close?"

"Yeah. My mother died when I was eight, and there was just the two of us after that."

"He never remarried?"

"No. When I was grown, I asked him once why he never married again. He said he only fell in love once in his life." Mark looked pensive. "I think he missed my mother even more than I did."

After a moment, he went on. "Were you close to your father?"

Up to a point, Kate thought soberly. Aloud, she said, "Yes."

She didn't want to dwell on that subject, however, so she asked a question she'd been curious about since they'd stopped at the memorial. "Why did you go to Vietnam? Were you drafted?"

Mark hesitated, then answered carefully. "No, I wasn't drafted. I volunteered."

"Why?"

He looked away, clearly uneasy. "It's hard to explain."

"Please try. I'd like to understand."

He looked at her once more. "Does it matter?"

"Yes." Somehow it mattered very much, though she couldn't have said why.

He began hesitantly. "Except for losing my mother, I had it pretty easy. My father loved me very much and spoiled me rotten. He had the money to indulge me in anything I wanted. Everything came easy for me—friends, school, life in general. I was in college when the Lottery happened. I was just old enough to miss it, but I watched friends who were just a little bit younger agonizing over whether they would get a high number or a low one."

It came back to Kate, who remembered seeing young men in the dorm celebrating because they'd drawn a high-enough number to keep them out of the army. Other young men looked stricken because they'd drawn a low number.

"But you weren't part of all that," she said.

"No, I wasn't, but it bothered me. A lot. I finally decided that for once in my life I should stop hiding behind privilege and plain good luck. I wanted

385

to put myself to the test, the same way so many others were being tested." He shook his head. "It seemed very idealistic in a way, and I knew my father, who had served in World War II, would be proud. I was so stupid."

"You were just young. We all were."

"I was totally unprepared for 'Nam. The minute I got there, I regretted it and would have given *anything* to be able to change my mind."

"What was it like?"

He gave her a disconcertingly direct look. "I don't talk about it."

"I'm sorry," Kate said in embarrassment. "I wasn't asking out of curiosity. I really wanted to know."

"Why?" he shot back.

"Because it obviously changed you terribly, and I want to understand why."

The answer clearly wasn't what he'd expected. As Mark took a sip of coffee, his hand shook slightly. She waited for him to speak, unaware that she was holding her breath.

"I can't . . ." Mark stopped, visibly gathered himself, then went on haltingly, "That is, I haven't really talked to anyone about it."

"Not even your father?"

"By the time I got back, he was sick with cancer. He was tough and determined and he fought like hell, but he was very sick for a long time. I couldn't . . . couldn't bother him with it. Things had changed between us, and all of a sudden *he* was leaning on *me,* you see."

"Yes, I see."

"He talked about the war a little bit, but he kept comparing it to *his* war. It wasn't the same, but I couldn't tell him that."

"Wasn't there anyone else you could talk to?"

Mark shook his head. "No. None of my friends who were still here had gone to 'Nam. Nobody wanted to hear about it. It was like . . . some ugly secret that everyone wanted to pretend didn't exist. I felt . . . ashamed."

Kate saw what that admission cost him; Mark couldn't meet her eyes. She knew that what she said next was critical.

"I want to hear about it, if you'd like to tell me."

Mark sat at the far end of the sofa from her, absolutely rigid, his hands gripping his coffee cup as if it were a lifeline and he was a drowning man.

In a slow, halting voice, Mark began to speak. Gradually, his words built into a soliloquy so devastating that Kate couldn't respond; she could only sit and listen in growing pain and sorrow as his words painted a vision of horror.

"It started with boot camp. They taught us that the Vietnamese weren't people. They were gooks, dinks, slopes, zipperheads, and slants. A contract airline flew GIs over. We sat there stone-cold because we knew where we were going and we wondered just how many of us would be going home in three hundred and sixty-five days. That was the tour of duty—twelve months exactly. Except for the marines. They had to stay for thirteen months to prove how much tougher they were than the rest of us. When I got there, the sergeant passed out a bunch of drugs along with the usual army gear, uppers, downers, pot. I joined a platoon and went into the bush right away, and from that first day, I realized there was no way in hell we could win that war because the enemy was everywhere, even among the people we were supposed to be protecting. There was one poor son of a bitch who was so desperate to go home that he shot his foot off trying

387

to get a medical discharge. There was a gungho lieutenant who wanted to cover himself in glory and didn't care how many of his men got killed. His own men executed him while they were out on patrol. They said it was an accident, but everyone knew the truth. Even the brass. They covered it up. They just didn't want it to get out. Every single one of my closest buddies in the platoon were killed in an ambush. They were all only nineteen. . . . After that, all I could think of was staying alive, making it through my twelve months so I could return to the 'world.' Once I went to China Beach near Da Nang. It was an in country R&R center. You were supposed to relax, have a good time there, but the beach was always covered with bloody bandages and the garbage washed ashore from the hospital ships *Repose* and *Sanctuary* out in the South China Sea. There was a lifeguard stand on China Beach, and it was real strange to see it there, with incoming medical choppers flying overhead.

"In a firefight, my lieutenant killed a four-year-old kid who got caught in the cross fire. The day before, he had just learned that he'd become a father for the first time. He broke down and cried, holding that little kid's body. And there was this real nice, uncomplaining kid who thanked me when I poked a cigarette into his mouth five minutes before he died. . . . Finally, after my three hundred and sixty-five days, I got on a plane for home with total strangers and a head full of confusion. I made the transition from rice paddy to California in less than thirty-six hours. There was no time to talk to anyone, to come to terms with what it meant, if anything. No time to deal with the guilt I felt for surviving when others died.

"In 'Nam, I clung to the fantasy that everything

388

would be all right once I got home. Everything would be the same. I would be the same as I'd been before I left. Instead of the hero's welcome my dad told me he got when he came back after World War II, all I got was insults. Somehow, while I was over there, the country changed. I changed, too. I felt isolated, numb. Old. After my father died, I thought about killing myself. I've got an old .38 that I snuck back from 'Nam. Once I sat with the barrel in my mouth and the hammer pulled back, but I couldn't do it. I see my friend Ronnie back in 'Nam with his brains smeared all over the bunker and I think, hell, I fought too hard to make it back. I can't waste it now. . . . But at night I have a hard time sleeping. I see old friends in my dreams, their faces, the ambush, their screams. I can't let myself feel anything. If I do then I'll have to thaw my numb reactions to the death and horror that surrounded me over there. If I let myself feel, I may never stop crying. I'm afraid I might completely lose control of myself.

"Every once in a while, something will happen, something small but happy, like when a foal is born or I see flowers blooming in early spring, and I realize how full life can be. But I always pull back, don't let myself enjoy the moment, because I feel like I'm betraying my friends who died. It seems wrong that I was able to go away and be healthy and they couldn't."

Mark was silently weeping. Kate took him in her arms, holding his head against her breast while rocking him gently back and forth, murmuring, "It's all right. I'm here. You're not alone. It's all right."

Her deepest instinct as a woman, to nurture, was aroused. Being needed so desperately was a feeling Kate had never known before. It transformed her, giving her a quiet strength that she'd never realized she possessed.

She stroked his hair and continued to murmur reassuringly, and when Mark raised his face to hers, she kissed away his tears. When he brushed his lips against hers, she didn't pull away. What began as comfort turned to passion. They made love on the sofa, but it was need as much as desire, and Kate was nearly blown away by the intensity. As she held Mark after, he confessed that she was the first woman he'd made love to since returning from Vietnam. Kate agonized over his isolation. His second confession was a shameful secret: he had a daughter back in 'Nam.

"I met this young Vietnamese woman," he said in an exhausted voice. "We established an exclusive relationship. We didn't talk about marriage. This was so common, most of the guys did it, but I cared for her more than I can possibly say. In a war zone, the relationships may be fleeting but they're intense. Then . . . she became pregnant."

When he didn't continue, Kate prompted. "What happened to the baby?"

"She was born just before I returned to the States. I saw her once, a tiny, brown little baby. The funny thing is, she had green eyes."

Kate asked gently. "What is her name?"

"Anne. Her mother wanted her to have an American name. She asked me what my mother's name was. It was Anne."

He stopped.

"What happened to them, the mother and child?"

"The mother died. The baby was taken in by relatives."

Mark spoke in neutral tones, as if those people had nothing to do with him. Despite her profound compassion, Kate was furious.

"How could you just leave her?"

"I tried to send money when I got back, but by then no one could find her."

As they talked on through the night, Mark gradually came to realize that more than anything else that had happened to him in Vietnam, he was haunted by the knowledge that he had abandoned his daughter.

"You can't put the war behind you until you resolve this," Kate insisted.

They sat close together on the sofa, wrapped in blankets that Mark had taken from a small chest in a corner of the room.

"You don't know what it's like over there now. I've checked it out. There are thousands of Amerasian kids in 'Nam. Finding my daughter would be impossible."

"Maybe, but you have to try. You came home seven years ago, but you didn't come all the way home. Part of you is still over there."

He didn't say anything, but she sensed that he knew she was right.

It was dawn now, and the first pale rays of sunlight were filtering through the large window of the study.

"I suppose I'd better get you back to wherever you're staying," Mark said tiredly.

Kate nodded. She didn't want to leave. She wanted to stay with him, but she couldn't. It was impossible.

In the morning light, Kate could see the ranch in all its glory, thousands of acres stretching as far as she could see in every direction. The house was situated on a slight rise, and below it were pastures, fields, and orchards. Bathed in the golden glow of a

California sunrise, with the air smelling fresh and clean, it seemed like the loveliest, most peaceful place on earth.

Kate hated the thought of leaving, of returning to L.A. and all the pressure and personal unhappiness that awaited her there.

As they neared the pickup, Mark turned and asked, "Can I see you again?"

The words touched her deeply and Kate was sorely tempted to say yes. However, her feelings for him were an even more serious threat to her marriage than Alan's casual infidelities. Seeing Mark again would mean the risk of losing everything she and Alan had achieved together.

"No," she whispered unhappily.

Mark looked deeply hurt but didn't argue.

As they drove down the winding drive away from the house, heading back toward town, Kate felt that she was leaving behind the first real happiness she'd known in a long, long time.

1980-1989

COMING OF AGE

ONE

Shelly

Chelsea was especially charming on this brisk, clear autumn day in late 1980. The sun was setting as Shelly let herself in to her ground-floor flat in a tall, narrow building on Cheyne Walk. The Thames wound smooth and placid beyond the embankment, only a few yards away, and the towering plane trees lining the walk were lush and green.

Chelsea was a chic residential area of old town houses extending for a mile and a half along the north bank of the river. For centuries, artists had congregated there, giving it a reputation as a bohemian enclave. Nowadays, rock stars such as Mick Jagger had homes on Cheyne Walk.

Shelly's small furnished flat was quite expensive, and she wasn't sure how much longer she'd be able to afford it. Since coming to London two years earlier, she had lived off her savings and the occasional modeling jobs that she got through Ryan, who had also relocated to London. The jobs weren't the high-paying ones she'd been used to at the beginning of her career in Paris, so she mainly lived off what she'd managed to save while working for Madame Justine. Nevertheless, London in the eighties was an extremely expensive city in which to live, and inevitably Shelly's savings dwindled.

She dropped her purse on a cherry-wood table in the narrow foyer and picked up the mail that her charwoman had put there, tiny lines of worry creasing her brow. She went into the sitting room and lit a fire in the blue-tiled fireplace, then curled up in a large, overstuffed chair. Pulling a cashmere afghan, a birthday gift from Barbara, around her shoulders, Shelly considered what to do next.

She'd just come from a job interview, the latest in a long line of futile attempts to secure decent, steady employment. As so often happened, the man doing the hiring didn't feel she was qualified for the position. However, he offered to take her out to dinner to discuss other options.

She turned him down.

Well, there was no point in dwelling on it, she told herself. She would just have to keep trying. If worse came to worst, she could return to L.A. and stay with Kate for a while. Kate had certainly made the offer often enough.

No matter how desperate Shelly got, she vowed she would never return to prostitution. Period.

During the first few months she'd been in London, before Ryan moved there and helped her start modeling again, Shelly had had a lot of time to do nothing but think. Losing Philippe had been a devastating experience, but the worst part had been the way he had looked at her when he realized what she was. His expression went deeper than mere disillusionment or even disgust. For the rest of her life, she would never be able to forget that look. It had made her feel filthy, degraded, worthless.

Now that she had some distance from the money and power and glittering surface of her former life as one of Madame Justine's high-priced call girls, Shelly could view that life objectively. What she saw was pathetic. For so long, she had been drowning in denial—denial that she hated being touched by those men, denial that she hated her life despite the luxury and superficial excitement. As she walked through Hyde Park on misty autumn mornings, browsed through musty old bookstores on rainy winter afternoons, or curled up by the fire in her little flat on long, lonely nights, Shelly knew she could never do it again. She had to make a new life for herself, one that would allow her some pride and self-respect.

Slowly, with a great deal of difficulty, she had begun to put together such a life: she found this wonderfully cozy flat; she took classes at the University of London; she forced herself to get beyond her shyness and make new friends. When she felt especially down, Ryan was always there to cheer her up, and that made all the difference in the blackest moments. He had long since stopped trying to get her in his bed, though she knew he would welcome her there at any time. Shelly didn't want sex from Ryan. She wanted friendship. He gave it, with no strings attached, and she was intensely grateful.

She told herself that she wasn't interested in sex with any man, though there were times when she wondered what it would have been like with Philippe. And Ryan. He was kind, generous, tremendous fun to be with. Shelly had never understood why he wasn't able to settle down with one woman.

With a sigh, she riffled through her mail. There was a postcard from Val with a stunning view of Maui and a scribbled note saying how perfect paradise was and what a terrific time they were having. She didn't explain who she was with, but Shelly assumed it was the mysterious boyfriend Kate had mentioned once. There was a thank-you note from Barbara's daughter, Allison, written in an awkward nine-year-old hand, thanking Shelly for the beautiful porcelain doll she had sent. Although Shelly had never met Allison, she kept up with her development through photos and letters from Barbara. Sometimes when she read a long letter from Barbara bringing her up-to-date on Allison's latest accomplishments or minor setbacks, it was a painful reminder of the loneliness of Shelly's life. Now facing thirty, she felt an overwhelming urge to have a baby.

More and more often, she found herself thinking of her abortion. Though she couldn't regret that decision, she was at a different place in her life now and she wanted a child by a father who would stay around to help raise it. Being a chic single mother wasn't for her. She wanted her child to have what she hadn't — a daddy.

To dispel her gloomy mood, Shelly turned on the television and caught the tail end of a news bulletin: ". . . thousands of horror-stricken fans have assembled in Central Park, near Lennon's residence, and are holding a vigil in his memory . . ."

His memory? What on earth was going on?

A photo of John Lennon flashed across the screen as the announcer continued in a grim voice, "In this chilling photo, we see John Lennon autographing his new album for Mark David Chapman, who hours later allegedly shot him dead near Lennon's Manhattan apartment house."

Shelly felt stricken. John Lennon *dead?* It was impossible! He was so young, the symbol of youth and energy. He was an icon of a time when the young ran the world and could do anything they damn well pleased with it.

Tears sprang to her eyes, and she brushed them away with her sleeve. Her thoughts were interrupted by the ringing of the phone. She was expecting a call from Kate to finalize plans for Kate and Alan to spend Christmas in London with her, so she wasn't surprised to hear Kate's voice; but instead of being cheerful, it was shattered.

"Shelly, did you hear about John Lennon?"

"Yes. Kate, I still can't believe it. How could it happen?"

"God, I don't know. Obviously Chapman is crazy, but that doesn't explain anything. I didn't even know Lennon, but I feel devastated."

"I know what you mean. I feel scared for some reason, like the world I knew is ending and I don't know what's going to take its place. What are the eighties going to be like if they begin with John Lennon being killed?"

Kate's voice was tight with sarcasm. "John Lennon is dead and Ronald Reagan has been elected president. I don't think this is going to be a great decade."

Shelly said wistfully, "When I look back on the past, when we were young and innocent and naive, all my memories are colored by the songs of the Beatles. They were so much a part of that time."

"Yeah. Even now, when I'm driving along and a Beatles song comes on the radio, it lifts my spirits. Now . . . nothing will ever be the same."

Later, Shelly sat lost in thought. *Nothing will ever be the same.* She had no idea what was to come except for the inescapable fact of change. Whether it would be good or bad was anybody's guess.

Two weeks later, she awoke to the ringing of the phone.

"Cheer-frightfully-ho, love!"

Recognizing Ryan's voice, Shelly laughed. "You are becoming disgustingly English. Have you been reading P. G. Wodehouse again?"

"As a matter of fact, yes. Shortly, I shall start carrying a brolly and wearing a bowler hat."

"That would look interesting with your cowboy boots."

"Actually, I didn't call to discuss my chameleonlike ability to blend in with whatever environment I find myself in. Put on your best duds. You're going to a party!"

She groaned. "Oh, Ryan, not tonight. I just want to putter around my tiny garden, do some reading, have some nice hot soup, and go to bed early. I'm not in a mood for partying."

"This is business, not pleasure. I think I've got a job for you. A *big* one."

"At a party?"

"No, of course not, but the man giving the party is the man with the job. Do you know Ben Rashad?"

"I've heard of him, of course. He runs a big cosmetics company, doesn't he?"

"Yup. Built it up from nothing. He's an interesting guy, half-caste, of course. His father was East Indian, his mother Irish. Anyway, he's looking for a model to be the face for Rashad Cosmetics. Print ads, TV commercials, photo on the products, the whole bit. An exclusive contract, of course."

Shelly's excitement quickly dissolved. "He'll want someone young."

"No, that's the great thing about this. The market his products are aimed at is slightly older — from thirty on up. He wants a quote mature unquote model, someone who women in that age group can relate to. He hired me to shoot the print ads and asked for recommendations. I showed him some pictures of you and he flipped."

"Are you serious?"

"Of course, I'm serious. Will I never get over this entirely unfounded reputation for levity? Anyway, he's throwing a big party tonight at his little place in the suburbs, only fifty or so rooms and enough land around it to qualify as a small national park back in the States. He wants to meet you, and I assured him you'd be there."

"Oh, Ryan, I don't know. I'm not prepared. I don't know what to wear. I look like hell. . . ."

Ryan chuckled. "You couldn't look like hell if you tried. I'll pick you up at seven. Be ready. 'Bye."

After hanging up, Shelly sat a moment, letting it all sink in. Lord, it would mean so much, the answer to her prayers. An exclusive contract would be worth a great deal of money, perhaps enough to finally give her the basic financial security she'd never had. Tears filled her eyes at the thought of never again having to worry about how she was going to pay the rent, buy food, live from one month to the next. Then she pulled herself back, afraid of wanting it too much. The odds were against her. Rashad might say he wanted someone older, but when it came right down to it, he would probably hire a fresh-faced twenty-two-year-old.

As she rummaged through her closet, searching for just the right thing to wear, Shelly told herself to calm down. She would simply go to the party and have a good time and not worry about the impression she was making on Ben Rashad.

The dress was one that Madame Justine had selected for her, an Oscar de la Renta original. Made of blue sapphire coup-de-velour, it hugged every curve of her body, falling in narrow folds to her feet. Cut high in front, with an open back, it was the most stunning gown that Shelly possessed. She hoped desperately that it would give her some confidence.

Her hair was pulled back in a sleek chignon. She surveyed her appearance in the full-length mirror and saw a beautiful, composed woman who bore no resemblance to the nervous, insecure person she felt like inside.

Remembering the lessons that Madame Justine had taught her, Shelly clipped on dangling sapphire earrings, picked up her silver evening bag, and straightened her shoulders.

It was showtime.

They arrived at Ben Rashad's palatial estate just outside London at eight o'clock. An old Tudor mansion, it was set in lavishly manicured grounds. The drive leading up to the house wound through a mile of woodland. Ryan hadn't exaggerated the size of the place or its magnificence.

The party matched the impressiveness of the estate. Rashad had hired a small circus for the evening. In the center of the broad back lawn that swept down to a man-made lake, an elephant performed tricks under the supervision of a gaily attired handler. Clowns juggled and did pratfalls.

Above the crowd, highwire artists performed amazing feats of balance.

At least one hundred guests mingled on the lawn, standing near brightly crackling bonfires to keep warm, and circulating in the downstairs reception rooms of the house. All of the downstairs rooms at the rear of the house had French doors opening onto a broad stone terrace.

Shelly was glad she had worn her best gown. The other guests were dressed in rich silks, satins, and brocades, and most wore fabulous furs and jewels. Beneath the string of Japanese lanterns stretching across the lawn, diamonds, emeralds, and rubies glittered in dazzling profusion.

"Ben likes to do things right," Ryan commented. "It's that poverty-stricken background, of course. He feels like he has to outdo everyone else just to be accepted, and he's right. Most of these people wouldn't give him the time of day if he wasn't rich. Come on, let's find him."

They made their way through the crowded ballroom and into an adjoining sitting room where people stood chatting in small groups.

"Ah, there's Ben," Ryan said.

Shelly followed his look and saw a tall, dark-haired, but surprisingly fair-skinned man, seemingly at ease in this glittering throng.

Ryan led her over to him.

"Here she is, Ben! The one and only face for Rashad Cosmetics!"

Shelly colored in embarrassment. Ryan was always supremely self-confident, but he was being far too pushy now. To her surprise, the handsome Ben Rashad didn't seem at all irritated with Ryan. Taking her hand, he said, "For once, Ryan isn't exaggerating. You are exactly what I've been looking

403

for. To be honest, I was afraid the photos he showed me might be misleading. Now, meeting you, I see that they didn't do you justice."

Shelly didn't know what to say.

Sensing her discomfort, Rashad went on, "I'm afraid Ryan and I are overwhelming you. Come, let me show you my house. I'm quite proud of it. We'll leave Ryan behind and have a nice chat, just the two of us."

His dark eyes bright with enthusiasm, Rashad took her through room after magnificent room, pointing out paintings, objets d'art, priceless antiques, all the while telling her about himself in unembroidered terms.

"My father was a professor in Pakistan. He left during one of the many periods of turmoil. In this country, the best job he could get was teaching in a second-rate public school. What you Americans would call a private school. The pay was poor, and he wasn't respected by the students or his colleagues, as he had been in his own country. My mother was an Irish barmaid who had come to London from a poor village in Northern Ireland. For her, marriage to a professional man, even if he was a poorly paid Pakistani, was a step up the social ladder."

He talked so frankly about his parents that Shelly felt she could ask a rather personal question. "Were they happy together?"

"No," he replied matter-of-factly. "They were quite miserable. Unfortunately, it didn't occur to either of them to end the marriage. The only intelligent thing they did was to decide not to have more children after I was born. I left home as soon as possible, when I was fifteen. To my father's everlasting disappointment, I didn't have

404

any desire to go on to university. School had always been an unhappy experience for me. Naturally, the other students derided me for being a half-caste."

"Children can be very cruel," Shelly said with feeling.

Rashad looked at her in surprise. "You must have always been an exceptionally attractive girl. Why would children make fun of you?"

"I was poor and didn't have the things they did, a nice house, the right kind of clothes, and . . . and other things," she finished lamely in embarrassment. She couldn't make herself add that the most important thing they had that she didn't was a father.

Rashad responded slowly. "Yes, I can see that you understand what it feels like not to belong. Well, at any rate, I had one goal—to make a great deal of money so people would be forced to accept me, whether they wanted to or not."

Shelly smiled. "Many people have the same goal. Most of them don't achieve it on a scale as grand as this. How did you do it?"

"I was smart enough to know that I should select a profession that provided the opportunity for rapid advancement and that would bring me in close proximity to wealthy people. So I apprenticed myself to a hairdresser, quickly became a hairdresser myself, and by the time I was twenty-five, I owned my own shop. Then it was a string of shops. Then I began manufacturing my own beauty products. Now, twenty years after I bought that first small shop in Islington, Rashad Cosmetics is the biggest cosmetics firm in Great Britain."

"You make it sound easy."

"No, it wasn't easy, but it was inevitable. I simply didn't allow for any other outcome. I was determined that one day I would be accepted by the people who had shown contempt for me. Along the way, besides making a great deal of money, I reinvented myself. I learned how to dress like the haut monde, how to talk like them, how to live like them."

Shelly felt a tremendous empathy with Rashad. She, too, had reinvented herself. Impulsively, she asked, "You've come so far and you have so much. Are you happy?"

His smile was vaguely sad. "I believe that's asking too much of life."

They were nearly back in the sitting room when he stopped and faced her. "I'll tell you right now, I want you to represent Rashad Cosmetics."

The abrupt offer caught her off-guard. She lost every bit of the composure that Madame Justine had so painstakingly instilled in her.

She burst out. "Why?"

"Because you are the most beautiful woman I've ever seen. Not just beautiful on the outside, but beautiful in your soul, as well. And because hiring you will give me a very good excuse to see you again."

No, not another seduction, she thought miserably. Her dismay must have been all too evident, for Rashad went on in a voice warm with compassion, "No, it's not what you're thinking. You don't have to sleep with me in return for the job. Being as desirable as you are, I'm sure many men have wanted something from you. I don't want anything."

Somehow, she believed him.

When they reached the waiting room, Ryan was waiting impatiently. Handing Shelly back over to him, Rashad said, "I'm in your debt, Ryan. You've done more for me tonight than you will ever know."

Suddenly, Rashad's eye was caught by a man standing across the room and an unspoken communication flashed between the two men. Turning to Shelly, Rashad went on. "I must be a good host and circulate among my guests now, my dear, but I will talk to your agent tomorrow. Perhaps, when your contract is finalized, we can celebrate by having dinner together."

"I'd like that," she replied.

When he left to join the man across the room, Shelly and Ryan hugged each other tightly. "I told you it would work out!" he said, triumphantly. Seeing the disapproving looks on the faces of some elderly people standing nearby, he said, "Let's blow this joint and go somewhere we can really celebrate!"

At a private club Ryan belonged to, they drank champagne and talked excitedly about the deal.

"I can't wait to start planning how I'm going to shoot you. The winter snows will be here soon; a backdrop of snow might be nice. You could be dressed all in white, with some fabulous diamonds. Ben wants a very sophisticated look for this."

"He's very nice, isn't he?" Shelly broke in. She was even more intrigued with Rashad himself than with the job.

"What? Oh, yeah, I suppose so."

Her feelings toward Ben Rashad were nothing like the romantic infatuation she'd felt toward Philippe, but she found him warm and sweet and she felt safe with him. He was just old enough to have the aura of a father figure, and that drew her to him in a primal way.

"He isn't at all like what I expected. There's something very kind and reassuring about him."

"I don't know about that, but I do know that he's going to pay you a great deal of money. Your face is going to be plastered all over the place. You're going to be rich and famous, and I'm not gonna do too badly myself."

"Ryan, who was that man he talked to after he left us?"

"Who? Oh, you mean Richard Ford, his partner."

"His partner in Rashad Cosmetics?"

"Yeah, and in his personal life, too."

"What do you mean?"

"You know, *partner*. They've been together for years. It's practically a marriage." At her shocked look, Ryan said, "Didn't you realize that Ben is homosexual?"

The deal was made for even more money than Shelly had expected. It wasn't enough to make her wealthy, but it was enough to give her a basic financial security if she handled it carefully.

True to his word, Ben took her out to dinner at one of the most exclusive restaurants in London to celebrate. Despite her disappointment at learning she'd misinterpreted his interest in her, she actually enjoyed being with him. There was something very safe in knowing that at the end of the evening he wouldn't make any demands of her.

She and Ryan began shooting the ads for Rashad Cosmetics. The results turned out even better than Ryan's inflated ego had predicted, and within a few months photographs of her face were everywhere and she became known as "the Rashad woman." During all this time, she saw Ben frequently—at his office, at lavish parties at his estate, on quiet dinner dates in the city.

After that first date, Shelly had stopped asking herself why Ben wanted to spend time with her if he was involved with Richard Ford. She simply enjoyed his company and the excuse it gave her to turn down dates with other men who would have expected more from her than interesting conversation and pleasant companionship.

Ben never talked about Richard or about being gay. Sometimes, especially at the office, Shelly would run into Richard and they would talk briefly. He was perfectly polite and didn't seem to resent her friendship with Ben. Every once in a while she would catch him watching her when he didn't think she was aware of his scrutiny. At those times, his expression was rather unsettling. He looked like he felt sorry for her.

One night in the early spring of 1981, when the first flowers were beginning to blossom in Shelly's tiny garden after a long, cold winter, Ben invited her to dine alone with him at his home. It was the first time she'd been his only guest there, and she sensed that this was significant, though she couldn't imagine why.

They had a marvelous dinner prepared by his chef, followed by coffee and brandy in his library.

"You never drink," he commented.

"I do sometimes."

"Very rarely. Why is that?"

"I don't like to lose control," she answered honestly.

He nodded approval. "That's good. Drunks aren't

classy, especially when they're women. My mother always drank too much. It was embarrassing."

Shelly didn't know how to respond to that very intimate revelation so she sipped her coffee and stared into the fire blazing in the marble-manteled fireplace.

Ben went on. "In a few months, your contract with me will be up. What will you do then? Model for someone else?"

She shook her head. "No, I'll be too old."

"How will you support yourself?"

He seemed genuinely concerned, and she was touched. "With what you're paying me, I'll get by," she reassured him.

"But getting by isn't good enough. What I'm paying you won't buy a nice house in a decent part of town and a really good car and beautiful clothes, all the things you deserve."

Shelly smiled. "I'm glad you think I deserve all those things, but I don't need them. I'll be all right."

"If you married me, you'd do much better than *all right.*"

She wasn't sure she understood what he had just said. "Are you asking me . . ." She stopped, then went on, "What are you saying?"

"I'm asking you to marry me."

When Shelly didn't respond, Ben continued in a perfectly reasonable tone, as if he was proposing a business partnership. "I could give you everything you want, and more. Financial security on a level far above *getting by.* Social position. You'd never have to worry about anything again."

Finally, she found her voice. "But Ben, *why?* Why would you want to marry me?"

"You mean because I'm gay," he stated as casually as if it were a subject they'd discussed often.

"Yes. You're not in love with me."

"No, but I like you a great deal. I enjoy your company more than any other woman I've ever known."

"Then why not simply go on seeing each other occasionally as we do now?"

"Because in my business it's bad public relations to be seen as openly homosexual. I have big plans for Rashad Cosmetics. I want to take it international. To operate on that level, it will help me enormously to have a wife, especially a beautiful, intelligent, charming one who represents everything I am trying to sell with my products."

Shelly wasn't angered by the cold logic of his proposal, but she was put off by it. "I see. You want to use me."

He reached out to cover her hand with his. "I'm sorry if I've offended you in any way. Please believe me, my dear, I didn't intend that. I'd like to think of this as a way we can help each other. You would help me professionally. I would take care of you financially."

"But there wouldn't be anything . . . personal in it."

"No. It would be a marriage in name only, which isn't as rare as you might think, especially in certain rarified circles."

"You would continue your relationship with Richard?"

"Of course. We've been together for many years. I care for him more than I've ever cared for another human being in my life, but I would be very discreet. As I would expect you to be, should you decide to have affairs."

It was all so cold. So sordid. Shelly couldn't believe he actually seemed to think she would agree to such a thing. She couldn't believe she was actually considering it.

Ben urged her to think about it, and she did—constantly—as she worked, as she sat alone at home, as she shopped. What had at first seemed to be unthinkable gradually came to appear reasonable. After all, he was offering her so much. If love and passion weren't part of the package, well, she'd never had much luck with those anyway.

More than the money and the social position, she was irresistibly drawn to the idea of the safety that Ben's proposal represented. With him, she would live in a golden cocoon, protected from the bad things in life, including all the men who wanted something from her.

One night while having dinner with Ryan, she confided in him that Ben had proposed. When he recovered from his immediate shock, he said, "Surely you're not considering it!"

"Why not?"

"The answer to that question is fairly obvious."

"You mean because he's gay."

"Yes!"

"Ryan, listen to yourself. You're saying that a marriage based on friendship and mutual support would be a mistake, yet your track record in that regard isn't so hot. I don't see that you have any right to pass judgment."

"I'm not passing judgment, Shelly. I'm just saying that marriage should be more than that."

"Oh? And how many marriages do you know that have even that much going for them?"

"Look, forget all the miserable marriages in the world. At least most of them started out with love and desire and an optimistic hope that they'd work

412

out just great. If you marry Ben, you'll be turning your back on a vital part of life."

"Sex." She dismissed the subject with a shrug.

"Yeah, *sex.*"

She looked at Ryan and said slowly, "Maybe I turned my back on it a long time ago."

The wedding of Ben Rashad and the model who represented his line of cosmetics, Shelly DeLucca, was one of the social events of the season. It took place in the summer of 1981 under gaily striped tents on the lawn of his estate before five hundred guests. Ben's private jet brought her bridesmaids, Kate, Valerie, and Barbara, to London and took them home again three days later.

Shelly was a gloriously beautiful bride in a fairy tale gown by the same designers who had fashioned the wedding dress worn by the Princess of Wales. As Kate, Val, and Barbara stood by the altar, wearing royal blue satin dresses and watching Shelly and Ben exchange vows, they assumed she must be blissfully happy. After all, she was living out the fantasy Barbara had predicted for her so long ago when they were teenagers—marriage to a wealthy Englishman and a happy-ever-after life in a beautiful country estate.

After the brief ceremony, the orchestra began playing and Ben swept Shelly into his arms for the first dance. When the waltz ended and another song began, their guests joined them on the hardwood floor of the ballroom. Kate, Val, and Barbara all danced with friends of Ben.

Ryan was first in a line of men waiting to dance with the bride. For once he'd shed his casual clothes and worn a tux. Shelly was surprised at how elegant he looked. But then, she realized, he had the perfect build for formal attire — broad shoulders tapering to slim hips. He almost looked like a different person, and she found herself feeling unaccountably awkward with him.

As one hand clasped hers gently but firmly and the other encircled her back, he said, "Forget what I said earlier, Shelly. I genuinely wish you and Ben well."

The tenderness in his voice, and the heady sensation of being held in his arms, had a profound effect on her. Her voice trembled. "Thank you."

Unable to quite meet his look, she went on, "I don't think we ever danced before."

There was a moment's hesitation, and the atmosphere was charged with a sense of poignancy. Then he said slowly, "No, we never did."

TWO

Valerie

As she drove up to Michael's isolated estate in the rolling green hills of the Napa countryside, Val was surprised to see his "outlaws," as he called his men, standing guard in full force. They were carrying guns, something she'd never seen them do before. Recognizing her car, they waved her on through, then quickly shut the massive, electronically operated iron gate after her.

Something serious must have happened, Val realized. Immediately, she thought of Michael and panicked. Bringing her car to a screeching halt in front of the house, she tore out of it and raced inside. The living room and his study were empty. Her panic growing, she ran up the stairs, calling desperately, "Michael!"

The door to his bedroom opened and he stepped out, looking sleepy, as if she'd awakened him from a nap. "Val, what's wrong?"

She threw herself into his arms. "I thought something had happened to you!"

"Nothing happened. I'm all right."

Taking her into the bedroom, he led her to the bed, where they sat on the edge, his arm around her.

415

"But all those men . . . and they had guns."

"I had a little disagreement with some guys. I had to turn down their business proposition. Anyway, I decided I'd better take some precautions for a while."

Val pulled back and stared at him. "What guys?"

Michael didn't answer. He didn't have to. She knew who they were. "They're Colombians, aren't they? With the cartel. Why didn't you tell me about this!"

"Because I knew you'd react this way," he snapped. "Look, it's no big deal. I can handle it."

"No big deal!" She was standing up now, glaring at him. "Michael, I know a little bit about those kind of guys. I've written about them. I've even interviewed a few of them. They're not like the cops you're used to outsmarting. They don't play fair. What do they want from you?"

"If you must know, they want to connect with me, use my boats and my distribution network. They said they could supply ten million dollars worth of coke a week."

"What did you tell them?"

"To go to hell. Look, I told you once, Val, I don't deal in the hard stuff, and I don't do business with scum."

"Oh, my God," she whispered. Gripping his shoulders, she forced him to face her. "No one tells guys like that to go to hell!"

A broad grin split Michael's face. "I did, and, baby, it felt good!" He laughed. "You should've seen the look on their faces when they walked out of here."

"It isn't funny, Michael! If they want your operation, they'll take it!"

His grin dissolved in an instant. "No way."

"Michael, you're in big trouble."

"I know they could be a problem. That's why I've got the outlaws out in force."

"And you really think that's all it will take to get rid of them? A dozen ex-hippies with small arms?"

"They can't get to me while I'm holed up here. I'll stay put as long as I have to, and eventually they'll get bored and go away."

Val shook her head slowly. "They won't go away. That's not how they handle things."

Kneeling down in front of him, as he sat on the bed, she pleaded, "You've got to listen to me. I know what I'm talking about. Get *out*, Michael! Right now! While you still can!"

"Give up? No way!"

"You've got plenty of money."

"I don't have enough to support the winery. When it starts showing a profit . . ."

"Bullshit! That's just an excuse, and you know it. You just want to go on being a smuggler."

"A smuggler . . . Yeah, that's just what I want to be. I like the sound of the word. I like everything it represents. Thumbing my nose at the Establishment, doing things my way, with no one telling me what to do. Following my own rules, not theirs. This is the only way of life for me. I can't even imagine trying to live a tamer life-style. I'd die of boredom."

Val stood, her expression bleak. She knew it was hopeless trying to make him see reason, but she had to try. "I know you think this is all fun and games. When your father was alive, it was a way to rebel against him and everything he represented. But he's dead now, Michael. He's been dead for a long time. You're not eighteen anymore, you're thirty-five. It's time to stop being a rebel

417

and start being a grown-up."

His jaw clenched. Michael was clearly angry but trying very hard to control it. "That's interesting amateur psychology, Val, but I don't agree with it. I'm not rebelling against anybody. I'm just being myself. You knew what I was when we got involved."

"Yes," she whispered in a tired, hopeless voice. "I knew what you were, and I found it tremendously attractive. But a lot of time has passed, Michael, and we're both getting older. What used to seem exciting just seems dangerous and stupid now. I want to be able to introduce you to my friends. I want us to be able to live together without being afraid of getting busted. I want to lead a normal life, like everyone else."

"I've never wanted to live like everyone else, and it *is* my life, not yours."

Val went cold inside. "I thought I was part of your life."

For one interminable moment, they stood facing each other, separated by anger, then Michael moved closer and said in a tender voice, "You *are* part of my life. I love you, Val. I know you have a hard time believing that, but it's true, more true than you'll ever know."

"Oh, Michael, I love you, too! But I need you to grow up now. I need you to be a man, not a little boy still playing cops and robbers."

"I can't be something I'm not, Val. Even for you."

She went rigid. From the beginning, Val had known this would be the inevitable end of the argument. She understood Michael too well to believe she could change him; but she had had to try.

A small sigh escaped her lips. "There's nothing left to say, then," she whispered. "Good-bye, Michael. I hope . . . you'll be all right."

She turned and started to leave.

"Val!"

She stopped but didn't look back.

"This is ridiculous! I don't want you to go."

Turning to look at him over her shoulder, she said, "I don't want to go, but I can't stay and watch you die."

She hurried out of the room, down the stairs, and out to her car. As she drove off, she saw that he'd followed her outside and stood watching as her car disappeared from sight. His figure was blurred by the tears filling her eyes and running down her cheeks.

The days were unbearable, the nights endless.

Val tried to throw herself into her work. She was much in demand now because of some live TV commentary she'd done during the 1980 presidential campaign. Her acerbic "end of an era" viewpoint when Reagan won had appealed to the enormous baby-boomer national viewing audience. In the wake of that exposure, she had been offered an interview show on a San Francisco network affiliate.

After her breakup with Michael, she found herself unable to concentrate or to generate the kind of energetic, no-holds-barred interviews her audience loved. It was all she could do to keep from bursting into tears while other people were around. The makeup man couldn't entirely conceal the dark circles under her eyes from all the sleepless nights. He suggested she consider plastic surgery.

419

Val knew she'd hit rock bottom when her producer, Ellen Delgado, asked her if she was drinking or doing drugs. She couldn't help smiling at the irony of it. From the moment she'd met Michael, she hadn't done anything more than occasionally smoke a little grass. She didn't even drink, except for wine, because Michael didn't like hard liquor.

"No," she answered. "It's been a long time since I've had that kind of problem."

"Well, something's wrong, and I want you to tell me what it is. *Now!*"

Ellen was as blunt-talking as Val. She had grown up in the worst part of Oakland and had escaped her family's vicious pattern of poverty, addiction, and crime by sheer intelligence and determination. She always said exactly what she meant and was brutally honest. It was one of the things Val liked best about her, and the reason why they made such a successful team professionally.

Ellen went on. "You look like hell, and your interviews have become aimless and superficial. What is it, Val?"

When she didn't reply, Ellen said, "If you don't talk to me, you'll have to talk to Sid." Sid Barlow was the owner of the station. "He's about ready to fire you."

That brought Val up short. "Are you serious?"

"Very."

"But my ratings are terrific. They're talking about syndicating the show."

"Your ratings have been slipping badly lately. Nobody's gonna syndicate a show with someone who looks like something the cat dragged in. Look, Val, you've got all the potential in the world. You could have it all, an E-ticket to the best rides. But you're blowing it, and I want to know why!"

It took a lot to unsettle Val, but the thought of losing the career that had come to mean so much to her really shook her. "I broke up with a guy."

"Shit, is that all? Why is it when a woman gets off track there's always some guy involved? Listen, you've gotta stop thinking with your crotch."

"All right, I promise you, I'll shape up."

"I hope so. A lot is at stake. Hell, *everything* is at stake! Trust me, Val, he isn't worth it."

She wasn't sure about that. Val only knew that she wasn't about to let her career go down the tubes.

The scare over her career didn't ease the hurt of leaving Michael, but it gave her something else to focus on. It made it imperative that she fight as hard as she was capable of fighting. Val was always at her best when fighting against overwhelming odds. That unquenchable spirit had propelled her out of Visalia and had enabled her to survive the self-destructive excesses of her generation. Now she harnessed all that considerable energy into saving her career.

She worked so hard during the day that she fell into an exhausted slumber at night. She concentrated intently on the interviews, as she had done so successfully until being blown away by Michael. She and Ellen devised new plans for the show, and they succeeded brilliantly. Ratings shot up, and once again there was talk of syndication.

On the surface, she was the old Val, incisive, ambitious, tough. Inside, she was empty. All the success in the world couldn't fill that emptiness. Only Michael could. Despite the fact that she missed him terribly, she never once considered going back. She had meant what she had said. She loved him too much to watch him die, and that was exactly what would happen if he continued dealing.

Val reached her lowest point after doing a show about comedian John Belushi's death in 1982 from a cocaine/heroin overdose, realizing all too well that she could just as easily have ended up like Belushi, a sheetcovered body on a morgue gurney. One of the guests on the Belushi show was Tom Hoffman, a highly regarded novelist and well-known drug advocate whom she'd met before while still doing coke. After they'd finished taping, he joined Val in her office, where he casually opened a little porcelain pillbox filled with white powder. When he took a miniature silver spoon from the pocket of his jacket, Val froze.

In an instant, she remembered the intensity of the feeling she'd once gotten from it.

"It's great stuff," he said with a smile. "You know me, only the best."

"You're really asking to get busted, walking around with that stuff," she said, trying to sound tough but failing miserably. After all this time, she still *wanted* it. Val knew that just a little would make her forget Michael. The pain would go away, replaced by a euphoria she hadn't felt since the last time she'd gotten high.

Just a little.

She was so close . . . she could almost feel the rush of euphoria. *No!* She'd come too far. She had too much to lose.

Val looked at him. "No, thanks. I don't feel the need any more to hit myself to make it hurt on the outside instead of the inside."

422

Tom shrugged. "Whatever. Well, see ya around."

When he walked out the door, Val saw Ellen standing there, watching in silence. For a moment neither woman spoke, then Ellen walked over to Val and gave her a big hug.

"Congratulations, *chica*."

A month after they'd parted, Val arrived home late one night after putting in an especially long day at work. As she trudged down the steep wooden stairs leading to her hillside apartment, she stopped short. A figure stood illuminated by the light on her front porch.

Michael!

She didn't stop to think. She simply dropped her purse and briefcase and flew into his arms.

He held her so tightly she could hardly breathe. "I missed you!"

She couldn't speak. She was too busy choking back sobs.

"You really got to me, Val. Nothing was any good without you. Come on, let's go inside. We've got a lot to talk about."

The Colombians hadn't tried to contact Michael again and things had been very quiet, so he still felt that she'd overreacted to the threat the Colombians presented. But he'd come to feel that it didn't matter who was right and who was wrong in their disagreement. If he had to make some changes in his life to have her, then he would do it.

Although when pressed for specifics, Michael resisted, clearly unwilling to commit himself yet to major changes, Val didn't force the issue. They fell into bed together, making love with an intensity

423

and need that they'd never experienced before. When they awoke together at dawn, they made love again, this time savoring the touch, the taste, the feel of each other. Afterward, as they sat curled up on the sofa, sipping coffee, Val wanted to know. Exactly how much was Michael willing to change? What kind of life was he offering her?

As he had the night before, he avoided going into details and Val's heart sank.

"This is no good, Michael. We're not getting anywhere. All you've done is open up the old wound."

"Val, you're being negative. Look, I've got an idea. Let's go away this weekend, to my place on Maui."

"That won't do any good."

"Yes, it will. It's quiet, peaceful, away from all the pressures we both have to deal with here. We'll talk and we'll resolve all this."

When she hesitated, he said persuasively, "Remember how happy we were there? We can be that happy again. I promise."

Val knew she shouldn't go. It was futile. He hadn't really changed and never would; but looking at Michael, his dark hair disheveled from their lovemaking, his eyes hopeful, she couldn't say no.

The house was located on an isolated promontory on the verdant north shore of the island and had its own private beach. Michael had hired a well-known architect to design it and had spared no expense. Like his house in Napa, it wasn't exceptionally large, but it was stunning. Built on two levels of ground, it centered around an indoor waterfall and small rock-lined pool.

Security hadn't been overlooked here, either, though the precautions weren't as extensive as in Napa. The entire grounds were surrounded by a tall spiked fence, and an electronically operated security gate barred the driveway. The house itself had an elaborate security system. Even without Michael's outlaws standing guard, Val felt safe there.

Standing on the patio, looking out at the lush tropical scenery of Maui and breathing the balmy air, she felt seduced. She thought it the most beautiful place on earth. Michael was right when he said they'd been happy there. The weeks they had spent in this house had been the most peaceful, most relaxed of her life.

They spent all of Saturday lying on the sandy beach, swimming and occasionally going inside to make love. She knew that given half a chance Michael would renege on his promise to face their differences; she didn't intend to let him do that. Still, she wanted them to enjoy this one day, at least, before again confronting issues that she knew were bound to tear them apart once and for all.

That night he suggested they go out to dinner at one of the restaurants in the luxury hotels lining Kaanapali Beach. Val said she'd rather eat at home and even volunteered to cook, something she rarely did.

"All right," he agreed with a wry laugh. "I know what your ulterior motive is. You want to stay here so we can talk."

"Yes. After all, that was the whole point of coming here, wasn't it?"

He sighed. "I guess so, but *I'll* cook and you buy the groceries. Here, I'll write down what we need."

Michael sat at a teak desk and quickly wrote out a brief grocery list. "I'll go for one last swim while you're gone. Come out to the patio and call me when you get back."

He walked outside toward the stairs leading down to the beach, as Val went into the bedroom to get her purse and the car keys off the dresser. She had just driven the car out of the garage when she remembered the grocery list that she'd left on the desk. Leaving the engine running, she ran back in and grabbed the list. Through the giant floor-to-ceiling window that overlooked the beach below, she saw Michael walking toward the water, a towel flung over one shoulder. Smiling and moving closer to the window, she saw him drop the towel on the sand. For some reason, he turned and glanced back at the house. Seeing her in the window, he smiled and waved.

Michael's smile was warm and loving and caught at Val's heart.

It was the last time she saw him alive.

Two dark figures dressed entirely in black came up behind Michael. Each carried a sawed-off shotgun. Both fired at once. Michael pitched forward, arms outflung, his contorted face expressing pain and shock and disbelief. As he dropped to the sand, the two figures fired more rounds into his still body.

It happened in less time than it took Val to scream in horror.

At the sound of her voice, the two ski-mask-covered heads looked up and saw her pressed against the window. In the instant they raised their guns, she dove for the floor. The shotgun blasts shattered the glass, sending it raining down on her. Crouching, she ran for the open front door. In the distance, she heard the sounds of running feet and knew they were coming for her. Professionals didn't leave witnesses behind.

Val threw herself into the car, shoved the gear shift into drive, and floored the accelerator. Nearly hysterical, she had to fumble with the remote control for an agonizing moment before finally getting it to open the security gate. She was at the end of the driveway, turning onto the road, when two more shotgun blasts rang out, shattering the car's rear window.

Terrified, crying hysterically, Val kept going and didn't stop until she reached the safety of a sprawling hotel complex a few miles down the highway.

At first, the authorities refused to let Val leave Maui. It was several days before they decided that she had had nothing to do with the murder that she knew would never be solved. There was no way the Hawaiian police would ever be able to identify the hit men. When she was finally allowed to leave, she took Michael's body with her for burial in San Francisco.

Since the moment of his death, Val hadn't been able to get the image from her mind of Michael smiling, waving. Except for the night it happened, she hadn't cried. She had simply dealt with everything in a daze of shock and pain. It was only when she arrived in San Francisco and was met at the airport by a compassionate representative from the mortuary that her brittle facade of composure collapsed. She fell into the man's arms and cried, never minding that he was a total stranger. The man simply patted her back and murmured, "There, there, my dear," in a soothing, professional tone. He'd had a lot of experience in dealing with grief.

When she got home, a sobbing Val called Kate, who caught the next flight to San Francisco after contacting Barbara and Shelly. The thought of being surrounded by her closest friends caused Val to weep anew in relief, and by the time Kate arrived four hours later, Val's tough facade was gone as sobs wracked her thin, wiry body.

After several cups of hot, strong tea and with Kate's arms around her, she was at last able to talk about Michael. Late that night, Barbara arrived, and the next afternoon, Shelly flew in on her husband's jet. Not one passed judgment upon hearing of Michael's smuggling, and when the short funeral service was held the following morning, all four women stood together arm in arm, as always, the bond between them strong in a time of need.

Although Barbara made a light lunch of a salad and white wine, no one had much appetite. This was the first time all four had been together since Shelly's wedding the year before, and Shelly said, "You know, seeing us all together like this, it really hits me that we're in our thirties! We're not young any more!"

Barbara grinned. "Hey, we're not exactly ancient. In fact, we look pretty damn good."

"I remember what my mother looked like at this age," Kate said thoughtfully. "At the time, I thought she seemed so old, but I don't feel that way."

"Maybe your mother didn't either," Val quipped, with an attempt at her old humor.

Kate shook her head. "No, I think she did feel old because she didn't have anything to look forward to."

"Well, *we* do," Barbara insisted. "Just look at us. We're not naive little girls anymore. Val, you're a TV journalist, Kate's a successful screenwriter, Shelly's married to a famous, wealthy man, and I've got the kind of life most women dream of—a terrific husband and an adorable child and enough money and freedom to do anything I want."

As Barbara spoke, Val looked at each of them in turn. If Barbara was right and they had so much, why didn't they seem more satisfied? She became so quiet that Kate said in concern, "Don't hold back. Cry if you feel like it."

Val shook her head. "No, I don't have any more tears for Michael, but I'd like to talk about him, if you don't mind."

"Of course not," Barbara responded. "He must have been very special for you to have loved him so much."

Val managed a faint ghost of a smile. "I thought he was. At first I thought he was exciting because he was even more of a rebel than I had been. Then I fell in love with him, and he fell in love with me."

She stopped and repeated slowly, *"He fell in love with me!* I couldn't believe it for the longest time. He was the only man who ever loved me. Maybe he was the only man who ever will."

Barbara started to protest but stopped at a warning look from Kate. Catching the silent exchange, Val said, "Don't bother trying to reassure me. I've come to terms with it. For whatever reason, I'm just not the kind of woman men find it easy to love." She sighed. "I have to think about

429

the future now. There's something I have to deal with. That's why I wanted you all to be with me. I have a decision to make, and I'm not sure I can make it on my own."

Looking at her three friends as they waited expectantly, Val finished. "You see, I think I'm pregnant."

THREE

Shelly

She sat in the sunny morning room, a pleasant room tastefully furnished in antiques and country-house chintz in a bold red-and-green cabbage rose print. This was one of the cozier, less overwhelming rooms in the mansion, and from the beginning of her marriage, Shelly had made it her base of operations. In here, she consulted with the chef about the daily menu, planned the lavish parties that Ben liked to give, and read her morning mail, sorting through invitations and sending replies.

In the two and a half years since her marriage, she had developed a reputation as one of the most influential hostesses in London. Ben encouraged her social ascent and was tremendously proud of her high profile because it reflected well on him. As he neared fifty, he had everything he'd yearned for when he was young and poor and a victim of ridicule. Shelly had already begun making preliminary plans for a party-to-end-all-parties for his fiftieth birthday. She knew he would be as excited as a child when it happened and deeply touched that she would care enough to go to so much trouble for him.

431

Her motivation went beyond mere gratitude for the luxurious life-style Ben had given her. She was genuinely fond of him. Once she'd gotten over her initial disappointment, profound as it was, that he merely wanted a marriage of convenience, Shelly had grown to care for Ben very deeply. In almost every way, he was the father she'd never had—kind, indulgent, strong, and wise. She could always turn to him when she had a problem, and if she wanted something, all she had to do was mention it.

Shelly told herself that she had just about everything any woman could possibly want—she wasn't interested in sex anyway—but sometimes as she lay awake at night, unable to sleep, she found herself thinking of Philippe and wondering what their marriage would have been like. She was lonely in her king-sized bed that Ben wouldn't share.

When Ben offered to let Gayleen live with them, Shelly politely rejected the offer. Her mother was part of a past that she wanted desperately to forget. Then, at fifty-two, Gayleen got married. Through letters from her mother, Shelly learned that his name was Fred Magruder, he was a retired civil servant, and he seemed to make Gayleen happy.

Now Shelly's only concern was that someone would recognize her as one of Madame Justine's girls. So far she had been lucky and hadn't run into any ex-clients. Gossip was rampant in her social circle, and she knew that if word of her background got around, she would soon hear of it. Although courtesans had always held a special place in European society, Shelly had no desire to test the theory that her past would not hurt her future.

As she sat at a rosewood desk in front of a tall window in the morning room, she was pleased to see a letter from Val, who was a terrible correspondent. She rarely wrote, but when she did, her letters were a joy to read. This one—a few scrawled paragraphs accepting Shelly's invitation to spend this Christmas of 1983 with her and Ben—was typical: "I'm looking forward to a real English Christmas," Val wrote, "with snow and roasting chestnuts and stockings hanging by the fire. Will there be carolers? Michelle would love it. She's only two, but she's already learning to sing 'Rudolph the Red-Nosed Reindeer.' Fortunately, she doesn't take after me in her singing ability. You won't believe how traditional I've become now that I'm a mum. I can't give Michelle the kind of family life she deserves, with a daddy and a house with a white picket fence and a mommy who stays home and watches 'Sesame Street' with her, so I'm doing my best to make up for it in other ways. I expect I'll join the PTA eventually and start wearing shirtwaist dresses just like Donna Reed wore.

"By the way, did you hear about the ERA defeat in November? What a bummer. People are so stupid. I can understand men being afraid of giving us equal protection under the law, but I don't get why so many women were against it. Did all those years in beauty salons, surrounded by God knows how many chemicals, kill a few brain cells? If I ever meet Phyllis Schlafly, I'm going to snatch her bald-headed. Anyway, it was ratified by thirty-five of the necessary thirty-eight states, but time ran out. Only six votes short! So, no equal status for women! Well, maybe in Michelle's lifetime.

"Gotta run. Michelle just woke up and Sarah, my nanny, is off with her new boyfriend, probably doing what I would have been doing at eighteen. Love ya."

Shelly smiled as she folded the letter. This would be the first time she'd see the baby. It would be so wonderful having a child in the house at Christmastime. She would have to get a very special present for Michelle. Maybe a giant stuffed panda or a rocking horse . . .

Her thoughts were interrupted by the sound of a car coming up the front drive. The morning room window faced the drive, and she saw Richard Ford stepping out of his gray Jaguar. She was rather surprised to see him because Ben was away and normally Richard only came to the house to see Ben on business.

True to his word, Ben had been discreet in his relationship with Richard. Shelly knew he must be spending time with Richard outside of business hours, but if so she had no idea when or where these liaisons took place. In spite of all this, she couldn't help feeling jealous of Richard because she knew that Ben loved him in a way he could never love her.

A moment later, Hastings, the butler, opened the door to the morning room and announced, "Mr. Ford, ma'am."

Shelly rose and smiled politely at Richard. "What a pleasant surprise! What brings you here this morning? I'm afraid Ben isn't back from Milan yet."

Ben had flown to Milan the day before to pick up a new Ferrari Testa Rossa that he'd ordered. He planned to drive it back himself, taking his time, getting used to the car, and Shelly had assumed Richard would accompany him. Obviously, that wasn't the case.

Richard, always rather quiet and soft-spoken, was even more sober than usual. For the first time, she noticed dark circles under his eyes. Normally an immaculate dresser, he had carelessly thrown on his clothes this morning and hadn't bothered with a tie. Shelly felt the superficial smile on her face fade as her hands clenched at her sides.

Taking those hands in his, Richard said in an exhausted voice, "Let's sit down, Shelly. I'm afraid I have some bad news."

For a moment she couldn't speak. Richard led her to the sofa, and as they sat down, she finally found her voice. "What is it? Is it Ben? Is he all right?"

Richard explained carefully. "He picked up the car yesterday at the factory in Milan. It was late, but instead of staying over, he decided he couldn't wait to drive it. They set out for Zurich."

"They?"

Richard hesitated. "Someone was with him. A young man."

Shelly immediately understood. Ben was involved with someone else. Looking at Richard, at the pain all too evident in his pale hazel eyes, she could only guess what it cost him to talk about this.

But the main thing was Ben. "What happened? Is Ben all right?"

"It probably would have been all right if Ben had been driving. He was familiar with Ferraris, knew how to handle them, but apparently he let the . . . the passenger drive. The young man wasn't used to the car. He took a corner too fast and went over a steep cliff. I'm afraid both of them died instantly."

435

"*No!*"

"The Italian police got hold of me early this morning. Ben's wallet was burned in the crash, but because he had bought the car through the company, the factory had a record of our business address and phone number."

Dead.

Ben dead.

"No," she repeated in a hoarse whisper.

"I know this is very hard for you, Shelly. It's . . . rather hard for me, as well. Would you like me to ring for Hastings, to have some tea brought in?"

She almost wanted to smile. The typical English response to tragedy—a nice, hot, strong cup of tea.

"No. No, thank you."

All at once, Shelly felt immensely cold. She wrapped her arms around herself and stared at the bright, cheerful morning room where nothing had changed, and yet everything was different.

Ben was dead.

She was alone again. She felt as bereft as a child who has suddenly been orphaned. She didn't know that her face had gone ashen, her deep blue eyes like two dark holes in her pale face.

In concern, Richard said, "If there's anyone you'd like me to call for you, to be with you . . ."

His words trailed off.

She looked at Richard and, to her surprise, realized that *he* was the person she wanted to be with right now. Her friends didn't know Ben as Richard did, they didn't love him as Richard did. Suddenly Shelly realized that she and Richard had a powerful common bond—both had loved Ben very much and both had been deeply hurt by his

436

inability to love them totally and exclusively.

For the first time, Shelly saw Richard not as a rival but as someone who could understand what she was going through better than anyone else possibly could. "There isn't anyone I'd like to see right now. Do you . . . have to leave? Could you stay for just a little while?"

His expression softened. "Of course. Shelly, I know we've never been close, but I want you to know that I will help you deal with this, in any way that you need my help. Ben told me once that if anything should happen to him, he wanted me to look out for you. He cared about you very much, my dear."

"He cared for you, too, Richard. I know this must be very hard for you."

He was clearly touched that she would say as much. "Thank you. I'm afraid he wasn't able to care for either of us quite as we would have wished, but he tried his best, you know. He never meant to hurt anyone."

"I know."

"I'm sorry to bother you with details at this time, but I'm afraid there are some things that must be decided rather quickly. I've arranged for the body to be flown to London, and it should be here this afternoon. Would you like to select a mortuary to handle it, or would you prefer to leave that to me?"

Shelly closed her eyes, trying to shut away the pain of a loss she hadn't yet fully taken in. After a moment, she opened them and said in a dull voice, "I'm sure you can handle that quite well. What . . . what happens next?"

"You must decide what kind of service, if any, you would like."

"Oh, Richard, I don't think Ben would have wanted a big, public funeral. Do you?"

"No, I don't think he would have liked that."

"Did he ever give you any indication of what sort of service he would prefer?"

"No. He didn't like to talk about death. Dealing with the idea of his own mortality was difficult for him. So it's really up to you. What would you like?"

She thought for a moment, then said in a firm voice, "Something simple and quiet. Private. Without a lot of gawkers. I know a lot of people were aware he was homosexual, and I couldn't deal with them staring at you and me and whispering behind our backs, speculating about our relationship with him."

"I agree."

Something occurred to her. "What about the business? What will happen to it?"

"You'll have to meet with Ben's attorney to go into the details, but I know that in his will he left a controlling interest to you and a significant number of shares to me."

Shelly was stunned. Ben had always refused to discuss the business with her, insisting that she shouldn't worry her lovely little head about it. She had felt frustrated and left out but hadn't wanted to press the issue. Now she couldn't understand why Ben hadn't left the entire business to Richard.

"But why would he do such a thing?"

Richard said simply, "We discussed it and decided it was the right thing to do."

"You agreed?"

"Yes. Look, I know that Ben had old-fashioned ideas about women and business, but he was faced with a clear-cut choice—either you or I would run the business if anything happened to him. I told him I wasn't interested in doing that. Besides, as his wife, it was only right that control of it should go to you."

"But you've been so instrumental in making it a success."

Richard managed a faint smile. "I've always worked behind the scenes, handling the mundane day-to-day details. I'm the money man, the one who holds creditors at bay during the rough times and the one who decides which investments are wisest during the good times. Ben was the visionary, the one with that rare combination of energy and charisma to make it a success. I could never do what he did, and I wouldn't want to try. If you truly don't mind, I would like to continue in my same capacity when you take over."

"*Me* take over? I can't! I don't know anything about business!" Shelly panicked at the thought of having to step into Ben's shoes and try to run a multimillion-dollar business.

"I can teach you what you need to know about the business. You won't have to handle it alone. I'll be there every step of the way. Don't worry about that. Whether you realize it or not, you've been identified with Rashad Cosmetics almost as much as Ben was. You're the face the public associates with the company. I'm confident you're the best, the only, person to run it. There are some crucial business issues we'll have to deal with, but they can wait for the moment. Right now, you have enough to deal with."

"Richard, there's something I want to ask you, but I know it may be painful for you."

His lips trembled slightly and his eyes glistened with unshed tears. "Nothing could be as painful as

439

losing Ben. I understand there may be some questions you'd like to ask. Go ahead."

"After he told me he was gay, he never talked about it again. It was almost like he wanted to pretend that he wasn't homosexual."

Despite his determined air of composure, Richard was obviously profoundly hurt by this insight. "Yes . . . he always felt a . . . a tension in his life because of his homosexuality. He knew the truth about himself from the time he was thirteen, but he wouldn't admit it to anyone but me."

"You knew him then?"

He nodded. "We grew up together, lived on the same shabby little street in Islington. We were drawn to each other because of . . . what we were, but also because we both wanted very much to get out of there and have something better in life."

"You must have always been his closest friend."

"And he was mine." Richard's voice broke and he looked away.

"Did his parents know?"

"Eventually. They suspected for a long time, of course, but didn't want to face it. Then one day his father confronted him with it and Ben admitted the truth. His father turned his back on him, refused to even speak to him again. Years later, as he lay dying, he still refused to see Ben. Following her husband's wishes, Ben's mother turned him away from the funeral."

Shelly could only imagine how devastated Ben must have been by such rejection. No wonder he encouraged her to maintain a relationship with her mother. The concept of family must have mattered a great deal to him because he had been deprived of his. Perhaps, she thought, that also partly explained his marriage to her. At least on the surface, it gave him a socially acceptable family unit.

"No wonder he tried so hard to lead a double life," she whispered.

"Yes. Ben and I were from an older generation. Younger people have less hypocrisy about it nowadays. The average twenty-year-old gay person is a lot less neurotic about it than us old fellows in our late forties. For Ben, because of the position he was in, it just made everything easier to be seen with a companion of the opposite sex. Especially one who was so beautiful and who other men desired."

Richard went on carefully. "I know Ben used you, Shelly, and at times I've sensed how terribly hurt you've been by that. I've understood the depth of your loneliness because I've experienced it myself. As much as you and I were hurt by that, it was equally hard for Ben. Homosexuality was a terrifying thing for him to live with. He was expected to laugh at jokes about it and was afraid not to."

"But he always had you. He wasn't alone."

"No. He wasn't alone. I was always there for him and always would have been, but it was still hard. We were companions but we had to hide, and gradually I wasn't enough. He . . . turned to others."

"Why?"

"I'm not sure. I loved him so much, I never needed anyone else." He looked at her and smiled gently. "I think you felt the same way."

Yes, she had, but it hadn't done either of them any good.

"As Ben grew older, he increasingly turned to younger partners. These liaisons never lasted long, and I always took him back. Hurt and angry as I

441

was at times, I always understood that it was part of his basic self-hatred, a way of acting out the worthless feeling he had because of his father's rejection."

"Do you know who was with him in Italy?"

"No. The Italian police told me his name, Mick Geeson, but it meant nothing to me. I'm sure he was just the latest in a long line of attractive, opportunistic young men who used Ben financially."

How sad, Shelly thought, how utterly sad. Ben had two people—her and Richard—who loved him deeply, but it wasn't enough.

Looking at Richard once more, Shelly asked, "When . . . when will he arrive?"

"He'll be at Heathrow at six o'clock. You don't have to be there if you don't want to. I can deal with it."

"No, I want to be there. To . . . to meet Ben one last time."

Respect shone in Richard's eyes. "I think he would have appreciated that."

Ben's death was announced by the media before Shelly had a chance to contact people privately. Although Kate, Val, and Barbara all offered to come, she preferred to face the ordeal alone.

Ben's graveside service took place in the cemetery near the small country church close to the estate and wasn't publicized. Richard, Shelly, and a few other close friends and high-ranking employees of the company were present. Richard had contacted Ben's mother, but she had refused to come. The vicar, a kindly, elderly man, gave a short but reassuring speech. The casket was lowered into the grave. It was over.

From the moment Richard had broken the news to her, Shelly hadn't been able to cry. She wished she could find the physical relief that tears would bring, but somehow they wouldn't come. It was as if she had closed off completely now and was devoid of emotion. As she lay in bed that night, she decided that perhaps it was better this way. If she was no longer capable of feeling anything, then Shelly could never be hurt again.

One week later, in December 1983, Shelly Rashad presided over an emergency meeting of the board of directors of Rashad Cosmetics. The board members, all middle-aged men, all wealthy, and most of them from aristocratic backgrounds, were wary. Beneath their hollow condolences was fear. Clearly, they were worried about what would happen to the company now that its founder and guiding light was gone. Richard had informed them that Shelly would be taking over, and they clearly had no confidence in her ability to handle the job.

As if a hostile male board and a job she wasn't at all sure she could do weren't enough, there was still more to deal with. As Richard gave a comprehensive report on the financial state of the company, Shelly realized that something was very wrong. A destructive pattern emerged—Ben's lavish overspending, taking the company public too soon, expanding into new markets without sufficient financial resources—in short, Rashad Cosmetics was in desperate financial trouble. The crisis had been brewing for a long time, but Ben had always been able to charm the board members out of their mounting concern and to stave off disaster with brilliant short-term solutions. But Ben wasn't here any more. Shelly faced this crisis alone.

She stopped Richard in the middle of a sentence and asked in dismay, "Are you saying the company is about to go under?"

Clearing his throat, he responded, "If we don't find solutions to these urgent problems — yes, I'm afraid so."

"Ben borrowed heavily from the company," he added uncomfortably. "I'm afraid that by the time that personal debt is repaid, there will be little left in terms of personal assets."

Shelly could not believe it. Ben's death wasn't the only trauma to deal with; now she faced losing the financial security she had sold her soul to achieve. It would all be gone — her social position, her home, the money, everything. She would have to go back to having nothing and worrying about how she would support herself. It had been difficult enough when she was in her twenties. Now, in her thirties, she couldn't face starting over again at the bottom.

While the board members muttered angrily among themselves, Shelly gave Richard a stricken look. To her amazement, he smiled.

"Ben used to say that there were no problems, only opportunities. We have some serious financial problems, it's true, but we also have a product line that is highly regarded and a corporate name that means a great deal. If we tighten our belt, financially speaking, make some cutbacks in nonessential areas, and move aggressively to increase our market share, we can survive. All it takes is the right leadership. I have every confidence that you can provide that leadership, Shelly."

She deeply appreciated his vote of confidence,

but looking at the highly critical faces of the board members, she realized that they didn't share it. Her immediate thought was to simply give up, turn the company over to Richard, let him do what he could with it, and concentrate all her energy on figuring out how she was going to support herself.

"With all due respect to Mrs. Rashad," one of the board members began irritably, "she has no business experience. There's no way she can deal with such serious problems. Our only option is to sell the company, if we can find a buyer; if not, file Chapter Eleven and liquidate."

Sell the company . . . liquidate . . .

"But Ben worked so hard to build this company," she began. "He wouldn't want to see it go under."

"Ben isn't here," the man snapped, no longer making a pretense of politeness.

Shelly looked at Richard, but he didn't say anything. He simply watched her, waiting for her response. She realized he wasn't going to make any decisions for her. He'd made it clear that he hoped she would fight, and he felt she stood a chance of pulling it off, but it was up to her to make that commitment.

"Do you really think I can do it?" she asked in a low voice.

He nodded. "I believe that if Ben were here, he would tell you that you could do it."

"I don't know . . . I need time to think."

"Why don't we adjourn the meeting," Richard suggested, "and return tomorrow, while the out-of-town board members are still in London. We can finalize our plans at that time."

Clearly anxious to leave and discuss the situation in private among themselves, the board members quickly agreed.

That night, Shelly sat alone in Ben's private office. She had hoped that the atmosphere of the office, so redolent of Ben's strong personality, might help her reach a decision. So far, all she'd come up with was confusion and despair. She looked at the clock. Nine o'clock; six A.M. California time. Should she call Kate, Val, or Barbara? No. When she had married Ben, she had abdicated responsibility for herself. Now she was being forced to take it up again. She was on her own.

"All right," she said aloud, her voice sounding strange in the empty, silent room. "Enough of this! Let's get to work!"

Hours later, she had finished examining the annual reports and the description of the product line. Something was missing with Rashad Cosmetics, but she didn't know what it could be. Looking up, she saw Richard standing in the doorway.

"I saw the light on and knew it must be you. I hope I'm not intruding."

"Of course not. Come in."

Seeing the papers spread out across the desk before her, he smiled as he sat down. "I see you're hard at it."

"Yes, but I'm not sure I'm making much progress."

"What do you think of the company — the products, the direction we're going in?"

"Somehow I have a feeling that we're doing something wrong, but I can't quite put my finger on what."

"Ben always said that women can all be persuaded to buy youth in a bottle and hope in a jar.

446

You're our typical buyer—upscale, thirtyish, concerned with presenting just the right appearance. What appeals to you about our products? Or doesn't appeal to you?"

She shook her head. "It isn't that simple. The cosmetics are fine, but so are a lot of other high-priced lines. Rashad needs something to set it apart, above the competition. Something very contemporary. My generation isn't like our mothers. We want something more from cosmetics than just covering up the inevitable wrinkles."

Richard began to look alert and interested. "Such as?"

"Well . . ." Shelly thought for a moment. "We don't want to get that matronly look our mothers have. I remember how my mother looked in her thirties. She looked middle-aged. I want to look young as long as possible. I want to push back the boundaries of middle age."

He nodded enthusiastically. "Yes, I can see that. Ben and I never thought of it that way. Go on."

"Well, for instance, skin care. My generation's getting older. We didn't have to think much about skin care before, but now we do. I'd rather use products that keep my skin looking young rather than using products that merely camouflage aging skin. After all, women are so health-conscious nowadays. We want our faces to look as healthy as the rest of our bodies."

"Of course!" Richard leaned across the table, his eyes alight with excitement. "We could focus on skin care as well as cosmetics. It's exactly the kind of bold step Ben would have taken."

His enthusiasm was contagious. Shelly's voice quickened with eagerness. "We could add a whole line of skin care products and change our cosmet-

447

ics so that they improved the condition of skin. We could open up clinics in all the major cities."

She stopped and her expression sobered. "This is ridiculous. I'm really getting carried away."

"No, your thoughts are right on target. Our research and development department can come up with new products to keep skin nourished and resilient. Cleansers and moisturizers to combat daily exposure to urban pollution and dehydrating environments, such as air travel."

"Exactly! Maybe women can't avoid character lines eventually, but we want them to look good when they get here."

"We'll have to come up with a whole new approach to marketing and promotion," Richard said, furiously jotting down notes.

Shelly rose and began pacing around the room. "The key is the word *natural*. I keep reading that the environment is going to be a big issue in this decade. I know that my generation is concerned about it. Maybe we could promote these new products by keeping them simple and natural."

"How do you mean?"

"Don't test them on animals or make them from animals or rare resources. Make sure they're biodegradable." She stopped and faced Richard. "Can we do all that?"

"Of course. Ben used to say if we can dream it, we can do it. Now you're the one doing the dreaming, Shelly, and I'd say you're every bit as good at it as he was."

"But the board . . ."

"Hang the board. They have no choice but to go along with you, for the time being at least. I'll make the necessary financial changes to keep us afloat while we change direction and put all your ideas into effect."

"Oh, Richard, do you really think we can succeed?"

"There's only one way to find out, Shelly. I won't pretend it will be easy. There's the board to deal with, creditors, all the naysayers who want you to fail spectacularly. It may turn out that the company is just too far gone to save. I can't promise you anything but a long, bloody fight. The only question is—are you up for it?"

Her excitement had dissipated as he reeled off the list of problems. She knew perfectly well how tough it would be. Once she started, she couldn't back out. Shelly would have to see it through, possibly to the bitter end.

For some reason, a memory, vivid in its intensity, flashed into her mind—Barbara telling all of them that they could do anything, be anything. She'd been right. Shelly might have stumbled along the way, but she had come even farther than she'd dreamed. She wasn't about to give up now.

Looking at Richard, she nodded slowly. "I'm up for it."

FOUR

Kate

Michelle Katherine Simpson, named for her father and her godmother, was born on a gorgeous late September day in 1981. Val went into labor a week ahead of schedule, in the middle of taping a show. She immediately called Kate, who flew in just in time to coach her through the birth.

When Val had told them she was pregnant and had asked for their advice, her three friends had all urged her to have the child. Kate knew that Val didn't want to have another abortion, especially since she knew this was Michael's child. When Val worried about her ability to raise a child alone, Kate said, "You won't be alone. We'll help."

And they did. Barbara found her a good obstetrician and gave her books on child care. Kate flew to San Francisco every week to be her partner in Lamaze classes. Shelly found a nanny she could rely on, an English teenager named Sarah, who had a lot of experience in caring for younger brothers and sisters and who was thrilled at the opportunity to go to the States.

In spite of their support and encouragement, Val continued to agonize over whether she'd made the right decision. "You know what a fuck-up I am,

Katie. I have no business being a mother. I can't even give the baby a father! And what about all the drugs I used to do? What if something's wrong with the baby?"

"You've had all the tests, and the doctor says everything looks fine," Kate reminded her. "As for not having a father, well, a lot of kids don't, and you're not a fuck-up anymore. You're successful and responsible."

Val refused to be reassured. She was a mass of nerves right up to the moment when she gave the final painful push and her daughter came into the world.

When the doctor laid the loudly protesting, dark-haired baby on Val's breast, her face was transformed by an inexpressible joy.

"She's beautiful!" she whispered tearfully. "She looks just like Michael."

At that moment, Kate knew that Val's decision to have the baby had been the right one.

When Kate took Val home two days later, Barbara was there, with baby clothes, formula, diapers, and a daunting array of other baby paraphernalia. Sarah wasn't due to arrive for a few days, so Kate and Barbara gave Michelle her first bath at home and took turns getting up with her in the middle of the night so an exhausted Val could rest.

The first time Kate took her turn at a 3 A.M. feeding, she sat in the pink-and-white antique rocking chair that Shelly had sent from London and held the tiny infant wrapped snugly in a soft yellow blanket knitted by Kate's mother. The room was dimly lit by one pale lamp in a corner. Through the bay window, Kate could see the lights of San Francisco twinkling like fairy lights, even at this late hour. It was quiet and still. A feeling of peacefulness, unlike anything Kate had ever felt before,

451

stole over her as she held the tiny infant in her arms.

This is what it would have been like with my baby, she thought, and tears stung the corners of her eyes.

When she returned to Trancas Beach a few days later, Kate was quiet and pensive. Going through Val's pregnancy and childbirth, then helping to take care of little Michelle, had brought home a profound truth. Despite the success she and Alan had achieved together, something crucial was missing at the core of her life. It wasn't just a baby, it was everything that represented — commitment, permanence, *family* — something beyond grosses, reviews, and deals.

She hadn't been ready to be a mother before, but she was now. Kate was prepared to handle the sacrifices, the physical exhaustion, the loss of independence and freedom. She knew it would affect her career to a certain extent. It would probably mean giving up writing for a few months because she wanted to do this right, *she* wanted to raise her child.

Because Val worked at a job outside the home to support herself and Michelle, she had no choice but to turn over Michelle to someone else for a large part of the day, but Kate was financially secure now and could stop working for as long as she wished. When she returned to work, she would still be at home. There was no need to rely on someone else to take care of her child.

She knew a child would drastically alter the lifestyle she and Alan had grown used to. It would be a little more difficult to go to Cannes for two weeks to attend the film festival, or to drop everything and

452

go rushing off to location when a movie ran into problems that only the writer or producer could fix, but she was willing, even eager, to make those adjustments.

She just hoped Alan was.

That night, Kate prepared his favorite dinner—not an easy accomplishment since cooking still wasn't one of her talents. She set the table with their finest linen, china, crystal, and silver and lit two tall candles in silver holders. A silver bucket filled with ice held a bottle of champagne.

When Alan came through the door at eight o'clock, he grinned in delight. "What's the special occasion? Are we celebrating something or drowning our sorrows?"

"Neither." Taking a deep breath, Kate plunged in. "I just thought it would be nice to make this night as romantic as possible since it could be the night our baby is conceived."

For a moment, he stood still, then he laughed and shook his head. "I knew you'd come back from Val's wanting a baby. That old biological clock's ticking awfully loud, isn't it?"

Kate let out a sigh of relief. He wasn't upset; he was amused; and, so far at least, he hadn't said he didn't want a baby.

"Well, I am in my thirties now. I don't have that much time left to put it off. How do you feel about it?"

Alan put his arms around her shoulders and kissed the tip of her nose. "Whatever you want, babe. The only question is, do we start trying before dinner or after?"

Kate couldn't believe how easy it was. No argument, not even a discussion, just "Whatever you want."

Nuzzling her ear, Alan whispered, "I vote for before dinner."

As they walked up the stairs to their bedroom, Kate told herself she should be thrilled. She had gotten what she wanted — Alan's agreement — but she couldn't help feeling that something was missing. She wished Alan could be enthusiastic rather than merely going along with it. She wished he could want this baby as much as she did, for the same reasons she did.

After they made love, she lay there thinking, *We might have just created a baby.*

Somehow, Kate didn't feel the fragile hope she'd expected to feel.

When her period came right on schedule two weeks later, she felt a twinge of disappointment followed by undeniable relief. She understood all too well what prompted the relief. Here in Trancas, her euphoria over Michelle's birth had faded. She was faced with the harsh reality that having a baby wouldn't change anything between her and Alan. It wouldn't make them close again, as they'd been at the beginning of their marriage. It wouldn't stop his occasional infidelities. They would only be a family on the surface. Underneath, there wouldn't be any of the qualities that Kate had grown up with in her family — unswerving loyalty and a deep and abiding love.

At the end of her period, Kate started taking her birth control pills again. Alan didn't ask if she was still trying to conceive, just as he hadn't asked how the abortion had affected her.

On a warm, early fall evening in 1984, Kate and Alan drove up to the security gates that

454

guarded the small, exclusive residential area known as the Colony in Malibu.

"This is the most important night of my life."

At Kate's skeptical look, Alan went on. "I'm not kidding! Do you know how important this meeting is?"

"I thought it was a dinner."

"Dinner, meeting, what's the difference? It's all business. The point is Bryan Yates is the head of the most successful studio in town."

"I know who Yates is."

She was irritable because the hot, dry Santa Ana was blowing especially hard that evening, sending eucalyptus branches falling to the ground, creating tiny whirlwinds of dirt and sand. On top of that, Alan's nervousness over this dinner was beginning to grate. From the moment their agent had called to say that Yates wanted to meet with them, preferably in a casual setting, such as dinner at his beach house, Alan had been tense and jumpy.

"Yates is thinking of offering me an independent production deal. I wouldn't just be producing our movies under an executive producer who gets all the glory and most of the money. *I* would be the exec, and *I* could develop other projects besides ours."

Kate felt a return of the panic that had gripped her when their agent had first explained the situation to them. What if Alan got so involved in doing other projects that he was no longer interested in working with her? Their work together, with Alan producing the screenplays they cowrote, was the strongest bond between them. Without that, there was very little to keep them together.

The guard at the gate checked their names off the list of people approved to enter and raised the barrier so they could turn onto Malibu Colony Road, which was lined with magnificent houses

455

built only inches apart, their garages facing the road, fronts facing the broad white beach. Per square foot, this was the most expensive real estate in L.A.

"We're gonna live here some day," Alan vowed.

"Do you realize what these places go for?"

"If this deal goes through, we'll be able to afford it."

He smiled at her, the first time he'd relaxed enough to smile all day. "This deal will give us everything we ever wanted. We'll make the biggest, most successful movies anyone's ever seen. I told you we'd go straight to the top together, Kate. I'm finally making good on that promise."

She felt a rush of relief. They were still a team, still in this together.

Kate envisioned the two of them in one of these houses—driving in and out of the guarded gates, living right on the beach instead of looking at it from a distance, being part of the exclusive little community of movers and shakers. It would be the culmination of nearly ten years of hard work. It would mean they'd arrived in a big way, succeeding even more spectacularly than Kate had hoped for in her wildest dreams.

All of it depended on how they got along with Yates.

They found his house, a starkly modern gray structure with lots of stained glass, and were admitted by Yates himself. "I hate having servants hang around at night if it isn't absolutely necessary," he said with a disarming smile. "I hope you don't mind, but this is going to be very casual tonight. We'll serve ourselves from a cold buffet."

Kate had read a great deal about him, so she was prepared for the fact that he was young, barely forty, and attractive in an Ivy League way, with

456

short blond hair, blue eyes, and a preppie style of dressing. Yates had come to Hollywood from the Yale School of Drama, had become an agent with one of the top agencies in town, and then had opened his own agency, which had quickly become enormously successful. By the early eighties, top agents were being offered jobs at the studios, and Yates took over R&M Studios, one of the oldest in town. His contacts with top talent soon turned around the ailing R&M. He was known for signing talent to exclusive, highly lucrative production deals. That type of deal was exactly what Alan wanted very badly.

They had drinks on the wooden deck that was partially protected from the wind by high walls on either side. The sun sank out of sight on the horizon in a blaze of gold, orange, and lavender. Kate, who rarely drank, had a couple of the margaritas made with fresh limes that Yates pressed on her. She was as nervous as Alan now and hoped that a little liquor might calm her.

"So, Alan, I hear your last film is doing great overseas," Yates began.

Alan responded, and they spent the next several minutes discussing the overseas market and the growing international nature of the film business, foreign financing, co-ventures with European TV networks and film studios, and other technical subjects that Kate understood but cared little about. Unlike Alan, she had never enjoyed the deal-making part of the business.

She was relieved to see that Alan's nervousness was gone; he and Yates seemed to be hitting it off very well. When darkness fell, Yates suggested they go in to dinner. The casual buffet he'd mentioned turned out to be a lavish spread of cold lobster, shrimp, crab, and pasta salad. Kate was too nervous to eat much and instead concentrated on the excellent wine he kept pouring into her glass.

By the time they adjourned to the elegantly furnished living room with its cathedral ceiling and massive stone fireplace, Kate was uncomfortably aware that she was a little drunk. Terrified that she would embarrass herself and hurt Alan's chances at the deal, she abruptly stopped drinking, hoping Yates would offer coffee soon.

Yates mentioned having a tape of the latest, as yet unreleased album of one of Alan's favorite singers. "Would you like to hear it?" he asked.

"Yeah, that would be great!" Alan answered enthusiastically.

When the music came out over the state-of-the-art stereo system, it seemed to fill the entire room with its slow, seductive beat. At that moment, the mood altered in a subtle yet critical way. Yates began telling Alan about an erotic suspense script that he had just bought. He mentioned, as if in passing, that he hadn't decided on a producer for it.

Alan was clearly interested. He made some suggestions as to how that type of film should be handled. Soon he and Yates were discussing what was sexy, cinematically speaking, and what wasn't.

Kate, sitting slightly apart from the two men, didn't participate in the dialogue. She knew she wasn't expected to. She had been invited only because she was Alan's wife and this was ostensibly a social occasion.

The liquor made her feel drowsy. Closing her eyes for a moment, she concentrated on the music rather than following the conversation. Suddenly she opened her eyes with a start, afraid that she might actually have dozed off.

She saw Alan and Yates bending over the large glass coffee table on a marble pedestal. Several lines of cocaine were laid out. She wasn't really surprised. Coke had become the currency of Hollywood society, and she had been at many parties where it was passed around freely. Sometimes it replaced dessert at the end of a dinner.

Kate had never tried it herself, though Alan occasionally did. Now she watched as he and Yates each pinched a nostril and inhaled the pristine white powder. Noticing that she was watching them, Yates smiled and said, "Why don't you join us, Kate."

The look Alan gave her spoke volumes. Don't insult him, he telegraphed. Everything's going so well. Don't blow this for me!

She hesitated, profoundly torn about what to do.

Taking her silence for assent, Yates brought some coke to her in a tiny gold spoon. She hesitated for just a fraction of a second, then thought, Why not? Just this once. After all, so much was at stake. As she inhaled, Kate felt a strange, uncomfortable sensation. Whatever she'd expected, it wasn't this overpowering numbness.

Yates laughed. "You look like you feel dead."

It was as if she'd been given an anesthetic. His voice seemed to come from far away.

"I think I'm going to faint," she whispered.

"Don't worry. The feeling will pass."

There began a nightmarish dream. Far away was Alan, kneeling by the table, doing more coke. Then, immediately in front of her, Yates, seeming larger, more dominant than he'd seemed before, pulling her to her feet and murmuring something about going to his bedroom.

Coke whore!

She'd heard men use the phrase often enough to describe a woman who would do anything sexually for coke. It was always said with a special disgust that never seemed to be applied to men who did coke.

That was exactly how she felt as Yates led her away. Like a coke whore.

Even in her lethargic state, Kate knew she didn't want to do this. She tried to tell Yates to let go of her, but she didn't seem to have the energy to pull away from him.

They were nearly out of the living room when she stopped and looked back at Alan. For one moment, her mind cleared and the scene was crystal clear to her. Yates beside her, quietly insistent. Alan sitting on the floor by the coffee table. Kate herself, feeling helpless and disoriented and scared.

Her eyes locked with Alan's. Don't let him do this to me, she begged.

Alan lowered his eyes and went back to the uneven lines of white powder in front of him.

She awoke at sunrise in her own bed with no recollection of how she'd gotten there. Alan lay beside her, dead to the world. Both were fully clothed.

Kate's mouth felt unbearably dry, as if she hadn't had anything to drink for days. When she sat up, her head exploded with the worst headache she could ever remember having. She dragged herself into the bathroom and splashed cold water on her face. Then, cupping her hands under the tap, she guzzled the water.

After a moment, she turned off the faucet and leaned against the hard, cold edge of the white-tiled counter. She didn't want to think about last night. She didn't want to think about anything. She just wanted to stop this horrible pounding in her head; but she couldn't shut off her mind. Disturbing images, painful memories assaulted her. She thought she'd been deeply unhappy before: when she learned of Alan's infidelities; when she realized there was no place in their relationship for a baby. Kate knew now that she hadn't begun to understand what real unhappiness was. At that moment, she was at rock bottom emotionally. She couldn't sink any lower. She was beyond tears. She felt too cold and empty inside to cry. For a split second, Kate felt that she couldn't live with such pain; anything, even death, would be preferable. The fleeting consideration of suicide frightened her. She didn't really want to die, but she couldn't go on living like this.

She no longer knew who she was or what she believed in. Right and wrong were a blur. *What would Daddy think if he could see me now?*

Since his death, Kate had tried desperately to redeem herself through her ambition. Last night, she had prostituted herself for that ambition. In doing so, she had lost any hope of redemption. She knew that in order to survive, she had to leave, had to get out of there immediately and go as far away as she possibly could. She knew with absolute certainty that it was the right thing to do. Leaving Alan, walking away from everything they'd built together, would take courage. She felt she didn't have any left.

Staring at her drawn reflection in the bathroom mirror, Kate knew she had to find the courage to save her life. Without hesitation, she yanked a duffle bag out of her closet, and shoved some clothes in it as quietly as possible so as not to awaken Alan. She took her passport and, pausing once to look back at her husband, thought about leaving a note. Even though she was a writer, at that moment, Kate had no idea what to say.

She left, closing the door gently behind her.

461

At ten o'clock that night, London time, a taxi pulled up to Shelly's front door. Kate stepped out, holding her bag, and handed the cabbie a fifty-pound note. Waving aside his offer of change, she hurried up to the front door and rang the bell.

It was the servants' night out, and Shelly answered the door herself, looking pale and lovely in a black velvet robe.

"Kate! My God, you look terrible! What's happened?"

The tears that wouldn't come before poured out in a deluge now as she fell into Shelly's arms.

"It's all right," Shelly murmured, holding her friend up. "You're safe now. Come on inside by the fire."

Kate let herself be led inside to a cozy room where a cheerful fire crackled. She thought she would never be able to stop crying. Shelly sat her down on a small, wonderfully comfortable sofa and continued to hold her.

"There, there," Shelly said, "it's all right now. Whatever happened, it's all over now and you're okay."

"You don't understand," Kate sobbed, her voice barely intelligible. "I did something shameful."

"Haven't we all?" Shelly whispered.

Kate stayed with Shelly through the autumn and winter of 1984 and into the spring, when her divorce from Alan was final.

After she'd been with Shelly for a few days, she wrote to Alan telling him where she was and letting him know that she intended to file for divorce. He immediately flew to London, full of remorse, begging Kate to return, mentioning rather uncomfortably that he'd gotten the deal with Yates. Without arguing or repeating all the reasons why, she simply kept saying, No. It was over.

Kate was immensely relieved when Alan finally accepted the fact that nothing could make her change her mind. Perhaps driven by guilt, he offered her a generous settlement, including the house and everything in it. She didn't want the house, where she'd never really been happy, or anything that would be a physical reminder of their marriage. She took half the money in their accounts because she wasn't stupid, and that was it.

When she finally explained to Shelly what had happened that night in Malibu, Shelly's expression darkened with cold fury. "You're well rid of him!" she snapped. "Alan isn't worth another tear. Not one!" That was the last time Shelly deigned to mention Alan's name.

For the first few weeks Kate was in England, she hardly left Shelly's house. She slept late, read, went for long walks, and waited for Shelly to come home at night from the office. She didn't talk very much, even to Shelly, but she listened with interest as Shelly described her efforts to extricate Rashad Cosmetics from its financial problems and make it an international success, as Ben had once planned.

Gradually, she started going into town to meet Shelly for lunch or dinner or a play. Christmas was a quiet, low-key celebration since Shelly was still in official mourning for Ben. Kate sent presents to her family, who were all gathered together in Visalia, and called them on Christmas day.

It was more wonderful than she had imagined to hear their voices. She congratulated Scottie on his engagement to Cheryl, the girl he'd dated throughout high school and college. When Thomas, trying very hard to be the man of the family, demanded to know what rotten thing Alan had done to cause their divorce, she actually managed to laugh and say, "None of your business, little brother."

When he told her that his wife, Carol, whom Kate was especially fond of, was expecting their first child, Kate felt a rush of emotion. Another generation. A little niece or nephew for her to shower with love and gifts as she did with Michelle and Allison.

"Daddy would be so thrilled," she whispered.

"Yeah, I know," Thomas responded, his voice suddenly gruff.

When her mother got on the phone, she merely asked Kate how long she would be away. Kate replied, "I honestly don't know."

"When you come back, please come home for a visit, at least a short one. We miss you."

It was the first time her mother had ever said those words to her. Kate knew that "We miss you" really meant "I miss you." It was the closest her mother had ever come to admitting that she was lonely and needed her daughter's company.

Kate was touched beyond measure, and although she wanted to cry out, "I miss you, too, Mom. I need you so much. What was your secret, you and Daddy? How did you stay in love so long?" all she said was, "I'll come. I promise" in an unsteady voice.

The holidays passed; Kate spent the long, cold English winter reading by the fire. When spring came to the countryside in early April and the flowers in Shelly's garden began to bloom, Kate felt herself come alive again. She began to feel strong enough to return to L.A. and deal with everything she'd left behind, especially her career.

In May, she received the final dissolution decree. She glanced at it then tucked it away in the bottom of her duffle bag because she couldn't bear to look at it again. Later, she realized that her marriage ended nine years to the day from the first time she met Alan.

One evening, Shelly came home to find Kate packed up and ready to leave on the midnight flight to L.A.

"I have to go now, quickly, while my courage is up," Kate explained, "or I'll stay here, hiding away, forever."

"You're welcome to stay," Shelly replied. "I'll miss you terribly when you're gone."

"I'll miss you, too. I don't know what I would have done without you. You gave me a safe haven when I thought I wanted to die. I'm not sure I would have been able to make myself whole again without your support."

Shelly smiled. "What are friends for?"

When she returned to L.A., Kate rented a small house in Malibu because, despite everything, she still loved the beach. She chose an area far from Alan's house in Trancas. She called her agent, whom she hadn't talked to except for one brief call shortly after leaving, and asked if someone else in the agency could represent her, feeling it would be too awkward if she was represented by the same person who handled Alan.

When he agreed enthusiastically, Kate should have realized something was wrong, but she was so anxious to get back to work that she didn't analyze his response. She was turned over to a new agent, Christie Wells, who immediately began setting up meetings for her with networks and studios.

At the first meeting, she discovered why her ex-agent was so willing to let her go. The midlevel studio executive confirmed her worst fears. Without Alan, she was considered a has-been.

"You mean you and Alan aren't working together any longer?" the executive, a young man in his late twenties, asked in surprise.

"No." Kate couldn't help wondering if perhaps instead of a divorce decree there should have been a notice in the trades announcing the end of her collaboration with Alan.

"Your agent really should have informed me. I was under the impression you were still a team."

"We're no longer a team, but I'm still a screenwriter," Kate said, trying very hard to contain her anger.

"Of course, but . . ." The executive looked intensely uncomfortable as he searched for an excuse to get rid of her. "The thing is, you see, we're looking for the male angle on this project, so . . ."

Kate knew there was no point in arguing. She rose and said, "In that case, I won't waste any more of your time."

Outside the building, she stopped in the middle of the sidewalk and took a deep breath to steady herself. It was going to be the same everywhere else, she knew. Alan had signed a big contract with R&M and was in preproduction on his first feature for them. Nobody questioned his ability to work without her, but they definitely questioned her ability to work without him.

The reality of the divorce finally sank in. Kate was truly on her own, not just personally but also professionally in a town where a woman's value was directly connected to the man in her life.

FIVE

Kate

The Saloon was a Malibu bar/restaurant that appealed to a wide range of clientele, from movie industry professionals to the blue-collar types who lived on the cheaper land back in the canyons. It had a rough-hewn decor, with sawdust on the floor and wood siding on the walls. Kate rarely went there because it had a reputation as a pickup joint and she hated the meat-market atmosphere, but Val had insisted.

"We are not going to celebrate your thirty-fifth birthday by doing something boring like having dinner at some overpriced restaurant and taking in a movie that you'll criticize because the structure is off, the dialogue is amateurish, or the characters are stereotypes," Val said firmly before dragging Kate to the Saloon.

Now, as they sat at a tiny round table in a corner, listening to country and western music on the jukebox, Kate said, "I'm not *that* critical."

"Yes, you are. It's one of your least attractive qualities. We're going to have *fun!* We might even meet some men, if we're lucky, and *really* have some fun!"

"I am *not* going to let myself get picked up

by the kind of losers you meet in bars."

"You're such a fucking pain in the ass. I'll bet you haven't even gotten laid since you and Alan broke up."

"How can I?" Kate snapped. "Do you know what the competition is like in L.A. for the scarce number of single, straight men? *Young,* incredibly fit girls who don't have an intimate relationship with cellulite."

Val sighed. "I know. Disgusting, isn't it? While they're doing all this research into chemical weapons, I wish they'd invent something that would get rid of every woman under twenty-five. Make that thirty."

"Speaking of celibacy, how's *your* sex life?"

Val groaned. "Don't ask. I wonder how long you have to go without sex to revert to being a virgin again?"

"I'm not sure, but I think I've reached it."

"You work in a business full of men. Isn't there anyone you're even vaguely interested in?"

"I'm not working, remember? I'm semi-retired."

Kate tried to keep her tone light and ironic, but it was hard. In the year since she had returned to L.A. she hadn't worked. It was humiliating taking meetings with executives who lost interest as soon as they learned she was no longer the other half of Alan's team. Now she understood how Eleanor Perry, the award-winning screenwriter of *Diary of a Mad Housewife,* must have felt. When her husband, director Frank Perry, left her for a younger woman, his career continued but hers died.

Kate gave up on trying to get an assignment and instead concentrated on ideas for original spec scripts, but she had a massive case of writer's block and couldn't seem to finish anything. Her agent had given up on her, and they hadn't talked in months. Kate's career seemed over.

She had earned enough money with Alan so that she didn't have to work to support herself, but she *needed* to work, needed to be productive, to feel there was a reason for getting up each morning. More than anything else, she needed to prove to herself that she did have talent and that Alan wasn't the sole reason for their success together. Her worst nightmare—that she was nothing without him—seemed to be coming true.

Having so much time on her hands, Kate found herself thinking about Mark—a lot—but she'd heard through Barbara that he had married, so she didn't try to contact him. For his sake, she was glad that he was no longer alone. She just wished . . .

"Look at us," Val went on, "here we are, at what they say is supposed to be our sexual peak, and we don't have any men in our lives."

"At least you have Michelle." It was downright depressing to think that at the halfway point in her life she was divorced, childless, her career a shambles. This definitely wasn't where she'd expected to be at this age.

Val's tough expression softened, as it always did when she talked about her little girl, whom she'd left in San Francisco with her nanny, Sarah. "Yeah, I've got Michelle. She's incredible. I don't know how I could have produced such a sweet kid. Maybe there isn't anything to genetics, after all."

Then she returned to the topic that always seemed to dominate their conversations. "Men. Where the hell are they, anyway?"

"They're all around," Kate replied. "The problem is trying to have a permanent relationship with one. Look at us, neither of us has been able to find a man willing to make a real commitment. Pretty soon we'll be forty. Our parents had been married for more than twenty years when they were forty. We're not kids anymore. It doesn't seem right to be

469

emotionally unencumbered."

"I'm not sure it's possible to have permanent relationships anymore," Val said thoughtfully. "The only single, straight men who are willing to commit are the needy ones, the ones who take and take emotionally but don't have anything to give. Healthy, attractive guys act like the world is their candy store, and they're not gonna stop sampling all the sweets as long as there's more sugar left on the shelf. God forbid they should settle down with one woman when there's a chance someone even prettier and sexier might come along. All the married men I know cheat on their wives. Hell, half the wives cheat on their husbands. Eventually, that catches up with you and you split."

"Barbara and David seem to have a solid marriage."

Val grimaced. "I don't understand what she sees in him. He's such an ass."

"Apparently, he's a faithful ass."

"Yeah, but who cares?"

"Barbara does. She seems to think he's great."

"Do you really think she does, or is she putting up a good act?"

Kate frowned. "I don't know."

She thought of Barbara's wedding, when Barbara had pretended to be so happy. Only Kate had known that the wedding, and especially the return to Visalia, weren't what Barbara really wanted, but Barbara would have died before she would let the others see that.

Val went on. "Maybe she's lying to herself. You know, when I call her at night, David's never home, he's always working late, and Allison's just like we were as teenagers, she wants to be off doing stuff she's not supposed to be doing with her friends. I think Barb spends a lot of time alone. She's got to be bored out of her mind with that empty ritual

of tennis-shopping-charity work-Medical Auxiliary-
PTA, ad nauseam."

"Maybe it wouldn't be enough for you and me,
but just consider something. We don't have a man.
She does."

"That was a low blow."

"But true."

Kate started to add something else, then stopped
as her attention was caught by a young man entering the bar. He had sandy hair streaked with gold,
dark brown eyes, and the bronze skin and muscled
body of a construction worker.

Looking from Kate to the man and back again,
Val said with a wicked grin, "See something you
like?"

Kate looked back at Val. "Are you kidding? He
can't be a day over twenty-five."

"I know. That means he has stamina."

"You're incorrigible," Kate replied with a laugh.

Unabashed, Val went on, "Judging by the bulge
in those tight jeans, I'd say he's really hung, too."

"Val!"

"And look at those buns . . ."

Kate hissed, "Stop it! He'll hear you!"

"I hope so."

"If you're so interested in him, why don't *you* go
after him?"

"Because, unfortunately, *I'm* not the one he's staring at."

In spite of herself, Kate couldn't resist glancing at
the man as he sat down at the bar. Val was right.
He *was* staring at her, but as their eyes met, he
looked away in embarrassment.

"Oh, God, a shy hunk," Val quipped. "Is there
anything more irresistible?"

"No!"

"What are you waiting for, an engraved invitation
on a condom? Go get him, woman! It's the eighties,

remember? We're smart! We're tough! We're in charge of our lives!"

"We're frustrated," Kate added dryly.

"So do something about it. This isn't high school. We don't wait for the guy to make the first move, in or out of bed."

"Valerie Lynn Simpson! I am not going to risk making a fool of myself."

"Then you're not gonna get laid."

"What am I supposed to do? Walk over to him and try to pick him up?"

"Guys do it all the time. If they can handle it, with their fragile egos, we sure as hell can. Go on."

"Wait a minute. Have you thought about AIDS? Ever since Rock Hudson died last year, casual sex has seemed a lot less casual."

"So use protection. You're an intelligent woman. You know about safe sex. Damn it, Kate, stop making up excuses and go for it!"

Why not? Kate thought. The worst that could happen was that he would reject her. Lately, she'd had a lot of experience dealing with that. As for protection, at home she had a handy little kit, complete with condoms and spermicide, that Barbara had sent her as a divorce present.

Val was right. She could handle it.

Quickly downing the rest of her drink for courage, Kate walked over to the bar. Assuming a confident attitude that she didn't really feel, she smiled and said, "Hi. My name's Kate. Mind if I join you?"

"No, that'd be great. I'm Danny. Can I get you a drink?"

Three hours later, they were in bed.

To Kate's surprise and delight, making love to Danny had been wonderful. As she showered early

472

the next morning after he had left to go to work, she thought about his tremendous energy (Val had been right) and his uninhibited enjoyment of the physical pleasure she offered. His sensitivity and sweetness reminded her of Roger. He didn't have Roger's intellect, but then she wasn't interested in him for his mind.

There was none of that awkward first-time, you-take-off-this-while-I-take-off-that. No fumbling with buttons and zippers or embarrassment about going to the bathroom. Everything just seemed to happen naturally as they teased each other and laughed and wrestled like kids.

They had simple, uncomplicated fun together. Danny brought out something in Kate that she thought she'd long since lost—an appreciation for the sheer joy of being alive, being sexual, being a woman. He was a different generation than Alan and felt no sense of competition with her, no need to diminish her in order to build up his own ego. He didn't care about her career status, her age, her cellulite; when she was with him, she didn't either.

Sex with Alan had been so complicated, weighed down by a heavy load of emotional baggage. From the very beginning she'd sensed the fragility of his ego and had felt burdened by the need to cater to it. Only once had she tentatively ventured to suggest that she needed just a little more foreplay to become completely aroused. He looked stricken and said in a tight voice, "Maybe we're just not compatible. If I can't satisfy you, then let's forget the whole thing."

She felt a rush of guilt at hurting him, and quickly reassured him that everything was fine. She never again tried to talk to him about her sexual needs. Her own physical fulfillment seemed far less important than his happiness.

But with Danny it was all so different. He asked

473

her what she wanted him to do to her, asked what felt good and what didn't. "When I touch you here, does that feel good? And here? Do you want me to go faster? Slower? Is there something you'd like to do that you've never done, some private fantasy?"

And he was forthright in his own requests, making it clear what really turned him on. "Hold me tighter, I won't break . . . bite me—lick me there—squeeze me when I'm inside you . . ."

She'd never talked so openly about sex with a man before, even with Roger. Such intimate communication was the most erotic experience she'd ever known. When he finally left her, after they'd made love twice, she felt not only physically satiated but emotionally stimulated.

Danny called her the next night and asked her out to dinner. From that moment on, she saw him nearly every day. He didn't have a long, angst-ridden story to tell her, as most men did. He was twenty-three, had been born and raised in the San Fernando Valley, and worked in construction while waiting for his big break as an actor. He hadn't really studied acting, but his high school drama teacher had told him he had talent. Somehow he'd managed to luck into finding an agent who had gotten him a few small roles in commercials.

He wasn't particularly ambitious, unlike most of the actors Kate had met, who would kill for a good part. He enjoyed working outdoors, and maybe someday he'd go for his contractor's license. Danny's lack of ambition was refreshing after Alan. Kate appreciated the fact that he never asked her to help his career. He was unaware of how successful she'd once been. When she told him she was a screenwriter, he said, "That's nice," then he bent down and kissed her toes, taking them into his mouth one by one and sucking on them. He smilingly referred to it as "shrimping."

The gesture was so innocent and yet so erotic Kate thought she would die if he didn't tear off her clothes and make love to her immediately! Sometimes when she was with him, she worried that it was wrong of her to only be interested in him physically. After all, that was what men did to women so often, and it really pissed her off. Then he would make love to her, and she stopped thinking and simply let herself enjoy him.

Danny was as at ease with her body as his own, touching her in all the right places, in just the right progression. Earlobe, throat, breasts, stomach, mound of golden brown hair. Sex, to Danny, was play and was supposed to be fun and creative. They made love in the loft bedroom of his tiny house way back in Encinal Canyon, in the grassy meadow outside, on the bank of the stream running nearby. She came with his mouth on her, with him inside her, outside her, on top of him, and under him. The longer she was with Danny, the more she realized how starved she had been to be touched, to make physical contact with another human being. The day she left Alan, she had felt as if she never wanted to have sex again. Now she realized how cold and empty life was without an intimate connection to another person. Life was too short to waste precious time being alone and unloved.

Kate thought of Shelly. During the time she'd stayed with her in London, Shelly had finally told her of Ben's homosexuality. She knew that in spite of that Shelly had never been unfaithful to Ben and even now didn't date at all. She couldn't understand how Shelly, who was so beautiful, so desirable, and could have nearly any man she wanted, could be so . . . *frigid*. As soon as the word occurred to her, Kate dismissed it. It was too cold and harsh a word to describe someone as warm and giving as Shelly. Still, Kate felt immensely sorry for her, sleeping alone every night in that big, empty house.

Her thoughts of Shelly were interrupted by Danny climbing into bed beside her and whispering, "I've been meaning to ask you. What's your most secret fantasy . . ."

Kate was at her house, working in her garden, when Danny drove up in his battered pickup, honking the horn maniacally all the way up the private drive. She straightened up, feeling a twinge of pain in her lower back in protest at the abrupt movement after an hour of bending down to plant flowers.

Damn, I'm getting old, she thought.

Danny jumped out of his pickup and ran over to Kate. His handsome face was lit by tremendous excitement. Before she could say a word, he burst out, "I did it! I got the part!"

Picking her up, he swung her around, laughing crazily.

"What part?" Kate finally managed to ask when he put her down.

"It's a spaghetti western and I'm the second lead and the producer thinks I could be the next Clint Eastwood!"

"Danny, that's wonderful! But you never said anything about it."

"I didn't think I stood a chance, so I tried to forget about it! I took a screen test a few weeks ago! My agent just called me!"

He swung her around again and laughed. "Kate, I did it! I still can't believe it! I never really thought it would happen. I thought I'd be pounding nails forever!"

"We have to celebrate. I'll change, then I'll take you out for the best dinner in Malibu."

His grin dissolved to a seductive smile. "I know a

476

much better way of celebrating." Sweeping her up in his strong arms, Danny carried Kate toward the house. "And you don't need a knife and fork."

They lay together in Kate's huge bed, with its gleaming brass and white enamel headboard. Kate was starving, but she was too tired to get up and make something to eat. Getting dressed and going out to dinner seemed like it would take more energy than she would ever again possess.

I wonder if it is possible to live on love, she thought with a thoroughly contented smile. Well, perhaps she would find out.

Danny talked on and on about his role, the movie, the director, and the other actors. His voice was tired but still filled with enthusiasm. "Thank God, I know how to ride. My uncle has a ranch up in Canyon Country and I spent a lot of time there when I was a kid, riding, roping, all that stuff. The only problem is finding someone to take care of Desperado while I'm gone."

Desperado was his dog, half wolf and half Saint Bernard. Kate had nearly fainted the first time the dog had come running toward her, barking excitedly.

"Are they shooting out of the L.A. area?" she asked.

"Didn't I tell you? They're shooting in Italy! I'll be gone for two months."

Of course, she thought with a sinking sensation. Spaghetti westerns were shot in Italy. Stupid of her not to have realized that immediately.

Kate's silence and the still way she held herself finally got through to Danny. "Wait a minute. You didn't think I was gonna leave you behind, did you?"

"You . . . you want me to come with you?"

He laughed. "Of course! What did you think?"

When she didn't reply, he went on. "I know you don't have a job or anything, so I figured you could just pack up and come with me. We'll have a ball, Kate. When I'm not working, we can go sight-seeing and eat pasta. It'll be so much fun!"

It would be, too. Kate had no doubt of that. It was so tempting to contemplate. He was right, she didn't have a job or anything. She could just pack up and go; but she'd run away once, to London and Shelly. It had been necessary, but she couldn't justify doing it again. It was time she stopped doing that. It was time she stopped looking for people to lean on and started trying to make something of her career again.

Kate sat up and looked down at Danny, lying there with a self-satisfied grin. "You know that I care for you very deeply."

"I know," he whispered. "I care for you, too."

"I know, but I don't think you realize what you've done for me. You brought me back to life when all I was doing was just existing. I'll always remember our time together with such warmth and such gratitude that I found you. It was a time of healing, of regaining my confidence."

"How could you not be confident? You've got so much going for you. You're smart and pretty and nice, and you've got more class in your little finger than most of the women I've known have in their whole bodies."

She grinned. "You silver-tongued devil." However, the grin was bittersweet, and there were tears at the corners of her gray eyes.

Danny frowned, then sat up beside her. "Wait a minute. You're not coming with me, are you?"

She reached out to trace the line of his mouth. "I love every inch of your body, and I love your sweet soul." She finished in a whisper. "No, I'm not coming with you."

"Why not? There's nothing keeping you here."

"Danny, this is your chance at the brass ring and you've gotta try for it. I grabbed that ring once, and I'm telling you, there's nothing like it. It's more fabulous than you can imagine. But I lost it and now I've got to try to find it again. I can't do that in Italy. I can only do it here. I've got to show these people that Kate McGuire's back in town, and this time she's here to stay!"

She could see that he didn't really understand. "But I want you with me," he said the way a very small child insists on having his own way.

"Oh, love, I *want* to be with you, but it would mean giving up my dream, once and for all, and I'm not ready to do that."

"There's nothin' I can do to change your mind, is there?"

She shook her head slowly. "No."

"Can I write . . . or call?"

"Of course. I want to hear all about how it's going. If there's a problem, if you need someone to talk to, I'm always here for you."

"Then when I get back, we can see each other again?"

She nodded, but she knew that at his age, two months was a very long time. A lot of changes would take place. The young man who left L.A. wouldn't be quite the same as the slightly older, infinitely more experienced man who would return.

She knew this was good-bye. She would probably never see Danny again. There was no point in telling him that now. He wouldn't want to hear it, and he wouldn't understand.

"What do we do now?" he asked helplessly.

Kate leaned over to kiss his chest. "I'm sure we'll think of something."

SIX

Kate

"Did you watch the royal wedding on TV?" Barbara asked.

"You mean Chuck and Di? That was ages ago," Kate replied before taking a mouthful of chicken salad.

It was a warm, late summer day in 1986, and they had met for lunch at a small outdoor café in the new mall on Mooney Boulevard. Each time Kate returned to Visalia for a visit, she complained about it looking more and more like L.A., but Barbara loved the new shops, which were far more sophisticated than anything Visalia had known in the past.

"No," Barbara responded, "I mean Sarah and Andrew. Didn't you watch it?"

"Nope."

"But it was so beautiful! Her dress was gorgeous, and he looked so handsome in his uniform. It was a love match, unlike Charles and Diana, where he had to marry a virgin and she was about the only one he could find. This was truly like a fairy tale."

"Fairy tales are an anachronism in this day and age. Look at Chuck and Di—they didn't live happily ever after."

"I think we need fairy tales more than ever now. When Allison gets married, I'm going to plan her wedding to be as close to Sarah and Andrew's as possible."

"You're going to invite eighteen hundred people to Westminster Abbey?"

"*No!* You know what I mean!"

Barbara motioned to the waiter for another glass of wine. She'd had two glasses before lunch, and this was her second during the meal.

Lately Kate had noticed that Barbara seemed to be drinking much more than she had ever done in the past. When she had hesitantly mentioned it to Val, she had responded matter-of-factly, "Barb's an alcoholic. I've seen it coming on for a long time."

Kate immediately denied that Barbara, of all people, could have a serious drinking problem.

"Hey, you're talkin' to an expert on addiction. I'm tellin' you, she doesn't just have a problem, she's a full-blown alcoholic. Sometimes when I talk to her at night, she's drunk."

"If you're so sure she's an alcoholic, why don't you say something to her about it?"

"I tried. She denied it, just like you did."

Now, watching Barbara concentrate on the wine and barely pick at her salad, Kate had the uncomfortable feeling that Val might be right, but what could she say to her? What could she do? Barbara had always been the dominant one in their relationship. Kate was used to leaning on Barbara, on turning to her for advice. The one time she'd tried to tell Barbara what to do, when she had urged her not to be forced into returning to Visalia, Barbara had ignored her.

Before Kate could say anything, Barbara asked, "So how's your new little niece doing?"

Kate had come to Visalia because her brother Scottie and his wife Cheryl just had their first child, a girl named Whitney Katherine (after her aunt). Already everyone was calling the one-week-old infant Katie.

"Katie's doing just great! She's going to be a big girl. She weighed nine and a half pounds when she was born, and when Cheryl took her to the doctor yesterday because of a slight rash, he weighed her and said she's gained a couple of ounces. I'm supposed to drop by there this afternoon. Want to come?"

"Sure. God knows I don't have anything more urgent to do."

Something in Barbara's tone made Kate look up sharply at her. To cover the sudden tension in the atmosphere, she asked, "How's Allison?"

"Oh, you know, already looking forward to graduation, and it's still two years away. She wants to go back East to college, probably to get as far away from here as possible."

"Can you blame her? We felt the same way at her age."

Barbara's expression hardened. "Yes, and look how far I got."

For fifteen years Kate had felt, deep inside, that Barbara must have bitterly regretted her accidental pregnancy, precipitate marriage, and forced return to Visalia, but her life had looked so serene and happy on the surface that Kate had ignored the truth. She needed to believe that everything was perfect with Barbara because Barbara was the one reliable constant in her life. She could always turn to Barbara because she always had her life together. As long as Barbara seemed to have found peace, love, and happiness, Kate could hope that maybe someday she would, too. As she had been when

482

they were young, Barbara was still Kate's inspiration.

Now Kate felt a deathly stillness inside. If Barbara was as bitter and unfulfilled as her comment strongly suggested, what was Kate to do? How could she respond? It would mean that everything about Barbara was a lie. If Barbara's life was nothing more than a superficial fantasy, then what hope was there for lesser mortals like Kate, Val, or Shelly to find real happiness?

Kate looked at Barbara and knew that everything—the reality of their shared history, hope for the future, *everything*—hung in the balance.

Suddenly, as if it never happened, the tension vanished with Barbara's laughter. "Oh, come on! Don't look so worried! I'm just in a bitchy mood today. I've got raging PMS and Allison has been impossible. Let's go see that new niece of yours."

Kate felt a rush of relief. Everything was okay, after all.

Wasn't it?

They paid the bill. As usual, Barbara insisted on treating Kate. Getting up to leave, Kate turned and came face to face with Mark Jensen.

It shouldn't have been such a shock, really. After all, Visalia was still a small town, though not nearly as small as it had been when she was growing up. Each time she came for a visit, Kate was just a little bit nervous because she half-expected to run into him.

She hadn't. Until now.

He looked so different from the last time she'd seen him that for an instant Kate didn't recognize him. Mark had put on a little weight and his skin was tanned. His eyes were as bright and tinged with an irrepressible air of mischief as they had once been. He was no longer the pale, almost emaciated

483

young man she'd last seen. It was amazing, in fact, how much he looked as he had in high school, brimming with strength and confidence.

"Kate!"

"Mark!"

Her heart was beating erratically and she seemed to have lost her voice. Finally, he was the one who rescued the situation.

"It's been a long time."

"Yes."

"How have you been?"

"Fine." I sold my self-respect for my husband's ambition, had a minor nervous breakdown, got a divorce, had a fling with a younger man, and saw my career go from hot to freezing cold. "Just . . . fine."

"Good."

"And you?"

"Very well, thank you."

They were like distant acquaintances who had absolutely nothing to say to each other. It was impossible to believe that the last time she'd seen him, she'd lain in his arms and listened to a confession torn from his very soul. Kate had given of herself to this man, both physically and emotionally, as she'd never done with another man.

Noticing Barbara, Mark said politely, "Hi. How are you?"

"Good, thanks."

Barbara looked from one to the other, and Kate knew that she understood.

Barbara went on in a breezy way that amazed Kate with its casualness, "Well, we've got to be going. Kate has a brand-new little niece that we're going to ooh and ah over."

For a moment, Kate thought that Mark looked as if he didn't want her to leave, then he said, "How

484

nice. Well, it was good seeing you again."

"Yes . . . good seeing you, too." I sound like a moron, she thought miserably.

As soon as they were out of Mark's sight, Barbara turned on her. "All right, what is it?"

"What do you mean?"

"You told me you danced with him at the reunion after Val and I left, but you guys did a lot more than dance, didn't you?"

They got in Barbara's silver Mercedes, a gift from David for their fifteenth anniversary, and Kate looked away.

"What happened between you two?" Barbara demanded. "And why didn't you tell me?"

"I didn't know how to tell you. Hell, I didn't know *what* to tell you. I was still very much married to Alan, and I was afraid it would sound like a sordid little one-night stand. I was afraid you'd think I was a slut or something, but it wasn't like that, it was . . ."

She stopped, unable to explain.

Barbara's mouth turned up in the barest hint of a smile. "Don't you know by now that nothing you could possibly do could shock me? I need you as much as you need me. You've never understood that, have you?"

Kate felt infinitely better. "Mark and I spent the night together," she explained. "He had been in Vietnam and had never quite recovered from it. I was so desperately unhappy with Alan. We comforted each other that night. I think it meant a lot to both of us. I know it did to me, but it was over the next morning. I had to go back to Alan." She finished, "At least, I felt I did then."

Barbara was silent for a long moment. "That's why you asked me later if I ever saw him around town."

485

"I wanted to know how he was doing. I was concerned about him, and . . . well, even if I couldn't be with him, I wanted to know how he was doing."

"Kate, he's divorced."

She was too stunned to speak.

Barbara went on. "I didn't mention it because I didn't think you were especially interested in him beyond that perfectly natural initial curiosity after running into him at the reunion."

"When did it happen?"

"Eight months ago." She grinned. "I read the divorce notices in the paper every day. Now that all my friends are in their thirties and have been married long enough to be disenchanted, I'm beginning to take a morbid personal interest in that part of the paper."

"They weren't married long."

"Nope. Obviously, it didn't take. Maybe because he's carrying a torch for you."

Kate gave her a skeptical look, but inside she wondered if it could possibly be true, and she realized something else. As far as Mark knew, she was still married.

Throughout that afternoon, she chatted with Scottie and Cheryl and made appropriately silly baby noises at adorable little Katie, but she couldn't get her mind off Mark. If they were to meet again, she would have to make the first move. Mark wouldn't contact her as long as he thought she was married.

Barbara dropped her off at her mother's house, where she was staying overnight. Bending slightly to talk to Barbara through the open car window, she said, "I'm going back early in the morning, so I won't see you. Give David and Allison my love."

Barbara gave her a no-nonsense look. "Call him."

Kate didn't have to ask who she was referring to. "I don't know . . ."

"I do. *Call him!*"

"What if it was just a one-night stand, as far as he was concerned?"

"Are you crazy? Didn't you see the way he was looking at you today?"

"Barb, maybe it just isn't meant to be. We couldn't get together in four years of high school. I've only seen him once in the seventeen years since then. My life is in L.A., his is here."

"Those are just excuses because you're scared."

"You're damn right, I'm scared. He may not want to hear from me."

"That's not what you're scared of. *Call* him!"

As she walked inside, Kate knew Barbara was right. She wasn't afraid of how he might feel toward her. She was afraid of her feelings for him.

Having an affair with Danny had been so easy. It was fun, sexy, uncomplicated. There was enough emotional involvement to make it pleasant but not enough to risk real pain when it ended.

With Mark, there was a very real risk. He could hurt her far more deeply.

After dinner that night, Kate sat in the living room with her mother reading a book while Lea sewed. Since her return from England, she had spent more time with her mother, coming up for frequent, brief visits. They still found it difficult to talk to each other, and Kate knew that would never change, but they'd settled into a fairly comfortable way of relating that was a great improvement over their past awkwardness with each other.

Her mind wasn't on the book. She'd read the same page twice and still couldn't remember what she'd read. Looking up from the book, she said, "Mom?"

Lea glanced up from the skirt she was hemming. "Yes?"

"Can I ask you something about Dad?"

Her mother was clearly surprised by the question. They'd rarely talked about Kate's father in the years since his death. Now she put down her sewing and said, "Of course. What is it?"

"He told me once that he wouldn't have been anything without you. I never quite understood what he meant."

Lea smiled. "You mean you didn't understand how someone like me could have made that big a difference in his life." Before Kate could protest, she said, "It's all right. Your father was so exceptional in so many ways, it's hard for you to see why he could have needed me."

Lea hesitated, then went on carefully, as if it was very important that she get the words just right so there would·be no misunderstanding. "Your father was born with all the natural gifts anyone could wish for. He was handsome, charming, bright. Everyone liked him. Well, you just couldn't help it. But somewhere along the way, he got the idea that he could get away with anything and it would be all right. People would forgive him. There wouldn't be a price to pay. When we met, he was just back from the war and was at a crossroads in his life. He could easily have gone either way. He was running with a pretty wild bunch, half of whom ended up in jail or dead after only a few years.

"I fell head over heels in love with him the minute I laid eyes on him. I never thought he would give me the time of day. I wasn't his type, you see. He went out with the flashiest girls around. We saw a lot of each other because my sister, your Aunt

488

Hope, and his best friend, Jack, were dating. Well, one day he asked me to go on a double date with the two of them. You could have knocked me over with a feather, I was that surprised, but I pulled myself together and said no."

Kate asked, "But if you liked him so much, why didn't you go?"

"That's what your father said, too. He knew I was interested in him. Well, most girls were. So he couldn't believe I would turn him down. I gathered up all my courage and told him the truth—that I cared about him too much to be with him and watch him throw his life away."

"What did he do?"

"He was mad, though he tried hard not to show it. Didn't speak to me again for weeks. I didn't see him, but I heard he was being wilder than ever."

"Were you unhappy during that time?" Kate asked.

Her mother didn't quite meet her look. "Yes. I was very unhappy, but I meant what I said, and I wasn't going back on it."

"Then how did you get together?"

"He showed up on my doorstep one morning at dawn and pounded on the door till my father opened it. My father was furious and was about to take his twelve-gauge shotgun to him, but Harry said just as calmly as could be, 'Sir, I'd like to ask for your daughter's hand in marriage.' "

Kate gasped. "You're kidding! What did Grandpa do?"

"He looked your father up and down, and I must say he looked a sight that morning. He'd been up all night, doing God knows what. Anyway, your grandpa said, 'I think my daughter can do better than you.' "

"What did Dad say?"

"He said, 'You're absolutely right, but I can't do better than her.'" Lea's voice shook a little and her face was flushed with pride. Kate had never seen her look this way before. She was amazed at how striking her plain mother looked at that moment.

Her mother went on, "Well, your grandpa let him in then and said it was up to me, he wouldn't stop the wedding if I wanted it. I came in from the hall where I'd been listening to the whole thing. Your father looked kind of awkward, but he cleared his throat and asked me to marry him."

"Do you remember his exact words?"

Lea smiled again. "How could I forget them? He said, 'I need you, Lea. If you'll marry me, I promise you, I'll never do anything to make you regret it.'"

She finished quickly. "So we were married the next week. After all, there was no point in waiting around."

Kate couldn't believe that she'd lived for thirty-five years without hearing this story. It completely changed her view of her mother, her father, their marriage. She was immensely moved but didn't know how to express what she was feeling. As always, Lea took charge. Clearing her throat, she said in her clipped manner, "It was a risk, of course, for both of us. He might not have lived up to his promise to me. I might not have made him happy. But when you love someone, *really* love them, you have to take a risk."

Kate was quiet for a moment, then she stood up and said in a subdued voice, "Excuse me for a minute. I've got to make a phone call."

Before leaving the room, she did something she had never done before in all the years she'd grown up in this house. She stopped, bent down, and tenderly kissed her mother's forehead.

They met for a drink in the bar of the Holiday Inn, the nicest place in town. Kate began without preamble. "I was sorry to hear that you're divorced."

Mark looked uncomfortable but not really sad. "It was for the best, for everyone's sake. It was a mistake from the beginning. I think we both knew it, but we were each so tired of being alone."

"I'm divorced, too."

He set down his drink so abruptly that he spilled some of it on the small, round table that separated them. "Was it —" He stopped but Kate knew what he meant to say. Was it because of him, somehow, and the night they spent together.

"My marriage was actually over long before I saw you at the reunion," she explained. "I just didn't have the courage to face it. It took . . . something rather ugly to make me face the fact that there was no real love between us, just a lot of need."

Mark nodded slowly in understanding. "Most of my friends have gone through divorce. Yours probably have, too. It seems to be the curse of our generation. We don't seem able to find the answer to the question, 'How do you make love stay?' "

Kate mused, "So many people I know, especially in the film business in L.A., orphaned themselves for their careers. *I* did. We broke from our families, then watched the new families we made get broken. We didn't care enough to patch them back up again. Or maybe, unlike our parents, we just didn't know how."

Mark said thoughtfully, "We searched for love, trust, the idea of *home,* but we never found it."

"Maybe, because of the way life is nowadays, so complicated, with so many temptations, it's impossible to find those things."

491

"You don't really believe that."

"I'm afraid I do."

He asked gently, "Am I going to see you again, or is this going to be another dead end the way it was seven years ago?"

Kate gave the only answer she could. "I want to see you again but I'm scared."

He took her hand in his. "Why? Don't you know I would never hurt you?"

She wanted to believe that.

He went on. "If we are going to see each other again, there's something you need to know."

Kate waited in an agony of curiosity as several terrible ideas went through her mind.

"I found my daughter."

That hadn't been one of the terrible ideas. She was so relieved, and so happy for him, she wanted to laugh and cry at the same time. "You found Anne? Where? When? What happened to her? Is she with you?"

He smiled. "I'd better start at the beginning. It's a long, involved story, and for a long time, even after I found her, I didn't think it would have a happy ending. After I saw you at the reunion, I thought a lot about what you said. I started going to a veteran's support group and it saved my sanity. Talking to you was a real breakthrough for me, Kate, but I needed to talk to other vets, who could relate to what I'd gone through. Anyway, one day I told them about my daughter, and to my surprise they encouraged me to try to find her."

"Oh, Mark, I'm so glad!"

"The first thing I did was to consult with the Amerasian Registry in San Jose. It's a nonprofit agency that tries to track down Amerasian children and their families. They put me in touch with the Office of Displaced Persons run by the U.S. government in Bangkok. After two years of letters and calls, I finally got the necessary papers to go to Vietnam."

"It must have been strange going back."

"Oh, yeah. Everything was changed. The banks had closed long ago for lack of currency. There were a lot more beggars on the streets than I remembered. The streets were empty except for some jerry-built cars and trucks trailing fumes. Anyway, to make a tedious, frustrating story short, after a long search, I finally found Anne on the streets of Ho Chi Minh City with the other Untouchables. Amerasians. They're the unlucky, the abandoned, the unwanted. People teased her because with her green eyes she was obviously Amerasian. They called her *con lai*, half-breed, and *bui doi*, the dust of life. They told her to go back to her own country. She was barely ten years old, but the expression in her eyes was that of a hardened adult. She sold cigarette butts for a living."

"Oh, Mark." Kate choked back the feelings that made her throat constrict and brought tears to her eyes. She couldn't bear the thought of any child having to live such a degrading existence.

"She lived in a three-room house with relatives of her mother. It was a patchwork of dirt, cement, and tin lit by a single bulb hanging from a wire strung crudely across the ceiling of the living room. She slept each night in a dingy room with twelve other people. It took months to get Anne into the States. Once we got back, our relationship was pretty rocky. She was remote and defensive, totally untrusting. Well, who could blame her? She stole food and hid it, afraid of going hungry again. Certain sounds—a car backfiring, a helicopter flying overhead—would remind her of the war, and she would cower under the nearest cover. It was ironic because

493

that's what I did for the first couple of years after I came back from the war. But she never cried. It was almost as if she had no tears left."

Kate couldn't help asking. "How did she feel about you?"

"She hated me. She blamed me for her mother's death. She blamed me for abandoning her. She refused to let me comfort her. Then during one of our many arguments, all of my anger, guilt, love, and frustration made me explode. I told her that I couldn't change what happened. I couldn't make it go away, for either of us. I had been twenty and terrified of dying. That was no excuse, but it was the truth. I told her that no matter how much she hated me, I would never leave her again."

Mark sighed heavily. Clearly, it was emotionally draining for him just remembering all this. "Anyway, that got through to her. When I hugged her, she didn't pull back. She began to cry. I wiped away her tears and told her I loved her. It was another year before she could say those words to me. When she did, it was the happiest day of my life."

A tear escaped down Kate's cheek and Mark reached out to lightly brush it away. "There's no need to cry. This story has a happy ending."

Kate smiled, blinking back the tears.

"Now we're just like any other father and fifteen-year-old daughter. I yell at her for playing her stereo too loud. She tells me I don't let her do any of the things her friends get to do."

He stopped and they looked at each other, neither saying anything. Kate felt the old chemistry returning in force, and she knew that Mark felt it, too. They were falling in love all over again, but they were both wary. Both had made serious mistakes. Both had been hurt.

Still, they wanted each other terribly.

Kate said hesitantly, "I'd love to meet Anne. That is, if it's okay."

"Of course. I'd like you to meet her. She's away at summer camp right now, but she'll be back next week. When do you have to go back to L.A.?"

She had planned on returning first thing in the morning. Kate needed to get back to work. She had started a new script, and although it was extremely difficult, at least she felt that she was finally on the right track with it. That was a feeling she hadn't enjoyed for a long, long time.

Now, looking at Mark, she answered, "I don't have to go back for a while."

His smile lit his handsome face and made her heart do somersaults. "Good."

Over the next week, they spent every possible minute together. During the day, they went horseback riding around the ranch, had picnics, and talked. At night, they prepared simple dinners together, nothing fancy because neither was much of a cook. They played chess or Scrabble and talked some more. They never seemed to run out of things to say to one another or things to laugh about together.

Then one night, without having to say a word, both knew they were ready to make love. When they kissed, neither held back. Mark led her upstairs to his bedroom. Standing only inches apart, they slowly undressed, feeling at once awkward and excited. As they lay down in the bed together, Kate thought that her heart had never beat so fast.

"I feel as nervous as if this were the first time. That's silly, I know, but . . ."

"No, it's not silly. In a way it *is* the first time — the first time we've come to each other without any barriers between us. Tonight it's just you and me. The war is finally over for me. I'm free. And you're free of Alan."

Free. She hadn't thought of it like that, but Kate knew he was right. She was finally free of everything that had kept her emotionally tied to Alan long after she'd left him.

She smiled up at Mark. "Do you know when I first noticed you?"

He shook his head.

"We were in freshman English, and you read a poem by Donne. A love poem. I was amazed at your audacity."

He chuckled softly. "Ah, yes. I think I wanted to embarrass the teacher. She had said we could choose *anything*, but the joke was on me because I discovered I actually liked poetry, especially Donne's. Of course, I wouldn't have admitted that to anyone at the time."

"I don't remember which poem it was, but I do remember that it took my breath away."

Mark frowned in concentration. "I remember some of it, I think . . ." He recited slowly, reaching for the words:

> My Myne of precious stones, My
> Emperie,
> How blest am I in this discovering thee!
> To enter in these bonds, is to be free;

Reaching out to encircle Kate's waist, Mark finished:

> Then where my hand is set, my seal shall be.

Kate was deeply moved. The timeless words of passion, spoken in Mark's husky voice, aroused a flurry of emotions. Happiness. Desire. Love.

His arm around her waist was strong and comforting. As she lay there, trembling with anticipation, she needed the reassurance of his tender strength. Instinctively, she reached up to cup his face in her hands and draw it down so their lips could meet.

When she finally pulled away, Kate said, without stopping to think, to censor her feelings, "I love you."

For all she knew, she'd just made a bloody fool of herself, but she didn't care. The words were said and couldn't be unsaid.

His lips curved upward and she thought he had the most dazzling smile she had ever seen.

Mark said, "I think I've always loved you. Since high school, when you were too uppity to have anything to do with me."

She laughed, a low, throaty chuckle. "That's only because I knew if once I gave way to you I would go up in flames."

"Then give way now . . ."

Mark held her so close that Kate could hardly breathe. She felt his skin against her skin, his heart beating against her heart. Her cheek was pressed against his shoulder and her fingers twined in his golden hair. She pulled back and took a deep breath; a moment later, they were kissing again. They kissed as only lovers can who have been separated for long, lonely years.

I've come home, Kate thought, repeating the words over and over like a heartfelt avowal of faith. It was like reaching a safe harbor after a perilous journey and knowing you were finally, and forever, safe. Knowing that no one, nothing, would ever again come between you and the only person in the world who mattered.

497

She lay on her back, on the cool white sheets, her hair a tangled mess from his fingers twining in it.

"Oh, Mark, there's so much I want to say, so much I'm feeling, but I'm not capable of speaking coherently."

"Good. Because we have better things to do, my love, than talk."

As his smiling mouth came down on hers, Kate knew that words weren't necessary. Each knew exactly how the other felt.

Their lovemaking was magical. Kate felt transformed, as if she'd become an entirely new and much wiser, much happier person.

Afterward, in a deep peace unlike any she could ever remember feeling before, they lay quietly together, legs, arms, fingers entwined.

"Please marry me."

The words were spoken so softly Kate wasn't sure she'd heard right. "What?"

Mark propped himself up on one elbow and gazed down at her. "I said *please marry me!*"

"But . . ." She stopped, unable to think what to say in response. Finally, she stammered, "But it's so soon . . ."

"Not soon, *late!* We've known each other a long, long time. It just took a while to get together."

"But you don't really know me."

"Oh, but I do. I knew the girl who went away years ago, and I know the woman who is lying beside me now. You can't say you don't know me. You know me better than anyone ever has or ever will."

For an instant, fear flashed in those turquoise eyes. "I can't bear the thought of losing you again, Kate. I love you so much. *Marry* me!"

She pulled herself up to a sitting position next to

him so their eyes could meet. It was absolutely critical that she make him understand how she felt. "Oh, Mark. I love you so much, too, but marriage . . ."

She froze inside at the thought of making that kind of commitment again.

"I can't," she said, hating herself for the hurt look that came into his eyes. "Please understand. I lost my own identity once, I even did things that went against everything I believe in. All because of a man I thought I loved. I can't risk that happening again."

His mouth hardened in an angry line. "I'm *not* Alan."

"Oh, love, I know. I'm sorry. Please don't try to force this. I just can't. Not yet."

To her surprise, he didn't argue. Instead, Mark said, "I think I understand. At any rate, I'll try to, but even if you can't marry me, you can live with me."

She couldn't think of a reason to say no. She didn't want to say no. So she smiled at him and said, "Yes, I'll live with you."

Kate beat down the tiny surge of fear she felt at the thought of making even that loose a commitment.

SEVEN

Shelly

She stepped off the Concorde, a stunning figure in a dove gray suit with a short skirt that revealed long legs in shimmering silver stockings. A helicopter took her to the Rashad Cosmetics and Skin Care Salon on Park Avenue for a brief conference with the new manager, who had recently been wooed away from a competitor.

Like everyone else in the country in the spring of 1987, the manager was eager to discuss the Gary Hart situation. Hart, the Democratic front-runner in the upcoming presidential race, had been caught spending the weekend aboard a yacht called the *Monkey Business* with a model named Donna Rice. Hart's sexual escapade was the subject of front-page headlines and rampant speculation.

Shelly always felt intensely uncomfortable gossiping about anyone's sex life, even a politician who had dared the media to "put a tail" on him. She cut off the manager's scathing comments and pointedly returned the conversation to business. Two hours later, she was on a flight to Tokyo. When she arrived there, she officially opened the newest Rashad salon, presiding over a cocktail party on the thirty-third floor of a skyscraper in the heart of Tokyo's

500

business district. The party featured a glittering array of guests, including members of the government.

The next day, she flew back to London.

In three days, Shelly had been in three different countries, England, the United States, and Japan, had conducted several business meetings, had accepted an invitation from *Harper's Bazaar* magazine to be included in its pictorial layout of "The Most Beautiful Women in the World over Thirty," and had approved a new ad campaign, which touted the new "natural beauty" that Rashad Cosmetics promised every woman could have. The epitome of the new look was Shelly herself. Her face, seemingly devoid of makeup and naturally glorious, was in all the ads, photographed, as always, by Ryan.

In the four years since Ben's death, Shelly, with Richard's invaluable help, had completely turned the company around. Rashad had the most successful cosmetics and skin care lines of all the upscale companies. Its success was inextricably entwined with Shelly herself. She was not only the CEO, handling the day-to-day business decisions, she was also the face of the company, the focal point of all the ads.

By the late eighties, it had finally become chic to be older. Shelly was symbolic of her generation of women, baby boomers who had become part of the group they had once said they couldn't trust. She couldn't have done it without Richard's support and advice. Hers was the creative vision, his the practical business expertise. Together they forged an astounding success that left other companies lagging far behind.

During the course of eighteen-hour days at the office, teetering on the brink of financial ruin not once but several times, fighting a skeptical board of directors, and dealing with hard-nosed financial institutions, they became as close as two people can be who aren't physically intimate. Richard became Shelly's best friend, and she relied on him even more than she had ever relied on her old friends, Kate, Valerie, and Barbara. He was the first and only man she had ever known whom she trusted completely.

Now, as she arrived back at her house outside London in the early evening, she hurried to change into a comfortable and chic lavender silk caftan. Richard was coming to dinner to discuss plans to open a Rashad salon in the Middle East. When she came downstairs a few minutes later, she was just in time to see her butler admitting him.

She smiled warmly. "Richard, how are you?"

He frowned. "I must warn you to keep your distance. I've had an irritatingly persistent cold that I can't seem to shake. I'm going to see my doctor tomorrow to see if he can't give me something for it. How are you after your whirlwind trip?"

"Tired. Jet lag has turned my brain to mush."

"We don't have to talk business tonight. Let's make this a quick meal so you can turn in early. You look like you could use the rest."

"No, there's too much to do. Tomorrow's Sunday. I'll sleep late and spend the afternoon reading the *Sunday Times*."

As she led him into the dining room, she went on, "I know you like steak and kidney pie so I've persuaded the cook to make it. She was rather huffy about it, implied it was beneath her, gastronomically speaking."

Richard chuckled. "Ben wooed her away from a duke by making an offer she couldn't refuse. She never quite forgave him for tempting her to choose filthy lucre over her integrity."

Shelly felt a sharp stab of guilt as she thought, He did the same to me!

Sensing her feelings, as he did so uncannily, Richard said gently, "It wasn't that way with you and Ben."

"He bought me, Richard."

"No. He offered you security, something you must have needed desperately."

They sat down at the round oak table in the breakfast room, so much cozier than the dining room, with its massive table seating twenty. "That's all in the past now, anyway. I've a bit of advice for you from your old Uncle Richard."

Shelly smiled. "Am I going to enjoy hearing this advice?"

"No, but I shall give it anyway. It's just this; Ben has been gone for quite a while now, and to my knowledge you haven't so much as gone out on a single date."

"Richard!"

"I told you that you wouldn't want to hear it. Shelly, you're a young, vibrant, immensely appealing woman, with a warm heart and a fascinating mind. You have a great deal to offer a man."

"I don't need any other man. I have you."

"You know what I mean. Why do you remain locked up in this ivory tower?"

"I hardly remain locked up here. Last week I visited our Paris and Rome salons, I just got back from New York and Tokyo, and next week I go to Sydney."

"That's all business. There's more to life than work."

"Is there? I'm not so sure. Men come and go,

but a satisfying career is always there."

"Your tone is light and bantering, but I think you're actually quite serious. There was a time when you had to work very hard to keep the company from failing, but that time is long past. You no longer have to devote yourself entirely to it, yet you still do, forsaking any sort of private life. Why? What drives you?"

She didn't answer. She couldn't tell Richard there was a demon chasing her, a black, ugly memory of graduation night and the sick shame she couldn't seem to escape. She knew that beneath her mask of a beautiful, supremely self-confident woman was the daughter of a small-town whore, someone tainted, unworthy, someone who didn't deserve to be treated with love or respect. Only more and more success could keep the demon at bay.

Now looking at Richard, Shelly said in a slightly wistful voice, "Maybe the same thing drives me that drove Ben. Maybe that's what drew us to each other. At any rate, it's no use talking about it."

"I've always sensed that you were very deeply hurt at some point in your life. I'm sure that's why Ben was able to seduce you, in a sense. Even though he offered nothing of a really personal nature, he did provide a safe haven from that pain. But, my dear, please understand that scars from pain can turn into an ability to love and be loved. If only you can find the courage to let them."

An air of cool reserve stole over her. "Those are lovely words, Richard, but that's all they are, words. I'm simply not interested in anyone."

"What about Ryan?"

"What?"

"You know perfectly well what I mean, so don't pretend otherwise. The man's been in love with you as long as I've known you, and probably well before that."

"Don't be silly. Ryan's a womanizer. He's only interested in conquests."

"I'd say he's only interested in the one conquest he never made."

Shelly forced a smile, trying to appear amused. "If he is, it's only because his ego is suffering."

"You're determined to stereotype him, aren't you?"

"It's easy to do, considering how he gets around."

"Did it ever occur to you that perhaps a lot of that is just talk? I suspect he prefers to maintain the image of a Don Juan rather than wearing his heart on his sleeve. He does have a fierce pride, you know. Just like you."

"This is ridiculous. Why are you determined to give Ryan so much credit?"

Richard lifted one eyebrow quizzically. "Why are you so determined not to give him any?"

Shelly had no response.

Richard went on gently. "I've watched him when he's around you and he doesn't think anyone is looking. My dear, what he feels for you is touchingly obvious. Unlike so many people, he cares for the *real* you, the person you are inside. When he photographs you, it's almost as if he's using the camera as a device to get close to you because you won't let him close in any other way."

"You give him far too much credit, Richard."

"And you obviously prefer to cast him in only one light—almost as a buffoon you hire because he's a good photographer. You're reluctant to see the whole man and to admit that he might have feelings and needs that go far deeper than a cartoon character's."

505

"Why are you so determined to throw me together with Ryan, of all people?"

"Because I sense that he represents what you fear most—passion. You must deal with that fear, or you'll never fulfill yourself in the way you have every right to do."

She went cold inside. "I don't agree." Abruptly changing the subject, Shelly went on in a no-nonsense tone, "Now, then, about Sydney . . ."

After dinner, they put business aside and played a quiet game of Scrabble. Richard won, as always, but this time Shelly came much closer than she usually did to winning. As she walked Richard out to his car, he said, "I'm afraid you might beat me next time. Perhaps I should quit while I'm ahead."

She laughed. "Oh, no, you can't quit just when I might have a chance to finally win one. Come to dinner next Friday and we'll see what happens."

"Very well. If this cold's better. See you at the office on Monday."

On Monday Richard was in the hospital. He had tested HIV-positive for AIDS.

Eight months later, Shelly sat beside his bed in an exclusive private hospital outside London. Richard was a shell of a man. His skeleton hand gripped her wrist like a steel claw, and his eyes were wide with the terror of dying.

"I love you," she whispered. She felt awkward saying the words because she hadn't said them in a long, long time. Now she finally found the courage to express an emotion she'd felt for years. Unable to speak, he moved his other hand, sketching circles around his heart, then pointing a shaky finger toward her: *I love you, too.*

Shelly swallowed the sobs that filled her throat. In a moment, she knew, she would lose all control; she couldn't bear to let Richard see her that way. She needed to be strong and unafraid for his sake, so she said, "I must go out for a minute, but I'll be right back, I promise. Rest now. I'll see you again soon."

As soon as she was out of his room, Shelly leaned against a wall and held herself to keep from shaking. What a nightmare it had been since the day his doctor had given Richard the news that was a death sentence. He hadn't realized that the lingering cold, recurrent flu, and all the other ailments that had bedeviled him for some months were a sign of his immune system breaking down.

When he had told her, Shelly had felt an even greater sense of loss and panic than she'd felt when Ben had died. Her first thought was, what will I do without him? Immediately it was followed by a scathing self-indictment. You selfish bitch! Stop thinking of yourself and think of Richard!

She did what little she could. She respected his wishes not to tell anyone, especially his parents, who lived in a nursing home. She let him continue to work until the last possible moment because he needed to feel useful. Even then, when he lay in a hospital bed, she spent hours each day with him, asking for his advice and keeping him informed of the latest successes of the company he was so much a part of.

Shelly dried her tears and squared her shoulders. She had to go back to Richard now. No matter how hard it was for her, she reminded herself that it was much harder for Richard. If it took every last ounce of courage she possessed, she had to stay with him until the very end.

Shelly couldn't let Richard die alone.

The next day, he slipped into a coma. She continued to hold his hand and talk to him, just in case he was still aware of his surroundings. Shelly couldn't bear for him to make that final journey in lonely silence.

Richard's breathing grew more erratic, with longer pauses between each breath. When he took one last tremulous breath, she waited, holding her own breath, but Richard didn't take another.

The nurse, who had hovered in the background for the last half hour, came over and felt for a pulse. Looking at Shelly, she shook her head.

Still, Shelly continued to hold Richard's hand, unwilling to let go of him, as tears poured down her cheeks.

Afterward, she threw herself into her work with even more of an obsessive dedication than before. Without Richard to rely on, she felt the demon's presence more strongly, a constant threat to her sense of self-worth.

It was her past buried alive.

Then in 1989, Terrence Westen came into the picture. Her greatest threat yet.

A self-made tycoon who had grown up on a sheep station in the Australian outback, he had a voracious appetite for successful, high-profile companies. He made an unexpected, stunning two-hundred-and-fifty-million-dollar bid for Rashad Cosmetics. The financial community saw it as merely another in the wave of mergers and acquisitions that seemed to be escalating by the late eighties, but for Shelly, it was nothing less than a matter of survival. Rashad Cosmetics wasn't just everything to her, it was the *only* thing.

When she went into an emergency meeting of the board of directors to discuss the offer, she assumed that of course they would reject it. After all, the company was doing great; there was no need for Westen's money. When she walked out an hour later, Shelly's face was grim. She had badly underestimated the greed of her board and overestimated their loyalty to her. They had agreed to meet again the following day, but Shelly knew that meeting would be even more acrimonious than this one.

That night, she sat alone in her office, long after everyone else had left, trying to think of a strategy to fight off Westen. As she had done so often in the year since Richard's death, she wished desperately that he could be here. With his help, she was certain they could beat Westen. At the very least, with him by her side, she wouldn't have to go through the bruising battle alone.

Shelly jotted notes on a piece of paper as random thoughts occurred to her. Maybe recapitalization, buying up as much of the company's stock as possible, would work. With the stock she already owned, including the significant amount Richard had left her, she might just be able to become a majority shareholder. Then she could vote down Westen's offer, and it wouldn't matter what the board of directors wanted. She could even appoint a new board, sending the old one packing. The thought brought a smile to her lips, but it was only fleeting. Recapitalization wasn't as easy as it sounded. She would have to liquidate *everything* to come up with that kind of money, and even then she might not have enough. It was a big risk, and she would have to shoulder it by herself.

"Hey, lady. Did you order a pizza?"

Shelly looked up, startled. Ryan stood framed in the doorway, wearing his uniform of faded jeans, scuffed boots, and ancient, creased brown leather jacket. He carried a flat, round box into the office and plopped it down in the center of her desk.

Opening the lid, he took a deep breath. "Ah, smell that pepperoni."

It smelled delicious. To Shelly's surprise, she actually felt hungry. Taking some napkins out of his jacket pocket, Ryan handed one to Shelly before giving her a big slice of pizza.

"You need to keep your strength up if you're gonna fight the bad guys."

She smiled. "I take it you heard about the board meeting tomorrow."

"Of course. The old company grapevine, you know."

He sprawled in the chair facing her desk and took a big bite of pizza.

After she'd eaten some, Shelly asked, "So what does the grapevine think of my chances?"

"The odds seem to be running about eighty-twenty."

"For or against?"

"Against. Personally, I'd give you better odds than that. At least sixty-forty."

"Thanks."

"Hey, I know what a tough cookie you are. They don't."

"A tough cookie, huh? Well, even tough cookies can crumble."

He shook his head. "No way. You're not gonna

crumble. Not with that remarkable air of self-possession."

She was intrigued. "What do you mean?"

Ryan finished the slice of pizza, wiped his hands
on a crumpled napkin, then leaned across the desk,
arms folded in front of him, looking directly into
her eyes. "The way you hold yourself as carefully as
if you were made of glass and are terrified you
might shatter."

He paused, letting the full impact of his words
sink in. "It could simply be the result of being a desirable woman doing business in a man's world. But
it isn't, is it? We both know there's a lot more to it."

Shelly couldn't speak. She could only meet his
probing look, trying hard not to flinch.

"I understand what was done to you, Shelly. I understand how scared you are of ever being hurt that
way again. I won't hurt you, I promise."

She was intensely aware of Ryan, of his face only
inches from hers, his big hands resting on the desk.
He was so strong, so physical, so male. Richard
had been right, she reluctantly admitted to herself.
Everything about Ryan spelled passion, and it terrified her.

For twenty years, she had tried to numb herself
psychologically, suspending her feelings because that
was the only way she could ensure her safety. She
had split between herself and her experiences, especially the gang rape and then, later, her life as one
of Madame Justine's call girls. She had frozen the
pain of the rape and had buried the feelings that
hurt too much to feel. She had survived the prostitution by denying all emotion.

Somewhere along the way, those frozen feelings
had blocked Shelly from herself and others. As far
back as she could remember, she hadn't said "I love

511

you" to anyone. Not to her mother. Not to her friends. She couldn't even say them to Richard until he lay near death.

Now this man, this disturbingly attractive man, was making a direct assault on those cold defenses. Shelly thought of all the long, lonely years, the narrowness of her existence, the lack of warmth, the complete absence of hope for anything more. Yet in a single moment, this man had managed to breach those defenses.

Intimacy . . . to touch someone and be touched back, not just skin to skin but heart to heart.

Shelly looked at Ryan, who was waiting quietly, and she was filled with panic.

"I have to go," she said, rising abruptly. "I have things to do to get ready for the meeting tomorrow."

She knew he could see through the lie. At that moment, Shelly felt utterly transparent and wondered just how much he saw.

Ryan's expression gave nothing away. He stood up and faced her. "I'll be around tomorrow. In case you should need me."

Shelly couldn't respond. She could only hurry out, as if she were running away from danger.

EIGHT

Kate

She moved most of her clothes, her typewriter, and her most cherished possessions onto the ranch. Kate kept the little house in Malibu as a place to stay when she was in L.A. on business. Though, she thought ruefully, with the state of her career, she wasn't likely to need it much.

In the peace and quiet of the pastoral countryside, her writing flourished. The script that she'd had such problems with in L.A. seemed to flow from her in a steady stream of creative energy. When Kate sent it to her agent, she attached a note saying, "I don't know if you can sell this, but I do know it's the best thing I've ever done."

At the same time, she discovered that her feelings toward Visalia itself had changed. In the warmth and closeness of the small town, she took pride in and comfort from its simple virtues. Getting back in touch with her roots, and the down-to-earth values she'd been raised with, filled a deep void she had felt all those years in L.A.

Kate had been apprehensive about living with Mark, sharing the same space day in, day out. What if they got in each other's way? What if they grew bored with each other? She could imagine any number of potential conflicts. Mark might resent her commitment to writing. She might realize they really had nothing in common after all.

To her relief, none of her worst fears materialized. Mark was busy working the ranch during the day, leaving her plenty of time to write. He was fascinated with her work, and she found that she enjoyed discussing it with him and getting his viewpoint. The melding of their two disparate lives was amazingly seamless.

The only problem was Anne. A strikingly pretty fifteen-year-old, she had inherited her father's intelligence, as well as his green eyes, and her mother's dark coloring and piquant features. Kate liked her immediately, from the moment they first met when Anne returned from summer camp, but the girl was extremely reserved. She politely rebuffed every suggestion Kate made for the two of them to go shopping, go out to lunch together, go to a movie, *anything* that would mean developing a closer relationship.

At first, Kate thought that perhaps Anne was merely shy, but as she watched her interact with her friends and with other adults, she realized Anne was actually very warm and outgoing. She didn't have a problem with other people. Only with Kate.

One day Kate overheard Anne talking to a friend on the phone. The friend must have asked about Kate, for Anne replied dismissively, "Oh, she's just my dad's live-in girlfriend. She probably won't be around for long."

Kate felt both insulted and deeply hurt. Leaving the house, she went for a long walk by herself, thinking hard about herself and Anne and Mark. By the time she returned, it was all perfectly clear.

Anne bitterly resented this interloper. She was afraid of losing her father again.

She knew she could go to Mark, explain the problem to him, and leave it to him to deal with, but that wouldn't actually resolve anything. At best, Anne would be even more determinedly polite, but she wouldn't accept Kate and there would certainly be no real closeness between them.

Somehow Kate had to work this out herself. Her experiences with children — with her younger brothers and with Barbara's and Val's daughters — had taught her that you can't force kids to like you. It might take a while to progress from cool civility to friendship to genuine caring, but that didn't matter. Kate wasn't going anywhere.

When Anne started her sophomore year in high school, she immediately focused on becoming a cheerleader. Day after day, Kate watched her practicing on the front lawn, her young face set in intense concentration as she did cartwheels and splits. Kate sensed that for Anne being a cheerleader represented acceptance in a culture where she didn't entirely fit in. Kate understood about not fitting in. She found herself praying for Anne's success with an even greater fervency than she had felt in hoping for her own.

The day of the tryouts came. That afternoon, Kate waited anxiously in the living room. The moment Anne came through the front door, Kate felt her heart sink. Disappointment was all too obvious in the girl's stricken expression. Mumbling a barely audible hello, Anne immediately went to her room, slamming the door behind her.

Mark was away at a livestock auction and wouldn't be back for hours. Even if he had been there, Kate doubted that he could help Anne. After all, he'd been one of the chosen in high school. Despite his fierce love for Anne, he wouldn't be able to empathize with her. He would sympathize, but that wouldn't be enough.

Kate went into the kitchen and made a pot of hot tea. She put the teapot, two cups, and a small plate of chocolate chip cookies on a tray and carried it to Anne's room. When she knocked on the door, she heard a listless voice say, "Come in."

She carried the tray inside and set it down on the nightstand next to the pink-canopied bed where Anne lay. She asked, "Do you mind if I sit down?"

Anne clearly minded but was too polite to say so. She nodded without looking at Kate.

Kate sat down in a white wicker rocking chair and began carefully. "I'm sorry it didn't work out."

Anne shrugged. "It doesn't matter."

"Oh, I think it did. I think it must have hurt a lot. I know how hurt I felt when the same thing happened to me."

Anne's glance flickered briefly toward Kate.

"When I was a freshman, my friend Barbara and I tried out to be cheerleaders. Barbara made it, but I didn't. The ironic thing is, it didn't really matter to Barb. She even made fun of it, and after that one year she never tried out for cheerleading again. But it mattered to me! Barbara could afford not to care about it because she knew she was accepted, popular, all those things that mean the difference between success and failure in high school. I wasn't popular, but I knew that if I could only be a cheerleader I would be. It would mean that the other kids accepted me even though I didn't come from a rich family or wear really nice clothes."

Anne murmured, "It's hard to be accepted when you're different."

516

"Yes. From what your father has told me, you must have felt that you didn't fit in back in Vietnam, and you probably feel that you don't entirely fit in here."

Anne's lower lip trembled. "In grammar school, a little boy called me a half-breed."

"I know it doesn't make you feel any better, but he was just repeating what grown-ups taught him. Stupid grown-ups."

For a long moment, Anne didn't say anything. Kate felt at a loss for words. She sensed that she and Anne were on the brink of something, but she didn't know how to breach the remaining barriers.

Then Anne admitted reluctantly, "I think, maybe, the kids didn't vote for me to be a cheerleader because they think I'm a half-breed, too."

Kate's heart ached for Anne. She felt a rush of protectiveness, exactly as she'd felt when Scottie and Thomas had been hurt as little boys. She would have given anything to be able to keep Anne from being hurt, but she knew she couldn't do that any more than she'd been able to do it for her brothers. All she could do was show how much she cared, and be honest, because anything less than honesty wouldn't do Anne any good.

"Maybe some of them felt that way," she said slowly. "Unfortunately, prejudice exists here. It exists wherever there is fear and stupidity, and that means pretty much everywhere. I'm afraid it's probably something you'll come up against your whole life. But, you know, I suspect it really didn't have that much to do with not being named a cheerleader."

For the first time, Anne looked directly at Kate. "Then what did?"

"I don't know, but I know it doesn't have to do with anything that really matters."

517

"What did you do when you didn't get to be a cheerleader?"

"I went to my room and cried, and for a few days I slunk around school, trying not to be noticed, convinced I had been personally rejected and was a total failure. Then one day I realized that if I was a failure because I wasn't a cheerleader, then that meant that the couple of hundred other girls in school who weren't cheerleaders were failures, too. That was obviously ridiculous, and I felt a lot better."

"But you're such a big success, how could you feel like a failure?"

Kate smiled. "I'll tell you a secret, something I haven't even told your father. When I was at the top of my career, at the point when other people thought I was the biggest success, inside I felt like a failure."

"But why would you feel that way?"

"Because I hadn't learned an important truth—that it isn't what other people think of you that matters, it's what you think of yourself. I had all the outer trappings of success, but I didn't have a sense of fulfillment inside."

Anne sighed. "My friend Jenny tried out and she didn't make it either."

"I'm sorry. I imagine she was pretty hurt, too."

"No. Jenny's tough. She said it was the school's loss."

Kate laughed softly. "She sounds like my friend Val. Nothing could ever keep her down for long."

"When I found out I didn't get chosen, it was the worst feeling. All the way home, I thought, I'll never feel good again."

"I know."

"I still feel bad, but I'm not so sure I'll go on feeling this way forever."

"I'm glad."

Kate picked up a cup and took a sip of tea. After a moment, Anne sat up and did the same.

"This is good tea."

"It's cinnamon." Kate smiled. "I'm not much of a cook, but I *can* boil water and stick a tea bag in it." She looked around the room, at the pink-and-white flowered wallpaper and the white lace curtains. "This is a lovely little girl's room."

Anne grimaced. "Yeah, but . . ."

She stopped, and a guilty look crossed her face.

Kate had a sudden insight. "Your father decorated this room for you, didn't he? When he first brought you here?"

Anne nodded.

"He must have wanted to give you the perfect room for a little girl, but you're not a little girl anymore, are you?"

"No. But I don't know how to tell him that I want to put posters of Bon Jovi and Prince on the walls and get a bed that doesn't have a canopy. It would hurt his feelings."

"In a way it would because he would have to face the fact that you're growing up. He missed so much of your childhood, he's reluctant to let go of it."

Kate hesitated, then said, "I could talk to him, if you'd like, maybe explain things so he wouldn't feel too hurt."

"Would you!" Anne's expression was animated. "That would be so great!"

"You know, there are some fabulous stores in the Design Center in L.A. They have the latest furnishings. We could go down some weekend and you could get something really high tech."

"You know what I'd really like? There was this bedroom set in *Seventeen*, it was all sleek and modern . . ."

Seventeen. Kate felt a jolt of déjà vu.

Anne's bedside phone rang, interrupting her. She picked it up. "Hello? Oh, hi, Jenny. You're right, they're scum. Listen, I'll have to call you back, I'm talking to Kate. We might go down to L.A. to get some new bedroom furniture for me. You wanna come?" She looked up at Kate. "Is that okay?"

"Of course. We could do some shopping at the boutiques along Melrose Avenue. You and Jenny would love it."

Anne spoke into the receiver again. "Hey, she says we can shop for clothes, too. Yeah, bitchin'! Listen, I'll call you back."

When she hung up the phone, Anne picked up a cookie from the tray and asked as she took a bite, "What do you think about gray and white?"

"I like it. What exactly did you have in mind?"

Anne explained in detail what she wanted to do to the room. Listening to her ramble on, Kate felt suffused with warmth.

Kate couldn't pinpoint the exact moment when she felt they had become a family. It was a long, sometimes difficult process of growing closer, arguing, growing closer again. Over the next two years they settled into a pattern of living together that worked. She couldn't imagine not having Mark and Anne in her life.

While she grew happier with each passing day, Mark grew more dissatisfied. He called their arrangement "playing house." He wanted and needed permanence and commitment. He was ready to

520

offer it and needed to receive it in return.

Kate's fear of a legal, permanent commitment didn't lessen. Then one day her script sold.

The Seekers, the first screenplay Kate wrote without Alan's collaboration, sold for a cool million dollars after a hot bidding war between three major studios. When the dust settled, it was turned over to a top producer who had an exclusive deal with the studio. He hired a brilliant director who attracted a major actor and actress. When the movie was released in the fall of 1988, it was a big commercial and critical success. There was even talk of Oscar nominations, especially for the script.

The romantic drama about a divorced man and a divorced woman finding the courage to love again after miserable marriages struck a chord in an audience that included millions of divorced people. It was also more than a little autobiographical. The passion Kate felt for the subject injected the script with energy and sensitivity.

From the moment the script sold, she was in demand again, as word spread through the industry that she was "hot." She spent so much time on the phone, talking to people in L.A., she had a separate line installed so she wouldn't tie up Mark's phone. Her agent called frequently with new offers, and Kate was in the enviable position of being able to pick and choose the projects she wanted to work on.

The only drawback was having to spend so much time in L.A., meeting with producers, directors, studio executives, and actors. She began staying in the Malibu house more and more often. It didn't make sense to return to Visalia after a meeting if she was only going to have to come right back to L.A. in a day or two.

It was all so exhilarating—the success, being in demand, the vindication of her ability as a writer separate from Alan. Her faith in herself and her talent was reaffirmed after three years of self-doubt and waning self-esteem. Kate was something without Alan, after all. Hell, she was *really* something.

Everyone seemed to have forgotten that for a while she'd been unemployable. She was back in the movie game. If there was an Oscar nomination— and *if* she actually won—she would be one of the undisputed winners of that game.

The quiet, serene life she had led with Mark and Anne changed abruptly. She went from writing in the mornings, then spending the afternoons reading, horseback riding with Mark, gardening, or taking Anne shopping to a hectic schedule of nonstop work. The evenings that she'd once spent curled up beside Mark, watching television or simply reading quietly together, were taken up with planning her whirlwind schedule. Time became a scarce commodity, and Kate found herself having to turn down things she would like to do—visiting her family, planning vacations in New York and London so Val and Shelly could meet Mark, taking Anne on a tour of colleges in L.A. and San Francisco to decide which one she would choose.

The numerous assignments her agent got for her meant that she had to work harder than ever, without a break, and the strain began to tell, especially in her relationship with Mark. Kate became short-tempered and irritable, but when he suggested that maybe she was under too much stress, she took it as a criticism and insisted she could handle it just fine, thank you.

After all, she told herself during the many times when she felt desperately overworked, this was what she'd striven so hard for ever since leaving Alan.

One night in early November, she returned very late from a trip to L.A. Kate had planned on being gone for only three days, but her agent had scheduled some additional meetings and before she knew it she'd been gone a week. Now, climbing the stairs to the master bedroom, she walked softly so as not to awaken Mark or Anne.

She felt guilty about Anne. They'd hardly spent any time at all together for weeks. Kate knew that Anne was excited about deciding on a college and was looking forward to going away next year, but she also knew that Anne was extremely nervous about the profound changes she faced. Because of the horrendous experiences she'd had to deal with so early in life, she was frightened of giving up the security she'd found on the ranch with her father.

Kate wanted to talk to Anne about these very natural conflicting feelings. She understood them so well, herself, and wanted to help Anne deal with them, but there never seemed to be time to sit down and talk, just the two of them, as they'd done before. Maybe next week, she thought, then remembered that she was supposed to fly back to New York for a brief meeting with a producer who operated out of there. Well, maybe the following week, she told herself.

She carefully opened the door to the master bedroom and was surprised to find Mark sitting in a chair, reading. He looked up as she entered.

"Hi, sweetheart. I was getting worried about you. I thought you might have had an accident in this fog."

She came over to him and kissed him lightly.

"The fog wasn't that bad. I was held up in L.A. at the last minute."

Kate shoved her suitcase aside, too tired to unpack it tonight, and yawned. "Lord, that's a miserable drive. Three hours of sheer boredom."

"So tell me about your trip. Anything interesting happen?"

She talked as she undressed and slipped into a white silk nightgown. "Not really. Just meetings, meetings, meetings."

"Who with?"

"The usual. Egomaniacal producers, directors, actors. All of whom are convinced they know more about writing a good story than the poor dumb writer does. Honestly, I'm tempted to say to them, 'If you know so much about writing this story, why bother with me?' Except I can't because writers are supposed to be like children, seen and not heard."

She yawned again, then finished, "I'd rather not even talk about it. It just makes me mad. My agent actually suggested I think about producing next time around, so I can have some real power, and I may just do it."

Mark frowned. "I thought you didn't want to produce. You said it was too close to the seamy side of the business."

Kate felt unaccountably irritated with him for repeating an opinion she'd voiced many times. "Maybe I've changed my mind. If Alan can produce, so can I."

Mark's tone was even, but there was an undercurrent of something—jealousy? concern?—in it as he replied, "I didn't realize this had anything to do with Alan."

"It doesn't. I was just using him as an example.

Look, it's late and I'm exhausted. Let's just drop this, okay?"

"Okay."

She slipped into her side of the bed; a moment later Mark joined her. Normally, she would have immediately snuggled up to him, and after such a long separation they would have made love with a great deal of eagerness and joy, but for some reason tonight, she just wanted to be left alone. He sensed it and stayed on his side of the bed.

Mark said quietly, "We need to talk. Lately we seem to be growing further and further a-part."

"That's not true. I'm just tired tonight from the trip."

"It isn't just tonight. You're spending more time in L.A."

"That's where my work is," she snapped.

"I understand that." Mark's patience was clearly wearing thin. "But I get the feeling that you stay down there longer than you really have to."

"That's ridiculous!"

"Is it? Did you *have* to be there for an entire week this time?"

"I could have come back for a couple of days, but I would've just had to go back again. It wasn't worth it."

"It wasn't worth coming back, even though I missed you terribly and needed to see you, if only briefly?"

"I don't need this crap, Mark. I won't let you make me feel guilty about my work."

Finally, his anger flared. "I am totally supportive of your career. I encouraged you to go on writing when you were having so much trouble, and no one was more thrilled than I was when *The Seekers* sold.

This has nothing to do with your career, and you know it!"

"I don't know it! You sound a lot like Alan right now, totally concerned with yourself, ignoring my feelings and needs . . ."

"Damn it, Kate, I won't be compared to him! I've told you in every way I know how that I'm not Alan. I am not just concerned with myself, and I sure as hell don't ignore your feelings and needs."

"I don't want to talk about this anymore tonight." She rolled over with her back to him.

After he turned out the light, Kate pretended to go to sleep, but it was actually a long time before she found refuge.

For several days, Mark kept bringing up the subject of their growing estrangement, trying to get her to talk about it and even suggesting they get counseling. She refused, insisting that she didn't have a problem and if he did, he should deal with it.

The truth was, Kate was emotionally and physically exhausted from trying to give one hundred percent of herself to her career and one hundred percent to Mark and Anne. She was profoundly torn between the demands of the career she'd worked so hard to resurrect and the demands of her relationship with the people who needed her. She tried to meet both demands. There were many times when she needed to be in L.A. but wanted to be with Mark and Anne for some special occasion — Mark's birthday, Anne's first date.

She began to feel that she was on a constant emotional seesaw, forever having to decide which was more important, the needs of her career or the needs of the people she loved. Terrified that she might once more lose her career, Kate couldn't bring herself to sacrifice any part of it. At the same time, she was consumed with guilt for not being there when Mark or Anne needed her.

Balance. The newest buzzword for women as the eighties wound down and the nineties came hurtling across the horizon. It was an appropriate word, conjuring up, as it did, images of someone doing a high-wire act. With no net.

At last, Mark's dissatisfaction and Kate's stress combined in the worst argument they'd ever had. It began when she told him she would have to spend a few weeks, maybe longer, in New York doing research for a new script that was set there. She wasn't sure when she'd be back, she said, but she'd let him know as soon as she had an idea.

Mark was silent. When he finally spoke his voice was deceptively quiet. "I get the strong impression that you need to get away from me, and your career is just an excuse to do that."

Kate didn't deny the awful accusation. She couldn't. It was true.

The longer she was with Mark and the closer they became, the more she came to depend on him emotionally, and the more afraid she was that this was all just a replay of her relationship with Alan. She had needed Alan, and look where that got her. She refused to let herself need Mark.

But she couldn't talk to him about these feelings, so she denied the accusation and their conversation quickly escalated into a full-blown argument that left Kate in tears and Mark looking grim.

The next morning she packed up her belongings and moved back to Malibu. As she drove away, watching the ranch recede in the distance in her rear view mirror, she felt a devastating sense of loss. Only once before had she felt such emptiness — when her father died.

Thanksgiving and Christmas were miserable. Kate didn't dare spend them with her family in Visalia because she might run into Mark, or worse, be tempted to call him, so she spent Thanksgiving in New York with Val, who had moved there when her talk show sold to syndication.

She spent Christmas in London with Shelly, who was touchingly pleased to have her company. Kate told herself it was idyllic, a real Dickensian Christmas. When she spent a lot of time on the phone with her agent, Shelly didn't criticize her. She could boast about how well her career was going and know that Shelly's response would be unqualified support. Shelly wouldn't question the ratio of work to personal fulfillment in her life because Shelly was a workaholic, too.

Kate insisted to herself that her breakup with Mark was healthy. It saved her from repeating her mistake with Alan. Back in Malibu, her life at the beginning of 1989 was an endless round of business lunches, industry parties, meeting after meeting. Her agent piled up assignment after assignment until Kate was booked well into the following year.

She told herself that her life was perfect. Her career was skyrocketing. She was completely free to do as she pleased, not tied down to anyone, not responsible for anyone other than herself. However, in spite of her reluctance to face it, she gradually became painfully aware that her entire sense of herself was defined by her work. Kate's whole self-image was based on the perceived success—power—of her position in the film business.

When she left Alan, and no one would hire her, they took away her work and with it her sense of dignity. During that bad time, she reminded herself that this was a business of rejection. Pursuing success for its own sake wasn't a healthy goal because if they could give you success, they could take it away again. Kate came to realize that power was derived from the process of doing good, worthwhile work, not from what other people in the industry thought of her. It was the single greatest lesson she had learned in her career, and she swore she would never forget it.

Yet now, as she submerged herself in the business once again, a nagging inner voice asked why she was once more having trouble writing. Why didn't she feel a greater sense of joy at her success, especially when she was nominated for an Oscar?

Kate didn't have an answer.

NINE

Barbara

She watched Allison tear open the letter from Sarah Lawrence College — the letter Allison had been eagerly, almost desperately, awaiting for weeks. Allison had already been accepted by Brown and Boston U, but Sarah Lawrence was her first choice. It had just the right cachet for a bright, ambitious young woman who wanted much more than Visalia had to offer.

At that instant, when Allison was totally focused on the letter, Barbara looked at her daughter, really looked at her, as she hadn't done in a long while. The girl was the spitting image of her mother. The older Allison got, the more alike they looked. Allison had the same chestnut hair and brown eyes and air of supreme self-confidence.

Funny, Barbara thought, that she'd inherited nothing from her father, except, perhaps, her life-long desire to be a doctor. Even that, too, came from Barbara, in a way.

Allison squealed in delight. "They accepted me!" She turned to her mother. "I'm in!"

Barbara had to force herself to smile. "That's wonderful, sweetheart." Why didn't she feel happier for her daughter? she wondered. Why did she have this sick feeling of jealousy? Because Allison was young and had her whole life ahead of her, with limitless possibilities? She hadn't screwed it up yet, and probably never would. She hadn't made the wrong choices and then had to live with the bitter consequences. An unplanned pregnancy would never ruin her chances. She was probably on the Pill now, for all Barbara knew, and even if she did accidentally get pregnant, she could simply have a safe, legal abortion.

It was the late winter of 1989. In a few months, Allison would graduate from high school and then would be gone. Her grandmother was taking her to Europe for the summer as a graduation present, and she would return just in time to leave for college. The house would be empty. Just Barbara and David and a long, long stretch of boringly predictable, empty years ahead.

"I'm going to call Daddy and tell him," Allison said. "And then I'll call Grandma. She wants to start planning our trip back East to visit the colleges."

When Allison left, Barbara took a bottle of white wine from the refrigerator and poured a glass. She didn't bother putting the bottle back in the refrigerator because she knew she would be having more. A lot more.

When David came home late that evening, following a medical society meeting, he found Barbara curled up on the sofa watching an old Marx Brothers comedy, *A Night at the Opera*, on the late show. She looked perfect, as always, her hair pulled back with a pink silk ribbon, wearing a pink velour jogging suit. Looking good was critical to Barbara, and even when she drank, she didn't let herself become slovenly.

When she'd heard his new Jaguar pull into the garage, she had quickly buried the empty wine bottle at the bottom of the kitchen wastebasket and had hid the wine glass under the sofa until she could wash it in the morning.

Now she smiled as he walked in. "Hi, darling."

It was no use. David could tell immediately that she'd been drinking. He could always tell.

That look came over his face. The look that said so clearly, I'm disappointed in you, Barbara! How could you do this to me? To Allison? How could you let us down like this?

Dropping his briefcase on a nearby table, he said, "How much longer do you expect me to put up with this behavior?"

"I don't know what you mean . . ."

"Stop it! Just stop it." He shook his head in frustration. "I don't understand why you do this, Barbara. You have everything—plenty of money, this house, a wonderful child. Other women would appreciate those things, but you . . ."

He stopped, then went on with the same old dialogue she'd heard a hundred times before. "Why can't you be more like your mother? She appreciated how hard your father worked to provide a good life for his family. She supported him . . ."

Normally, Barbara listened in guilty silence as David listed her failings and compared her to her mother, that rigid paragon of virtue, but tonight something inside her snapped and she felt that she couldn't bear to hear the comparison one more time.

"Don't!"

"What?"

"Don't compare me to my mother!"

"You're right. Why bother? There's certainly no comparison. She would never humiliate your father like this."

"I've never humiliated you!"

"You haven't fallen down drunk at a social event, but that doesn't mean people haven't noticed your drinking. Max gave me some literature on the Betty Ford Clinic recently. He said I might find it *useful*."

Max was a new young doctor who had recently joined David's practice. His wife, Lorie, a psychologist, had talked with Barbara a few times at Medical Wives Auxiliary functions. Barbara felt uncomfortable at the way Lorie seemed to watch her carefully.

Now she found herself fighting back a surge of panic. How much did Max and Lorie guess? Had they talked to other people about her? Were her friends in the Auxiliary even now gossiping about her behind her back?

As David went on, "Can you imagine how that made me feel? For a junior partner to suggest my wife is a drunk." Barbara sat in miserable silence, unable to respond. "You might think about Allison," David said. "This is hard on her, you know."

"Allison's doing just fine!" Barbara shouted, surprising herself at the force of her words. She never yelled like this because it might suggest that she was out of control, but at this moment, she couldn't help it. "She'll be going off to college in the fall, happy as a clam!"

"My God, you actually sound jealous of her. Your own daughter. Thank God, her grandmother is there for her. You're certainly not."

Barbara found herself overwhelmed by a terrible

irony. Her life had come full circle. Her mother hadn't wanted her to achieve more than she had done. Now Barbara felt threatened by Allison achieving more.

She murmured softly, "You don't realize how much like my mother I really am."

The next morning, Barbara took her Mercedes into the dealership to be serviced and was surprised when a new service manager came out to greet her.

"Morning, ma'am. What can we do for you today?"

There was something vaguely familiar about him. Tall and muscular, he had blond hair and hazel eyes and looked to be about her age, in his late thirties. The name tag on his blue work shirt said "Rick."

A sharp, vivid memory suddenly filled Barbara's mind of Steven Ashe and Rick Paxton cruising in Steven's black El Dorado on graduation night.

She froze.

He repeated, "Can I help you, ma'am?"

"Um . . ." she cleared her throat nervously. "Yes, I, uh, keep hearing a rattle when I get up to a certain speed."

The man smiled, showing even white teeth. There was something predatory about the smile that Barbara found intensely erotic. He really is very attractive, she thought, much more attractive than he was in high school.

She wasn't surprised Rick was still in Visalia. While he'd been a first-string football player, he hadn't been quite talented enough to get an athletic scholarship to college; and he certainly wasn't especially bright. Nevertheless, he was sexy in a coarse way that she found stimulating after the dull refinement of David and the other men, mainly doctors, in their social circle. She was bored to tears with cerebral men.

"Well, now, why don't I take it for a short drive and see what happens. Want to come?"

Barbara hesitated.

"It would be helpful if you came."

They got in her car and he headed for Highway 198. Barbara was very aware of his body in the close confines of the car, his flat stomach and thigh muscles bulging in his tight jeans.

"You're new," she said after a while.

"Yeah, just started last week. I used to work at the Chevy dealership. This is sure a step up from there. There's nothing like a Mercedes for quality and class."

After a moment of silence, he went on, "I know you. You went to Redwood, too, didn't you?"

"Yes."

"Barbara Avery, right?"

"Browning. I'm married now, but I'm surprised you remember me. It's been twenty years."

"Oh, I remember, all right." The glance he swept over her was frank in its appraisal. "You really look terrific, if you don't mind me saying so."

She felt at once embarrassed and flattered. "Thanks." She added boldly, "So do you."

He grinned.

Barbara was reminded of something she'd read once about the dangerous stranger with the killer grin.

They were on Highway 198 now, outside of town, and Rick had taken the car up to sixty-five.

"I don't hear a rattle," he said. "We'd better turn around and head back."

As they made their way back to town, Barbara

535

was glad the irritating, now-you-hear-it-now-you-don't rattle wasn't showing up today. It gave her an excuse to come in to the dealership again soon.

She returned one week later, just before noon, when she assumed he took his lunch break. When they got back from the brief test ride, she invited him to lunch. They didn't talk much, but then she wasn't interested in him for his conversation.

That day he was able to identify the source of the rattle and arrange for a mechanic to fix it, but Barbara wasn't dismayed. She knew she could always come up with another mechanical problem.

A few days later, she took her car in just before five-thirty, when the service department closed, complaining of a recurrence of the rattle. This time when they took the car out together, they ended up at a motel on Mooney Boulevard with a bottle of whiskey. It was hot and fast and sweaty. Rick didn't seduce Barbara, he simply took her, and she found it thrilling. She loved having everything reduced to a physical level. She clawed at him as he rammed into her with little finesse but tremendous energy. When she came, the intensity of it overwhelmed her. Finally, after years of growing more and more numb, Barbara felt alive again. From that moment on, Rick had a hold on her that both excited and frightened her. She knew she would do anything he asked.

They saw each other one or two evenings a week, heading straight to the motel when Rick got off work and staying just long enough to fuck and to drink a great deal. David rarely got home before nine or ten at night, so Barbara didn't have to explain her absences to him. Allison had stopped wanting to have anything to do with her mother once she became a teenager, so she didn't seem to miss her.

Barbara couldn't keep her mind off Rick. When she played tennis at the club or presided over Medical Wives Auxiliary luncheons and PTA meetings, she thought of his hard, muscled body and the things he did to her, uninhibited things that David had never done. She craved the sensations she felt with Rick, and it was all she could do to maintain an air of decorum until she could escape from her stifling environment and meet him at the motel.

Once, when he arrived late, refusing to explain what had kept him, Barbara berated him for keeping her waiting. Instead of arguing, Rick simply tore her clothes off and took her roughly. She was so desperate for the orgasmic release that only he could give her that she clutched his shoulders, digging her nails into them, begging him to fuck her.

Looking down at her, he flashed that killer smile. "The fucking homecoming queen who wouldn't give me the time of day wants me, doesn't she? *Doesn't she?*"

"Yes," Barbara moaned. "Oh, God! Yes!"

Soon Rick started bringing marijuana so they could get high before having sex. Barbara hadn't smoked pot since college and hadn't particularly liked it then, but she smoked it now because it added to the illicit aura of their meetings.

At one rendezvous, after having several drinks before coming to the motel and smoking a couple of joints with Rick, she began a boozy, stoned monologue of frustration and bitterness as Rick leaned against the headboard, listening.

"My mother's the biggest bitch in the world," she said, slurring her words badly. "She was always jealous of me, didn't want me to do anything that would show her up. Well, she got what she wanted. I'm stuck here, doing just what she did. I tried to get out. I tried, but David got me pregnant and there was nothing I could do, nothing at all."

She sighed heavily and took another drag on the joint. "Kate and Val and Shelly got out, but I didn't . . ."

Barbara was so stoned that she didn't sense Rick becoming alert. "Are you talkin' about Shelly DeLucca? That woman who's in the TV commercials?"

Barbara nodded.

"You guys were friends in high school, weren't you? Yeah, I remember, you were always together, you and Kate somebody and that red-haired girl." He stared at her intently. "You guys were all together on graduation night. I remember Steven and me talkin' to you. You had that new Mustang, a real cherry car, then Steven picked up Shelly and took her to the party . . ." His voice trailed off as his mind struggled to put it all together.

Finally, he said slowly, "Steven died that night, after the party. Somebody ran him down. I always wondered who it could've been. The rest of us left. Nobody else was there, 'cept Shelly, and she didn't have a car."

Barbara could see the logic of what must have happened that night beginning to be apparent to Rick, and she went cold inside. The warmth of the marijuana and the booze was gone now.

"She wasn't there when the police found Steven. How did she leave? Who came and got her?"

She knew what was coming. She braced herself as if she were about to be hit.

538

"She called *you*, didn't she? 'Course, who else would she call. *You* had a car. *You* came and got her, and *you* ran down Steven."

"*No!*"

"Shit, yeah! It must've happened like that! And nobody ever knew."

"It's all Shelly's fault," Barbara insisted. "If she hadn't gone with Steven, none of it would have happened." Her voice grew whiny. "I didn't mean to hit him. He walked right in front of the car. I didn't mean to hit him, but Val was screaming at me to get him and somehow my foot pressed down on the accelerator and then he was lying in the road, just lying there, not moving . . ."

She finished in a whisper, "And nothing was ever right again . . ."

Barbara began to cry softly; after a while, she fell into a drugged stupor. She didn't realize she'd fallen asleep until she awoke hours later with a dry mouth and a raging headache.

Rick was gone.

Barbara had a vague feeling of unease but no recollection at all of anything she'd said to him.

The next evening, when she met Rick at the motel, he didn't immediately undress her as he normally did. His hazel eyes glittered with a barely suppressed excitement that somehow wasn't at all sexual. When Barbara tried to kiss him, he pulled back.

"We need to talk." His voice was cold, calculating.

There was something different in the atmosphere, something menacing. Barbara tried to laugh it off. "Come on, neither one of us is interested in talking."

"You did a lot of talking last time."

She went rigid. What had she said last time? She tried desperately to remember but couldn't. Lately, she was having a hard time remembering things. She'd missed a Medical Wives Auxiliary meeting because she'd forgotten about it. Allison got mad about some clothes that she said she'd asked Barbara to take to the cleaners, but Barbara didn't remember the conversation.

Now this.

"What . . . what do you mean?"

Rick was clearly in no hurry to answer her question. Sitting down in a chair, he crossed his arms over his broad chest and looked up at her appraisingly. He began slowly, "You know, I was at Steven's party that night. I left with a bunch of other guys. Steven was the last to leave. The last time I saw him, he was getting in his car to drive back to his mother's place here in town."

Rick looked intently at Barbara. "I always wondered who ran him down. The police never caught the person. After a while, people stopped talking about it. I stopped trying to figure out who did it, but I was still curious."

Barbara couldn't move, could hardly breathe. She stood mesmerized.

Rick finished with a slow smile. "It's nice to have my curiosity satisfied after all this time."

She panicked. "Look, I don't know what you think I said, but you're wrong . . ."

"No way! You did it! I thought about it all last night and I figured it out. That little blond bitch was a friend of yours. She probably called you to come and get her. That red-haired girl, Valerie. She was there, too, huh? You were all together that night, drivin' around in your new car. That other girl, what's her name? Kate? Was she there, too?"

Barbara didn't say a word. Her throat was so tight, she couldn't swallow.

"You think I'm stupid. I'm good enough to ball, but that's all I'm good for. Well, lady, I'm a hell of a lot smarter than you are. I'm smart enough to know an opportunity when I see it."

"What do you mean?" The words came out in a tremulous whisper.

"You drive around in your fuckin' Mercedes and look down on me because I'm just a stupid mechanic. Well, I want nice things, too, but it takes money. And you're gonna give it to me."

"I don't have any money . . ."

"The hell you don't! I seen your house. I know exactly how much your car costs. I know your husband's a big deal doctor. You got money. So do the others. At the reunion, I saw their pictures on the wall 'cause they were such fuckin' big shots. All of you are gonna pay, or I'll go straight to the police. I don't think your friends would like that kind of publicity, do you?"

Barbara gathered what little courage she had left and tried desperately to fight back. "It's just your word against mine."

"There were other people there, too. You think your friends will risk their own hides to protect you? When the police start asking them questions, they'll turn on you so fast it'll make your head spin."

"They won't do that!"

"You sure about that? Anyway, all I have to do is tell that husband of yours, and you're finished. He'd be pretty pissed off to hear his wife has been ballin' someone else, and when I tell him you killed somebody . . ."

"No!"

"Everybody in town will be talkin' about it. You won't be able to raise your head around here."

Barbara knew he was absolutely right. It didn't really matter if he could convince the police of her guilt. Once the story got out on the grapevine, she'd be through. David would certainly leave her; her friends would drop her. She would have nothing. She would be nothing.

And Val and Kate and Shelly—especially Shelly, who'd endured so much—would be ruined.

For twenty years, she had feared this nightmarish moment. Now it was here. She looked at Rick and felt revulsion toward him. How could she ever have been attracted to him? If he touched her right now, she would be sick.

"I don't have very much money of my own," she said dully. "My husband controls most of it."

"Well, you'd better figure out a way to get it out of him because if you can't, I'll go to him, and see if *he'll* pay me to keep quiet."

"How much do you want?"

"Ten thousand. For now. Later, we'll set up a regular payment schedule. And I want the others' phone numbers. I'm gonna give them a call."

Oh, God! It would go on forever! It would never end! He would bleed them all dry for the rest of their lives.

"Please, you must understand, I can't come up with ten thousand without asking my husband, and he'd want to know what it's for."

Rick laughed. "Tell him it's to buy your boyfriend a new car. There's a nice little Mercedes 560 I've had my eye on."

He got up and looked down at her. "I'll meet you here Friday. You'd better have the money."

After he left, Barbara stood there for a moment,

before falling to the floor in a crumpled heap, sobbing hopelessly.

Over the next few days, she considered and discarded a number of plans. She only had about five thousand in cash that she could get her hands on without making David suspicious. She couldn't go to her mother. Constance would demand to know what Barbara needed such a large sum for.

As she kept coming back to the inevitable realization that she would have to tell David, she trembled. There was no way he would understand, no possibility that he would forgive her.

Maybe, she thought, she wouldn't have to tell him the whole truth, at least not the worst part, the part about Steven. Maybe she could just confess that she'd had an affair and was sorry and it would never happen again. She could say that Rick was threatening to tell everyone about the affair and she needed to give him money to keep him quiet, to protect their reputation and social standing.

Maybe, just maybe, David would forgive her if she was sufficiently contrite. Maybe he could figure out a way to stop Rick from demanding any more money, by threatening to sue him for harassment or something.

Barbara clung desperately to the hope that just this once David would be there for her when she really needed him.

As soon as she told him, she knew it wasn't going to work out.

"You had an affair!" he stormed at her.

They were in their bedroom and he'd just gotten

543

in from a particularly late, hard day. Barbara knew as soon as she saw him that it wasn't a good time to try to talk to him, but she had no choice. Tomorrow was Friday.

She answered quickly. "I'm sorry, David, I'm so sorry! I'd give anything if I could erase it, make it never happen."

"Who was it?"

"No one you know."

"How long has it been going on?"

"Just . . . just a couple of weeks," she lied, hoping he wouldn't find out that it had actually been longer.

"How could you do this to me? Does anyone know? Do our friends know?"

"Of course not! It's not like I would have told anyone."

He stared at her as if she'd sprouted a horn in the middle of her forehead. "How could you do this to me?" he repeated.

"David, I'm sorry! I would give anything not to have to tell you this."

"I was never once unfaithful to you."

He was telling the truth, she knew. He always did.

"I could have. There were plenty of willing women, nurses, women doctors, even some of your friends in the Auxiliary. But I never did. I wouldn't do that to you."

He looked at her as if everything he'd ever admired in her had turned to shit.

"There's . . . more," she said in a small voice.

His face grew even more hard. "How could there be more?"

"He's threatening to tell everyone about the affair. He's blackmailing me."

"He wants money to keep his mouth shut about this?"

She nodded miserably.

"How much?"

"Five thousand," she lied. She could raise the other five thousand herself. She hoped David would never know just how much Rick had actually demanded.

"I could give him the money," she said in a hurry, "and then maybe you could talk to a lawyer, find out if we could force him to stay quiet somehow."

She said nothing about Kate, Val, and Shelly. If she mentioned them, then she'd have to explain about Steven Ashe as well, and she couldn't do that.

"I'm not giving him a dime!"

"You don't understand! We have to give him the money tomorrow or he'll tell people. Let's just make this one payment, then we'll figure out a way to deal with him."

"Not one dime!"

Without saying another word, David went to his closet, took out a small suitcase, and began carefully packing.

"What are you doing?"

He didn't look at her. "I'm leaving. As soon as I've got an apartment, Allison can move in with me. I don't think it would be good for her to stay with you."

For the first time since Rick had confronted her, Barbara faced the fact that she was completely alone in dealing with this.

"But . . . we can work this out."

"*No!*"

"David . . ."

He had finished packing. "Your drinking was bad enough, but I won't put up with this, Barbara. I'll be filing for a divorce immediately."

He turned and headed toward the door.

"But what about the blackmail?"

"Everyone will just have to find out. There's no way to avoid a lot of unpleasantness. At least if I'm no longer with you, it will be a little easier."

"For who? Maybe it will be easier for you, but what about me?"

"I no longer feel any sense of responsibility for you, Barbara."

He was nearly out the door.

"David! I can't deal with him alone!"

"You should have thought of that before you went to bed with him."

Then he was gone.

She drank so much that night she passed out and slept all the next day. She didn't hear Allison leave for school and didn't hear her return in the afternoon. When she finally got up, she found a note from Allison on the kitchen counter. It said that she had left with her grandmother on the trip they'd planned to check out colleges back East.

Barbara poured another drink. Her fingers shook as she held the glass.

David was methodical, she knew. He would do exactly as he'd said. He would find an apartment and would move Allison into it. She knew Allison would choose to stay with her father. It had been a long time since she and Barbara had been close. David would hire an attorney and file for divorce. Nothing she could do or say would change his mind.

Her eye was caught by the flashing red light on the telephone answering machine. Pressing the but-

546

ton, she listened to three messages, all from members of the Auxiliary board saying they'd heard that David had left and asking her to call them.

It was beginning. Barbara knew they would pretend to offer support while trying to get her to step down as president and resign from the group as quickly and quietly as possible. After all, she wasn't going to be a doctor's wife much longer.

She saw the future clearly. She would lose everything—her husband, her daughter, her so-called friends, her social position. Barbara had given up everything for David and Allison—her education, her dream of having a career as a doctor, a life outside Visalia. All this, only to be abandoned, with no resources, no identity of her own. If she wasn't Mrs. David Browning, she didn't know who she was.

And if Rick followed through on his threat to go to the police . . .

Kate, Val, and Shelly had a great deal to lose as well.

She had thought about calling them but felt guilty. She had gotten them into this by having an affair with Rick. She couldn't bear to think of it so she poured herself another drink. By the time Barbara was supposed to meet him at the motel, she lay sprawled on the living room sofa, passed out cold, an empty bottle of whiskey lying on the floor beside her.

When she awoke the next morning, there was a new message on her answering machine: "This is Rick. You can't avoid me. Meet me at my house at eight o'clock tonight with the money or I'm going straight to the police. You got that? I'll tell them all about you and the others killing Steven. Don't even think about not showing up this time."

Her first thought was to have another drink, but her mind was clear enough to realize that she needed to sober up. Rick wasn't going away. She had to deal with him. Not just for her own sake but for Kate, Val, and Shelly. Sitting on the edge of the bed, her head hanging down tiredly, she noticed the nightstand. In the drawer was a gun. David had given it to her years ago for protection because he had to work so late at night, leaving her and Allison alone. She hadn't wanted to keep a gun in the house, but he had insisted.

It was an old gun of his father's, from his service during World War II. When David had given it to her, he had told her to get it registered, but she had never gotten around to it. Getting up, she went over to the drawer and opened it. The gun was still there under some papers and odds and ends.

Barbara hadn't touched it in years. Now she gingerly picked it up as if it might go off of its own volition. Checking, she saw that it was full of bullets. It all came back to her—David showing her how to hold it, how to click off the safety, how to fire it.

Barbara slipped the gun into her bag and left.

Rick rented a rundown clapboard house in the middle of a grape vineyard outside of town. Barbara had only been there once before and had refused to return because it was so filthy. When she asked him why he didn't move into a decent apartment in town, he replied that he liked the isolated location. He could do as he pleased without nosy neighbors watching.

As she drove out to the house, passing row upon shadowy row of grapevines, almost invisible in the darkness, she was glad of the isolation.

He stood waiting on the front porch, staring out at the road. When her car pulled up, he came down the rickety steps to meet her.

"You'd better have the money and your friends' phone numbers," he said impatiently. "I didn't like being stood up last night. Do it again and I'm goin' straight to the cops."

She got out of the car, clutching her purse tightly in both hands. "It's cold out here," she said. "Let's go inside."

He hesitated, then said, "Yeah. Let's go in the light where I can see the money."

Turning his back to her, Rick started back up the steps.

In less time than it took to take one ragged breath, Barbara opened her purse, took out the gun, carefully aimed, and fired.

Rick pitched forward, face down, and didn't move. A crimson stain spread across the back of his gray sweatshirt.

Forcing herself to walk closer, she looked down at him. He didn't seem to be breathing. She knew she should fire again, just to make sure, but she couldn't. Nausea was rising in her throat, and she knew she would be sick if she didn't get out of here immediately.

Reaching down, she pulled his wallet out of his pocket in an attempt to make it look like robbery, then she stumbled back to her car and peeled out of the driveway in a squeal of burning rubber.

A little way down the road, she had to pull over to be sick out the window. When she finally pulled herself together, she drove to a nearby reservoir and threw the gun in after carefully wiping her fingerprints off it, just in case.

At home, she went straight to her bedroom. She crawled into bed with her clothes on and lay there shivering, cold to her very bones. She didn't fall asleep until exhaustion finally overtook her sometime after dawn.

On Monday morning, Barbara went down to the Federal Express office and mailed off letters to Kate, Shelly, and Val. After another sleepless night, she had realized that she couldn't deal with this alone. She didn't know what to do, but she knew she needed them with her.

She had just returned home and was making some coffee when the doorbell rang. She didn't want to answer it because she was afraid it might be someone wanting to talk to her about David. Peering surreptitiously through the curtains, she was surprised to see a man dressed in a suit standing there. He didn't look like a door-to-door salesman. For a moment, she thought of just waiting until he left, but she was worried. Who was he? What did he want?

There was only one way to find out.

Opening the door, she said with a forced smile, "Yes?"

"Mrs. Barbara Browning?"

"Yes."

He showed her his badge. "I'm Detective Alex Pinero with the Visalia Police Department. May I come in and talk to you for a minute, ma'am?"

She tried very hard not to react. "Of course, but what is this about? Are we having more burglaries in the neighborhood?"

"No, ma'am. This has to do with something else."
As they sat down in the living room, he took out
notebook and pen and asked, "Do you know a
ick Paxton?"

She pretended to think for a moment. "No . . .
, I don't believe I do."

"Are you sure, ma'am?"

"Yes."

"He was the service manager at the dealership
here you bought your car."

"Oh, yes, that blond man. He's fairly new. I've
nly talked to him a couple of times when I took
y car in. I didn't pay much attention to his
ame."

"So you haven't seen him very much?"

"Oh, no. Not more than two or three times, and
en only for a minute while I explained what I
anted done to the car."

"Did you ever see him away from the dealership?"
She thought furiously. Had anyone seen her at
e motel? She had been careful always to park on
e street and slip in the back way to avoid being
en by the manager.

"No," she said definitely. "I'm sure I've never seen
im outside of the dealership." She tried to sound
aturally curious as she asked, "Why?"

"Mr. Paxton was killed this weekend."

"Oh, dear! How awful!"

"He was shot. A farmhand found him lying in
ont of his house out in the country."

"He had your unlisted phone number in his
ook."

"How odd. Where would he get my number?"

"We wondered the same thing. That's why I'm
ere."

The look he gave her now was shrewd and ob-

servant. She knew he was gauging her reaction. She
had to be very, very careful.

"Detective Pinero, I'm sorry to hear about this
poor man's death, but as I said, I barely knew him.
He certainly wasn't part of my social circle."

"I'm aware of your background, Mrs. Browning. I
was a patient of your father's, and I know that your
husband is the head of surgery at Municipal Hospital. It seemed ludicrous that someone like Paxton
could have anything to do with you, but I had to
check it out."

"Of course. If that's all . . ."

He gave her a brief smile. "Sure. Thanks for
your time, ma'am."

When he left, Barbara stood at the window,
watching him drive away. Was that the last she
would see of him? Did he believe her? He had accepted her denial so easily. Too easily. He didn't
look like a stupid man. Would he somehow be able
to trace her involvement with Rick? Had she left
fingerprints at his house the one time she had gone
inside there? If he found out about Rick's frequent
visits to the motel, would he find a maid or someone else who had seen her sneaking in and out?

Panic seized her. Pinero was just pretending to
accept her protestation of innocence. He would be
back. With proof. And it would all come out. Not
just about Rick but about Steven Ashe, too.

Barbara couldn't bear it, couldn't bear the
thought of being arrested, going to jail, being the
object of ridicule and scorn. She could just see
the way Allison would look at her, with such shame
and revulsion. And her mother . . .

It wouldn't end with Barbara. It would lead inevitably to Kate and Val and Shelly.

She went into her bathroom and took out the

bottle of Elavil that her doctor had prescribed for the severe depression that had plagued her for some time. She'd just picked it up from the pharmacy three days earlier and the bottle was nearly full. Taking it into the kitchen, she opened a bottle of wine and began shoving fistsfull of pills into her mouth, washing them down with the wine.

TEN

Valerie

Val sat alone in the passenger cabin of the jet, sipping mineral water with bitters and lemon and making calls to a network executive in Rockefeller Center, bankers, and business reps. At one point, she just had to stop and laugh at how the worm had turned. It was all such a trip, as she would have said during the sixties. Only then she would have been sitting cross-legged on the floor of some cheap apartment with a bunch of hippies gathered around a hash pipe.

Now she sat in the luxurious confines of a private jet belonging to a broadcast magnate. He had sent it to New York to pick her up and fly her to L.A. to discuss her possible purchase of one of his TV stations. Now she was returning home.

Flying from coast to coast in a private jet to talk about a multi-milliondollar deal was just one example of how dramatically her life had changed over the last few years. Val had moved to New York when her TV show was syndicated. At the same time, she formed her own production company, People Productions, and took over ownership of the show. With its phenomenal success, she found herself transformed almost overnight into an extremely wealthy woman with a lot of cash to invest.

When the call had come from the broadcast magnate, she hadn't been surprised. Word was out—she was not only a media darling, she was a savvy businesswoman. "Who would've thunk it?" she asked herself wryly, remembering the wild-eyed radical she'd once been. Now she was a yuppified capitalist with a co-op facing Park Avenue, an accountant who knew far more about her finances than she did, and a full-time housekeeper. While she was still a self-declared crusading journalist, the truth was she worried more about her daughter Michelle's grades and the lack of daylight between her thighs than she did about the political viability of the radical left.

Val was thirty-seven years old, and forty was just around the corner. Despite the crow's feet at the corners of her eyes and the gray hair among the red, she still felt like a kid. Sometimes when she took Michelle to the park or to their new country place in Connecticut, she played with her with all the giggly enthusiasm of another seven-year-old.

In a way, she knew, she would never entirely grow up. Considering the stuffy, old-before-their-time grown-ups she knew, she decided that wasn't so bad. She made more than a million dollars a year but still related on an elemental level to her audience—the unemployed, house-wives, the young. "I'm a surrogate for them," she often said. "I ask the questions they'd ask if they had the chance."

Sometimes when she talked to Kate, they commiserated with each other over how strange it felt to no longer be lower middle class. They admitted to each other, as they couldn't admit to any of their new friends or co-workers, that they felt like frauds. At some point, someone would come along and say,

"We've found out who you really are and you don't belong."

At that moment, the pilot's voice came over the intercom, announcing that they were about to land at Kennedy and asking Val to fasten her seat belt. As the plane circled, then landed and taxied to the terminal, she switched her thoughts from high finance to romance. She had a date that night with an entertainment attorney she'd been seeing for a few weeks. He was everything she'd ever wanted in a man — successful enough not to feel intimidated by her high profile, attractive without being male-model-handsome, smart, with a rapier wit to match her own — and he was terrific in bed.

He was also seven years younger than she was, which made their relationship very with it.

There was just one problem. He had absolutely no intention of ever making a commitment to her. Val was merely one of several women he dated, and she wasn't even at the top of the list. He rarely made plans far in advance with her, and often called on Saturday afternoon to see if she was free that night. Obviously, he'd tried other women before settling for her.

They would never get married. He would never be the father figure she wanted for Michelle. He didn't even particularly like kids because, he said, they tied you down.

Val knew what would happen. At some point in the not-too-distant future, either he would stop calling because he'd found someone else or she would start turning him down because she was tired of his bullshit. Either way, it would end as all her relationships ended.

Failure to commit. The disease of the eighties, she thought as she stepped into a cab in front of the airport. She'd even done shows about it, but despite all the shrinks she'd interviewed, all the women authors with books like *How to Catch the Man of Your Dreams*, she still had no idea how to find what she wanted: someone who wasn't just passing through.

At home, she gave Michelle a big hug and a kiss, helped her with her homework, ate dinner with her, then turned her over to Sarah, the nanny who'd been with them since Michelle's birth. She showered and changed into a nifty little black-and-white original she'd picked up in London on a trip to visit Shelly. Analyzing her appearance in the full-length mirror, she decided she'd definitely improved with age. Val would never be conventionally pretty, but maturity had filled out her thin frame nicely and the sharp planes and angles of her face were now often described as "interesting" in profiles of her. With a five-hundred-dollar haircut and an air of self-confidence that came with success, she was a striking woman.

Val grinned at her reflection. Definitely not bad.

She left just in time to make her nine o'clock cocktail date with Stan, the attorney. It went according to script. He asked about her trip, she asked about his latest case, they had two drinks, then went back to his place to make love. She didn't spend the night with him because Michelle would expect to see her when she awoke in the morning. Besides, Stan didn't ask her.

When she went into work the next morning, Ellen, her producer, asked about the trip. Val respected Ellen's opinion enormously and often relied on it when making decisions concerning her career. Now she asked Ellen what she thought about the network executive's ideas regarding a new prime-time talk show he wanted Val to host.

After discussing it for a few minutes, Ellen said, "Enough business. Let's talk about what really matters. How are things with you and Stan?"

Val scrunched up her face in a thoughtful expression. "You know what I realized last night?" she asked, answering Ellen's question with a question.

"What?"

"That I'm dating the same man I've always dated. He's got a different name, but essentially he's like every man I've ever gotten involved with. *Unattainable*. I'm involved and he isn't."

Ellen nodded. "I know. Well, dump the bum and start looking elsewhere."

"You think I haven't looked elsewhere? Even though I hate sports, I've gone to sports events because there are so many men there. I've gone to parties that bored me stiff because someone said there'd be someone there I really should meet. When I used to have some free time, I took university extension classes in male-oriented subjects like money management. I've gone grocery shopping at six o'clock in the evening because that's when men are getting off work and doing their shopping. I've gone to cultural events, and you know I'm the most uncultured person in the universe. I've volunteered in political campaigns, gone to the 'in' restaurants and nightclubs. Hell, I even tried a singles club in San Francisco where the members are all tested for AIDS before they join."

Ellen laughed. "All right. I give up. I don't have any other suggestions."

Val looked at Ellen. Despite the fact that they had worked closely together for several years now and were good friends, she realized that she knew almost nothing about Ellen's romantic life. Unlike most of the women Val knew, Ellen never discussed who she was dating.

"What do *you* do?" she asked curiously.

"About men?"

"Uh-huh."

"I don't do anything. I gave up on them after my second divorce."

"I didn't know you'd been divorced twice."

"Yup. My first husband was Hispanic, like me. He hit me. *Once.* I walked out the door and never looked back. My second husband was very successful, very attractive, a terrific guy in a lot of ways. Only problem was, he couldn't keep his pants zipped."

Val grinned. "I know the problem. Sometimes when I'm with Stan and he's kind of in a hurry to get me home or get me out of his apartment, I get the feeling I'm the first shift and the second shift is due any minute."

"We should go out for a drink sometime and spend the evening trashing men," Ellen joked.

"How about tonight? Michelle's spending the night with a friend, and frankly I hate staying in my apartment alone."

"Okay. I'll be in my office. Come by when you're ready to leave."

They sat in a booth in an upscale bar in Greenwich Village, drinking and laughing. Val rarely got drunk anymore because she was so obsessed with being a responsible mother to Michelle, but tonight she let herself go and was having a helluva good time.

"So there we were," Val said. "He practically had his entire face down my throat, I mean, I'm talkin' major tongue action, and we're both starting to shed clothes and he stops and says in this serious

559

voice, 'You realize I'm just offering friendship.' I mean, can you believe the guy's timing?"

Ellen nodded. "Yeah, I can."

"*I* didn't go after him! *He* pursued me! I didn't even particularly like him. I just wanted to go to bed with him. He was so paranoid about me expecting something from him that he felt he had to make it clear where he stood. What an asshole."

"So what did you do?"

"I told him I don't fuck my friends and left."

Ellen laughed. "Good for you."

Val's expression sobered. "The thing is, I'm pretty happy with my life. I mean, what's not to be happy with? I get paid obscene amounts of money and I have the smartest, most beautiful little girl who ever lived. I still can't believe how much joy she brings to my life. Part of my mind is always on her — Is she okay? Is she wearing her coat when it's cold? Because of her, I'm never entirely free, but that's okay because she keeps me from getting too far down when I'm depressed. When she's gone, like tonight, I hate the empty feeling of the apartment. There's nothing but the sound of my own footsteps on the floor."

"I always wanted to have children," Ellen admitted, "but it never worked out. When I turned forty and wasn't involved in a relationship with a man, I accepted the fact that I would never have kids. But there's a big hole in my life. I envy you."

"My life is far from perfect, you know. For a long time, I totally concentrated on my career and Michelle and didn't even want to date. At the back of my mind was the assumption that some day, when I was ready, someone would come along. Then a few months ago, someone asked me when I made the decision to choose career over marriage. I hadn't realized I'd made that decision."

"There are so few men available at our age," Ellen said. "The men of our generation were killed in Vietnam or psychically wounded or messed up by drinking and drugs—or they're gay—or they don't want to settle down with one woman because a better one might come along and they want to keep their options open."

Val mused. "You know, I've never, in my entire life, found a man who was willing or able to give me what I need—emotional intimacy and commitment and support."

She finished sadly. "Aside from Michelle, there's no one who really loves me. And there may never be."

"I have a solution," Ellen announced.

"What?"

"More piña coladas!"

Two hours later, they stumbled into Ellen's apartment. She had said, "Let's have a slumber party!" and Val, who was more than a little drunk, thought it a great idea.

They put on warm flannel nightgowns because it was a bitter cold March night, climbed into bed, drank hot toddies, laughed, and were just plain silly together. Through a drunken haze, one thought was crystal clear to Val—This is what love is. Feeling connected, feeling understood. She had never really felt it with a man, even Michael.

She felt closer to Ellen than she'd ever felt to another adult. Then somehow the innocence of their affectionate hugs changed. The air between them was charged with a physical awareness. Reaching out to Val in her moment of vulnerability, Ellen turned warmth and caring to passion.

Their lovemaking was spontaneous and deeply

satisfying. For one stunned moment, Val felt shaken by the discovery that she could respond physically to a woman like this. After all the men she'd been with, it was a shattering realization, but it seemed so natural, so right, and was so comforting that she simply went with it. Inside her head, she experienced an epiphany of such transcendent sweetness that she felt forever changed.

Afterward, as they nestled together in bed, Ellen made a confession that wasn't nearly as startling as it would have been an hour earlier.

"I'm a lesbian. Long ago I gave up trying to find a man who could give me what I need. I met an older woman, Grace, in San Francisco, and we were together until she died, shortly before I came to New York with you."

Having lived in San Francisco for so many years, Val had known many gay men and a few gay women, but she was amazed at Ellen's rationale.

"I didn't grow up with a preference for women. It was a pragmatic decision on my part as I got into my thirties, with two failed marriages behind me. It just seemed to me that there were a lot of first-rate women and second-rate men out there."

At Val's stunned look, she smiled and said, "You'd be amazed how many women have reached the same conclusion. I've met a lot of them, in one way or another. Here's another hot topic for the show. A major cultural phenomenon that no one wants to talk about, and a devastating commentary on the state of male-female relationships as the eighties dissolve into the nineties."

"On an emotional level, it makes so much sense," Val agreed. "But . . ."

"But it's terrifying to think of being labeled a lesbian," Ellen finished for her. "I know."

Looking intently at Val, she said, "But it's what I

am. Does it change how you feel about me?"

"Of course. But . . . but not in a bad way."

"Good. Because there's something else you must know. I love you, Val, not just as a co-worker or even as a friend. What just happened between us is something I've been wanting for a long time. When Grace died, I was afraid I would never again care that deeply for someone, but I care even more deeply for you. I want . . . I *need* this to be the beginning of a permanent, committed relationship between us."

Val had no idea how to respond. The harder she examined herself, the more she realized that she had always looked to women, not men, for support and love. A memory that had lain deeply buried in her subconscious suddenly came to her — Myrna hugging her at the end of the People's Park conflict and the intense way Val had responded to her. At the time, she'd denied that response. Now . . . she realized she had been happier tonight with Ellen than she'd been with a man in a long, long time, but the thought of defying the taboo that separated them was terrifying.

What about Michelle? Would such a relationship hurt her?

A Biblical quote flashed through her mind. "The sins of the fathers . . ." She knew damn well it applied to mothers as well.

All the warmth and love she felt with Ellen dissolved in an instant as the religious doctrine of her childhood came back to haunt her, bringing with it a rush of guilt. As a child, she had been taught that any window left open in one's own faith can let in the evil that strikes down loved ones. Now, years later, she felt the remembered feeling of suffocation. She was bad, what she had just done was bad, and she would be damned to hell for all eternity.

563

No matter how hard Val tried to tell herself she didn't believe in all that religious cant, on some level she was still affected by it.

"I must go," she whispered in a shaky voice, not quite looking at Ellen.

She kept her face averted as she dressed quickly.

Ellen didn't say a word, but Val sensed the terrible rejection Ellen must be feeling—just like Val felt when the men she slept with got out of her bed and left.

Val didn't sleep well that night. She thought about Ellen and how good it had felt to be with her, but at the same time she felt frightened and guilty. Always, at the forefront of her thoughts, was Michelle.

The next afternoon when Michelle returned from her friend's house, Val asked her if she'd had a good time and what they'd done. When Michelle had finished chattering on about all the fun she'd had, Val asked carefully, "How would you feel if someone else came to live with us?"

"Who?"

"Someone like Ellen, perhaps."

"I like Ellen. When I go to your office, she doesn't treat me like a little kid. She explains stuff to me instead of saying I'm too young to understand."

"So . . . you wouldn't mind if she came to live with us?"

"For how long?"

"Maybe a long time. Maybe forever."

"That's okay."

"Would you like her to be part of our family?" Val pressed, wanting to be absolutely certain that Michelle didn't mind.

"We're not a family."

"Of course we are. What makes you think we're not?"

"Two people aren't a family," Michelle said with all the conviction of childish certainty. "It takes three people to be a family."

"You mean a mommy, a daddy, and a child?"

"Sure, but it doesn't have to be a daddy. A lot of kids don't have daddies, but they have brothers or sisters or grandmothers or somebody. Just as long as it's three people."

Where on earth did she get this from? Val wondered. She seemed absolutely convinced of it. A vague, half-remembered phrase flashed through her mind. *A lonely little couple.* Is that what she and Michelle were? Is that why Michelle thought two wasn't enough for a real family?

Michelle went on, "So if Ellen lived with us forever, then there would be three of us and we'd be a family."

"And that would be good?"

"Of course."

Of course.

When she went to work the next morning, she received the letter from Barbara.

Spring 1989

COMING HOME

ONE

Kate

Kate, Valerie, and Shelly remained at Barbara's bedside until Dr. Garcia came by on his rounds early in the morning. Seeing how exhausted they looked, he said, "Go get some rest. There won't be a change in her condition for a while."

As they left her room, a man walked up to them and flashed a badge. "Detective Alex Pinero with the Visalia Police Department. May I have a word with you ladies?"

For an instant, Kate couldn't understand what he would want with them. Then she remembered that suicide was a crime and that the police were always notified.

"What do you want?" Val asked sharply before Kate could respond.

"I understand you ladies are old friends of Mrs. Browning."

"So?" Val was at her most belligerent.

"Val, it's all right," Kate said. Turning back to Pinero, she replied, "Yes, we are, but we don't know anything about her suicide attempt."

"How did you find out about it?"

"She wrote to each of us, asking us to come. Obviously, she was upset about something, but before we could get here, she . . . she took some pills."

"Did she say what she was upset about?"

"No."

"Had anything happened recently that you're aware of that could have prompted her suicide attempt?"

They all shook their heads.

"Everything seemed fine," Kate replied. "We have no idea why she would do this."

Val interjected, "Why don't you ask her husband? I'll bet he knows what was wrong."

"I've already talked to Dr. Browning. He insisted he knew of no reason why his wife would do such a thing. However, he admitted that they recently separated. Then he refused to say anything further without having an attorney present."

Kate was amazed. Barbara hadn't said anything to her to suggest that she and David were having serious problems. Of course, Barbara, as the wife, might have been the proverbial last one to know.

Val frowned. "The jerk. She probably did it because he left her. I'll bet he had a little nurse on the side."

Pinero asked Kate, "When did she send these letters to you?"

"They were sent by Federal Express, overnight delivery. We all got them yesterday. The time on them was 9:30 A.M. Monday."

"She was brought to the hospital late Monday morning," Pinero said thoughtfully, "so she must have sent them right before I saw her. That means she was worried about something even before I talked to her."

"What did you talk to her about?" Val asked quickly.

Instead of answering the question, he asked, "Do any of you know a man named Rick Paxton?"

The name was vaguely familiar somehow, but Kate couldn't quite place it. "I don't think so," she began, then stopped. "Wait a minute. I think we went to high school with him, didn't we? But I don't think any of us have seen him since then."

She looked enquiringly at Val and Shelly, both of whom shook their heads, but Kate caught a look in Shelly's eyes — a momentary flicker of something — before Shelly assumed a blank expression.

"Did you ever hear Mrs. Browning mention him?"

"No," Kate answered for all of them. "If she'd known him, recently, I mean, I'm sure she would have mentioned it to one of us."

"What does he have to do with this?" Val demanded.

"He was killed over the weekend. Mrs. Browning is implicated in his death."

Shelly gasped.

Kate was stunned. "But that couldn't have anything to do with Barbara!"

"That's what I thought," Pinero replied. "They didn't seem to have anything in common. He worked as a service manager at the local Mercedes dealership and was a small-time drug dealer, though he never got caught for that. Did a little time in Roadcamp for drunk driving. Not the kind of guy you'd expect someone in her position to know. When I talked to her, she denied having a relationship with him, but as soon as I left, she tried to kill herself. Now, that's pretty suggestive."

Val jumped in. "Barbara wouldn't have given someone like that the time of day! I don't know why she tried to off herself, but I'll bet it had to do with her husband, not some minor league slimeball."

Pinero looked unconvinced. "Maybe." He took out

571

a notebook and pen. "Can I have your names, addresses, and phone numbers?"

When Val gave her name, he looked at her with interest. "I thought I recognized you. You have a TV show, don't you?"

She nodded coolly.

Recognizing a snub when he saw one, Pinero got back to business. "Are you going to stick around for a while?"

"Are you telling us not to leave town?"

"Let's just say I'd like to talk to you again before you leave."

"We're not going anywhere until we know what's happening with Barbara," Kate answered tiredly.

"Okay. I'm going to wait around here, in case she regains consciousness. If any of you happen to think of anything helpful, you can find me right here."

With that, he sat down in a chair just outside Barbara's room.

As they walked over to the elevator, Kate was uncomfortably aware of his gaze following them.

None of them had any idea where to go. Kate didn't want to go home and deal with her mother's questions yet, so she suggested they go back to Barbara's house. She knew where Barbara hid an extra key outside, and there was certainly plenty of room in the huge house.

They let themselves into the marble-tiled entry that rose two stories tall. Kate was immediately struck by the ghost-town atmosphere of the place that had once seemed the epitome of the American dream.

"It's eerie," Val commented, echoing Kate's thoughts.

"That's just because it's empty," she insisted.

She felt intensely ill at ease. In this house, almost

exactly twenty-four hours earlier, something had snapped within Barbara and she had tried to take her life. It wasn't a hysterical attempt to get attention or even a cry for help. As a doctor's wife, she knew how many pills it took to do the job. She'd taken that many.

Why? Was Val right? Could Barbara have been reacting to David leaving her? *What*, if anything, did Rick Paxton have to do with it?

Those questions preyed on their minds as they made their way to the three guest bedrooms.

After a couple of hours of fitful sleep, they straggled into the ultra-modern, black-and-white kitchen, one at a time. Kate had spent a lot of time in the house and knew exactly where all the ingredients were to make coffee. As she prepared it, Val and Shelly sat at the small pine table at one end of the kitchen, looking exhausted and worried.

Even Shelly had lost her air of composure this morning. Her clothes were wrinkled, her hair disheveled. Kate knew that the haunted look in her lovely deep blue eyes wasn't just concern for Barbara. She was deeply affected by being back in this town.

Val and Shelly made desultory small talk while Kate busied herself with cups and saucers, cream and sugar. She sensed among the three of them an atmosphere of thoughts unspoken but not, as was usual with them, of thoughts unspoken but understood.

She noticed something out of the corner of her eye—the blinking red light on the answering machine attached to the kitchen phone. There was nothing unusual in that. One of Barbara's friends in town had probably tried to call her.

Yet somehow it seemed significant. Looking at

Val, she said, "There's a message on the answering machine."

Val's instincts as a reporter were immediately intrigued. "Let's see who it's from."

"I don't know if we should."

"It could be urgent," Val insisted, getting up and walking over to the machine. After a moment, Shelly followed. "Maybe it's from her mother or Allison. For all we know, they aren't even aware she's in the hospital."

"You're right. Okay, let's see who it is."

She pressed the playback button. After a moment, a male voice began, "This is Rick . . ."

None of them said a word. They stood in a small semicircle around the machine, rooted to the spot.

What they had all feared since receiving Barbara's letter was just confirmed. When the machine clicked off and automatically rewound the message, Kate broke out of her paralysis. "How could he have known about Steven?"

Suddenly she became aware that Shelly was as white as a sheet. "I know," she whispered.

Val turned on her. "What is it?"

Shelly sat down heavily on a chair and held herself tightly, protectively. A range of emotions played across her lovely face — fear, anxiety, shame. With a horrible sense of déjà vu, Kate realized that she'd seen those same emotions twisting Shelly's face into a tortured mask on graduation night. Now Shelly was experiencing again the terrifying feelings she'd felt as a result of the gang rape.

When Shelly didn't answer, Val went on angrily. "Look! This proves that Barbara not only knew Rick, she was being blackmailed by him! And that means she probably killed him!"

"No!" Kate shouted.

"We've got to face the truth if we're going to help Barb. Running from it won't do any good!"

"Running from it is exactly what you told us to do twenty years ago! And look where it's led — Barbara's nearly dead!"

"Stop it!" Shelly screamed hysterically, then buried her face in her hands and sobbed.

Dear God, Kate thought, it's just like that night. It's all coming back, and this time we can't pretend it didn't happen.

Val bent down to Shelly's level. Her voice was gentle yet persistent as she said, "We have to know how Rick could have found out what happened."

Without looking up, Shelly murmured into her hands, "He was there. He was one of them."

Val straightened and looked at Kate. For a long moment, neither spoke. Then Val said, "If he knew what happened, why didn't he say anything at the time?"

"He can't have known then," Kate answered, thinking furiously. "Barbara must have accidentally let it slip when she was with him, or he guessed somehow. I don't know, but I'm sure she wouldn't have told him on purpose."

"She was probably drunk," Val said in a matter-of-fact tone.

Ignoring the blunt assessment, Kate said, "At any rate, it must have happened quite recently. He wouldn't have waited very long to start blackmailing her."

"And us," Val added. "Apparently, he was a greedy little bastard. He was going to shake us all down." Val shook her head in confusion. "Why would she get involved with scum like that?"

Kate didn't answer, but she thought she understood how it might have happened: the same way it

575

had happened the night she'd gone to bed with Bryan Yates, when, for reasons too dark to contemplate, she'd allowed herself to be drawn into something terribly destructive.

"Hell, it doesn't matter," Val went on. "The point is, he knew and he was blackmailing her. She must have killed him."

"If she did, it was to keep our lousy secret!" Kate said furiously. "She was protecting us as much as herself. It's all your fault! If you hadn't persuaded her to try to hide what happened that night, none of this would have happened now!"

"*My* fault? Look, I kept her out of jail. I saved her ass, and you know it!"

"If you saved her, then why is she lying in the hospital right now, nearly dead?"

"If we'd gone to the police back then, we'd all have gotten in trouble. Especially Barbara, because she was driving."

"But it was an accident . . ."

"Was it?"

"Are you saying you think she ran Steven down intentionally?" Kate asked slowly.

"I was sitting right next to her. I saw her face. She meant to kill him."

"No! He was drunk, he stumbled in front of the car, she couldn't miss him!"

Val didn't respond, but Kate knew that she was convinced Barbara had meant to hit Steven. Kate desperately wanted to believe it was an accident. For all these years, she'd told herself it was and had used that belief to justify their actions in not going to the police.

She remembered something she'd long since forgotten—the rage she'd felt when she'd realized what those boys had done to Shelly and her desire to se

576

them all dead. Especially Steven. Barbara would have felt the same rage.

"If you're right," she said in a deathly voice, "then we should have gone to the police."

"No way! What she did to Steven was justice, pure and simple."

"Without going to the police and the courts, there couldn't be any justice!" Kate insisted, remembering her father and all he believed in.

"How can you talk about justice, knowing what he did to Shelly? She wouldn't have gotten any justice in the courts. Every one of those guys would've walked, and Shelly would have been hung out to dry in front of the whole town. As far as I'm concerned, we had the right, as women, to defy a legal system that wouldn't give us justice. I thought so then, and I still think so!"

Suddenly, Shelly, who had kept her face buried in her hands, looked up at them with tear-filled eyes. "Stop talking about it! I can't bear it!"

Kate knelt beside her. Her voice was soft with compassion. "I'm sorry you have to go through all this again, but don't you see, we have to talk about it. We've been running away from it for twenty years. We've tried to deny it, but it didn't work. We've all been affected by it. I know I have. I think you and Val have, too. And Barbara certainly has. It's finally caught up with all of us."

"I can't bear to remember it," Shelly repeated.

"Yes, you can. You're a lot stronger now than you were then. You *can* deal with it. You have to." She looked at Val. "We all have to. We have to face this, once and for all."

Val said stubbornly, "What we did was right. We live in a society that condones violence toward women. It's always been that way."

577

Kate didn't argue. Turning back to Shelly, she said, "We've got to talk about what happened that night. For twenty years, we haven't talked about it but it's always been there, eating away at us. We were all devastated by it."

When Shelly tried to look away, Kate took her chin in her hands and forced her friend to look at her. "It's like going back to the house you grew up in, walking through each dark room, turning on the lights, exposing the secrets, and dealing with the feelings. We have to do that, Shelly. We have to look at this terrible thing we've been denying all these years."

"You don't understand the fear and shame and rage and pain."

"I know, but the shame isn't yours. It doesn't belong to you. You were a sweet, innocent girl. You still are deep inside. What those boys did to you wasn't your fault. Do you hear me? It wasn't *your* fault."

"They made me hate myself," Shelly whispered.

Val put her arms around her. "You should hate *them,* not yourself. *They* did something wrong, you didn't. They did something criminal. You didn't deserve it. Do you understand? *You didn't deserve it!*"

Kate added, "You'll never be able to see it the right way until you deal with it."

Shelly nodded slowly. "Yes . . . oh, God, you're right. When it was happening, when they . . . were raping me, all I could think of was that I just wanted it to end. But it never ended. Four months later, I had to deal with the abortion. Even then, it didn't end. I've lived with a constant feeling of terror. I'm afraid, I'm always afraid . . ."

She broke down and began sobbing again.

"They had no right to do that to you!" Val

578

shouted furiously. "It wasn't your fault! You didn't ask for it! You didn't deserve it! You've got to understand that."

Kate sat down next to Shelly. "You can say anything you want right now. Get it all out. Say what's been in your heart since that night."

Shelly looked up at her, gulping back tears. "I hate them," she whispered.

"Say it louder," Kate urged.

"I *hate* them," she repeated in a stronger voice. Then, shouting, "I hate them! I'm glad Steven's dead! I'm glad Rick's dead! I wish they were all dead!"

The tears poured out of her then, as twenty years of suppressed feelings came rushing to the surface. Kate and Val held her, rocking her back and forth, murmuring reassurance. As the three held onto each other for dear life, Kate realized that she couldn't blame Val. It hadn't been her fault any more than it was Shelly's for going with Steven in the first place. They had all been victimized. They had all paid a price.

Especially Barbara.

Later, an emotionally exhausted Shelly sat on a white sofa in the living room sipping hot black coffee. Despite her tear-streaked face and the tired way her body slumped on the sofa, Kate thought she looked better, lighter somehow, than she had in a long time. She no longer held herself rigidly, as if constantly expecting to have to ward off attack.

Kate and Val sat in nearby chairs, also drinking coffee, trying to come to terms with a twenty-year-old tragedy that still haunted them.

"It would have been different if Barbara hadn't gotten pregnant and married David and come back

579

here," Val insisted. "None of this would have hap
pened."

"I'm not so sure," Kate mused. "I think, deep in
side, she felt she had to atone for Steven's death
She atoned by getting pregnant and giving u
everything she wanted in life."

Then she shook her head in confusion. "I don
know. Maybe her pregnancy *was* an accident an
she simply couldn't face an illegal abortion afte
watching Shelly go through it."

Shelly looked at Kate. "It was so horrible, but
honestly don't regret it. If I had it to do over again
I would do the same. I couldn't have done other
wise."

She added softly, "Still, I would so like to have
child now."

"I know," Kate said. "I feel the same way. I ha
a perfectly safe, legal abortion. At the tim
it seemed the right thing to do. Even though
couldn't admit it to myself, I knew Alan and
weren't going to make it, and I couldn't fac
raising a child alone; but not a day goes by tha
I don't count the years and figure out how old h
would be."

She stopped, then went on wistfully, "Somehow
always imagine him as a little boy. I can see hin
playing on the beach with a little pail and spade
smiling and playing tag with the waves." Her eye
filled with tears. "But I can't decide what color hi
eyes would have been . . ."

Brushing away her tears, she went on, "For com
pletely selfish reasons I chose to deny life to tha
child."

She looked at Val. "I think that's why I encour
aged you to have Michelle—because I bitterly re
gretted having an abortion. I didn't have the guts t

ake responsibility for the life I'd allowed to begin. I ook the easy way out."

"But it wasn't easy, was it?" Val asked gently.

"No."

Val shook her head. "Poor Katie. You were always so hard on yourself. Barbara may have been ur fearless leader, but you were the one we all urned to when we were hurt or scared. You always lt like you had to make it all better."

Kate's expression hardened. "I don't think I made nything better. I was a perfect little yuppie. No inonvenient kid was going to spoil the precarious alance of my life. It might affect my marriage or, od forbid, my career. The awful irony is that my arriage ended anyway and my career went to hell or a long time. During that time I would have had child to love, who would have loved me. Maybe I ould have realized a lot sooner that success isn't verything."

Val responded, "For our generation it was the nly thing."

Kate met her look. "We wanted so much, didn't e? More than anything, we wanted change for its wn sake, to break all the rules laid down over housands of years of male rule. We wanted everying our mothers had—marriage, motherhood—nd we wanted more—careers and freedom. But we ad no experience in handling freedom. I think at's why we felt so lost and scared. Maybe that's hy Barbara married David and returned to Visa-a. It was so tempting to return to the old ways, e old security."

Kate broke down and began to cry softly. "I could ave had a child. I could have had something real nd true and lasting with Mark. Why did I make many bad choices?"

581

Val got up and went over to Kate. Kneeling down by her, Val hugged her and whispered, "The only thing I still hold onto from all those miserable years in church is the idea of forgiveness. It's the one part of that whole mind-set that makes sense. Forgive yourself, sweetie. You deserve it."

Kate looked into her eyes. "Still, I can't help but wonder, what if? What if I'd made different decisions?"

"You could say the same about Barbara. What if she'd decided not to have Allison or marry David and went on to achieve the kind of life she wanted instead of imprisoning herself here. There's no point in asking *what if.*"

"You're right," Kate said, pulling herself together. "There's no point in questioning our choices now. All we can do is face whatever mistakes we made and come to terms with the past."

She looked at Shelly. "I think we were all victims of what happened on graduation night."

Shelly nodded slowly. "Yes, but it will take a while to fully come to terms with it. All this time I felt responsible because I went with Steven. I thought the way I looked, being sexy, triggered the assault, so on some fundamental level I rejected my own sexuality. I couldn't let any man get close to me."

"But Philippe . . ." Val interjected.

Shelly shrugged. "He was a fantasy figure to me. We didn't have a *real* relationship. Neither of us was looking for one. He wanted someone to put on a pedestal, not a flesh-and-blood woman with imperfections. I wanted Prince Charming, not a real man who would force me to get in touch with my sexuality again."

She stopped, an expression of sudden enlightenıent energizing her expression. "Like Ryan," she ·hispered.

Kate said, "I'm just now beginning to realize how ·st I felt when I lied to my father and he knew it ·nd it ruined our relationship. That's why I turned · Alan, why I was so dependent on him. I was ·esperate for a man to fill that void." And why she ·as so frightened of making a real commitment to ·lark, she realized, because she was afraid of mak-·ıg the same mistake. Rather than risk failure ·gain, she was willing to spend the rest of her life ·lone.

Val looked at Shelly. "What happened to you just ·onfirmed my mistrust of men. I think that, more ·ıan anything else, is why I insisted we cover it up, ·ot go to the authorities. Because the authorities ·ere men, and I was convinced I couldn't trust ·ıem."

She shook her head. "I'm sorry. I'm so ·orry."

Looking at Val and Shelly, Kate articulated what ·ıey all felt. "The fact is, we're stuck with the deci-·ons we made when we were too young to realize ·ıeir consequences. We can't undo the choices we ·ıade when we were young. All we can do is accept ·ıem and go on. At seventeen, we were inexperi-·ıced and naive. Now we have a strength that ·ɔmes from surviving. We don't have to let what ·appened on graduation night continue to affect our ·ves. After all, we've come pretty far. We're tough. ·/e're survivors."

"What about Barbara?" Shelly asked.

"I don't know what to say about Barbara, but I ·now what to do."

Getting up, she went into the kitchen. Val and ·helly followed and watched in silent consent as

583

Kate punched the erase button on the answering machine.

They returned to the hospital to find Detective Pinero still sitting outside Barbara's room. He looked at them but didn't say anything as they entered her room, closing the door behind them.

Once again, they ranged themselves around her bed. Looking down at her, still lying there silent and pale, Kate said, "Barb, we're here. All of us. Val and Shelly and me. We came, just like you asked. You can wake up now. You're not alone."

She paused, hoping to see some flicker of recognition, some sign that Barbara might regain consciousness, but there was nothing.

Val tried to sound like her usual breezy self. "Hey, kiddo. It's me. Come on, wake up!"

Barbara's eyelids fluttered but stayed closed.

Shelly said, "Barb, it's me. Shelly. Please wake up."

Her eyelids fluttered again, opened briefly, closed, then opened again.

The excitement the three women felt was short-lived as they saw the hopeless expression in Barbara's eyes.

Forcing her voice to sound calm, Kate took Barbara's hand and said, "We're with you, Barb. We know what happened with Rick and we'll stand by you. We'll help you just like you were trying to help us, to protect us from him. It will be all right," she lied, hoping desperately that Barbara would believe her. "You just have to fight, that's all. Don't give up."

A bittersweet smile gently curved the corners of Barbara's perfect mouth. When she spoke, her voice was so low and so hoarse that they had to bend down to catch the words.

"Don't you know," she whispered, "I've always taken the easy way out."

Her eyes closed again and in a moment she stopped breathing.

"No!" Shelly moaned.

A red light began flashing on one of the machines monitoring Barbara followed by a loud beeping sound. In seconds, a nurse rushed in, closely followed by Dr. Garcia. The three women were forced out of the room. They stood together in the doorway, watching while the nurse and doctor tried in vain to revive Barbara.

When it was over, Dr. Garcia covered Barbara's face with the sheet. As he and the nurse left the room, he said to her, "Call Dr. Browning. Tell him if he wants to talk to me, I'll be in my office."

In a moment, he was gone and the nurse was back at her station, making the call.

Suddenly everything was very still and quiet after the hectic efforts of the doctor and nurse to save Barbara. Kate, Val, and Shelly stood there staring, almost in disbelief, at the lifeless form under the sheet, trying to comprehend the finality of it.

Kate couldn't grasp it. It was impossible! Barbara dead? No! It couldn't be! Barbara had always been there, and Kate had counted on the fact that she always would. They would grow old together, reminiscing about their youth, sharing jokes that only the two of them understood. Each would be comforted by the knowledge that no matter where she went or what she did, somewhere in the world there was someone who knew everything about her, the bad as well as the good, and who cared deeply for her anyway.

585

Men might come and go, children would grow up and leave to start their own lives, but a friend — a best friend — was forever. Nothing could come between them, not anger or physical distance or even tragedy.

Nothing but death.

In her mind, Kate saw Barbara's smile, warm and reassuring, heard her voice, brimming with confidence. It was impossible to accept that she was gone forever.

Val and Kate looked at each other, tears in their eyes.

As always, Val hid her deepest feelings with anger. "Damn it!" she exploded. "Why couldn't she fight!"

Memories of Barbara followed one upon another in Kate's mind: that day up at Three Rivers when they were sixteen, Barbara predicting what kind of men each of them would fall in love with, somehow making each of them feel special; Barbara arranging the abortion for Shelly, selling her jewelry to pay for it, driving to Tijuana; Barbara choosing to have Allison, to give her life, at the expense of her own dreams; Barbara urging Kate to call Mark; Barbara protecting all of them from Rick Paxton.

She was always there for them and never, until the very end, expected anything in return. By the time she did ask something of them, it was too late.

Kate said slowly, "I think she gave away so many pieces of herself that finally suicide was an easy option because there was nothing left to kill . . ."

Her voice broke. Val hugged her, then Shelly.

As they stood close to each other for support, Detective Pinero came over to them. "Did she regain consciousness?"

"Yes," Kate answered, her voice shaky, "but only for a moment."

"Did she say anything? Was she involved with Paxton? Did she kill him?" he demanded.

They looked at each other. Without saying a word, they reached a mutual decision. As they did twenty years earlier, they banded together.

Speaking for all of them, Kate answered, "She didn't say anything."

Shelly and Val nodded in agreement.

TWO

Kate

The next day, Kate was sitting in the living room of her mother's house when the doorbell rang. She had just talked on the phone to Val and Shelly, who were staying at the Holiday Inn, so she knew it couldn't be them. No one else, not even her brothers, knew she was there because she'd told her mother she didn't feel like seeing anyone just yet.

Who could it be? she wondered as she walked to the door.

When she opened it, she was stunned to see Allison standing there. She looked taller than Kate remembered from the last time she'd seen her, nearly a year earlier, and even more slender. She had her mother's stunning, long-legged figure. With her long, dark brown hair, brown eyes, and finely sculpted features, she looked so much like Barbara had at seventeen that she nearly took Kate's breath away. It was like seeing the ghost of a younger Barbara who thought the world was hers to do with as she pleased.

Without saying a word, Allison burst into tears and threw herself in Kate's arms. They held each other very tight, Kate filled with an overwhelming feeling of love for Allison and a profound pity. Until that moment, she'd focused entirely on her own

588

nearly unbearable sense of loss at Barbara's death. Now she realized that as hard as it was for her to lose her best friend, it was infinitely harder for Allison to lose her mother.

"It's all right," she whispered, patting Allison's back exactly as she'd done when Allison was a baby. It wasn't all right, but she didn't know what else to say.

Later, when Allison had her tears under control, Kate asked, "How did you know I was here?"

"I heard Dr. Garcia tell Daddy that you and Aunt Val and Aunt Shelly were with Mom when she died. I knew you'd stay for the funeral, so I got out her address book and found your mother's address."

"I'm so glad you came, Alli. I wanted to talk to you, but your father . . ." Kate paused, unsure how to go on. She didn't want to hurt Allison by insulting her father, but she was so furious with him for his cold behavior throughout this terrible time that she couldn't trust herself to speak of him.

"It's all right," Allison responded. "I know Daddy's been real mad for some reason. Did you know that he and Mom separated a few days ago?"

"Yes. Were you aware of that?"

"Not at the time. I was back East with Grandma, looking at colleges. Daddy called and told us that Mom had died, and when we got back and I started asking questions about it, he said he didn't know anything because they'd separated."

"I'm sorry, Alli. That must make a difficult time even harder for you."

"I wasn't really surprised. They weren't getting along for years. Daddy was always working and Mom was alone. And she, well . . ." She stopped, looking embarrassed, then went on awkwardly. "You probably knew she drank a lot."

589

Kate nodded.

"That's why I was gone so much, over at friends' houses or at Grandma's. It was just so unhappy at home."

All this time, Kate thought, we were so convinced that Barbara's life was perfect. How sad that she couldn't tell us the truth and ask for our help.

But she *had* asked for their help, Kate remembered. It had just been too late.

Looking at the dark circles under Allison's eyes and her drawn expression, she asked, "How are you holding up under all this?"

"Okay. Daddy's back in the house, but somehow I just can't face it yet, so I'm staying with Grandma."

It amazed Kate that Allison could feel as close as she obviously felt toward Constance, whom Kate had always seen as a cold, intimidating figure. Maybe Constance was different with her granddaughter. Maybe with Allison there was none of the competition, even jealousy, that had kept her from being close to Barbara.

"The thing is," Allison went on, "I wanted to make sure you knew the funeral is tomorrow at ten at Hansen's."

"Yes, I know. Your father was kind enough to tell me."

Actually, David had asked his secretary to call Kate and the others with the information, but she didn't think it was necessary to tell Allison that.

"There's something else, Aunt Kate. I'd like you to deliver the eulogy."

"Oh, Alli, I'm deeply touched, but I couldn't."

"Please! There's no one else, and you knew her best. You were her closest friend."

Kate really didn't want to do it. The thought of getting up there in front of an audience, including

David and Constance, and talking about Barbara, whom they had treated so harshly, was extremely upsetting.

"I wouldn't know what to say," she insisted.

"Just say the truth about her. It's what she would have wanted, I'm sure of it."

Looking into Allison's dark brown eyes, still moist with tears, Kate knew she couldn't refuse.

"All right. I'll do it."

"There's one more thing," Allison said, not quite meeting Kate's look.

Kate knew what was coming and braced herself.

"I know Mom was unhappy, but I still don't understand why she . . . why she killed herself." She looked up at Kate. "Do you know?"

For the first time, Kate truly understood what it must feel like to be a mother. She felt the intense pressure of having to give just exactly the right answer and not being at all certain she could come up with it. Allison would insist that she wanted the truth, but which truth? There were so many.

Aware that her answer would color Allison's view of her mother forever, Kate began slowly, "Your mother loved you more than you will ever know."

When Allison started to protest, Kate rushed on. "Oh, I know you haven't been close for a long time, and maybe she wasn't the kind of mother you needed her to be. Love doesn't have anything to do with being perfect. Sometimes it's strongest in imperfect situations. The important thing is, she chose to have you instead of pursuing dreams that meant a great deal to her. That was how much she loved you."

"You mean she could've had an abortion but she didn't," Allison said pragmatically.

"Yes."

Allison was thoughtful for a moment. "When I go away to college, I'm going to participate in the NWPC. Do you know what that is?"

Kate had to suppress a smile. "Yes. I know that it's the political arm of the women's movement. I was active in it before you were born, young lady."

"My mom was always talking to me about the women's movement, and for a long time I couldn't care less. She was so excited about Geraldine Ferraro, but I just didn't see the point. After all, women aren't discriminated against or anything any more."

Kate said briskly, "I'm not sure I agree with that."

"Then the Supreme Court decision came along and the pro-life movement and all, and I really began to think about things. I have friends who got abortions, and it was definitely the right thing to do. There was no way they could be mothers at fourteen or fifteen. The idea that they might not be able to make that choice anymore is scary."

"Yes. Very scary. Because no matter how you feel about abortion, it's the most difficult and most personal decision a woman can make. She should be able to make that decision herself."

"I agree. I think abortion is the Vietnam of my generation."

Kate looked at Allison thoughtfully. "You may be right."

"I always wanted to be a doctor, like my father and grandfather, but lately I've been thinking about going into politics. Women in office can really make a difference on the abortion issue, especially on the state level. Do you think I'd be a good politician?"

Kate smiled. "I think you'd be a great one."

"I might eventually run for Congress and get involved in environmental issues. This planet is being raped, you know, and something's got to be done about it. Who knows, I might even end up running for president. After all, anything's possible for women nowadays."

Kate found herself buoyed by a sense of optimism and endless possibilities that she hadn't experienced in years.

"Yes, Alli. Anything's possible."

Allison rose. "Thanks, Aunt Kate. I'll see you tomorrow."

"Will you be all right?"

"Yeah. I'm pretty tough, you know."

"I know."

When she left, Kate had the uncanny sensation that she'd just seen a vision of what Barbara might have become. If only things had been different on that hot June night twenty years ago. . . .

When the minister of Constance's church finished speaking, he nodded toward Kate in a prearranged signal that it was now her turn. As she rose and walked to the front of the funeral chapel, she was uncomfortably aware of all the eyes on her.

There was David, looking stiff and coldly angry; Constance looking disapproving, as if her daughter had committed a particularly serious social faux pas; Val and Shelly looking grief-stricken.

Kate stood at the podium, gathering her thoughts. She had stayed up late the night before, trying to write a speech. She was a professional writer, she kept telling herself, she should be able to do this without any problem. Somehow, none of what was in her heart could be put down on paper. She finally gave up, trusting instinct to get her through the ordeal.

Only now that she stood there, with Barbara lying in a white coffin behind her, she didn't think of it as an ordeal. She thought of it as an opportunity. In a moment of clear vision, Kate saw that it wasn't necessary to give a speech recalling the aspects of Barbara that were safe to relate to this audience, most of whom had never known the real person beneath the carefully constructed facade of perfection.

All she had to do was say good-bye. From the heart.

"We loved Barbara as a friend who shared some of the best, and the worst, times of our youth and who touched our hearts and encouraged our dreams. I only wish that when she finally asked for our help, we had had the chance to give it, as she gave it to us so many, many times."

Looking out at the crowd of people, she saw Allison smiling proudly through her tears, and she knew that she'd given her mother back to her, in a way.

Kate finished in a voice choked by emotion. "She sacrificed herself for the people she loved. I wish . . . she were here now so we could tell her how much she meant to us. Good-bye, Barbara."

She couldn't go on. Her eyes were filled with tears as she left the podium, and she nearly tripped on the steps. Suddenly Val and Shelly were there, helping her. When she sat down, they sat on either side of her, each tightly clutching her hand.

We'll get through this together, Kate thought, just as we've gotten through everything else.

At the cemetery, the ceremony was brief. The minister recited in a mournful voice, "Remember now thy creator in the days of thy youth, while the evil days come not, nor the years draw nigh. Man goeth to his long home, and the mourners go about the streets; or ever the silver chord be loosed, or the golden bowl be broken. Then shall the dust return to the earth as it was; and the spirit shall return unto God who gave it. Amen."

Then the coffin was lowered into the ground. A grim-faced David and Constance started to lead Allison away, but she drew back and paused just long enough to toss into the grave one of the white roses from the arrangement that Val, Shelly, and Kate had sent.

Barbara had always loved white roses.

Suddenly Kate fell apart. She had cried over the past three days, but she hadn't cried like this, as if a dam had burst within her, as if she would never stop crying. It was so unfair, so damn unfair! Barbara never had a chance.

Kate's heart and spirit were broken. She didn't know where to turn, what to do. It seemed as if there was no hope, no solace.

A man walked toward her. His figure was hazy through her tears, shimmering like a mirage. She wasn't at all sure he was real.

Until he spoke. Just one word. *"Katie."*

And she knew he was real.

She threw herself into Mark's outstretched arms, and felt them encircle her with the strength of his love.

EPILOGUE

Val sat at her desk going over the list of topics suggested by the young associate producer, Lenny Stern, who had taken over in Ellen's absence. One by one, she crossed them off, muttering under her breath irritably. "Women involved with married men—Lord, but that's been done to death . . . problems with in-laws—*boring!* . . . sports group-es—give me a break . . ."

Lenny hadn't come up with one idea that was either original or searingly topical. None of his suggestions would appeal to Val's audience and, even more important, to her own sense of curiosity. Damn, but she missed Ellen. Ellen had an unerring instinct for what worked and what didn't. She had a real feeling for the kinds of stories Val could do best, stories with heart and passion.

Lenny would have to go, Val decided. Maybe he could get a job with Geraldo Rivera. His interests were certainly much more male-oriented.

"Hello."

At the sound of the familiar voice, Val jerked her head up sharply. For a moment, she couldn't trust herself to speak. Then she said, "I left messages on your answering machine every day."

"I know. I was away and I didn't call in for my messages for a couple of weeks. I'm sorry."

"That's okay."

Val stopped, unsure how to continue. It had been easy talking to a machine, but talking to a real, live person was something else again. Suddenly she said, "Fuck this shit," and got up and walked over to Ellen. "Welcome back," she said, hugging her warmly.

For once Ellen didn't look like the unemotional, efficient automaton most of the staff assumed her to be. Her eyes filled with tears and her voice shook when she asked, "Did you mean what you said in your messages?"

"Don't I always mean what I say?"

"You don't have a problem with this . . . with us?"

Val shook her head. "No. I've made a choice and I'm at peace with it. Something happened recently that made a big change in me. I let the truth into my life. I feel stronger now, strong enough to let *you* into my life. Into my heart."

"I'll be good to Michelle. I would never do anything to hurt her."

Val smiled. "I know."

Grabbing her coat, she went on. "Let's go for a walk in the park. There's so much I want to share with you and get your thoughts on."

They walked out of the office, side by side, and Val asked, "Did I ever tell you about my friend Barbara?"

"You mentioned her a few times. She lives in your hometown, Visalia, doesn't she?"

"Yes. That is, she did. She's dead now."

"Oh, Val, I'm so sorry! What happened?"

How to explain? Where to begin?

At the beginning, of course.

600

"Twenty years ago, we were friends, Kate and Shelly and Barbara and I. It's funny, we were all so different, but we had one thing in common. We all wanted out of there . . . and Barbara showed us the way . . ."

Shelly stepped out of the company limo still wearing the same simple, elegant gray wool sheath she'd worn to Barbara's funeral the day before. She said to the driver, "I'm not sure how long I'll be. Why don't you wait for about fifteen minutes, and if I'm not back, leave."

He looked doubtful. It was late at night, and while this area near the river was hardly the East End, it *was* in the middle of the city and wasn't nearly as safe as her country estate. "Are you sure, ma'am?"

No, she wasn't sure at all. From the moment the limo had picked her up at Heathrow and she'd given the driver Ryan's address instead of her own, she'd been nervous as hell—but for once she wasn't going to let fear stop her.

Shelly smiled at the driver. "Don't worry. I'll be fine."

Her voice sounded much more confident than she felt, but then, she had a great deal of practice at hiding her true feelings.

She walked up the steps into the building, which had once been a warehouse but had been converted into expensive, river-view condos. She hurried, afraid that if she hesitated, her courage would fail her. Shelly had thought about calling Ryan first but knew that she needed to face him.

At the door of Number 19 she stopped, took a deep breath, then pushed the doorbell. After a moment, she heard the sound of footsteps and then the door opened. The words she had carefully thought out during the eleven-hour flight from L.A. to London died on her lips.

Standing at the door was a lovely, black-haired young woman. Behind her, Shelly could see packing boxes stacked one on top of another and white sheets covering the furniture.

"Yes?"

Shelly felt like an absolute fool. She had waited too long. After all, Ryan was only human. What did she expect? That he'd never look at another woman again once she let him walk out of her life? For all she knew, this young woman was going to the States with him.

She had no idea what to say, but she had to say something. "I . . . that is, I must have the wrong flat."

The young woman looked at her curiously. "Aren't you Shelly DeLucca? Ryan works for you, doesn't he? I simply adore your products. I won't put anything else on my face."

Before Shelly could speak, the young woman turned to shout, "Ryan! Come here!"

Embarrassment washed over Shelly; she wished that she could simply disappear.

Then Ryan was standing there, staring at her in amazement.

"Shelly!"

What could she say? She tried desperately to come up with a plausible excuse for her presence, something that would let her slink away with the tattered remnants of her dignity.

Before she could say a word, the young woman turned to Ryan. "You've probably got business to discuss. I'll just get Felix and take him to my place.

You can stop by in the morning and say good-bye, if you like. George will be home, and he'd love to see you before you go."

Ryan nodded without really looking at her.

The young woman picked up a cat carrier and left. Inside, Shelly could just make out the vague mewings of a frightened cat.

"Felix hates that thing," Ryan explained. "I only put him in it to take him to the vet. He'll be immensely relieved when Charlotte lets him out of it and he finds himself in her apartment. She's taking him, you see. Because of the quarantine laws, I can't take him to the States with me."

"Oh."

There was a world of relief in that one small word.

Ryan went on. "It's especially nice of her because her husband, George, isn't too keen on cats."

"I see."

The blank astonishment he'd shown when he first saw Shelly had been replaced with an expression of curiosity. He asked her in. "I'm afraid the place is a mess. I'm leaving in the morning. Everything's packed, so I can't offer you anything, but we can probably find something to sit on."

He threw back a sheet, uncovering a white sofa.

Gathering her courage, Shelly said what was in her heart. "When I saw Charlotte, I thought I was too late."

Ryan looked at her with such transparent love she couldn't understand how she could have ever dismissed it as mere desire. "Don't you know by now you could never be too late?"

She couldn't speak, couldn't even stand. She nearly fell onto the sofa.

Sitting down beside her, he said with that devilish

grin that turned her insides to mush, "I've got Shelly DeLucca the way some people have got measles. I've had it from the first moment I focused a camera on you in L.A. all those years ago. When I realized I couldn't have you, I tried to put you out of my mind, but I couldn't."

Shelly knew there had to be absolute honesty between them now. Nothing less would do. She forced herself to confront an extremely painful issue. "How did you feel about me when I worked for Madame Justine?"

The pain in Ryan's eyes tore at her heart. "It nearly killed me, thinking of you with other men. But I knew that it nearly killed you, too. That was even worse."

Tears filled her eyes.

He took her hands in his big strong ones; this time she didn't pull away. "Don't cry now," he whispered. Then he smiled. "If I'd known that all I had to do to get you to come to me was to play hard to get, I would've done it years ago."

Shelly laughed softly. "You always make me laugh."

His smile dissolved. "I want to do much more than that."

"I know."

She felt the first faint stirrings of desire deep within her. Her hands trembled in his. She wanted to kiss him, and knew that he wanted to kiss her, but there was still something critical to be resolved.

"Ryan . . ."

"Yes, love."

She went on determinedly. "There's something I must tell you before . . ." She stopped, uncertain how to proceed.

"Shelly, you don't have to make any confessions. I

604

don't care what happened in your life before. All that matters is what we build together."

Her smile was warm with gratitude. "Thank you for that, Ryan, but there *is* something I must tell you so you'll understand why I . . . well, why I ran from you as if from the devil for all these years."

"All right."

"Kate told you in Paris that I was . . . raped." His hands held hers a little tighter and she took courage from his strength. "She didn't tell you all of what happened that night. It affected all of us deeply. Ultimately, it killed Barbara . . ."

Shelly told Ryan everything. The gang rape. Steven Ashe's death. The abortion. Barbara's suicide. At some point, he pulled her against him, holding her with a fierce protectiveness, and she continued to speak, her voice muffled against his chest. Ryan listened intently, rarely speaking, letting her say everything that she needed to say. When she finished, he brushed the tears from her wet cheeks and kissed her forehead and the tip of her nose and then, lightly, her lips. He said, "I thought I understood, but I didn't. You must have been so hurt and so frightened. But it's over now. All of it. It can never hurt you again."

Shelly felt the last part of a heavy burden being lifted from her shoulders. She knew he was right. It could never hurt her again.

He told her about his own background growing up in rural Texas with his abusive, alcoholic father and a loving mother. His determination to escape the anger and pain and poverty of his life. An unhappy early marriage to a free spirit who wanted the sixties ideal of free love, drugs, and rock 'n' roll to go on forever. When they finally stopped talking, Shelly realized they had been at it all night. It was

nearly dawn. Suddenly, they weren't talking anymore. They were just looking at each other. At that
moment, Shelly saw right into Ryan's very soul and
knew she could trust him.

Love, like everything else in nature, has its season. Now, in the summer of her life, she had finally
found it. She knew she wanted him.

Shelly made the first move, leaning over to kiss
him tentatively. Ryan responded with tremendous
restraint each step of the way, clearly not wanting to
frighten her. She wanted to tell him not to worry;
for the first time in years, she wasn't frightened.

They moved closer.

In the bedroom, the physical and emotional intimacy she shared with him there was unlike any of
the intimacies men had taken with her body in the
past. She let down her guard completely. The line
separating them dissolved as their boundaries and
borders merged. She surrendered to the relationship
and to the moment. She became vulnerable.

When it was over and she lay in his arms as he
talked of all the nights they would spend together
forever and ever, she knew that in vulnerability she
had finally found her true strength.

Kate sat at her typewriter in front of an uncurtained window. In the flowerbed bordering the lawn,
boldly colored tulips swayed gently in a mild breeze.
Long-legged foals gamboled in a nearby pasture.
Beyond lay endless orchards of fruit trees in blossom, their tiny pink or white flowers looking delicate against clear, azure skies. And in the distance
rose the massive Sierra Nevadas, colored a dusky
green.

Springtime, when the air was filled with the first

signs of new life, was her favorite season at the ranch. She smiled to herself. Actually, all the seasons here were her favorite because she shared each of them with Mark.

He braced himself against a whitewashed fence, watching the foals, idly chewing on a piece of straw, a bucolic figure except that he was so damn handsome. Next to him, Anne stood with her head leaning against his shoulder.

My family, Kate whispered out loud, loving the sound of the words. Once she would have assumed family was a question of blood ties. Now she knew that ties of love had nothing to do with blood. Anne was her daughter as surely as if she'd given birth to her. Mark was her husband, and always would be.

Reluctantly tearing her eyes away from them, she tried to make herself concentrate on the piece of paper in the typewriter, but it was hard because she was so filled with happiness, all she wanted to do was dwell on it, in a thoroughly maudlin, unproductive way.

Kate especially wanted to dwell on the baby growing within her. She hadn't seen a doctor yet for a pregnancy test — it was too soon — but she knew there was life inside her. She had known from the moment of conception.

She felt so serene, so totally and completely fulfilled. She had learned to trust her own heart again, in a way she hadn't done in a long while. Finally, Kate was able to claim her roots, to honor and embrace them. For so long, she had tried to avoid them because there was pain there.

Now she was free of that pain. She had learned that it was necessary to go home again if she wanted her work — and herself — to be whole. She remembered something T. S. Eliot had said: The end of all our travels is to return to where we began and to know the place for the first time.

She knew this place now, and she knew herself.

Kate was nearly forty, at an age when it was crucial to start to define what a successful life is. She had defined hers with a simple equation — home, family, work. Success no longer meant moving up yet another rung on an ever-upward ladder. It meant fulfillment and inner peace and doing the work that mattered to her rather than the work that would bring the greatest notoriety. Unlike Alan, she no longer paid attention to scorekeepers.

She had begun writing her most ambitious script yet, the story of the women of her generation. Forcing her gaze away from the foals and Mark and Anne, and back to the page, Kate began typing a voice-over that was the opening of the new script.

"I grew up in a small town . . ."